WEAVER STREET AT WAR

CHRISSIE WALSH

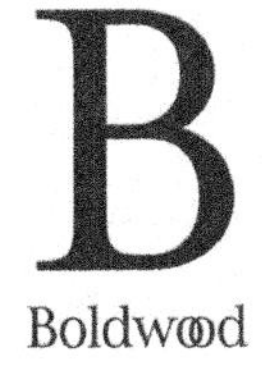

First published in Great Britain in 2024 by Boldwood Books Ltd.

Cover Design by Colin Thomas

Cover Photography: Colin Thomas

A CIP catalogue record for this book is available from the British Library.

Paperback ISBN 978-1-80280-960-2

Large Print ISBN 978-1-80280-961-9

Hardback ISBN 978-1-80280-959-6

Ebook ISBN 978-1-80280-963-3

Kindle ISBN 978-1-80280-962-6

Audio CD ISBN 978-1-80280-954-1

MP3 CD ISBN 978-1-80280-955-8

Digital audio download ISBN 978-1-80280-958-9

Boldwood Books Ltd
23 Bowerdean Street
London SW6 3TN
www.boldwoodbooks.com

For my grandson, Harry Walsh.
My grateful thanks to all the wonderful readers who have followed the lives of the folks in Weaver Street.

1

LIVERPOOL, FEBRUARY 1941

Anna Carswell sensed the shift in the motion of the train as its racketing pace gradually slowed to a clanking, grinding halt. Startled, she opened her eyes, her dream dissolving. All around her passengers in the overcrowded carriage were on the move, hauling bags from the overhead racks above the two long seats then crowding the space in between. Gathering her wits, she smoothed her skirt then struggled to her feet, and squashed between the plump rear of a woman smelling of fried onions and the stout frame of a burly man in a donkey jacket, she reached up to the rack for her kitbag.

'Here, let me.' Donkey Jacket shot out a beefy hand, and lifting the kitbag as though it were a bag of feathers, he balanced it on the seat Anna had just vacated. He gave her an admiring smile. 'Women's Auxiliary Air Force,' he said, referring to her blue WAAF uniform and acknowledging her thanks with, 'It's a pleasure to help a brave young lass like you.'

Anna smiled up into the friendly brown eyes in a fleshy face under a flat cap set at a jaunty angle. Then one of the passengers in front of them opened the carriage door and the passengers behind surged forward, buffeting Anna and her helper. Caught off guard, Anna wobbled but Donkey Jacket steadied her before lifting her kitbag and then handing her down onto the platform. Anna stood to gather her bearings and retrieve her luggage, but her kind guardian had already hefted it onto one shoulder and his own tool bag onto the other. 'Come on, love, this way. Let's get out of here,' he said, parting the crowd with his bulk. Desperate not to lose sight of her kitbag, Anna matched her step to his along the platform.

'Welcome to Liverpool Lime Street,' he said as they jostled their way through the throng on the busy station, many of the men and women who were arriving or departing wearing blue or khaki uniforms. 'Not that you'd know it since they've taken down all the signs so that Hitler's spies won't know where they are.' He chuckled and Anna joined in.

On the platform up ahead, three women in the distinctive uniform of the Women's Voluntary Service were doling out cups of tea. Anna wouldn't have minded one, but her companion seemed eager to be on his way and she didn't want to lose him, or her kitbag. He might be able to provide her with directions once they were out of the station.

'It's my first time in Liverpool,' she said as they made their way to the exit. This wasn't strictly true. Her adoption certificate named her place of birth as Liverpool, but that had been twenty-one years ago. Liverpool held no memories for Anna. Up until now it had just been the name of a city in the north, and home a Victorian terrace house in Salisbury, Wiltshire with her adoptive parents Jane and Norman Carswell. Anna pushed the thought aside.

'It'll be Derby House then that you'll be going to.' By now they were on the pavement outside the station and Donkey Jacket set down Anna's kitbag.

'Not today. I need to get to Edge Hill. I'm billeted there. I don't have to report to Derby House till tomorrow.'

'Then you'll need to take a tram; Edge Hill's a fair bit out of the city centre. Now, never let it be said that Con Mulligan failed to rescue a damsel in distress,' he jested, and hoisting her kitbag to his shoulders again, he set off walking. 'Come on, love, I'll take you to the tram stop. I'm for Scottie Road meself, lived there all me life, a true Scouser born and bred.'

Matching her step to his, Anna observed how different the city was from the Wiltshire town she still thought of as home, and the RAF camp in Oxfordshire that she'd left that morning. *So, this is where I was born*, Anna mused as she strode along the damp pavements rimed now with a coating of frost in the rapidly cooling air. The late afternoon was overcast, its greyness exaggerating the gaping holes in between buildings; the result of previous German bombing raids. The streets were busy with people going about their business, many of them shabbily dressed. *But then who wasn't in these days?* thought Anna. The war was in its second year and new clothes were only available when you had enough coupons to buy them. It made her appreciate her smart blue uniform: she was able to save her coupons to purchase something special if the need arose. Yet no matter how down-at-heel some of the people looked, she couldn't help but notice their cheery greetings and stoic smiles as they passed one another by. If Hitler had hoped to destroy the fighting spirit of the Liverpudlians by sinking the ships that brought food and arms into the port, Liverpool being the eastern end of the transatlantic chain of supplies from North America, it seemed to Anna that he had seriously underestimated the inhabitants of this city.

'You'll like Liverpool once you get used to it,' Con said as they walked past the damaged St George's Hall, 'although it's not the same as it was before Jerry blitzed it last Christmas.' He nodded at the Hall's broken stonework. 'They firebombed this place, and down by the docks where me ma lives took a right hammering. The bastards even bombed St Anthony's school air raid shelter. Killed eleven people, two of 'em priests.'

Anna shuddered. 'I must say it all looks rather dismal and depressing after what I've been used to. I was stationed in Oxfordshire, lots of sleepy villages surrounded by leafy woods and meadows, but I'm sure I'll like the city once I get to know my way about. Thanks again for showing me the way.'

'No problem, queen. Lucky for you I was working down Knotty Ash today fixing a roof what got blown off by Jerry flying low over it. The bloody bastards don't care who they harm, if you'll pardon the language.'

Anna, inwardly amused that he should think she would be offended by his use of the epithet, and at being called 'queen' said, 'No need to apologise. I've heard much worse.'

'Aye, I suppose you have, although I would have thought the RAF lads were dead posh and didn't go in for cursing, you know, public school an' all that.'

'Don't you believe it. Some of them can be right bloody bastards,' Anna replied, thinking of one RAF man in particular.

Con was wishing he was twenty years younger and more or less voiced his words. 'It's a pity there's a war on and that you're needed at Derby House and I'm busy shoring up bombed-out buildings, otherwise I could have shown you the sights, taken you out on the town.' He gave a rueful grin. He would have enjoyed spending the evening with this tall slender girl whose creamy complexion and auburn hair were a delightful combination. 'Instead, I'll be cosying up to me old ma,' he continued, 'making sure she's safe in the shelter when the sirens go off. She's a game old bird but I worry about her when I'm not there.' They turned a corner into a broad thoroughfare. 'Now this is William Browne Street. You'll get a tram for Edge Hill from this stop.' He came to a halt, his eyes lingering on her pretty face and eyes that were the palest greenish-grey above a scattering of golden freckles on the bridge of her nose. 'Now, you take care and I'll get off home in case Jerry comes calling.'

Anna felt a fleeting moment of panic. She'd been enjoying Con's company and now he was leaving her all alone in a strange city.

'Thanks ever so much, Con. You're a real gentleman. Your mum's lucky to have you.' Anna held out her hand. 'I'm so glad I met you, and thanks for giving me directions.'

'Think nothing of it,' Con said, gripping her hand in his meaty paw. 'And if you're ever at a loose end give me ma a shout. Her door's always open for a jangle and a cuppa. Number 320, Scotland Road.'

'I might just do that,' Anna said, laughing as the tram clanked to a halt. Con handed her up to the platform and dumped her kitbag beside her. 'Best of luck, Con. Take care.'

'You an' all, queen. Good luck in Liverpool,' he called back as the tram rattled away.

Anna found a seat, and when the conductress came to take her fare, she asked to be put off at Weaver Street. 'New to the city are you, love?' the conductress asked as she handed Anna her ticket. Anna nodded. 'If I was twenty years younger, I'd have joined the WAAFs or the ATS,' the woman told her, 'but I suppose I'm doing me bit on the trams.' She moved off down the aisle, singing out, 'Any more fares to paradise.'

Anna sat back to enjoy the ride although her heart was in her mouth. She wondered if her new landlady in Weaver Street would be as friendly as the two people she'd met so far. She dearly hoped so. Her life had been filled with misery for far too long. In the past eighteen months there had been too much anger, sadness and heartbreak to cope with and she was sorely in need of respite.

In Anna's experience, the entire twenty-one years of her life had never been what you might call happy. Her adoptive parents had been a strange pair: lazy, disillusioned Jane, a one-time dancer with a theatre company, and Norman, the unsuccessful insurance salesman with an erratic temper and a liking for strong drink. When Anna had asked Jane why they had adopted her, she'd replied, 'I was bored and lonely. Norman was always out chasing sales and I thought a baby would be nice to play with.'

Jane had drifted through life in a fantasy world of *Red Letter* magazines and old theatre programmes, salving her misery with vodka and forty cigarettes a day. Norman had drowned his in the whisky bottle. Growing up with two people who seemed to care nothing for each other, and even less for her, had been gruelling to say the least. They had made no secret of her adoption, and it had taken Anna less than ten years to arrive at the conclusion that she had been adopted on a fleeting whim to plug a gap in their meaningless lives, one that she had failed to fill.

Over the years the gap had become a chasm. By the time Anna was nineteen and working as a typist in a solicitor's office, Jane had disappeared so far into her dreamworld that she was out of reach. Norman grew more irascible by the day, and his drunken rants more dangerous.

Had it not been for Anna's naturally ebullient spirit, life might have been unbearable. Things had come to a head at the beginning of September 1939. War had not only broken out in Europe, it had broken out in the unhappy terrace house in Salisbury. Norman had arrived home sodden with drink and raging at his lack of sales. As usual, he had vented his anger on Jane. She'd had a brain haemorrhage and died two days later, and the following week Norman had been killed outright when he'd staggered into the path of an army lorry on its way to the camp in Tidworth. Anna couldn't honestly say she missed them; she had never really known them, and they had never taken the trouble to know her. Before the year ended, she had sorted out her affairs, put the house on the market and joined the WAAF. Like school and the solicitor's office, the training camp was a haven after too many years of living in the shadows of Jane and Norman.

Now, as the tram to Edge Hill trundled its way out of the city centre, Anna gazed out of the window to familiarise herself with what was her new home. It didn't matter much to her where she lived. In her opinion she didn't just come from a broken home, she came from one that had completely and utterly disintegrated. And if that wasn't bad enough, just recently her heart had been shattered into a million pieces; the love of her life had betrayed her with her best friend. Unconsciously, and despite the fact that she was wearing her uniform issue gloves, the fingers of her right hand strayed to her left and circled her bare ring finger. An agonising sharp pain stabbed her chest and annoyingly caught in her throat. *Forget about him*, she told herself. *It's over and done with so concentrate on the future.*

Taking a deep breath and sitting more upright, she focused her gaze, staring in shocked compassion at the blitzed and bombed-out streets. Great gaping holes and masses of debris, rafters clinging precariously to exposed wallpapered rooms of houses that had once been family homes, and empty buildings that had been work places. After the green fields of Oxfordshire, it really was a depressing sight. *But one I'll have to get used to*, she thought. If she was to be stationed here for the foreseeable future, she'd do what she'd always done: she'd make the best of it. A lifetime of living with Jane and Norman Carswell had taught her to make her own happiness.

'Next stop for Weaver Street,' the cheery conductress sang out. Anna stood, and holding her kitbag in front of her and nudging it with her foot, she shuffled down the aisle.

'Mind how you go, love,' the conductress chirped as Anna alighted.

'You too, and thank you.' Anna gave her a grateful smile. The tram rattled off and Anna looked around to gather her bearings. She was on a broad pavement lined with shops and offices, the nearest being a bakery, a hardware store and a tiny fancy goods shop amusingly called Betty's Bijou Bazaar. There were sandbags stacked outside some of the premises, and the windows were crisscrossed with broad bands of brown sticky tape. Other than that, there was little sign that Edge Hill was at war. Intrigued by the silly name, Anna decided to go into the Bijou Bazaar and ask exactly where Weaver Street was. There seemed little point in setting off in the wrong direction. The bell tinkled above the door as she pushed it open. A pleasant-looking young woman greeted her with a smile.

'Can I help you?' the woman asked, coming from behind the counter into the small space, its walls and shelves bedecked with displays of brightly coloured scarves, gloves, pottery ornaments and cheap jewellery.

'I hope so,' Anna replied. 'I wondered if you could point me in the right direction for Weaver Street.' She plumped her kitbag on the floor.

The young woman's smile widened. 'I most certainly can. You're a WAAF, and I'll bet anything that you're Mavis's new lodger.'

Anna looked surprised. 'Miss Mavis Robson? Number fifteen, Weaver Street?'

'That's right,' the woman chirped. 'She told me she was expecting you today.' She glanced at her wrist. 'Look, just give me two minutes to cash up and I'll take you to Mavis's.'

Somewhat nonplussed, Anna looked at the items on display as she waited for her to empty the till and put the takings into a canvas bag, then turn out the lights. Suddenly the little shop was plunged into gloom, and Anna realised how late in the afternoon it was.

'Okay, I'm ready.' Jangling a bunch of keys, the woman made her way to the door, letting Anna out first. Then she locked the door and said, 'Mavis here we come.'

They didn't have far to walk before they came to the end of the row of shops. A wide lane led off to their left, and at the end of it, Anna's guide paused. 'This is the back way into the houses in Weaver Street, and seeing as how we all usually just use our back doors, I suppose you'll do the same.'

Anna looked up the unmade lane. On the right-hand side was a row of terrace houses and on the left a detached house then a line of wooden fencing. Before she had time to take in any more, her guide said, 'Come, I'll show you round the front.' They walked past the gable end of the first house in the row and came to the end of a tarmacked street with a public house on the opposite corner. Here the fronts of the houses that she'd seen in the back lane faced an identical row built in the same red brick. The house doors, blue, red, black and green, opened straight on to the street, and straggly plane trees grew every few yards on the edges of the pavements.

'This is Weaver Street proper,' the woman told Anna waving an arm expansively, 'and that's the Weaver's Arms pub and up at the top of the street you can just see St Joseph's Church. So' – she turned and smiled warmly – 'welcome to Weaver Street.'

Anna thought it looked rather drab but she kept her thoughts to herself, and as they retraced their steps and entered the lane, she learned that her guide was called Rose Walker.

'Anna Carswell,' she responded. 'I've just travelled up from Oxfordshire.'

They walked alongside the row of houses, each one with its own little garden, some better tended than others, and by the time they arrived at the gate to number fifteen, her new billet, Anna had learned that Rose lived at number three with her three-year-old son, James, that her husband, Joey, was serving in the navy, that his parents lived at number five, and that the newer, more modern house with a garden planted with colourful shrubs and neat borders on the left-hand side of the lane next to an allotment belonged to Kitty and John Sykes.

'You'll soon get to know everybody,' said Rose, pointing to houses where people called Maggie, Lily, Molly and Beth lived. But the most surprising thing she learned was that Rose had once lived with Mavis when she first came to Liverpool from Buckinghamshire.

Anna's mind was buzzing as Rose led the way to number fifteen's door.

'You'll love living with Mavis, she's the best in the world,' Rose gushed, pushing open the door and calling, 'Yoo-hoo, Mavis. Look who I found.'

A small, neat woman with mousy hair and beady eyes came rushing to greet them. Her fluffy brown jumper and fluttering hands had Anna thinking that she looked like a friendly sparrow. 'Oh, you're here at last. Come in, come in,' Mavis Robson trilled, 'you're more than welcome.'

'Pleased to meet you, Miss Robson.' Anna dumped her kitbag and shook Mavis's bony hand, at the same time taking in the tidy, cosy living-room-cum-kitchen. The black iron range gleamed as did the polished sideboard, and the brightly coloured pegged rugs and pretty cushions let her know that her new landlady was house-proud. *Not a dump by any means*, she thought, having been warned by one of the WAAFs in her unit, a snooty girl from a wealthy background and fond of spouting that she was *just doing her bit for king and country*, and that *up north was all muck and whippets, and clogs and shawls.*

'You must be tired and parched after such a long journey, so take your coat off and sit yourself down. Make yourself at home.' Mavis indicated an armchair by the hearth. Anna slipped off her greatcoat then took off her cap, and relieving her of them, Mavis scurried through an open door into what Anna presumed was a hallway. Next to go was the kitbag. Mavis left it at the foot of the stairs, and coming back into the kitchen she said, 'We'll have a cup of tea and a chat for starters, then there's a shepherd's pie in the oven for later.' She flicked a thumb at the black-leaded range with shiny brass knobs.

'I knew who she was the minute she came into the shop,' Rose said, laughing. 'I gave her a little tour of the front street on our way here just so she gets the lie of the land.' She smiled at Anna. 'You'll find it a lot different from Oxfordshire, just like I did when I came up from Buckinghamshire, but you'll be glad you came. I know I am – it changed my life.' She gave Mavis an endearing smile then said, 'I'd best get off and collect James. May will be wondering what's kept me. Not that she'll want to give him back to me. Granny May spoils him something rotten.' Chuckling, Rose let herself out and Mavis boiled the kettle.

'Lovely girl is Rose; she used to live with me,' Mavis said as she put leaves into a round brown teapot and poured on boiling water.

'Yes, she told me,' Anna replied, and Mavis wondered what else Rose had divulged.

Mavis filled two cups then asked if Anna took milk and sugar.

'Just a drop of milk,' she said, not wanting to use up Mavis's precious sugar rations although she did prefer sweet tea. In the camp at Harwell there had been a plentiful supply of basic foodstuffs, but Mavis would only have rationing coupons for a single person and practically everything was in short supply. At first it had just been sugar, butter and bacon, but recently the government had extended the list to include all kinds of meat as well as tea, jam, eggs, cheese and biscuits. Of course, Anna would give her food coupons to Mavis but even so, she'd make sure she didn't take more than her fair share. She'd already got the feeling that Mavis would be a generous landlady.

Mavis handed her a cup then sat with her own in the other chair by the fire.

'Now, tell me a bit about yourself and ask me any questions you like, and I'll do my best to answer them. I want you to feel comfortable, so it's my job to make life as pleasant as it possibly can be, considering the situation the country's in.' Mavis shook her head and tutted impatiently then took a sip of tea. 'You're a long way from home doing a responsible job, and most likely you're missing your friends and family.'

By now, Anna had drained her cup. Never had tea tasted so good, it being the first drink she'd had since changing stations for the second time on her journey from Oxfordshire that morning. When Mavis lifted the teapot and offered a refill she readily accepted. Her empty stomach rumbled and the tantalising smell from the pie in the oven made her mouth water.

'So, what did your parents think when you joined the WAAF?' Mavis asked. 'I'll bet they were proud but worried.'

'Actually, no,' Anna said softly. 'Both my parents are dead. Mother died the day after war broke out and my father two weeks later.' She didn't want to talk about Jane and Norman.

Mavis gasped. 'Oh, you poor child. I'm so sorry. Me and my

thoughtless tongue.' She sounded so utterly contrite that Anna pitied her.

'Yes, it was a shock, but I try not to dwell on it,' she said, thinking that although she had been truly sorry for Jane and Norman's untimely deaths, her sadness had been more for their wasted lives rather than that she missed their love and affection. What you never had you never missed.

Mavis, her composure recovered, said, 'You're a very brave girl,' and sensing that Anna wasn't inclined to dwell on the sad event she asked in an overly bright voice, 'Now what is it you'll be doing whilst you're at Derby House?'

Anna briefly explained that she was a teleprinter operator and that her work was all to do with communications. She was careful not to say too much. *Careless talk costs lives.* Not that she thought for one minute that her landlady was a German spy, but she didn't feel like getting into a long conversation about her work or about her past. She had too many bad memories, the worst of them being Simon Grant. In fact, what she wanted to do right now was empty her bladder, the two cups of tea having rushed through her empty system. She was about to ask where the lavatory was when the back door opened and a man limped into the kitchen, a broad smile on his face.

'Oh, so you've arrived then,' he said, looking at Anna with his one good eye. A ragged lid covered the empty socket of his other eye. 'She's been on pins all day waiting for you.' He grinned at Mavis then sat down at the table, lifting the teapot and pulling a face when he discovered that it was empty. 'I see I'm too late for a cuppa.'

'Never,' said Mavis, getting to her feet and adding, 'Anna Carswell, meet Jack Naughton.'

She began making a fresh pot. Jack seemed so much at home that Anna presumed he too must live with Mavis.

'Did you have a good journey, Anna?'

'It could have been better. I had to change stations three times and the trains were packed with service personnel all being shunted from one end of the country to the other.'

'Mobilisation, that's what they called it in the last war. I lost track of the different places they sent me. I just did what I was told, that was until they had to pension me off.' He winked with his good eye and patted his leg.

'Did you...?' Anna glanced from his disfigured face to his stiff leg.

'Aye, I copped this lot in France. Mind you, if I had the chance I'd go again. We can't let Jerry win. Hitler might have his bloody Gestapo and his SS, but we've got Winston Churchill and we'll show the buggers that we won't be beaten.'

'Language, Jack!' Mavis expostulated as she handed him a mug of tea.

'Sorry, love.' He gave her a rueful smile then started telling her he'd planted cabbage and set some onions, and would get the early potatoes in tomorrow. Anna tried to recall if she had seen something outside the back door that served as a lavatory. The snooty WAAF had remarked that they didn't have indoor plumbing up north.

'Excuse me,' she blurted, feeling as though she might burst. 'Please could you show me where your lavatory is?'

Mavis clapped her hands to her cheeks. 'Oh, my goodness! Whatever was I thinking. I should have asked if you wanted to freshen up when you first arrived. How remiss of me.' She hurried to the door leading into the hallway. 'Come on, love, this way.'

Anna jumped to her feet and followed, Mavis insisting on humping the kitbag upstairs step by step. When they reached the landing, Mavis pushed open the nearest door. 'This is your room,' she said, leaving the kitbag in the doorway then scampering along the narrow landing to tap a door at the far end. 'This is mine, and this is the bathroom.' She opened the door at right angles to her own bedroom door with a flourish. By now her cheeks were flushed partly because of her oversight at not having shown Anna the facilities earlier, and partly because of the speed she'd mounted the stairs. 'I'll leave you to it,' she panted. 'Come down for your dinner when you're ready.'

So, they did have indoor plumbing after all. Thank goodness for that. Gabbling her thanks, Anna dived into the bathroom, closed the door then felt for the light switch. Finding it, she flicked it down, dashed for the lavatory and plumped down on the seat. Along with the relief she felt as her bladder emptied was the feeling that she'd got lucky with her new billet. Grim stories told by some of the more experienced WAAFs had made her anxious when she'd heard that some landladies were mean and pernickety and only doing it for the money, or that she might be expected to share a cramped, little room with two or three other girls in a squalid house with no comforts. The bathroom, like everywhere else in the house that she'd so far seen, was spotless. She washed her hands and face, drying them on fluffy towels that smelled of lavender. As she switched off the light, she gave a sudden gasp.

In her hurry she'd forgotten about the blackout. Nervously she turned the light back on, her breath rushing out of her when she saw that the window panes were blacked-out. Fines were issued for showing a light after dark. Even the faintest glimmer might attract the German bombers. Just another of the bugbears that a country at war had to suffer, and how embarrassing it would have been if her thoughtlessness had led to a member of the Air Raid Precaution team knocking on her landlady's door on her very first night in residence. Her panic subsiding, she flicked off the light and walked the length of the landing, noting that the panes in the tall window at the head of the stairs were also painted over.

Now to investigate my bedroom, she thought, but this time she wouldn't be so careless.

Inside the dark room she could just make out the window. The curtains were already drawn. Retracing her steps, Anna switched on the light.

Her heart soared when she saw the decent-sized room with its single bed, wardrobe and dressing table. The pretty blue and white patchwork quilt on the bed matched the mats on the dressing table, Anna guessing that they were Mavis's own handiwork, as might be the blue and grey pegged rug and the curtains: blue forget-me-nots on a white background and lined with heavy black cotton cloth. She couldn't have wished for more.

Wasting no time, she stripped off her uniform tunic and hung it over the back of the chair at the dressing table then she unpacked her kitbag, shaking the creases from the tightly rolled garments before hanging dresses, shirts, skirts and cardigans in the wardrobe. Two pairs of shoes went under the bed and underwear and other bits and pieces either in or on the dresser. Then sitting on the edge of the bed, she unlaced her thick-soled black RAF issue shoes, and coming upright she took off her skirt. Keeping on her blue shirt and tie and the hateful grey lisle stockings, she pulled on a grey tweed skirt and cardigan and slipped her feet into a lighter pair of shoes. Next, she checked her uniform for any stains it might have acquired on the journey. Relieved to find none she gave the skirt and tunic a good brushing then hung them carefully in the wardrobe. It wouldn't do to turn up at Derby House looking anything less than immaculate: she didn't fancy being hauled over the coals by her commanding officer on her first day.

Before she left the room, she turned out the light and went to the window. Parting the curtains an inch or two, she peered out into the darkness. A watery moon lighted the lane she had walked up with Rose and she could just make out the stark shapes of large trees beyond the allotment. No lights shone from the windows of the modern house on the other side of the lane, the blackout forbidding it, but frosty crystals coating the garden walls and stones in the lane glistened in the pale moonlight, lending an almost ethereal quality to the scene below.

I think I'm going to like living in Weaver Street, Anna told herself as she let the curtains fall back into place.

Relieved and refreshed, she went downstairs. The distinct greenish smell of boiled cabbage mingled with the smell of shepherd's pie. Anna's tummy rumbled. She was starving. Jack was nowhere in sight, and Mavis was scooping food onto plates. The gaily patterned oilcloth that was covering the table on Anna's arrival was now hidden under a snowy white tablecloth. The table was set for two. Anna wondered why. Where was Jack?

'Sit yourself down,' Mavis said, coming to the table with two plates of shepherd's pie and cabbage. Anna dithered. *Which of the four chairs should she choose?* 'I usually sit here.' Mavis put a plate on the left-hand side of the table. Anna murmured her thanks and sat in a chair on the right. Mavis set down the second plate. 'Now, eat up. I'm sure you're hungry.'

Anna tucked in. It tasted delicious; good home cooking was certainly preferable to the stuff they dished up in the canteen at Harwell. Noticing how eagerly Anna attacked the pie, Mavis silently ate her own. *She seems like a nice, well-bred girl*, she mused as she munched.

'That was marvellous,' said Anna, sitting back, her plate scraped clean. 'I don't know when I last ate such a tasty meal.'

'It was only a bit of mince and potato and one of Jack's winter cabbages,' Mavis said offhandedly, but she had flushed at the compliment. 'It gets harder by the week to put decent food on the table. What with only being allowed one shilling and tuppence worth of meat each week and just four ounces of ham and two of cheese, my brain's addled when it comes to concocting recipes. The wireless programmes and the magazines are full of suggestions, but I can't say I'm fond of sardine fritters and Lord Woolton Pie.' She curled her lip. 'And as for mock bananas made with parsnips and milk, you can keep them.'

'Well, your shepherd's pie was a triumph compared to the stuff they served in the canteen where I was stationed,' Anna said.

Beaming with pride, Mavis got to her feet to put the kettle on. 'I gather you wouldn't say no to a cup of tea and a piece of eggless sponge to finish off then.' Anna agreed and when the tea was brewed and served, she demolished the slice of cake in three bites, declaring that you'd never know an egg hadn't been within a mile of it.

'I'm pleased you think so; making cakes and buns is my job.' Mavis then went on to tell Anna that she worked in the Adelphi Hotel as the pastry and cakes chef. 'I've worked there for years. Before the war I would have gone in every day but what with eggs and flour so scarce I just do three mornings each week. If the Germans keep targeting the ships bringing food stuff into the port, we'll soon be eating grass. If it wasn't for the greens and spuds Jack grows on his allotment, I don't know how we'd manage.'

At the mention of Jack, Anna satisfied her curiosity by asking why he hadn't had his dinner with them and saying she had expected that he would.

Mavis chuckled. 'Jack doesn't live here. He lives next door, and he left us alone today so that we can get to know one another. I gave him some of the pie to take home with him. He's a grand man is Jack and a very special friend.' She glanced at the hearth. 'And that fire won't mend itself,' she said, referring to the glowing embers. 'I'd better get some coal.'

She disappeared into the space behind the back door and a moment later Anna heard the rattling of hard objects against metal coming from below. Reckoning that the house must have a coal cellar underneath it she made a mental note to take her turn at fetching the coal.

When Mavis reappeared with a full bucket, she was delighted to see that Anna had cleared the table and was at the sink washing the plates.

'You didn't need to do that,' she said.

'No bother,' Anna replied. 'It's only right that I share the chores.' She could have added that at home she hadn't shared them, she'd been responsible for all of them once she had grown old enough to be useful, but talking about Jane and Norman only made her unhappy so she turned and said, 'Is there anything else I can do?'

'Not a thing,' said Mavis, sparingly placing lumps of coal on the fire; it was also rationed. 'Sit you by the fire and we'll talk over how we're going to live together peacefully, like.' She went and washed her hands then sat in the armchair opposite the one Anna was now sitting in. 'As you've no doubt guessed, I'm a bit of a stickler for keeping things tidy' – she gave a self-deprecating grin – 'so I'll expect you to clean up in the bathroom after you've used it, and keep your bedroom in good order.' Chuckling, she added, 'When Rose came to live with me, she was useless at cleaning up after herself. It never occurred to her, what with coming from a house where servants had done everything for her.'

Anna showed her surprise. She hadn't got the impression that

Rose was anything other than a working housewife and mother. 'She didn't strike me as being grand,' she said.

Mavis laughed. 'Oh, no, not now. Rose has learned a lot of life's lessons since then, and all for her betterment.' Her reflective smile left Anna wondering what the lessons that Rose had learned were, but it was none of her business so she returned Mavis's smile then set about reassuring her that she would abide by the rules.

'I'll be at Derby House for most of every day, and if there's an emergency I might be expected to stay overnight, but when I'm here I'll do my fair share of cleaning and cooking. I'm used to it.'

'I could tell that by the way you had the dishes washed while I fetched the coal, but I'll not be expecting you to do too much as your job is very important to the war effort. You'll need to concentrate on that.'

Anna grimaced. 'To be quite honest, I'm nervous about what they might expect of me. I've only ever worked in Harwell where it was only RAF personnel, and my commanding officer told me that working for HQ Western Approaches – that's how it's known at Derby House – won't be what I've been used to because it's a joint effort run by the Senior Service,' she said, referring to the British Navy. She giggled. 'Apparently the Senior Service takes a pretty dim view of any careless behaviour and tend to look down on us. The CO warned me that it was my duty to make a good impression to uphold the honour of the RAF.'

'And I'm sure you will,' Mavis said, sitting back with a satisfied smile. 'And I'm sure we're going to get along just fine. You'll soon get to know my friends and neighbours in Weaver Street and they'll make you more than welcome. Salt of the earth they are, good hard-working people always ready to help one another out. We stick together in troubled times like these, and believe me it makes blackouts, curfews, rationing and fear of air raids all that easier to bear.'

'If they're all as helpful and as pleasant as Rose, and as welcoming as you and Jack, I'll be glad to meet them,' Anna said. 'I really appreciate my lovely bedroom, and the dinner was a proper treat.' Then unable to suppress a yawn, she covered her mouth with her hand. 'Sorry, it's been a long day.'

'I'm sure it has,' said Mavis, getting to her feet. 'Now off you go and get ready for bed. You can have a bath if you like; there's plenty of hot water tonight, but I suggest you restrict them to two a week to save on the coal. I'm just popping round to Jack's to say goodnight.'

'Thanks ever so much for the lovely welcome. Will you promise to give me a shout in the morning in case I sleep in?' Anna said as she went towards the door into the hallway and Mavis headed for the back door.

'I'll do that. I'm always up before seven. We don't want you to be late on your first day.'

The back door closed behind Mavis and Anna wearily mounted the stairs.

It wasn't until after she had taken a pleasant, hot bath and was putting on her nightdress that the full impact of transferring from Oxfordshire to Liverpool hit her. She'd most likely never see Simon Grant again. There would be no opportunity for him to tell her he'd acted badly, that he'd never make such a crazy mistake again, and that it was her and only her that he loved. That part of her life was over.

Anna had met Flight Lieutenant Simon Grant at a camp dance shortly after arriving in Harwell. She'd been immediately attracted to the tall, handsome flyer with striking blue eyes. He'd whirled her round the dance floor, shown her how to do the Lindy Hop, and laughed when she'd confessed that she hadn't been to many dances before. She hadn't told him she'd been too busy carrying the burden of a mentally ill mother and a drunken father to have much of a social life. She'd only told him about her dysfunctional upbringing some months later when she had thought they would spend the rest of their lives together. Simon had seemed sympathetic, saying 'you poor old thing' and 'what rotten luck', in his cut-glass, public school boy accent and at the time she had been comforted, but looking back on it she realised that he hadn't been all that interested in her sad history.

When it became obvious that they were an item, the girls in her unit had congratulated her on landing such a catch. Her closest friend, Suzy Griffiths, had declared that Simon was absolutely gorgeous and given half a chance she wouldn't mind having him for herself. Anna had laughed at that, taking it as a compliment. She had never had a long-term boyfriend before and it was all new to her. In fact, she'd rarely made close friends with anyone from school or work. Close friends expected to be invited into your home and the shame of letting them witness the miserable life she led with Jane and Norman in the shabby house in Salisbury was too embarrassing. Instead, she was friendly with everyone but always kept them at a distance that didn't involve them discovering her secret.

Anna and Suzy had got to know one another during their training at West Drayton. Suzy was training to be a driver, and Anna a teleprinter operator, but they often attended the same general lectures. They had been sitting beside each other listening to a senior WAAF giving a lecture on appropriate behaviour now that they were part of His Majesty's forces. *A WAAF does not engage in flighty dalliances with her male colleagues*, the gawky, rather unattractive senior WAAF had said with a distinct curl of her lip. Suzy had giggled.

'I'll bet she's never had a flighty dalliance with a donkey let alone a man,' she whispered to Anna. This weird, somewhat crude remark struck Anna as hilarious and she almost choked on her suppressed laughter. When the senior WAAF advised that *an approach from a member of the opposite sex should be dealt with courteously but firmly leaving him with the clear understanding that you must not be distracted from your work*, Anna muttered, 'Thanks for eyeing my breasts and patting my bum, Captain, but my teleprinter needs me more than you do. Adolf might call at any minute.'

A stern reprimand to stop gossiping and pay attention from the senior WAAF had them shaking in tandem as they tried their best not to laugh out loud. Since then, they had been inseparable. They hadn't seen much of one another in working hours, Anna on duty in the communications rooms and Suzy in the garage or out on the road driving the officers to various locations, but whenever they were off duty, they had made trips to the cinema in Hillingdon or into London, and of course they attended the dances on camp.

At first, after Anna and Simon became a couple, Suzy had often tagged along with them, sometimes with one of Simon's fellow flyers in tow. They'd had great fun. From March to November Anna had been deliriously happy; at last, she had found someone to love who returned that love fulsomely. It had been a dreamtime filled with hope, even when her heart had been in her mouth during every mission Simon flew, dropping leaflets over France and Belgium to assure the citizens of those countries that the British RAF had their backs, or in the later months of their courtship flying on bombing raids over Berlin or Hamburg. Her fear had always been that he might not make it back. She had been too happy to consider that it was their love that might not survive.

Even when Suzy suddenly stopped spending her free time

with Anna and Simon, Anna had thought nothing of it; Suzy's long blonde hair, baby-blue eyes and bubbly personality attracted a raft of admirers. Anna had been far too much in love to give much thought to anyone else's romances. She'd found the man she would love forever, God willing.

Now, as she sat at the dressing table in her bedroom at number fifteen, Weaver Street, she was swamped by a deluge of memories of her time at Harwell. Feeling slightly light-headed, she unpinned her hair then ran her fingers through it. The trouble with having a glossy auburn mane of naturally wavy hair was that she had to fashion it in a way that sat neatly under her peaked cap; sometimes a French pleat or scraped back into a neat roll at the nape of her neck. Both hairstyles made her scalp feel tight, and at the end of each day it was pure luxury to let her hair flow free. But tonight, it brought tears to her eyes.

Simon had likened its colour to the last rays of an autumn sunset. *You know the sort I mean?* he'd said, stroking her hair gently. *The smouldering embers that flare with passion.*

And he set me on fire with his slick tongue, she thought grimly as she tugged a brush through her hair, static crackling in the silent room.

He'd given her a ring, and hadn't objected to her wearing it on the third finger of her left hand. They hadn't talked about marriage. Life was far too precarious these days to make long-term plans; it seemed like tempting fate. He'd been flying with Bomber Command then, and if he didn't choose to spend all his off-duty time with her, she'd accepted that he needed to let off steam with his brothers-in-arms, and hadn't been the least bit worried. *I must have been blind as well as stupid*, she told her reflection in the mirror.

She still found it hard to believe that he had betrayed her with Suzy of all people. Or that her best friend had been able to look her in the eye, laughing and chattering in the way they always did when they met up at the end of each day in the dormitory shared with eighteen other WAAFs. It had been something of a ritual before going to sleep to whisper confidences, Anna singing Simon's praises and Suzy dreamily elusive about the man she was dating. Anna had said he sounded as wonderful as Simon. But, of course he did, she now thought, he was Simon. Suzy's cruelty still hurt.

Her hopes and dreams had been shattered on a miserably cold day in early December. She hadn't seen as much of Simon in the last couple of months, his time off duty never seeming to match with hers, but on the few occasions he'd sought her out they'd easily fallen into the same routine, a drive to somewhere interesting, a tasty meal in a country pub then back to his quarters to make love. She'd been sitting in the canteen hoping against hope that duties would allow them to spend the weekend together when Margaret Barnes sat down beside her. Although Margaret also worked in communications, Anna didn't know her very well.

Margaret had opened up the conversation by talking about work and the freezing weather. Then looking directly into Anna's eyes she'd said, 'Look, I know it's none of my business but I hate to see anyone being made a fool of so forgive me for what I'm going to tell you.'

Anna had felt sick. She'd rushed from the canteen to the cloakroom and thrown up her lunch. For the rest of the afternoon, her jangled thoughts made it difficult to concentrate and twice she was reprimanded, tears threatening to flow and make her look just like what she was: a complete fool. At the end of the shift, she went in search of Simon. She had to know if Margaret's words were true.

Simon had shrugged dismissively when Anna asked whether

it was true that he was having an affair with Suzy. 'We're having a bit of fun together, just like you and I, darling. Live for the moment is what I say. It doesn't interfere with what we have.'

What we have? Anna had shrieked that she thought they had something special, that she wasn't just another of his girls. He'd said she read too much into things, and when she'd asked him why he'd given her the ring he'd shrugged again. 'It was a gift. Nothing more. I got it from a chap who owed me money. It was no use to me so I gave it to you.'

Anna could hardly believe what she was hearing. As an icy hand clutched at her insides, the blinkers fell away and she saw him for what he really was: a smooth-talking playboy who was out for everything he could get. She'd ripped the ring from her finger and thrown it at him then stormed off. He wasn't worthy of her love and devotion or the tears she would no doubt shed. But it was hard to love a man who didn't love you back, and the next few days had been sheer agony.

Anna was good at hiding her feelings, and in front of the other girls she had kept up the pretence that it was she who had ended their relationship. Harder to bear had been sharing a dormitory with Suzy; she couldn't avoid her but she'd given her the cold shoulder whenever they were together. Suzy had seemed unperturbed, and that had hurt just as much as losing Simon. It wasn't unknown in these live-for-the-moment times for engagements to be broken off. Redeployment to a different camp meant they fizzled out, or worse still, if the man was a flyer, the awful fact that he hadn't made it back. Anna wouldn't wish that on Simon, even though he was a lying cheat.

So, she had put on a brave face right up to leaving Harwell. Now, alone in Liverpool, her heart broken, she had to convince herself that life with Simon was over and that this was a fresh start where no one knew her or her history.

She climbed into bed. The familiar pain that had tormented her nights for the past three months was building up again and she closed her eyes tightly, willing it to go away. From now on things would be different and it would be a long time, or maybe never, before she put her trust in any man. For now, her heart was hers and hers alone.

2

At the same time as Anna Carswell was preparing to spend her first night in Weaver Street, Lily Stubbs was writing in a ledger in the disused shop on Broad Green that was now being used as the headquarters for Air Raid Precautions. The door opened, and John Sykes walked in. Lily licked the end of her pencil, scribbled a few final words then greeted him with a cheery grin.

'I've finished logging where everyone is,' she said proudly, referring to the names of the wardens and the streets they were patrolling. 'Now, if it's okay with you I'll go to Durning Road; we're short-handed down there. Stanley's doing it on his own.'

Stanley Pickersgill was her mother's second husband, and although Lily liked him a great deal and thought he was good for her mam, she'd never thought of him as her stepfather. At twenty-three years of age, she was too old for that.

'Good girl, Lily,' said John, taking off his warden's helmet then running his fingers through his thick brown hair. As head warden, his helmet was white with a large black 'W' on the front whereas the one Lily was now putting on was black with a white 'W'.

John sat down behind the desk in the makeshift office and gave a weary sigh. 'I checked that Anderson shelter on Bradfield Street where they said they'd smelled gas. It was a sack of manure.' He rolled his eyes. 'And I gave Nellie Moss a ticking-off for breaking the blackout. That's the third time this week.' He chuckled. 'You don't think she could be in league with the Luftwaffe, or one of Adolf's spies, do you?'

'What! That barmy old bat?' Lily exclaimed as she checked her whistle was in the pocket of her tunic and her handbell in her haversack. 'Last time I spoke to her about her blackout she didn't even know there was a war on.'

'And don't we all wish there wasn't,' John replied, rubbing his tired eyes. He'd been working all day in the engineering factory that he owned, overseeing the making of small machine parts for tanks and anti-aircraft guns, a government contract, and he had to ensure it was completed to perfection. *Mr Churchill's relying on us, lads,* he had told his workforce.

Lily buttoned her black serge tunic and slung her haversack over her shoulder. 'I'll be off then. Let's hope it's a quiet night and Jerry stays at home,' she chirped as she tootled off out into the dark street.

'Ta-ra, love,' John called after her. He smiled fondly. Lily was a grand girl. He'd known her for most of her life. She was his step-daughter Molly's best friend, and Lily's mother, Maggie, was his wife's best friend. Maggie and Lily lived at number nine Weaver Street, and Kitty had lived next door in number eleven when she'd first arrived in Liverpool from Ireland. That had been in 1916. She'd been married to Tom Conlon then and had given birth to two children before Tom had been murdered. It hadn't been a happy marriage. Tom had been a bookmaker with delusions of grandeur. His adulterous affair with the daughter of a wealthy horse owner and trainer had almost broken Kitty, but being a woman of great spirit, she'd risen above it. She'd bought a little café on the towpath that ran by the river at the top of Weaver Street and turned it into a successful business to ensure her own and her children's future. John had fallen in love with Kitty from the moment he'd first met her, but respectful of her status he hadn't declared his love until after Tom's death. Now they were married and living in a house he'd had built next to the allotment in the lane behind Weaver Street. He'd had it built there because he had been adamant that he wouldn't live in Tom Conlon's house, and Kitty had been extremely reluctant to move away from her good friends and neighbours. After living in Weaver Street for fifteen years, John understood why. They were a great bunch, and young Lily Stubbs had grown into one of the best.

* * *

Lily cut a determined figure as she marched along Broad Green, past the Weaver's Arms and on towards Durning Road, proudly wearing her helmet and battledress. She'd surprised her mother and everyone else in Weaver Street when instead of dashing off and joining the ATS, the Auxiliary Territorial Services, or the WAAF, she had chosen to stay on at Holroyd's mill weaving miles of khaki and blue serge for the troops, and then volunteered for the ARP.

Lily loved being a warden, and tonight she had been thrilled when John asked her to man the headquarters whilst he went to check out the suspected gas leak; a great deal of the infrastructure in their area had been damaged by a German incendiary bomb in November 1940. Now, as she strode purposely on her way to join Stanley in Durning Road, she blessed the day she'd joined the ARP. For the first time in her life since becoming a member of the team of part-time wardens, Lily felt that she was doing something really worthwhile, and that her efforts to save lives were appreciated. None more than by John Sykes.

John was the kind of dad Lily would have liked, and in her younger days she'd been jealous of Molly. Lily had never known her birth father. The only thing she had of his was her mane of flaming red hair. When she'd been born, her mam, Maggie, had been the battered wife of drunken Fred, a regular in the army who from the start had suspected that a red-haired baby wasn't his. Proved right, he'd beaten her mam senseless and with Kitty Sykes's help Maggie had thrown him out for good. Lily hadn't seen him since, and had no desire to do so.

However, her mam was the sort of woman who needed a man in her life, and growing up, Lily had had a string of 'pretend dads', some who stayed for a few weeks and one who'd hung about for years until he'd been found out to be a cheat and a liar. That was the trouble with men, in her experience, and she wasn't going to make the same mistakes as her mam. Lily was on the lookout for a man as kind and trustworthy as John Sykes and, in the meantime, she was happy to share him with Molly.

At the corner of Durning Road, Lily gave an involuntary shudder, not because of the chill night or because it was pitch black. This was the road on which she had had her baptism by fire. She'd been on duty in nearby Gladstone Street checking that the inhabitants were adhering to the blackout, or were safe in the shelter at the end of the street. Eight hours of continuous bombing had rocked the city, sirens blaring, fires starting, and ambulances and fire engines screeching to wherever they were needed. It had been 29 November 1940 and ever since then, whenever Lily patrolled Durning Road, she felt as though she would never forget that night.

Overhead the sky had been black with Junkers and Dorniers flying at top speed, their ear-splitting howl terrifying. Across the distance Lily could see smoke and flames rising over the docks as the Germans bombarded the port. The answering clatter of ack-ack guns split the air and the incoming roar of Spitfires chasing the German bombers off target filled the night sky. Lily had just hustled a young woman with a baby into the safety of the Anderson shelter when word came that parachute mines had been dropped in Wavertree and the Botanic Gardens. Sam Cope, an elderly warden and a veteran of the First World War, had rushed over from Crossfield Street with the news.

'That's a bit too close for my bloody liking,' Lily's colleague, Brian Barraclough, had said as across the distance they watched smoke rising and flames leaping skywards. He had no sooner spoken than the whine of an approaching engine high above had them ducking for cover in an alley between the houses. A blinding flash followed by shock waves in the ground let them know that Jerry had dropped an incendiary very close by.

'It's hit something in Durning Road,' Lily yelled, charging out of the alley and running in the direction of the explosion. Brian ran with her, and Sam tailed off to bring other wardens in the nearby streets to assist. As Lily pelted down Durning Road, the Dornier's pilot executed a victory roll and zoomed eastwards. 'Bastard!' Lily screamed. 'Bloody bastard!'

Slowing her pace, she stared in horror at the flames engulfing the shattered walls of the Ernest Brown Junior Instructional Centre. It had taken a direct hit, piles of rubble where once had stood a grand, sturdy building. Lily's heart sank. She knew that this was a designated shelter, and that there were probably hundreds of people sheltering in its basement and boiler room. Trams brought people out of the city centre to buildings like this, their stout vaulted ceilings a strong protection against German bombs.

But not this time.

She took her handbell from her haversack and her whistle from her pocket and as she scrabbled over the rubble, she rang the bell and blew short sharp blasts in the hope of attracting the attention of anyone still alive in the ruins. Her eyes feverish, she sought for a raised arm and listened for cries for help. But she saw no bodies and heard no screams.

By this time Brian and other wardens who had raced to the devastating scene were frantically heaving broken masonry and wooden spars aside. Lily was doing the same, her gloves in tatters and her hands raw. Then she heard the roar of engines and an AFS fire engine screeched to halt, closely followed by two ambulances.

Lily scrambled off the mountain of debris, and as the firemen unreeled their hoses and the rescue crew set about trying to get to the people trapped below, she stood watching as jets of water arced through the air and men with spades and picks hacked at the rubble near to where the entrance had been. Flames hissed then died, metal sparked against stone as the rescue team tackled the marathon task. Tears made pale pink rivulets down Lily's grimy face. She felt utterly helpless. *Pull yourself together, Lily Stubbs*, she silently chastised. *When they get them out, you'll be needed so stop being a drama queen.* She checked her haversack for gauze, cotton wool and triangular bandages; she had been trained to deal with minor injuries.

A roar went up from the rescuers. They had broken through, making a space big enough for the men, women and children to escape from under the ruins. They emerged one by one, staggering over the rubble, their shocked faces pale and their garments covered in grey dust.

Lily sprang into action, rushing forward to help a young woman with a baby in her arms and a toddler clinging to the hem of her coat. Lily scooped up the toddler, and tucking him under one arm, she supported the woman with the other. The woman's teeth were chattering, and the baby's wails tore at Lily's heart. Leading them to safety and then ascertaining that they were uninjured she left them in the care of two ladies from the WVS. The Women's Voluntary Service were always on hand at times like this.

'Lily! Lily!'

At the sound of her name, Lily turned to see Molly O'Malley waving to her. Molly was a trained nurse. When she married Mickey, she'd had to give up working in the Oxford Street hospital, but her marital status did not prevent her from being a part-time member of an ambulance crew. Three nights a week she helped man an ambulance whilst her mother, Kitty, looked after her and Mickey's baby son, Ronan.

Molly was bathing a nasty gash in the head of one of the first men to emerge from the basement. Slumped on the steps of a nearby house that had escaped the blast, he was cursing the Germans for all he was worth. 'Fucking Fritz, targeting civilians. It's not bloody right.'

'No, it bloody isn't,' Lily agreed.

'There must be three hundred sheltering in that basement and the fucking boiler's burst,' the man roared. 'Them as wasn't crushed to death 'ull be bloody drowned in scalding hot water. None of 'em 'ull stand a sodding chance.'

Molly and Lily exchanged horrified glances.

'Hold still while I fix this bandage,' Molly said to her angry patient, and Lily said, 'I'd best get back, see what else I can do.'

She toiled into the hours of the morning, heartsore and weary as she led the injured to the ambulances, reunited frantic mothers with their children and helped carry the dead to the waiting lorries. When there was nothing more she could do, she trudged back to the headquarters to fill out her report. She found

John there, just back from organising evacuations and cordoning off the danger areas. They looked at one another, the horrors of the night plain on their faces. Lily filled out her form, her hands shaking and her heart heavy.

'Come on, love. We'll walk home together,' said John as Dave Garnet arrived to take over. 'Let's hope there's no more incidents like that tonight, Dave. Best of luck, mate.'

'I've never seen anything like it,' Lily said as they walked back to Weaver Street. John squeezed her arm tucked through his.

'Before the war, Lily, no one would have dreamed that patrolling the streets in the blackout would save hundreds of lives. There were some who laughed at us and called us army dodgers, but now they know what we do is vital. By the way, Brian told me you worked like a trooper tonight. I'm proud of you.'

'I did what I had to do,' she said lightly, but inside she was glowing.

Now, under a sky thick with grey clouds that held no threat of enemy aircraft, as she walked past the ruins of the Ernest Brown Junior Instructional Centre she remembered the 165 men, women and children who had lost their lives in its basement and were buried there; no headstones or flowers to mark their graves. Nearing the end of Durning Road she wondered if, whenever duty brought her to this road, she would always relive the horror of that night.

Stanley was standing guard on the corner of Nuttall Street and he gave her a smile. 'Quiet tonight,' he said as she came level with him.

'And I hope it blooming well stays that way,' Lily said wholeheartedly. She took a packet of Player's Navy Cut from her breast pocket. Lighting her cigarette, she dragged deeply on it.

'Them things 'ull kill you,' Stanley grunted.

'And so might Jerry,' scoffed Lily.

3

On Monday morning it was stingingly cold and Anna buttoned her greatcoat up to her chin as she stepped briskly out into the back lane ready to face her first day at Derby House. As promised, Mavis had wakened her early, given her a breakfast of tea and toast then wished her good luck in her new job. She hadn't got far when a pretty woman with a riot of tawny hair called out to her from the garden of the detached house on the opposite side of the lane. Well wrapped up in a tweed overcoat and woolly hat, she was holding a pair of garden shears.

'Good morning, ye must be Anna.' The woman walked up to the garden gate. 'Are ye settling in all right? I'm sure Mavis gave ye a great welcome.'

'She did,' Anna replied, somewhat taken aback. It seemed that not only Mavis Robson but everyone else in Weaver Street had been awaiting her arrival. First it had been Rose, then Jack, and now it was this woman leaning over the gate, her gold-flecked hazel eyes alight with friendly interest. Anna searched her mind for a name. 'You're Mrs Sykes, Kitty,' she said, hopeful that her memory hadn't played her foul.

'That's right. I just wanted to make ye welcome, an' I'll not keep ye 'cos I'm sure ye've a busy day ahead of ye.'

Anna grimaced. 'Something like that. It's my first and I'm dreading not being up to scratch. Still, I'll give it my best shot.' She gave a brave smile.

'Ach, I'm sure ye'll be fine. Now, off ye go. I'll no doubt see ye later. Ta-ra.'

'Nice to meet you,' Anna said as Kitty went back to the shrubs she'd been clipping and Anna hurried along the lane. She didn't want to miss the tram. Turning up late on her first day wouldn't earn her any credit, and as her old CO had reminded her, she had to uphold the honour of the RAF.

'Good morning,' a friendly voice called out as Anna drew level with one of the houses in the terrace. It was Rose. She was standing on the steps, a child in her arms, and an older woman beside her. 'Best of luck for today. Don't get lost in Liverpool,' she chirped.

'Good morning, I'll try not to,' Anna called back. 'Can't stop, I've a tram to catch.'

'See you later then,' Rose said.

Good lord, Anna thought, almost running out into Broad Green. *It's lovely to be made to feel so welcome, but if I miss the next tram, I'm a dead duck; good job I started out early.*

She caught it by the skin of her teeth.

'Hop aboard, love.' The same conductress as the day before grabbed her arm as Anna leapt for the platform. Anna gave her a friendly smile, and gasping her thanks she took a seat. The sights she'd seen yesterday didn't look quite so depressing in the pale February sunshine, and as the tram chugged its way into the city centre, she tried to imagine the day ahead. She'd feel confident if she was given her usual job operating a teleprinter but if she was assigned to something different, she'd have to be on her toes to show that she was up to it.

'Take care,' the conductress advised as Anna alighted in William Brown Street.

'I'll do my best,' Anna responded, and thinking how thoughtful and cheerful all the Liverpudlians she'd met so far seemed to be, she walked briskly down Dale Street towards Derby House. A cool breeze blew in from the nearby port on the eastern end of the Atlantic Ocean but she was warm enough in her greatcoat over her blue tailored skirt and jacket. Her peaked cap was set at just the right angle, and her auburn hair was neatly rolled. She couldn't help but notice the admiring glances of those she passed by and acknowledged their friendly smiles with one of her own, saying, 'Thank you' to an elderly bearded man who growled, 'Good on yer, girl,' and returning the smart salute from a man in a RAF uniform.

When she reached the Town Hall, she paused. According to her instructions, Western Approaches Headquarters were situated behind it. She found the unimpressive building easily, surprised that it wasn't at all grand. Later she learned that most of it was underground. In the foyer, Anna gave her name to the Wren on duty then followed her along corridors to Group Captain Sharp's office.

'She lives up to her name,' the Wren said with a grin, 'so make a good impression. You're not the only new recruit this morning,' she added as they turned a corner into a short corridor. A blonde, dumpy girl in a WAAF uniform was pacing nervously at the end of it. 'Well, I'll leave you two to it. Best of luck.'

The Wren strode away, and Anna smiled at the other girl. 'Hello, I'm Anna Carswell. I gather you're just starting today, as well.'

'Primrose Dobbins,' the girl mumbled. 'I've been transferred here from RAF Grimsby.' She sounded rather lost.

'RAF Harwell in Oxfordshire,' Anna said. 'Where's Grimsby?'

'The other side of the country, Lincolnshire, on the coast.' This time Primrose sounded utterly woeful. 'I come from Hull and the camp was that near I could go home on my days off.' Her sad, plump face reminded Anna of a painting she'd seen on a trip to a gallery in London, the cherub's innocent rosy face framed with golden curls and its limpid baby-blue eyes and pouting rosebud lips showing its discontent.

'You'll get over your homesickness once we get to know Liverpool and this place,' she said comfortingly, and at the same time thinking that she had never felt like that: she hadn't missed home at all. She'd been glad to see the back of it.

The group captain's office door swung open. A hawk-like, rangy woman in an impeccable uniform towered in the doorway. Her steely grey eyes looked Anna and Primrose up and down and Anna interpreted her expression as *not overly impressed*. She could almost feel Primrose trembling beside her.

'Welcome aboard, Carswell, Dobbins.' Elsie Sharp's head jerked from one to the other. 'I'll deal with you first, Carswell, alphabetic order you know. You wait here, Dobbins.' Primrose dithered, and Anna followed the group captain into her office. She went and sat behind her desk while Anna stood to attention in front of it.

'According to your previous CO you're a quick learner, Carswell, so you'll be joining one our new teams. Know much about the ops here, do you?'

'Some,' said Anna hesitantly, then hastened to add, 'and I'm sure I'll soon learn more.'

'It's to be hoped you will,' Elsie Sharp growled. She then delivered a battery of questions in staccato bursts, her hatchet face giving nothing away as Anna responded as alertly and accurately as she could. The group captain fell silent. Resting her elbows on the desk and pressing her clasped hands to her chin, her gimlet eyes scrutinised Anna from top to toe. The corners of her mouth twitched into a little smile. 'Dismissed, Carswell. Send Dobbins in.'

Anna saluted smartly, swung on her heel and marched out, closing the door behind her.

'Your turn, Primrose. She's not so bad.' Anna gave her an encouraging grin.

A few minutes later the girls were being marched through the building, doing their best to match Elsie Sharp's impatient long stride and take in snappy information. 'I'll show you round first. Explain what we do here. Get the hang of the place. Important to know the run of it. Vital in an emergency.' Anna thought it was like being spoken to by an ack-ack gun.

'In Derby House the Senior Service and the RAF work together. Joint ops to protect the convoys crossing the Atlantic. Senior Service has overall control. Our RAF reconnaissance planes provide vital forward info. You'll be working on that.' The latter was said almost threateningly.

They descended flights of stairs, down, down, into the basement. 'Nerve centre of the ops.' At the foot of the last flight, the group captain flourished her arm. 'Gas proof and bomb proof.' She ploughed onwards, pointing out emergency areas, dormitories, bathrooms, two recreational areas, the telecommunications room and the commander-in-chief's quarters. At last, they arrived at a pair of double doors. A naval rating on guard saluted and after returning his salute, Elsie Sharp said, 'Important to have your pass. Not allowed to access this part of the building without it. Carry it at all times.'

The guard opened the doors and they entered a vast room

with an enormous table in the centre. The tabletop was a huge map of the North Atlantic, and a similar map covered one wall. Around the table, Wrens and WAAFs were moving little models of the convoys to show their deployment, and others were perched on ladders updating positions or chalking reports on massive blackboards. The room seethed with activity, and the noise level was such that Anna and Primrose had difficulty hearing what the group captain was saying.

'This is where the Battle of the Atlantic is plotted out. Your job will be to trace and track submarines and enemy aircraft to protect the Allied merchant convoys on the dangerous approaches to Britain from the US and Canada,' the group captain told them as they toured the room, Elsie Sharp pointing out the purpose of each designated area.

Anna tried to blot out the various voices as Elsie pointed out the Aircraft State Board. 'Shows present situation of all RAF stations and ongoing operations,' she said. 'Info coming in from telecommunications.'

At the mention of telecommunications, Anna felt a longing for the teleprinter she was used to working. As though the group captain had read her mind, she said, 'I know you're both teleprinter operatives, but we're short-handed in here. This is where you're needed.'

Anna and Primrose exchanged anxious glances. Primrose looked shell-shocked, and Anna felt totally overwhelmed.

'Everything understood?' The group captain gave each of them a piercing look.

'Yes, ma'am.'

'Right, I'll leave you to it.' She turned and clicked her fingers. 'Somerville, all yours.'

To their relief, a pleasant-looking woman a few years older than Anna and Primrose hurried towards them with a kindly smile. 'Good to have you aboard,' she said. 'I'm Corporal Lucy Somerville. I'll be showing you the ropes. Have you worked in ops before?'

'No, Corporal Somerville,' Anna replied. 'I'm Anna Carswell and I was a teleprinter operator at Harwell. WAAF Primrose Dobbins was the same at RAF Grimsby,' she explained by way of introduction and noted the resigned look of disappointment on the corporal's face: *another pair of raw recruits.*

'Never mind,' Lucy said. 'I'll introduce you to the rest of the team.' She led them across the room and reeled off names: Poppy Montfort, Susan McIntyre and Denise Lawton. The girls smiled a tired welcome; Anna memorised their names.

'I don't need to remind you that men's lives depend on you,' the corporal continued, 'so we can't afford any mistakes. You need to keep a sharp eye and be alert at all times.' She gave them a warning look. 'I'll pair you off for the first few days. Anna, you go with Poppy, and Primrose you're with Susan.'

Anna gave Poppy a confident smile she didn't really feel. Poppy responded with a serious nod. She was a tall, big-boned girl with fair hair pulled back in a chignon, and Anna could tell from her cut-glass accent and assured manner that she'd most likely received a private school education, and that she came from a wealthy family, the sort who rode to hounds. She'd met her type at Harwell, and her haphazard upbringing with Jane and Norman left her feeling slightly inferior.

Then they got to work. Anna's first task was to chart the weather systems and the positions of sea and air craft, Poppy showing her how to mount the ladder and move it along the overhead rollers so that she could attach the little pin symbols to the gigantic wall map. Then they moved on to Aircraft State Board where Anna logged aeroplanes in and out of the many airfields across the country. The Derby House bunker was connected to

Station X at Bletchley Park where the codebreakers pieced together vital life and death information and Anna felt incredibly important as she responded to the incoming intelligence they were transmitting. Finally, she took her turn at the huge table in the centre of the room where a helpful Wren instructed her in the movement of the little model ships that represented the convoys. 'The Atlantic's riddled with German U-boats,' she said. 'They try to gather like packs of wolves round our ships but once they've been located, we can warn the convoy to change course. Then we keep track of where our ships are by moving them like this,' said the Wren, pushing a little boat an inch or so across the imaginary water with a long stick. She handed the stick to Anna then read out some coordinates. Gently, Anna pushed a ship in the merchant convoy into its new position. 'Well done,' praised the Wren.

There was an awful lot to take in and Anna felt that her brain was working overtime but by the end of the afternoon she glowed with pride as Poppy reported to Corporal Somerville, 'She's good; had most of it off in no time.'

The corporal's taut features relaxed into a satisfied smile. 'That's good to know. See you tomorrow,' she said and gave a smart salute. Anna raised her right hand with two fingers together and did likewise.

The five girls finished their shift, and as they made their weary way up to ground level, Poppy, Susan and Denise told Anna and Primrose what Liverpool had to offer other than working in Western Approaches.

'They have great dances at the Grafton,' Denise said. 'Loads of lonely soldiers and airmen all looking for a good time.'

Poppy rolled her eyes. 'And you intend to give them one, do you?' she said, tapping the diamond ring on the third finger of her left hand before adding, 'I won't be doing that.'

Anna felt a twinge of jealousy. She'd thrown her ring back in Simon Grant's face when he'd betrayed her. She didn't want to be tied to a lying cheat, but she still ached for the love she thought they'd shared.

Poppy must have noticed Anna's pained expression. 'Did you leave a chap behind when you came up here?'

Anna hesitated. 'No... no one in particular. I've no time for romance. I'm just out to enjoy myself,' she heard herself say flippantly. She didn't want their pity.

'I did,' Primrose said, finding her voice at last, encouraged by the friendly camaraderie. 'Collin's a leading aircraftsman, and we've been keeping company for nearly a year. He's still in Grimsby and I'm over here,' she said dismally.

Denise sniggered at Primrose's quaint 'keeping company' but the others were suitably sympathetic.

'My chap's a flyer, Spitfires,' Poppy said, 'and in this day and age you never know just how long they'll be around.' Anna presumed she'd made the gruesome remark in order to comfort Primrose and let her know that she wasn't the only one whose romance was in peril. Anna knew that Poppy most likely lived in fear and dread of her fiancé not returning from a mission one day. She'd felt like that, her heart in her mouth every time Simon's Avro Lancaster had taken to the air.

Out on Rumford Street and then into Dale Street, the girls walked past a bombed-out building where workmen were clearing rubble. Ignoring the wolf whistles and cheeky remarks about girls in blue they chatted about their personal lives before coming to Liverpool. Anna felt comfortable in their company, but she didn't divulge anything of any import. She wasn't ready for that.

Partway up Dale Street, Poppy and Denise went to catch a tram to their own billets and Anna, Primrose and Susan continued walking, Anna to the tram stop in William Brown Street and Primrose and Susan to their separate billets in Bold Street. 'It's a nice coincidence that Primrose and I are billeted in the same street,' Susan said.

'What's your billet like?' Anna asked.

'Very basic, but it'll do,' Susan said pragmatically. A Scot from Fife, and married to a soldier serving in Italy, she had been in Liverpool for almost a year. 'I've joined the local church and met some lovely people where my landlady runs a sewing circle,' she continued, her soft Scottish burr rolling the 'r's'.

'Mine's awful,' Primrose replied gustily. 'The landlady's a shrew, mean enough to nip a currant in half and as religious as the Pope and the Archbishop of Canterbury rolled into one. And she seems to have forgotten that cleanliness is next to godliness. What's your place like, Anna?'

Anna thought of lovely generous Mavis and her spotless house and the pretty bedroom. She deliberately played it down. 'Oh, you know, I've lived in worse,' she said, thinking of the house she'd grown up in.

'I think I'll request a transfer,' said Primrose.

'What? Leave Western Approaches before you've barely started?' Susan was shocked.

'No, just another billet, I mean.' Primrose sounded askance. 'Today made me realise how vital the job we're doing is, and I'm going to give it my best shot. What do shabby lodgings and a bit of homesickness matter when we can help save lives day after day?'

She spoke with such fervour that Anna thought she had misjudged this cherubic-looking girl who had been a bag of nerves when they first met. Underneath those bubbly blonde curls and behind those baby-blue eyes was a steely spirit that she now decided to apply to her own situation. She'd forget all about her disastrous love life and immerse herself in her work and having a good time.

'That's just how I felt,' Anna said. 'It's definitely more challenging than teleprinter operating and I was worried I wouldn't get to grips with it, but when I did, I felt proud. I think I'll like working and living here.' They were now at the end of Dale Street. 'See you tomorrow then,' she said as they were about to part.

'See you then,' said Primrose. 'I'll go and face the dragon and the miserable cold tea she'll have waiting for me. Last night she took so long saying grace that the boiled fish was clap cold.'

Anna thought it best not to mention Mavis's delicious shepherd's pie. 'Perhaps you could ask Corporal Somerville about finding you another billet. She seems more approachable than Group Captain Sharp.'

'And I can ask my landlady if she knows of anybody in the church with a spare room.' Susan tucked her arm in Primrose's and they went on their way.

'See you tomorrow,' they chorused, leaving Anna to continue on to William Brown Street to catch a tram that would take her back to Weaver Street.

4

Molly O'Malley was ironing in her kitchen at number eleven Weaver Street. Her baby son, Ronan, lay sleeping in his pram. At six months old he was bonny and bouncing, and blessed with his parents' best features. He had his mother's high cheekbones and finely sculptured chin, and his father's Roman nose and well-shaped mouth. Long dark lashes caressed his cheeks and behind his closed lids were eyes of the brightest blue. Everybody said Ronan was the image of his dad, and Molly never looked at him but she thought of Mickey. She missed her husband so much, it hurt.

Smoothing the creases out of the overall she wore when on duty with the Auxiliary Ambulance Service she told herself she even missed ironing his shirts. It was a Friday morning, another week without him and only his letters to bring him closer, but not close enough. He was so far away, and the distance seemed to get further by the day.

Molly Conlon had married Mickey O'Malley the day before war broke out. Her mother, Kitty, had thought they were both too young, Molly then nineteen and Mickey just twenty, but Molly had known that she wanted nothing more than to be Mickey's wife, she just hadn't reckoned on being a bride of less than three months before her husband was snatched away.

Mickey had joined the RAF, and after his training in Chester he'd qualified as a leading aircraftsman and was now stationed in Liberia, West Africa. Molly supposed she should be thankful that he wasn't in the thick of the war in France or Belgium. Mickey's letter assured that there was no fighting on the Gold Coast, and that his squadron were there to maintain British colonialism and assist in the supply of equipment to where it was needed. However, it didn't prevent her from feeling cheated out of married life. Ronan had been conceived during Mickey's embarkation leave, and he had yet to hold his son. Photographs could never make up for that, but it was all they had for now.

Molly unplugged the electric iron, smiling as she recalled what her mother had said when she had complained about how awkward Mickey's shirts were to iron. *If ye'd had to manage with a flat iron warmed on the fire like I did when I married your da, ye'd have had something to moan about, him wanting a clean white shirt every day for the race meetings. I'd no electric an' only an old black iron range to cook on.*

The memory made her appreciate the changes that had been made to what had been her childhood home. Gone was the black iron range, and in its place a neat tiled fireplace, and the drab brown cupboards were now painted a pretty shade of green. A shiny gas stove sat in the alcove flanked by an enamel-topped cupboard on one side and a white pot sink on the other.

Two comfortable armchairs at either side of the hearth, and a table and four chairs against the back wall, it was her dream home; she'd been born in this house and for the first three years of her life, Tom Conlon had been her father. She barely remembered anything about him but sometimes she recalled his flashing blue eyes – so like her own – and imagined she smelled the scent of his cologne. He'd been a bookmaker bent on joining the elite who frequented the racetracks. She'd heard tales about his nefarious dealings and knew the detail of how he'd come to lose his life: murdered one night behind the Weaver's Arms; assailants unknown. He was buried in the graveyard of St Joseph's Catholic Church at the top of Weaver Street, a name on a headstone and not much more. She sometimes visited his grave, took flowers, and she suspected that her mother, Kitty, did the same.

When her mother had married John Sykes and moved to live in the house across the lane, she had rented out number eleven to the O'Malleys. Molly had been six years old when she first met Mickey, and though they had grown up as friends, it had taken a near disastrous incident for her to realise that she loved him, and probably always had.

A cry from the pram let her know that Ronan had wakened. Scooping him up and burying her nose in the sweet-smelling folds of his neck, she carried him over to the armchair and sat down. Undoing her blouse then exposing her bosom, she began feeding her son. He sucked ravenously, the tingling in Molly's breasts a pure pleasure as she thought back to the time she had fallen in love with Mickey. In those days she had been involved in a silly, one-sided romance with Heinz Muller, a young German who with his parents had fled the horrors of Adolf Hitler's rise to power. Molly had thought that because she loved him, he must love her.

Heinz was a political fanatic, the seditious articles he'd written for a German newspaper one of the reasons he'd had to leave Munich. Once he was settled in Weaver Street, he'd continued fighting for what he thought was right by joining the hunger marches and protesting against the British government's lack of assistance for the thousands that the Great Depression had rendered unemployed. Then, Molly had thought that he was wonderful. Yet it was at one of the protest rallies that she had come to realise how little he cared for her. A riot had broken out, but in his frenzied zeal, Heinz had given no thought to her safety. It was Mickey who had rescued her from the mob.

The hideous experience had opened her eyes to who her true friends were, and she'd soon found that having fun with Mickey was far more enjoyable than Heinz's intense company. A few trips to the cinema and walks by the river, and Molly had learned what love was really all about. As for Mickey, he'd fallen in love with her when she was thirteen, or so he said.

Now her thoughts strayed to Heinz who was in an internment camp on the Isle of Man. One morning, men had raided number seven where the Mullers lived, and shouting 'Collar the lot', they had dragged Heinz and his father, Gottfried, out into the lane and into a black van. They were suspected of being German spies. No one had heard of them since. Heinz's mother had gone to live with relatives in London, and Rachel Dyson and her son, Philip, had come to live in number seven.

Poor Heinz, Molly thought as she changed Ronan from one breast to the other. *There was nobody who hated Hitler more than he did. He'd never have spied for him.*

The back door opened and her mother walked in, beaming when she saw her grandson latched onto his mother's breast. Kitty adored Ronan just as she did her own three children. Molly and Patrick, born a year apart and now twenty-one and twenty respectively were Tom Conlon's offspring, and fifteen-year-old Robert was her second husband, John Sykes's. Her children had always been her priority, and in the bad old days when Tom had been having an adulterous affair with the daughter of a wealthy horse-racing magnate and doing shady deals at the racetrack, Kitty had fought tooth and nail to ensure that her children didn't suffer. She'd worked all hours God sent to buy the café she now owned on the towpath. Then God had given her a second chance at happiness, and she'd married John. Molly loved her stepfather, and she adored and admired her mother: Kitty was a great example to follow.

'Aw, just look at that wee boy takin' his fill,' she crowed, her Irish accent still noticeable even though she'd left Roscommon more than twenty-five years ago. She stroked Ronan's chubby hand. 'Any word from Mickey?' she asked, taking a tea towel and drying the dishes on the draining board. She rarely sat still, and never overlooked a job that needed doing.

'Not since his last letter two weeks ago.' Molly dismally answered the question her mother repeatedly asked. 'Have you heard from Patrick?'

Kitty's face crumpled. 'Aye, I had one this morning. He never says much about what he's doing – I suppose he can't for security's sake – an' he always tells me something daft about what they get up to in the mess, but I can read between the lines. He's finding these flying missions tough, even though he's wanted to fly aeroplanes ever since he was a wee lad. He says he lost a good mate last week, a lad who didn't make it back.' Kitty began clattering the dried dishes into the cupboard above the sink. 'I hate to think of him flying that Spitfire of his an' being chased to hell by one of Hitler's ruddy Messerschmitts. It's no way for a young man to have to spend his life.'

'Our Patrick will be all right, Mam, he knows what he's doing,' Molly comforted unconvincingly. Fear for her younger brother's safety was never far from her mind, but worse still was to see her strong mother living in dread, day after day, for her beloved son. It was common knowledge that Spitfire pilots had very short lives.

In her childhood, Molly had sometimes been envious of her

serious-minded brother, accusing Kitty of favouring him over her. Whereas Molly had inherited Tom Conlon's black hair and blue eyes, and on rare occasions his stubbornness, Patrick had Kitty's tawny curls and hazel eyes. Not only did he look like his mother, he had the same rational mindset and sweet-natured approach to life. Molly, now older and wiser and a mother with a son of her own, knew how her mother felt. She put Ronan up on her shoulder and patted his back. He burped, and Kitty laughed.

'Hand him over. Let his granny have a cuddle with her favourite grandson.'

'He's your only grandson,' Molly reminded her as she placed him in Kitty's arms.

'Aye, he is until our Patrick gets wed an' gives us another one. That's if he ever marries.' He was never far from her thoughts, and Molly's heart ached for her.

''Course he will. He's so handsome I'll bet all the WAAFs in Duxford are dying about him.'

Dying was an unfortunate choice of word and Molly could have bitten her tongue off as she watched her mother bury her face in the curve of Ronan's neck. It was time to change the subject.

'Anything exciting happen at work?'

'No, an' we don't want it to,' Kitty scoffed. 'Tampin' shells an' grinding hand grenades doesn't call for excitement. It's steady hands an' your mind on the job.' Kitty worked three shifts each week in the munitions factory in Edge Lane as well as running her café with the help of a young assistant. She'd had a narrow escape when she worked in the factory during the Great War, an explosion that could have blown her to kingdom come had John not been there to rescue her. Still, it didn't deter her from going back to doing her duty. *Anything to make sure our troops have enough ammunition to finish off the Germans*, she'd told John when he'd objected to her putting herself in danger.

'Yeah, that's how we want things. It's been dead quiet round here these last few nights. The only call-out our ambulance had was to an old chap who'd fallen downstairs. Luckily, he didn't break anything except for a statue of Our Lady on his hall table.'

'Mary wouldn't take kindly to that. He'd better be seeking penance when he makes his next confession.' Kitty sat down, dandling Ronan on her knee. He rewarded her with a gummy smile. 'Ah, would ye look at him,' she cooed. She gave Molly an enquiring look. 'Talking of our Blessed Lady and all things holy, when are ye thinking of getting him baptised? It's long past time.'

Molly looked pained. 'Aw, Mam, don't start that again. You know I don't want to do it without Mickey being there. It wouldn't be right.'

'An' it's not right that this poor child hasn't been churched. You've no idea when they'll give Mickey leave long enough for him to come home all the way from Africa.' Kitty sounded positively aggravated.

'You're just looking for an excuse for a party, Mam,' Molly sneered before letting her face crumple. 'Sorry, I know you're right, but Mickey hasn't even seen him, let alone held him, and I just keep praying they'll send him back to us so we can get on with our lives as they should be.' She brushed away angry tears. 'I'll go and see Father Maguire next week.'

'There, there, love. Don't take on. I didn't mean to upset ye,' Kitty said contritely. 'This bloody war has a lot to answer for, wrecking people's lives, but we just have to get on with what needs doing even if them we love aren't here to do it with us.'

'I know, Mam. I know. Do you want a cup of tea?'

'Aye, the panacea for all ills. I'll have one then I'd best start making dinner. Your dad and our Robert will be coming home at six and God alone knows what I'm going to make. I wanted a bit of shin beef but the butcher didn't have any, an' I'm sick of sausage and spam. I can't even make a Yorkshire pudding. Jack gave me two eggs but I've hardly any flour. I'm thinking of getting chickens meself.'

Molly had brewed the tea as Kitty bemoaned her lot. She'd just filled two cups when the back door opened and Lily bounced in. 'Thank God it's Friday,' she trilled. 'Ooh! Have you just made a cuppa? Give us one, I'm dead thirsty.' She'd come straight from the mill and the smell of greasy yarn that she wove into serge and khaki hung in the air.

Molly filled another cup, and relieving Kitty of Ronan she put him in his pram then sat down at the table with her mother and her best friend.

'Are you on duty tonight?' Lily asked her.

'No, I'm off. Why?'

'I'm going to the Grafton. Do you want to come?'

'No thanks, I'm not in the mood for dancing, and I've Ronan to mind,' Molly said flatly.

'I'll mind Ronan. Ye get off with ye. Ye could do with cheering up,' said Kitty. She turned to Lily. 'She'll go with ye. It'll stop her sitting here moping.'

Molly looked uncertain, but Lily cried, 'Wahoo! A girls' night out. It'll do you good.'

* * *

Anna walked up Weaver Street's back lane to her billet. It had been a tiring two weeks filled with trepidation, information overload, and excitement. She felt wearily proud of her achievements and would have liked nothing better than a hot bath, a tasty dinner and an early night, but she had promised to go to the

Grafton with Denise and Poppy from Derby House so she would only manage two out of three of her desires.

'Your dinner's ready, love,' Mavis said as Anna entered the kitchen. 'It's fish and chips.'

Anna refrained from telling her that was what she'd had in the canteen at Derby House at lunchtime. Stripping off her jacket, she sat down to eat. 'This is lovely, Mavis,' she said appreciatively, the fish and chips being far tastier than the soggy offering in the underground bunker. 'If it's all right with you I'll have a bath when I've eaten. I'm going dancing with the girls from work.'

'Ooh, that's nice. You deserve a bit of fun after the weeks you've put in.' Her beady eyes twinkled. 'I loved dancing when I was young, and whenever me and Jack get the chance to waltz the light fantastic, we can still do it with style.'

Anna couldn't imagine Jack whirling round the dance floor, but she loved her landlady's enthusiasm. She always had something interesting to say, and during the past weeks in the evenings that Anna wasn't on night duty, they had found plenty to talk about. Anna told Mavis about the girls she worked with, and the camp in Oxfordshire. She didn't mention Simon, neither did she divulge that she was adopted and that living with Jane and Norman had sometimes been a nightmare, but she did say that Jane had once been a dancer with a passion for theatre. In return, Mavis delivered snippets of information about herself and the neighbours, and although Anna hadn't met all of them, she felt she already knew them.

'Leave the washing up, I'll see to it,' Mavis ordered when Anna took her plate and cup to the sink. 'You have your bath and make yourself pretty, ready for the dance.'

'Thanks, Mavis. I'll do my best.'

'You won't have to try hard. You always look lovely. I'm surprised some chap hasn't snatched you up already.'

Anna forced a smile and said, 'I'm not for snatching, Mavis.'

In the bath she mulled over Mavis's remark. She wondered if Simon was getting ready for the camp dance in Harwell; they usually had them on the last Friday in the month. Would he be dancing with Suzy, or had he tired of her and found some other poor girl to hurt? Telling herself she'd had a lucky escape, she dried herself and went to her bedroom. Now what should she wear? She didn't have much choice. Deciding that the green polka-dot dress was the best of the two, she slipped it on then carefully pulled on her one precious pair of silk stockings. She brushed her hair, letting it hang in glossy waves to her shoulders. A touch of make-up, and she was ready.

'You look a picture,' Mavis said when Anna went back downstairs. 'The Grafton's always packed with off-duty servicemen. You'll be beating 'em off with a stick.'

'Have you got one big enough,' Anna quipped. 'Don't wait up. I've got my key.'

'Oh, I'll want to hear all about it,' Mavis chirped as Anna left by the back door.

She walked down the lane, her feet uncomfortable in her high heels after wearing her flat WAAF-issue shoes all week. Even so, she felt ebullient. The bath had soaked away her weariness and she was quite looking forward to the dance. *This is one in the eye for you, Simon Grant. I'm getting on with my life and enjoying it.*

* * *

As Anna had been taking her bath, Lily Stubbs was in the bathroom of the house three doors down applying a liberal coating of gravy browning to her long, slender legs. Leaving it to dry, she streaked her cheeks with Pan-stick then rubbed it in with her fingertips, her naturally pale freckled complexion turning a deep shade of tan. Bright blue eye shadow, black mascara and fiery red lipstick finished off the look. Her legs now dry, she twisted her body at an awkward angle and cursing under her breath, she carefully drew a line up the back of each leg with a brown crayoning pencil – pretend stocking seams – she'd give her eye teeth for a pair of silk stockings.

She dressed and went downstairs, the blue satin halter-neck frock showing off every curve and quite a lot of bare flesh. Her mane of wavy red hair was caught up at the sides with glittery combs. When she sashayed into the kitchen her mam and Stanley were sitting either side of the hearth in a pair of shabby armchairs.

'Ooh, you look dead gorgeous, kid,' Maggie gushed. 'Are you for the Grafton?'

'Yeah, Molly's coming an' all. I'm going to call for her. Are you two going out?'

'We're popping over to the Weaver's for a few pints,' said Stanley. 'Now, think on. You mind how you go.'

'I always do, Stan,' Lily scoffed as she went out of the back door.

Molly was flushed and dithery when she let Lily in. 'Do I look all right? It's that long since I had a night out, I've forgotten what it's like,' she gabbled, 'and I feel rotten about it 'cos it's like I'm doing it behind Mickey's back.'

'You look dead on,' she said, admiring Molly's red silk sheath dress, 'and don't be thinking like that. Mickey won't be expecting you to sit moping every night. I'll bet he enjoys his nights off in Africa.'

Molly looked anxious. 'Do you think so?'

Lily shrugged. 'I don't know, and neither do you. Look, it's just a dance we're going to, not joining a bloody harem. Come on, else we'll miss the next tram.'

They stepped outside just at the same time as Anna walked by. They'd heard about her from their mothers, Mavis having told Maggie and Kitty, but they had only met fleetingly when one or another of them had popped into Mavis's, and with Anna being at Derby House all day and Molly and Lily out most evenings with the ARP and the Ambulance Service they had yet to form a proper acquaintance.

'Hello,' Molly said as they caught up with her. 'Are you going into town?'

'I'm meeting some girls I work with. We're going to the Grafton.' Anna smiled at the two friendly faces.

'Then you're in good company,' said Lily. 'That's where we're going.' She linked arms with Molly and then Anna. Anna felt a rush of appreciation for their company. This was far preferable to travelling into the city alone. Really, the nicest people lived in Weaver Street.

* * *

The queue outside the Grafton stretched along the pavement. Anna saw Poppy and Denise and when they joined them, she introduced Molly and Lily. Then they waited for the doors to open. The Grafton Rooms were Liverpool's first purpose-built dance hall and had been extremely popular for almost twenty years. An impressive triangular pediment topped the main entrance, and the fiery red brickwork panels, alongside and above it, were surrounded by cream stonework. Anna thought it looked very grand.

'Ooh, look at them chaps over there. Don't they look smashing in their uniforms.' Denise pointed to a group of soldiers lounging against the wall of a building on the opposite side of the street.

'Anything in trousers looks smashing to you,' Poppy reprimanded.

'But you have to admit they're all tall and handsome,' said Lily.

'They're all out for one thing, and I should know,' Poppy said.

'What's that?' Molly asked innocently.

'Getting into your knickers, that's what,' Poppy told her.

'I wouldn't mind that one with the blond hair getting into mine,' Denise said saucily.

'AC2 Lawton! That's not how a WAAF should behave,' mocked Poppy, doing a perfect imitation of Group Captain Sharp.

'No, it wouldn't meet Razor Sharp's high expectations,' Anna giggled. 'I'll bet no man has ever seen her knickers, let alone got into them.'

They were still laughing when the doors opened and the queue surged forward. Inside the dance hall they headed straight for the cloakroom.

'Have me seams smudged?' Lily lifted her dress and showed the backs of her legs to Molly.

'Have you got your pencil?'

Lily fished in her bag, and Molly repaired the lines on the back of Lily's calves. After much primping of hair, powdering of noses, reapplying lipstick and adjusting bra straps they trooped upstairs to the dance floor. As they entered the ornate ballroom with its vast circle of polished wood and walls painted in vivid red and gold, they were met by a blast of music and gyrating bodies swinging to the strains of 'Boogie Woogie Bugle Boy'.

'It's the Ivy Benson All-Girls Band. Brilliant!' Denise waved excitedly at the stage where a group of glamorous girls in fabulous dresses played saxophones, clarinets, trumpets and trombones. Their identical off-the-shoulder gowns were nipped in at the waist and their fully flared blue satin skirts shimmered like the sea as they swayed to the rhythm of the tune they were playing. It was plain to see that from the tops of their beautifully coiffed blonde, red, or brunette heads down to their shapely ankles and high-heeled shoes that these girls had been picked as much for their youth and glamour as for their musical skills. In front of them a flamboyantly dressed woman enthusiastically waved a baton and jigged up and down in time to the music.

'Will we try and find a table?' Anna's eyes ranged the crowded ballroom, and spotting one with empty seats round it, she said, 'Look, over there. Quick before anyone else grabs it.' Weaving their way round the edge of the dance floor, the girls hurried to the table only to arrive at it at the same time as three soldiers.

The soldiers grinned at the girls' consternation, and the dark good-looking one gallantly gestured for the girls to sit down. 'After you, ladies,' he drawled. 'We can't have pretty girls like you standing around all night.' He winked at Denise. 'Can I have this dance?'

Denise accepted like a shot. The rest of the girls hadn't been sitting down long before they were inundated with offers, and Polly, Anna and Lily took to the floor. Molly hadn't taken much part in the chatter, neither had she accepted a request to dance. She felt out place without Mickey by her side. She sat back, watching the other girls and admiring how relaxed they were as the music roared and the dance floor throbbed under hundreds of feet attached to hot swaying bodies.

Lily, sensing that Molly wasn't really enjoying herself, sat the next dance out.

'You don't have to babysit me, Lily, and I'm sorry I'm a wet blanket. I've got out of the way of enjoying meself.'

'I don't mind. I'm dead knackered anyway. Too many late nights.'

A soldier with a pint of beer in his hand swayed up to their table. He paused and stared.

'By bloody hell, if it isn't Lily Stubbs,' he exclaimed, beer slopping from his glass. Lily and Molly looked up, surprised.

'Hiya, Barry.' Lily didn't sound overly enthusiastic at seeing her old boyfriend but the gleam in her eyes and her smile let Molly know she hadn't forgotten him.

'It must be three years since I last saw you,' Barry said. 'How ya doing?'

'Can't complain. What about you? Enjoying the army?'

'You must be bloody joking. Come on then, give us a dance for old time's sake.'

Lily glanced at Molly. 'Go on,' Molly said, 'I can look after meself.'

Barry plonked his pint on the table then yanked Lily to her feet. 'Come on, Lil, let's show 'em how it's done.'

When Anna came back to the table for a refreshing drink of lemonade, Molly was alone. Anna sat down, and when Molly refused a big burly sergeant's offer to dance, so did she.

'I'm beginning to wish I hadn't come,' Molly said miserably. 'It doesn't seem right without Mickey.'

'I know what you mean,' Anna replied, for the more she had danced, the sadder she'd felt. It was all right telling herself to enjoy it, but it was Simon's arms she wanted to be in. She wondered if she'd really ever get over him. She hadn't wanted to think about him but the slow, smoochy music the band were playing more frequently now that the evening was drawing to a close made it impossible not to remember him.

Angrily, she emptied her glass, her annoyance at everything about the evening mounting.

'Might I have the pleasure?' A tall, handsome man with steely grey eyes was gallantly holding out his hand. He looked very smart in his service dress blues, the insignia on his sleeve letting Anna know he was an RAF wing commander.

'Go on,' urged Molly, 'don't let me spoil your night.'

Flustered, Anna accepted. Better to be moving than moping.

They danced a foxtrot and he said his name was Ross. She replied, 'Anna.' They danced in silence, Ross somewhat taken aback by her curt reticence.

Then Ivy Benson flourished her baton and over the microphone she announced, 'Last waltz, ladies and gentlemen. Make the most of it and thank you for letting us entertain you.' They began playing 'Somewhere Over the Rainbow'. The song was slow, sad and rather mournful and Anna blinked back tears. It had been a favourite of hers and Simon's.

'Did anybody ever tell you your hair's the colour of autumn leaves?' Ross whispered against her ear. 'You really caught my eye and I've been standing over there plucking up the courage to ask you to dance.'

Oh, here we go again, Anna thought tetchily, *the same old sweet talk that he hopes will lead to me jumping into bed with him.* She didn't reveal her thoughts. Instead, she snapped, 'You took your time, Wing Commander. It's the last dance, but no matter, I've heard it all before,' and with that she slipped out of his arms and strutted away, her back rigid.

Ross Penhaligon stared after her. He must have touched nerve, but he didn't know how.

Anna marched to the cloakroom, got her coat and waited for the others to join her. Polly and Denise arrived chattering excitedly about the dance and declaring they'd had a brilliant time, and Molly was eager to go home. Lily was nowhere in sight.

'You know the big blond I was dancing with?' Denise gushed.

'Well, he's walking me back to my billet.' She preened as she put on her coat, her gloating expression saying, *I pulled, but you lot didn't.*

Anna's eyes slid to Molly, and she pulled a face. Poppy said, 'So what? I came to dance, not to score with half the British Army, Denise, in case you got the wrong idea.'

Denise pouted and strode out of the cloakroom. The others followed her into the gaggle of people making their way outside.

A few paces from where Anna stood, she saw Ross the wing commander looking directly at her. He looked bemused but she turned her head away. Then Molly caught her arm, and after Anna had said, 'See you Monday then,' to Polly, she and Molly walked to the tram stop.

'Where did Lily go?' Anna asked.

'Off with an old boyfriend she hasn't seen for ages,' Molly said, 'and seeing as how she never came back it looks as though they've taken up where they left off.'

Anna wondered if she would accept Simon back into her life so easily, if they should ever meet again. She had a sneaky feeling she would. The tram rattled to a halt and they boarded.

'Did you enjoy tonight?' Molly asked.

'Not really,' Anna said. 'The dancing was okay but for some reason I felt as though I shouldn't be there.' She debated whether or not to tell Molly about Simon; get him out of her system.

'Do you miss your family, Anna?'

Anna surprised herself by saying, 'I don't have one. Both my parents are dead, and I'm an only child. They adopted me when I was a baby. Strangely enough, according to my birth certificate I was born in Liverpool. I never expected to end up working here.'

'That's a bit of a coincidence,' said Molly. 'Have you ever thought about trying to find your real mother?' Molly couldn't imagine life without Kitty and her family. She felt sad for Anna.

'Can't say that I have,' Anna replied, her tone casual. 'I didn't have a great relationship with my adoptive parents. They were...' She paused then said, 'Let's say they weren't suited to caring for a child, so I soon adapted to being independent and making the best of things. As for my birth mother, if she didn't want me in the first place, I can't see how she'd want me now.' She said all this without a trace of emotion.

Molly's heart went out to her. Anna was far from her home, had no family, and no idea where her roots lay. *Here I am, feeling sorry for myself and this poor girl has more than enough to bear.* She decided to go out of her way to befriend Anna.

'Well, you'll find a family of sorts now you're living in Weaver Street,' she said.

5

On Saturday morning, Anna slept late. Much to her surprise she'd had an untroubled, restful night. *It must have been all that dancing*, she thought, as out of the blue came a vision of the wing commander's hurt expression. It made her cringe. She needn't have been so ungracious, she silently chastised herself. He wasn't to know that she'd had her heart broken by someone who happened to have waxed lyrical about the colour of her hair, but then Simon Grant had a silver tongue that spun lie upon lie. She closed her eyes to dispel the memory.

She was off duty until Monday. *'Ease you in gently, Carswell,'* the group captain had said. Anna lay back on the pillows, staring at the ceiling and thinking that had she had a free weekend in Harwell she might have taken a trip into London with some of the other girls, gone to the cinema or a show. Or, once upon a time, if Simon had been available, they'd have spent the day driving out into the country then back to his quarters to make love. *He's probably doing that right now with some other girl*, she thought bitterly, and wondering why it was that now she was far away from the camp in Harwell she was wallowing in self-pity when in the weeks after she'd discovered his infidelity she'd put on a brave face, letting the girls and Suzy know that she didn't really care. And she'd been convincing. When she'd laughed and had fun with her friends, they had taken it for granted; love affairs on camp turned on and off like a tap.

Hearing sounds down below, Anna jumped out of bed. Now that she had no heart left to break it couldn't be broken a second time, so she would go out and dance and laugh, and take all the pleasure that life was prepared to offer her. Dressed in 'mufti' as those in service referred to clothes other than their uniforms, she went downstairs to be greeted by her cheery landlady. After tea, toast and a boiled egg – thank goodness Jack kept chickens, the rations in Mavis's house not reduced to just one egg per person per week – Mavis suggested that Anna accompany her to Kitty's house.

'We'll go over for a cuppa and a jangle,' she said. 'It'll give you a chance to get to know the neighbours better.'

There being no reason to refuse, Anna agreed. As they got ready, she recalled what Molly had said the night before: she'd find a family of sorts in Weaver Street.

* * *

Three doors down, Lily Stubbs was standing in Molly's kitchen, her expression not wholly contrite as she said, 'I'm dead sorry for leaving you in the lurch last night. I meant to come back but me and Barry had a lot of catching up to do and I sort of forgot the time.' She lit a cigarette and puffed furiously.

'It's all right. I knew where you'd be, and it didn't spoil the night,' Molly said as she lifted Ronan from his pram. 'And don't go blowing smoke all over him, Lily,' she added as Lily stepped forward, cooing at her godchild. Lily stepped back. She didn't want to be in Molly's bad books, and was relieved that her friend appeared to have taken her absence so lightly. 'In fact,' Molly continued as she began to dress Ronan, 'I already felt rotten about being there without Mickey. I felt as if I was cheating on him.'

'You'd never cheat on Mickey. You never do anything daft that you might regret.' Lily's mournful remark and the frown creasing her brow alerted Molly. What had Lily done?

'Where did you get to last night? You weren't on the last tram. I came home with Anna.'

Lily's cheeks burned. 'I stayed over in the city at a mate of Barry's,' she muttered.

'Did Barry stay there as well?'

Lily nodded as she dragged deeply on her cigarette.

'Oh, Lily, I hope you didn't do anything foolish.'

In their younger days, Molly had often worried about Lily's mad lust for life. She knew that much of it came from the way Maggie had brought her up, one man after another taking her mother's attention away from her, and Lily searching for someone to replace it. Her teenage years had been a crazy social whirl of one boyfriend after another, Molly commenting at that time that Lily changed her boyfriends as often as she changed her knickers. Barry had been the one she'd gone out with longest. Then he'd disappeared off the scene and since Lily had joined the ARP, she hadn't had much time for the opposite sex and seemed to have calmed down.

Lily answered Molly's comment with a shrug then stubbed out her cigarette. 'Here, give us a hold of him while you get ready,' she said, holding out her arms to take Ronan.

* * *

Rachel Dyson stood by the kitchen window in number seven Weaver Street. She saw May Walker and her daughter-in-law, Rose, making their way over to Kitty Sykes's house. The women often met up in one or another of the houses and when she had first arrived in Weaver Street, she had been invited to join them. Initially, she had accepted out of politeness but the women were so close-knit that she had felt as though she were intruding. Furthermore, she had no desire to be part of the cosy set-up, so she had declined any further invitations; the less they knew about her, the better. Women like them had noses for rooting into other people's affairs. A slip of the tongue on her part could open up a minefield of awkward questions.

Rachel, a native of Liverpool, had returned to the city from Carlisle after the death of her husband, George. She'd gone to live in Carlisle in 1921, escaping Liverpool and all its bad memories for the love of a good, kind man who had married her despite knowing about her unfortunate mistake.

Rachel, an only child, had been born shortly after her parents had returned to Liverpool. The house in Woolton was rather grand and she had grown up surrounded by the beautiful things her parents had brought back with them from the Kashmir where her father, Isaac, had been stationed with the British Forces. Although the Rigbys were not opulently wealthy, hers had been a privileged upbringing. After leaving school she had obtained a position in Blacklers department store as a junior in the ladies' mantle department: an impressive place to start a career in ladies' fashion. Three years into the job and nicely climbing the ladder to third saleswoman she had fallen foul of the charms of the manager, a married man with little sense of decency. Blinded by flattery, she hadn't realised how despicable he really was until she'd let him make love to her. It had been a gruelling and degrading experience; one she would never forget. When she had told him she was pregnant he'd had her dismissed on some trumped-up charge of being inefficient. Worse still, her extremely religious parents had disowned her. Cruelly abandoned, she had found a room to rent and work in a run-down café ludicrously called the Wishing Well until she'd had to leave and go into the unmarried mothers' home run by the nuns. The labour had been long and hard, and she had lingered between life and death for two weeks after the birth. By the time she was back in the land of the living her baby had been whisked away for adoption. She had begged to know whether her baby was a boy or a girl but none of the midwifery nuns had seen fit to tell her. They believed it was kinder for her not to know, so they said. *It didn't do to dwell on it. She had to get on with her life.* However, a young maid in the convent had told Rachel that she had given birth to a daughter with dark red hair just like her own. She had left the unmarried mothers' home feeling bitterly disillusioned yet relieved that she didn't have a baby's welfare to consider; she hadn't wanted it anyway.

After the birth she had gone back to work in the café to allow herself breathing space to plan what she should do next. It was there she had met George Dyson. They had started walking out, and whenever his job as a travelling salesman brought him to Liverpool, he'd sought her out. It was George who had taken to calling her Rachel – *Rachel at the well*, he had said in reference to the Bible story and the name of the café. She had been all too ready to change her given name and had called herself Rachel ever since. She did not love him; he adored her. She had only married him for security. They had gone to live in his hometown where she had borne him a son, Philip. It had been an unusual marriage dogged by George's ill health. His lungs had never recovered from a gas attack whilst he was serving in France. He had died when Philip was fourteen, and for a long time after that

Rachel had toyed with the idea of returning to Liverpool in an attempt to heal the rift with her ageing parents. When Philip joined the army at the beginning of the war, she had seen no reason to stay in Carlisle. Leaving her job in Binns, a grand department store, where she had been head of sales in the ladies' fashion department, she had returned to Liverpool in 1939 only to discover that her father had died and that her mother was bitterly unforgiving. In Elspeth Rigby's eyes, her daughter, Florence, had sinned and Florence/Rachel's hopes of living in the family home had been dashed. She had taken rooms nearby in an attempt to make amends, and when she applied for a position in Blacklers her credentials stood her in good stead. She was back in the city of her birth doing a job that gave her pleasure, but try as she might, the rift between mother and daughter had remained unhealed.

On her mother's death some six months later Rachel had been outraged to learn that she had bequeathed her entire estate to the church. In an angry exchange with the church wardens, Rachel had claimed some of the furniture and fine porcelain and ornaments that her parents had brought back with them from India and moved into permanent accommodation in Weaver Street. It wasn't what she would have liked, but it was all she could afford. It seemed that at every turn she had been cheated out of things that were rightfully hers. Working six days a week with one Saturday off in a month hadn't given Rachel much opportunity to socialise with her neighbours but she didn't care; they weren't her sort. Kitty Sykes was pleasant enough, and Mavis Robson was all right, but the Stubbs woman was dreadfully uncouth. She could well do without their company.

She was about to walk away from the window when Mavis and a young woman came into view, Rachel's attention caught by the colour of the younger woman's hair. Instinctively, she ran her fingers through the faded locks of her sleek 'roaring twenties' bob and focused on the stranger's vibrant glossy tresses; her hair had once been that same shade of reddish-brown that shimmered from darkest amber to fiery russet; a most uncommon colour, so people had often remarked. Gazing after the departing backs of the two women as they made their way down the side of Kitty's house, Rachel wondered who the stranger with the glorious auburn hair could be.

* * *

Kitty was smearing margarine on scones she had baked that morning. *Oh, for the days when I dolloped on butter*, she thought, wondering if she should also use some of her jam. At the beginning of the war, she had taken over a plot in the allotment and planted blackcurrant bushes. Last year the crop had been sparse, and whilst she'd made several pounds of jam, she had only a few jars left, most of them emptied by her own family and too many given away. John often told her she was too generous, but Kitty's kind heart would never allow her to see people go without if she could do something about it.

The kettle was simmering over a low light on her sleek gas cooker, and on the table were cups, a jug of watered-down condensed milk and a bowl of sugar. Kitty looked forward to these little get-togethers and her kitchen had hosted many of them over the years. It was a pleasant room with its pale green and cream cupboards and modern appliances. John had had the house especially built for Kitty before he married her. She had been adamant that she didn't want to leave Weaver Street and number eleven where Molly lived now. John had been equally determined not to live in the house that Kitty had shared with Tom Conlon. To Kitty's delight and eternal gratitude, he had built the house on spare land next to the allotment thereby giving them a new home in which to start their married life, with Kitty still able to live among the dearest friends she had ever had. More than once, they had helped her to overcome the worst days of her life. She was a naturally strong woman with the spirit of a lioness, but without their support, and Maggie's in particular, she sometimes doubted that she would have survived Tom's infidelity and betrayal of all she had held dear. They had helped her to achieve her aim of having a business that would ensure her and her children's future, and fighting tooth and nail she had made the café on the towpath a thriving enterprise. John was the icing on the cake, and her second marriage so wonderful that Kitty considered herself blessed. Staunch friends and a man who loved and respected her, she didn't want for more.

Of course, it hadn't been a one-way street. Her friends knew that they could rely on Kitty to help them through the bad patches, and she had done so many times. Sticking together through thick and thin was the essence of living in Weaver Street.

She heard the back door open and turned the gas higher to bring the kettle to the boil.

Beth Forsythe was the first to arrive, entering the kitchen diffidently although she and Kitty had been the greatest friends from the moment they'd first met when Kitty had been a waitress in the café she now owned. In those days, Beth had lived at number three, Weaver Street, with her domineering father, Walter Garside. The friendship had been sealed when Kitty had advised Beth to stand up to her father's bullying, obnoxious behaviour. Otherwise, he'd make her life a misery. Beth had taken her advice, and defying her father she had married Blair Forsythe, a young Scot who had come to work in Holroyd's mill. After the wedding they had moved into number thirteen, Weaver Street, Kitty their neighbour on one side and Mavis on the other.

However, Walter was still close enough to continually pester them and the marriage was in danger of collapsing and would have done so had not Kitty *given him the rounds of the kitchen* as she'd then put it. Sparing no mercy, she had frightened him into altering his ways by letting him know that he was an ungrateful curmudgeon who didn't deserve a daughter who still cooked his meals and did his washing and household chores. She'd warned him that Blair might well take Beth to live in Scotland, leaving him to take care of himself, and Walter had taken Kitty's words to heart. For this, and much more, Kitty had Beth's deepest gratitude. What was more, Kitty and Beth shared the same interests. They liked reading whereas Maggie had no time for it, and although prim and proper Beth sometimes objected to Maggie's rough manner and her casual love affairs these three young women were the closest of friends. They had supported one another in the early days of their married lives, helped in the raising of one another's children, and laughed and cried together.

'Hello, love, you're the first to arrive,' Kitty said in the full knowledge that Beth preferred it that way. She was still shy, and walking in on a group of chattering women was far more intimidating than being established before they arrived.

'Oh, you know me and my...' She needed to say no more. Kitty understood.

'How's Stuart doing with his exams?' Kitty asked, putting Beth at ease by engaging in her favourite topic. Stuart was Robert's best friend and Beth's only son. He was training to be an accountant with a prestigious firm in the city. Beth had been terrified of giving birth a second time and had even plucked up the courage to go to the Marie Stopes family planning clinic, a brave venture for Beth who was dreadfully prudish about things of a personal nature.

'He's studying hard,' she said then went on to give Kitty the detail of what that entailed. Kitty half listened as she poured boiling water on the leaves in the teapot. At times Beth's obsession with her son's career was tedious but she loved her friend so kept her thoughts to herself.

'Sit ye down, the others will be along any minute,' said Kitty with a sense of guilty relief as the back door opened again and Rose and May walked in. Greetings were exchanged. 'James not with ye?' Kitty asked.

'Grandpa Bill's keeping an eye on him,' Rose said, and May followed with, 'Aye, he loves having him to himself for a bit.'

Kitty smiled, remembering the time when May wouldn't have dreamed of leaving Bill in charge of the cat, let alone her grandson. But Bill's drunken days were a thing of the past. When Rose married Joey Walker in 1935, her father, James Brown-Allsopp, had advised Bill to get into scrap metal and to the amazement of the neighbours in Weaver Street he'd given up the drink, found an old pram and trawled the streets for scrap. A government contract in 1938 had turned Bill's business into a thriving enterprise, and he boasted that he was responsible for the removal of all the gates and iron rails within ten miles of Edge Hill. The pram had been replaced by a cart, then a lorry and now he had two of them.

'How's Stuart getting on at the accountancy?' Rose asked, sitting down next to Beth. Like Kitty, she knew how to engage Beth and Beth eagerly took up the reins.

'Yoo-hoo,' Mavis called out as she and Anna came into the kitchen.

'Hello, Anna,' Kitty said with a welcoming smile. 'I'm pleased ye could join us.'

'So am I,' Anna replied, keen to see what glued these women together *'through thick and thin'* as Mavis had said. She looked round the neat, tidy kitchen, admiring the décor and thinking that Kitty was a woman with very few needs. She smiled at Beth. They had met fleetingly when Beth had called to give Mavis some wool for a jumper she was knitting for Blair. Beth bobbed her head in response. Rose greeted Anna like an old friend.

As Anna sat between May and Rose at Kitty's table, she recalled what Mavis had told her about the fat, jolly woman and her husband, Bill. Mavis said he had once been a notorious drunk who'd led May a dog's life, but there was no sign of that now. May looked perfectly content, and Anna could tell that she and Rose got on well. Was this evidence of what Mavis had described as '*pulling together in the rough, tough times*', which had sustained May and Rose until things had got much better? she wondered.

Kitty had decided to put jam on the scones, and May commented on it. 'Ooh, lovely. Blackcurrant jam. Is it your own?' Kitty told her it was and that she hoped for a better crop come August. 'I sowed carrots and parsnips yesterday, and John's planted potatoes.'

'Aye, Bill got his earlies in last week,' May said in a tone suggesting that at one time the only thing Bill would have planted was his feet in the pub as he drank pint after pint. As they continued talking about their crops in the allotment, Kitty poured tea and invited everyone to help themselves to scones.

'Oi, leave summat for us,' Lily shouted as she and Molly walked in.

'Give me laddo here,' Kitty said, relieving Molly of Ronan and planting a kiss on his cheek. 'Who's Granny's favourite wee boy then?'

'Don't let our Robert and Patrick hear you say that.' Molly sat down and helped herself to a scone. She smiled across at Anna. 'You've recovered from last night's dancing then.'

Anna laughed. 'I haven't had that much exercise since I did my physical training.'

'I take it you all enjoyed your night out at the Grafton,' Mavis said perkily. The girls agreed, and that started all of them chatting about dancing, the older women reminiscing and the younger ones giggling at the stories when the door burst open and Maggie bounced in.

'Why didn't you give me a shout?' she snapped, giving Lily an accusing glare. 'What have I missed?'

'Not much, Maggie,' laughed Kitty. 'We were just talking about going to dances.'

'I used to be a dead ringer for Rita Hayworth when I got on the floor,' Maggie boasted as she took a seat and grabbed a scone. Anna could see little resemblance to the film star in the carelessly put together woman, her hair in curlers and a cardigan over what Anna presumed was a nightdress.

The chat flitted from dancing to rationing, Beth making them laugh when she described her disastrous attempt to make fudge out of caramelised carrots. The shortage of food led to comments on the recent bombing on the docks, then to Anna's whereabouts before she came to Liverpool, and Lily's and Molly's work with the ARP and the Ambulance Service. Everyone had something to contribute, and if someone aired a personal problem the others offered suggestions of how to solve it. They were all in this together, and it was all done with sympathy and good humour.

Mavis was telling them that Harry Lauder, the famous Scots entertainer, was staying in the Adelphi Hotel when Maggie interrupted her.

'Eh, I've only just noticed,' she cried, pointing her finger at Anna who was sitting across from her at the table. 'Who does she remind you of? Her hair's exactly the same colour.'

Eight pairs of eyes all turned to observe Anna who looked bemused.

'Aye, now ye mention it she does put ye in mind of Rachel,' said Kitty.

'Rachel who?' Anna's voice was high with curiosity.

'Rachel lah-di-dah Dyson, the snotty cow that lives at number seven. Haven't you seen her yet?' Maggie jeered. 'You can't miss her. She's always dressed up to the nines, and thinks she's better than everybody else.'

'Now, Maggie. Don't be unkind,' Mavis chided.

'Still, you don't see many folks with that colour of hair.' May looked closely at Anna.

Anna shifted uncomfortably in her seat, unwilling to be the centre of attention.

'See,' Maggie crowed. 'When it comes to hair, I'm...'

'Aw, shut up about hair, Mam,' Lily scorned, giving Anna a sympathetic look. 'To listen to her you'd think she was a top-class hairdresser, and to look at her...' Lily flourished her cigarette dismissively.

'Yeah, well, I didn't have time to do owt with it because you let me sleep in, you sarcastic mare,' Maggie retorted then puffed furiously on her cigarette.

'She does a good job putting highlights in mine,' said Rose, eager to keep the peace as she patted her long blonde locks. 'She did a smashing job on it for my wedding. I'll never forget that. Joey said I looked like a fairy-tale princess.'

'And you did, love. I never saw a more beautiful bride.' May began describing Rose's wedding for Anna's benefit.

Peace restored they continued chatting. Anna was enjoying herself immensely. When it came time for them to leave, Lily suggested that Anna might like to go into town with her. Anna readily accepted. It was an opportunity to make friends with someone her own age although she liked all the Weaver Street women. They were a lively bunch, and she had a feeling that they were just the sort of people to help her forget the hurt and pain that had clouded her life for far too long.

Kitty had cleared away the cups and plates after the women had gone, and was now making a lunch ready for John and Robert's return from the factory. She was glad that fifteen-year-old Robert showed no desire to dash off and join the forces as she had heard some other lads of his age had tried to do. He was more than happy to work with his father in the engineering works that John had founded before the First World War. Then it had only made parts for bicycles and other small machines. Now it had government contracts to make parts for aircraft and guns.

Robert had told Kitty that some of the lads he'd been at school with slagged him off for not wanting to join the forces. 'But I tell 'em, don't I make the parts that keep our aircraft flying and the ack-ack guns firing – and your dads' cars running. That shuts 'em up,' he'd said proudly. Kitty had laughed. He was just like his dad, straightforward, uncomplicated and honest to a fault.

Kitty popped slices of bread into the toaster. She loved her modern appliances, so much easier than kneeling in front of the fire, dangling a slice on a toasting fork and praying that it didn't drop into the flames. It never failed to amaze her how the world and her life had changed in the last thirty years. She'd moved from a small farm in Roscommon, then to Dublin, left Ireland for Liverpool, lost a husband then gained another, borne three beautiful children, and now even though the country was at war she still felt as though the world was her oyster.

Ye're blessed, Kitty Sykes, she silently told herself as she sliced a nub of ham that she'd been lucky enough to get from the butcher the day before. When she heard the back door open, she turned to greet two of her blessings. John and Robert entered the kitchen laughing and chatting. She smiled warmly at her husband then at her son. They were both tall with floppy brown hair and soft brown eyes, and although Robert had yet to achieve John's breadth of chest and shoulders Kitty knew that he would do one day. Like his father, making small machine parts fascinated him and the factory was as dear to him as it was to John. Sometime in the future it would pass into his capable hands and he would carry on the tradition, unlike Patrick who from being a young boy had wanted to fly aeroplanes. His desire had been fulfilled, but Kitty wished with all her heart that it wasn't a Spitfire he was piloting. They were instruments of death: a German pilot's, or Patrick's.

John dropped a kiss on her cheek. They might have been married for seventeen years but their love for one another was still fresh. For a moment as fleeting as thistledown, Kitty leaned into him, feeling the beat of his heart and the warmth of his strong body. He was her mainstay.

'What are ye for this afternoon?' she asked as she put plates of ham, pickles and toast in front of them at the table. 'I'm going to the café. This decent weather might attract a few hikers and bird-watchers, and those lads on bikes from Kirby usually drop by of a Saturday. I'll go and give Sheila a hand.'

'Lads from Kirby,' John hooted. 'There's not one of 'em under fifty; lads indeed.'

'Aye, that's as may be. Tis only the ould lads that are left. All the young ones are away fighting,' she said dismally. 'An' at least it's a bit of trade.'

'We're for the allotment. We're going to turn over that far plot and plant more spuds.'

'Aye, where would we be without spuds?'

Robert plunged his teeth into a pickled onion, and hoped that his mam didn't start on about the Irish Famine when all the potato crops had rotted. It was an interesting story but he'd heard it too many times before and it made him feel awfully sad and a little bit guilty. His dad saved the day by talking about the recent bombing on the docks, another miserable subject but one for which the English were not to blame. Quite the contrary.

* * *

Anna and Lily walked arm in arm around the city centre, Lily giving her a guided tour of the landmarks and commenting heatedly on the terrible damage that had been done to some of the fine buildings. They kept well away from the docks as it was there that the Germans were most intent on destruction. They both carried their gas masks in little cardboard boxes slung over their shoulders because although the bombing raids usually occurred after dark the girls were alert to any danger.

'This is what we locals call Holy Junction,' Lily said as they stood on one corner of a large crossroads. 'It's where Church Street meets Lord Street, Whitechapel and Paradise Street. Makes you laugh, doesn't it?' she commented sarcastically. 'You'd think the Good Lord would smile kindly on a city with such devotion, but look at it.'

'I'm beginning to think God takes no interest in what goes on down here,' said Anna. 'He just leaves us to get on with it.'

'Yeah, you could be right,' Lily agreed and as they strolled along Dawson Street, she told Anna about the night the school had been bombed in Durning Road. 'It was a designated shelter and hundreds of innocent men and women and their kids were in the basement when Jerry bombed it. Them that weren't buried alive were scalded to death when the boilers burst. Now, you tell me why He let that happen. It's not as though they were doing anybody any harm.' She shuddered. 'I'll never forget helping dig 'em out as long as I live.'

'That must have been awful,' Anna said. 'I feel the same whenever I mark up aircraft that have been blown to bits or ships that have sunk to the bottom of the ocean. All those men on board were somebody's husbands, fathers and brothers and I ask myself why they had to die.'

'None of it makes any bloody sense any more,' Lily grunted.

Anna was reminded of the recent things that had happened to her that seemed to make no sense and asked, 'Do you ever find yourself praying for something only for it to go unanswered no matter how hard you pray?'

'Can't say as I do. We aren't churchgoers. Is it something you do a lot of?' Lily sounded curious.

'No, my parents weren't religious, but about four months ago I wanted something really badly and I prayed then. Of course, it all came to nothing.'

'What was it?' Lily was intrigued. 'That's if you don't mind me asking.'

Anna wasn't sure whether or not she minded. She had never talked about Simon with anyone. She just kept all the hurt inside, festering.

'Was it something to do with a man?' It was as if Lily had read Anna's mind.

Anna bit the bullet and gave an emphatic 'Yes.' By now they had reached Eliot Street, and on the opposite corner to Blacklers, the upmarket department store, there was a small café. 'Let's go in there and have a cup of tea,' she said.

Over a weak cup of tepid tea, and encouraged by Lily's 'aws' and 'oohs', Anna gave her a sketchy version of having an affair with a man who turned out to be a rotten cheat.

'Yeah, they're all the same,' Lily scorned. 'I grew up watching one fella after another cheat on me mam. I swore I'd never let that happen to me so I just love 'em an' leave 'em before they ditch me.'

'Have you never had a long-term relationship?' Anna was surprised. Lily was beautiful and she seemed the sort of girl any man would like to hold on to.

Lily's face clouded. 'Yeah, that lad I went off with the other night at the Grafton. I went with him for ages but he wanted it all without putting a ring on me finger so I told him to bugger off.' She lifted her cup to her lips, gazing thoughtfully over the rim of it as she sipped. Anna thought she looked troubled.

'So, are you and he back together?'

'Nah, he's still out for what he can get for free.' Disgusted, Lily drank the dregs of her tea.

It felt good denigrating the opposite sex, like fighting back, and Anna realised that she was feeling lighter for having offloaded the pain she'd been carrying for too long. They left the café and as they were window shopping outside Blacklers she wondered what had made her say all those things to a girl she barely knew. Perhaps it was true that a problem shared was a problem halved.

It had been the same with Molly as they'd travelled home from the dance. She'd never divulged that she was adopted to her friends at school, or the staff in the solicitor's office, and her fellow WAAFs. She didn't want their pity, or for them to think she hadn't had a normal upbringing – even though she hadn't. Was this sudden change of heart anything to do with living amongst the friendly people in Weaver Street? she mused, as Lily pointed out a black evening dress and a pearl handbag that she'd never be able to afford, and Anna gazed longingly at a tailored bottle green suit. Whatever it was, she had to admit that being open and honest about things made her feel better in her own skin.

They were walking along a narrow street with the blank brick walls of warehouses on either side, a short cut so Lily said, back to William Brown Street to catch the tram to Edge Hill when three very drunken sailors came roistering towards them, jabbering in a foreign language as they barred the way.

'Bugger off,' Lily yelled, grabbing Anna by the arm and quickly sidestepping the pests before breaking into a run. The rejected sailors shouted what sounded like curses after them.

'Bloody foreigners,' Lily panted when it was safe to slow their pace. 'You've got to watch out for them when you're in the 'Pool. They come off the boats thinking all the girls are dying for 'em 'cos they have this idea that English women give it away for free.'

'They're not the only ones. Some of the English are just as bad.'

Reminded of Barry, Lily grunted, 'Yeah, you're dead right there, kiddo.'

They carried on walking to the tram stop, Anna thinking that she liked Lily and that she would make a good friend.

6

On Monday morning Anna arrived at Derby House ready to start another week learning more of the intricacies that working with Western Approaches Command involved. As she entered the operations room Primrose and the rest of the team were already there.

'We lost two of our planes south of Malta last night,' Poppy said dolefully. 'The team doing night duty were run off their feet the entire shift. Let's hope it's a bit calmer today.' Anna could tell that Poppy was thinking about her fiancé: he was a flyer with a squadron based in Duxford. Her thoughts flew to Simon. Was he still safe? She pushed the thought away. He wasn't hers to think about any more. Still...

Lucy Somerville came over, clipboard in hand to give them their duties for the day.

'You're up the ladder, Poppy. Denise, you're on Aircraft State Board.'

Denise groaned. Keeping up with the readiness of all of the RAF stations displayed on a huge board as well as the up-to-the-minute information about ongoing operations brought in by the girls on the teleprinters in the next room meant that she'd have to keep her wits about her for the entire day. Corporal Somerville ignored her displeasure.

'Primrose, the weather board's all yours, and you, Anna, you're on the table.'

Anna glanced over at the huge table that showed the positions of the convoys on a massive situation map. She'd be moving little model boats to show their exact deployment. She hoped she'd be up to it and not hinder the Wrens already working round the table.

'Oh, and before you go to your stations,' Lucy continued as the door opened and she gave the thumbs up to the person who had just entered, 'I'll introduce you to our new temporary member of the team.' As she spoke, the newcomer had made his way to her side.

Anna felt her cheeks reddening when she saw who it was. She stood to attention.

'Ladies, meet Wing Commander Ross Penhaligon. He'll be working alongside us to see how we operate in order to transfer the knowledge back to his squadron.'

Lucy rattled off the girls' names. Ross nodded and smiled at each of them. He gave no indication that he and Anna had already met – and had she imagined his silvery-grey eyes cooling to iron grey, and his smile fading when it came to her turn?

For the rest of the day Anna worked alongside Ross, his manner towards her no different from how he treated the other girls: courteous, friendly and efficient. Then, just as their shift was ending, the room began to seethe with activity: incoming German aircraft were sighted south of Norway and also off the east coast of England.

'The buggers are coming thick and fast from all directions

tonight.' The burr of a Scots naval officer had them all on their toes.

'You'll have to stay on, girls,' Group Captain Sharp informed them. 'All hands to the pump,' she added with a jolly smile.

'Just as I was getting in the mood for putting my feet up and finishing *How Green Was My Valley*,' Poppy groaned.

'You'd be better off reading *For Whom the Bell Tolls*,' Anna quipped. 'It's better suited to this moment in time.'

'I was meeting my big blond soldier,' Denise whined. 'He's called Lee and he's lovely.'

'My billet's that grim, a night spent here is a better option,' Primrose said as they went back to their stations, ready for what lay ahead. Further alerts came in, Anna's spine tingling and her wits sharp as she leaned over the table, plotting the manoeuvres of the convoys and aircraft. The room was tense with urgency as they worked on and on; men's lives depended on them.

'Enemy sighted north of Scapa Flow...' The staccato voice called out grid references from a naval corvette on convoy duty. As the code was interpreted, Anna concentrated on the area around the Orkney Islands, her nerves jangling with fear for the British naval base.

'Poor sods,' the Wren at her elbow muttered. 'Jerry's either after the base or the convoys. Our poor lads don't stand a chance up there. If they're not blown to kingdom come, they freeze to death in the bloody cold water.'

'Enemy aircraft overhead...' This time the staccato voice sent shivers down Anna's spine even though the temperature in the room seemed to have risen as the tension increased. Palms moist, she now concentrated on Liverpool Docks. There would be no going home tonight. She had warned Mavis this might happen and Mavis had given her Kitty's telephone number to call in an emergency. If she got a few minutes respite she'd call to put her mind at rest. As the Wrens checked the convoy's position, Anna and Primrose double-checked the positions of the aircraft. The city was taking another battering, but deep in the basement of Derby House those on duty could not hear the sirens blaring or the roar of the fire engines. Even if they could, they would have ignored them. They were too busy averting disaster.

As Anna was toiling over the ops table in Derby House, Lily Stubbs was patrolling Gladstone Street thinking about Barry. She hadn't seen him since the night of the dance at the Grafton, or should it be the following morning. In fact, the last she'd seen of him was when she'd been hastily pulling on her clothes in the scruffy bedroom at his mate's house in Hood Street. Barry had been lying in the rumpled bed smoking and saying it was a pity he had to go back to Catterick Camp the next day, and it being a Sunday he wouldn't be able to see her again. He'd told her he'd most likely be going overseas in the next week or two. He didn't know exactly where, it was all hush-hush, but word had it that it could be Belgium. He hadn't asked her to write to him and she hadn't suggested it. They'd parted with the most casual of good-byes, Lily feeling used and dirty, and silently cursing herself for having fallen into bed with him so easily. *I'm more like me ma than I think I am*, she thought.

'Penny for them,' said the new ARP recruit at her side.

Lily flinched. 'What...?'

'You were miles away,' Eric Kitson said. 'I was asking you will we check the shelter at the top of the street. Make sure that the folks using it have their gas masks and whatever else they might need.'

'You've a lot to earn, Eric. Some of the lazy buggers round

here always wait until the last minute to leave their houses. Then they complain like bloody hell, as if it's all our fault and nowt to do with Jerry,' she snarled then instantly regretted it. She was annoyed with herself on two counts: one, for not giving her undivided attention to the job, and two, for swearing. Eric didn't deserve it. He was a soft-spoken very polite young man. He was an industrial chemist at Buchanan's Engineering and had been to university. Not the sort that Lily usually spent time with.

'Sorry, Eric. I didn't mean to snap, but sometimes this job makes me mad,' she said. That wasn't true; it was her feckless night with Barry that had made her short-tempered but she couldn't tell Eric that.

'I can imagine it does when you've been doing it for as long as you have.' Lily heard the sympathy in Eric's voice and felt ashamed. 'But Warden Sykes says I couldn't learn the ropes from anyone better. He thinks very highly of you.'

Good old John, always ready to sing her praises. Lily searched for something to say that was instructional and at the same time give an explanation as to why she felt annoyed. 'What people don't seem to understand is that we're trying to protect them. I get cross when I go into houses where there are kids in danger,' she said. 'Last year I helped evacuate dozens of them to the countryside, then their dozy bloo—' She nearly bit off the end of her tongue. 'Their silly mothers went and fetched 'em back when there was no bombing, so if we find people still in their houses make sure you don't miss the kids who might be in bed, or hiding 'cos they're frightened to death.'

'I'll take particular care with that,' he said as they walked up the street. 'It beggars belief that parents wouldn't want their children to be safe in the country, but I suppose their mothers are reluctant to be parted from them.'

'The mothers could have gone as well. Some of them did but

they couldn't hack country life in somebody else's home, not after living in a city like the 'Pool.' She broke her stride to bang on a window. 'Put that bloody light out or fix your blackouts,' she bawled. 'Or better still, get up to the shelter.'

'Keep your soddin' hair on,' a voice yelled back. 'Nosy bloody ARP.'

Eric chuckled. 'I see what you mean.' They continued walking. 'Do you live round here?'

'Weaver Street, off Broad Green. What about you?'

'Aigburth until a month ago. We were bombed out and came to live with my mother's sister in Wavertree. Fortunately for us she has a big house close to the park.'

Posh, thought Lily, but said, 'Nice,' instead.

They'd almost reached one end of the street when the short sharp blasts of the air raid siren signalled an imminent attack. They both looked up as the high-pitched whine of an aircraft engine filled the sky. The dark shape of a Junkers broke through the cloud, swooping towards Edge Hill goods station. The heavens cracked open and an almighty boom signalled that Jerry had dropped his bomb. The smell of cordite wafted on the air.

'Bastard!' Lily yelled, shoving Eric into action as the sky turned black. The Junker's pilot had come with his mates. 'You do that side of the street. I'll do this one,' she ordered as ringing her handbell furiously, she banged on the nearest door then pushed it open. 'Anybody in here? Get to the shelter now.'

A bedraggled, pale-faced woman was struggling to get three children into their coats then slinging gasmask boxes round their necks. Lily bent to help then shepherded the family out into the street. 'Run for the shelter,' she shouted, pointing up the street. White-faced, the children dithered, their mother shrieking for them to get a move on.

Lily and Eric banged on doors, checking that the houses were empty and that the occupants were hopefully safe in the shelter in case the bombers dropped more lethal surprises. Lily looked up but she couldn't see the planes for the clouds. A short distance away, a bomb exploded, smoke and flames spiralling upwards. At the top of Gladstone Street, she waited for Eric to catch up with her. Then, turning the corner and hurrying down Peel Street, they continued their task, Lily angry that some of the children she led to safety were the same ones she had helped evacuate the year before.

'They shouldn't even be here,' she barked at one woman who was more concerned with having come out of her home without her cigarettes.

'You couldn't lend us a couple of fags till it dies down could you, pet?' she begged as Lily bundled the children and the woman into the overcrowded shelter.

'No, I bloody couldn't. I've better things to do than keep you in cigs.'

By now, Lily and Eric were joined by the other wardens who had dashed to the area, John Sykes among them. 'All clear in Gladstone and Peel,' Lily reported. 'What did they hit?'

'They were no doubt aiming for the goods station,' John said, referring to the depot with a huge arched entrance that was the last stop before Lime Street Station. 'The bombs fell short on Tunnel Road. We'd best get over there.'

On Tunnel Road they met with a devastating scene. The houses at one end of the street had taken a direct hit. Fire was spreading to their neighbours. Fire engines and ambulances were already in attendance. 'Check them collapsed Andersons,' Lily told Eric as she pointed to the wrecked shelters at the rear of the demolished houses. 'I'll check the others.' For the next hour, Lily and Eric searched the rubble for survivors, led the walking injured to the ambulances and the shocked to the WVS tea stall.

Eventually, when there was nothing more they could do, they took advantage of a refreshing cup of tea.

'You were magnificent.' Eric's voice rang with sincerity and his eyes were warm with admiration as he gazed at Lily. She was mud-stained and dusty and her hair had escaped from under her helmet in fiery tangles. 'You made me think of Boadicea charging into battle.'

Lily blinked. 'Who's he when he's at home?' She spoke flippantly, embarrassed yet thrilled by his words.

'Not he – she,' Eric explained. 'She was a warrior queen who fought to defend England against the Romans.'

'Oh...' Lily was lost for words. Not for the first time she felt rather ignorant. To hide the feeling she said, 'We could do with her sort to fight Jerry.'

'Why, when we've got you?' Eric chuckled. 'Look, I know we've just met but what do you say to a night out together when we're both free? We could go to the cinema maybe.'

Lily bit her lip. He had a lovely way with him, and he was good looking. Could she hold her own with somebody who was so refined and intelligent? She decided she'd give it a try.

'I'd like that,' she said.

In Derby House, shortly after midnight, Anna made her weary way to the canteen. She felt dead on her feet. The canteen was gloomy, only a couple of lights on and most of the tables empty. There was just one member of the catering staff behind the counter. Anna ordered tea and toast then sat at a table far away from the few operatives who were also taking a break. The tea was stewed and the toast tasted like sawdust. When she had finished it, she sat with her elbows on the table and her aching head resting in her hands. The scraping of a chair at the other side of the table had her peering through her fingers.

'Mind if I join you?' Ross Penhaligon stood with one hand on the back of the chair, waiting for her answer.

'Feel free,' she said although she would have preferred to be left alone.

'Busy night?' he said, putting his plate and cup on the table before sitting down.

Anna nodded. What was there to say?

'Anna, tell me if I'm talking out of turn, but why did you pretend we'd never met when Corporal Somerville introduced us?'

Anna's eyes met his. 'You did too,' she said, her tone accusing.

'True, but it's a lady's prerogative to speak first. I didn't want to embarrass you.'

'You didn't,' she replied curtly. 'Anyway, it's not important.'

He drank his tea and ate an Eccles cake, the silence between them swelling.

'What is it that I say or do that offends you?' Ross sounded both hurt and intrigued. Anna wondered if she was being unfair.

Then, reminded of Simon and the unfairness of all that, she said, 'It's not just you. It's all of your sort. You think you only have to say a few flattering words and give an admiring glance or two and girls like me will fall into your arms and be undyingly grateful for the attention.' Two bright spots coloured her cheeks. She pushed back her chair and marched out of the canteen.

Ross watched her go, a bemused and rather angry expression masking his face. What was that girl's problem? He was attracted to her, but she clearly found him obnoxious.

* * *

'Pass the biscuit tin,' Maggie said to Beth as she settled into one of the bunks in the Anderson shelter. Beth pursed her lips and did as she was asked, then went to assist Kitty who was boiling the kettle on a small Primus stove. Beth upturned cups that had been left top-down from the night before. The trouble with the shelter was that dust got into everything.

In 1939 when war broke out, John had told Kitty he was going to erect a shelter in the back garden for his family and their neighbours. True to his word, the shelter had been built. Kitty hadn't liked the idea. *What about my rose beds?* she'd objected.

The roses had been dug up and replanted down the side of the garden, and men from John's factory had dug a huge pit and then erected the shelter. Now, on nights like this, Kitty thanked her lucky stars that she'd let John have his way. He always knew best. Between them, Kitty, Maggie, Mavis and Beth had made it as comfortable as possible with blankets and pillows on the bunks and a ready supply of provisions to see them through the long, terrifying nights.

Tonight, as soon as they had heard the short sharp blasts of the sirens they had piled in: Kitty, Robert, Molly with baby Ronan, Mavis and Jack, Beth and Stuart, and Maggie, all well used to the disturbing nights that had troubled their lives for far too long.

'Room for any more?' May Walker gasped as she bustled in with Rose behind her carrying young James. A minute later, Rachel Dyson slipped in looking as though she'd prefer to be anywhere but there, and responding to Kitty and Maggie's welcome with the briefest of nods she tucked herself into a corner as far away from them as was possible. Jack, the only man amongst them, stepped outside, searching between the clouds for a patch of star-studded sky; he liked to see the stars. They gave him hope. Across the distance he heard the whine of the Junkers and the dull sound of explosions. He stepped quickly back inside and closed the door. 'Docks again,' he muttered.

Molly rocked Ronan in her arms, humming softly to lull him to sleep. Young James sat quietly playing with a toy boat. He knew by now that he mustn't cry or make a fuss. His daddy was somewhere out on the sea, keeping them safe from the bad men. Robert was curled up with a copy of the *Beano*. He loved how the comic ridiculed Hitler and the Nazis and how the British heroes won every battle. He thought of his brother Patrick up there in the sky fighting the enemy and made him a silent promise that he'd do his bit down below to keep his mam and his sister and baby nephew safe.

Cups of tea were passed round, and as they drank, each one of them knew that the others were thinking of their loved ones: Kitty saying a prayer for Patrick flying somewhere high in the heavens, and hoping that John wasn't performing any heroics with the ARP. Maggie's mind was on Lily and Stanley. She thought that Stanley was too old to be out with the ARP on nights like this, but he would have none of it. As for Lily, she was tough stuff, but still...

Beth sat with her arm round Stuart, both of them thinking of Blair somewhere on the Western Front. May worried for Bill out guarding his scrapyard, and along with Rose they both prayed for Joey Walker's safety. He was commanding a naval corvette, but where, he couldn't tell them: careless talk cost lives.

Rachel Dyson sat with her hands folded thinking of her son, Philip. Did life in the REME suit him better than the life he'd shared with her? He rarely kept in touch with her. Mavis remembered the young man she would have married had the First World War not snatched him away on Valentine's Day in 1915. He had a grave in Tyne Cot cemetery, and one day she and Jack might visit it. On nights like this she knew that Jack thought back to the time he'd lost his eye and the proper use of his leg. Whatever they were all thinking, they were all in agreement that war was rotten. It changed people's lives, sometimes irrevocably.

The air in the shelter had grown stuffy. 'Pooh!' Robert wafted his hand under his nose and glared at Maggie sitting next to him. 'Did you fart, Maggie?'

'Cheeky bugger!' Maggie rolled her eyes innocently. 'So what if I did? It's better out than in. Trapped wind's a killer. Just like them bloody Germans up there,' she said as the whine of a passing Junkers shook the roof of the shelter. Dust cascaded down. But Maggie's comical remark about her problematic intestines had set them off laughing, and the fear they might have felt dissolved in chuckles and groans. They settled down to await the all-clear.

7

On Wednesday evening, Anna arrived back in Weaver Street in the pouring rain. Two nights in Derby House was long enough, and she was looking forward to a nice hot bath and some of Mavis's home cooking.

'Eeh, we've missed you, love,' Mavis cried as Anna entered the kitchen. 'I'm sure you're glad to be home. I'll bet you've been worked off your feet.'

'Something like that,' Anna replied, sinking into the armchair she now thought of as hers. 'I gather you had a couple of near misses, Mavis. I heard that Jerry was targeting Edge Hill goods station but hit Tunnel Road instead.'

'That's right,' said Mavis as she made a pot of tea. 'I was talking to Lily earlier. She said it was awful, but thankfully no lives were lost.' She filled two cups. 'I went to the Adelphi yesterday and today to do a bit of baking, and it broke my heart to see the devastation in the city centre.' She handed Anna a cup then sat down. 'I hope you're safe in Derby House.'

'Oh, we are. It's so deep underground we don't see or hear a thing from up above. All we hear is the grim news coming in from wherever Jerry is doing his damnedest.' Anna's head was still aching from the repetitive staccato rattle of the voice calling out reference numbers and the urgency in which they had to warn the convoys and aircraft in danger, but the heat from the fire and the cup of tea was having a soothing effect. It was good to be home.

It had been a strange three days. Not only had it been fraught with life-threatening activity, she'd had to contend with the disquieting presence of Ross Penhaligon. After their brief exchange in the canteen, he hadn't spoken to her again about anything personal but every now and then she'd felt his eyes on her, questioning and confused. She'd tried to ignore those looks, but they had unsettled her. The other girls had nothing but praise for him, his kind thoughtfulness making him easy to work with. Perhaps she was being too harsh, tarring him with the same brush as she'd like to tar Simon Grant – and feather him – a fitting punishment for the lying cheat. But Ross wasn't Simon. He was really nothing like him, and maybe she should throw off the animosity she felt towards all RAF men. She just didn't know.

'You can hardly call these April showers.' Mavis looked out of the kitchen window on Saturday morning at the torrential downpour. 'It's been like this for the last three days but I suppose you don't know that where you were.'

Anna agreed. 'Let it rain, let it pour,' she replied cheerfully. 'I'm going to spend my two days off going absolutely nowhere. I've had enough excitement for one week.'

'Jack's like a box of weasels 'cos he can't work in the allotment,' Mavis continued. 'He's been...' She got no further as the door opened and Jack stomped in.

'I cut some fresh parsley to go with the fish,' he growled, shaking raindrops off his head and shoulders. 'I didn't have to go far in for it. It's by the gate, but the plots are turned to mud. It puts me in mind of the trenches.' He shuddered at the memory.

'Thanks, love, that's good of you, and don't be taking on 'cos you're not gardening. You know the wet weather plays havoc with your leg.'

Jack addressed Anna. 'You're back then. She missed you. We all did.'

Anna gave him a grateful smile. She'd only been away two nights, but it was nice to know they had been thinking about her. It was how she imagined it felt to have a loving family. 'I'm glad to be back; you can't beat home comforts,' she said.

Mavis and Jack exchanged pleased smiles.

'I'll bake the fish and make parsley sauce and mash for tea. It 'ud better be tasty; I queued nearly an hour at the trawler shop to get it. We'll be having it about half past five. Don't be late,' said Mavis.

'I won't,' Jack said. 'Any road, I must get on. I'm making a little cart for Rose's James.' He limped back out into the rain. Mavis smiled fondly after him.

'Jack likes nothing better than making stuff for the children. Young Robert and Stuart loved the forts and the little trucks he made for them, and now they're too big for such things he's doing the same for James. Next it will be Ronan's turn. I don't know what we'd do without Jack. He keeps us supplied with veg and tomatoes for most of the year. Not to mention the eggs from his chickens, and he's a grand handyman when it comes to a bit of plumbing or joinery. He's a good man is Jack.'

Mavis's little speech was heartfelt, the warmth in her eyes touching. Anna swallowed the lump in her throat. *She loves him, he's not just the next-door neighbour, and he clearly adores her.* She wondered why they weren't married. Perhaps one day Mavis would tell her.

'It's my turn to host the get-together.' Mavis was taking cups and saucers from the cupboard. 'They'll be round about eleven.' Anna glanced at the clock: ten minutes to the hour. 'You don't have to join in if you don't feel like it,' her landlady added. 'I won't mind if you don't.'

'I wouldn't miss it for the world. They're great company,' Anna said, feeling very much part of the Weaver Street family.

Kitty and Maggie arrived first, coats over their heads to fend off the rain, and laughing. It would take more than a downpour to deter these two, Anna thought as they bustled in tossing their coats over the back of a chair. 'Bloody weather! The sky's black. If it's not pissing rain, it's dropping bombs,' Maggie hooted, and Kitty added, 'If it keeps up like this, we'll need an ark, never mind an air raid shelter.' They plumped into chairs at the table. Maggie lit a cigarette. Mavis pulled a face and gave her an ashtray.

Next came Beth, buttoned up in a mackintosh and shielded by an umbrella. After shaking off the rain on the doorstep she carefully folded her umbrella, propped it behind the door, took off her mackintosh and hung it on the peg. Prim and proper, neat and tidy. Smoothing her skirt, she sat down with Kitty and Maggie.

How different they were from each other, thought Anna: Kitty neat and trim, her tawny locks and flashing green eyes a perfect foil for a woman who was full of spirit. By contrast, Beth was prissy and rather withdrawn, her tightly rolled dark brown hair lending a pinched expression to her solemn face. Then there was Maggie, who always looked as though she had been thrown together with her mop of bleached hair and garish make-up and untidy dress. Yet, for all their differences the bond between them was so strong that Anna felt she could almost reach out and touch it. Mavis had told her that these three had stuck together through thick and thin, commiserating or rejoicing at whatever life had seen fit to bestow on them. As Anna listened to their newsy, amusing gossip she thought how nice it must be to have such firm friends. Not like Suzy and Simon. *I thought I'd found a true friend and confidante in her,* she mused, *but clearly I'm no judge of character; I was daft enough to think Simon truly loved me.* A shout from Maggie broke her reverie, and pushing the unwelcome thoughts aside, she went and sat with them at the table.

'Hey, Anna, did you click with a snazzy airman when you stayed over in Derby House?' Maggie's lewd expression let her know she meant had she slept with one of them.

Anna grimaced and laughed. 'If I had, my group captain would have thrown me out on the street in my knickers.' She adopted a stern, rebuking tone. 'The RAF does not approve of WAAFs cavorting with the opposite sex.' They all laughed.

'I'm glad I didn't join up then,' said Maggie.

Beth gave her a disapproving look. 'Do you ever think of anything else, Maggie?'

'Yeah, I sometimes think you're a bit toffee-nosed.'

Anna drew a breath. Was there going to be a row?

'I am, and glad of it, Maggie,' Beth said calmy. 'One of us has to be.'

'Stop it, ye fratching besoms. Ye're like a couple of children,' Kitty intervened. That set them off laughing again.

'What's so funny?' said Lily as she bounced into the kitchen. 'What did I miss?' Her eyes heavy with sleep from another late night with ARP and her fiery hair a tangled mess, she still managed to look beautiful. Anna gave her a welcoming grin.

'Nothing worth hearing,' said Kitty. 'Maggie's on about sex and Beth's having none of it.'

'Nothing new then.' Lily yawned as she sat down next to Anna. 'Where's Molly?' she asked, glancing round the room.

'She'll be in shortly. She's just feeding Ronan.' Kitty had no sooner spoken than Molly dashed in out of the rain with her son bundled under her raincoat.

'Here, take him, Mam,' she gasped, shoving Ronan into Kitty's arms then shaking raindrops from her hair. 'It's bucketing down out there. I nearly didn't come.' She flopped down in a chair. 'By the way, Mavis, Rose sends her apologies. She's working in the Bazaar and May doesn't want to bring James out in this weather.'

'Can't say I blame her,' said Mavis. She poured tea and a lively conversation began about the recent air raid. Then, when the older women began to chatter about people and events that were foreign to Anna and of little interest to Molly and Lily, they talked to each other. Lily told them about the lovely new ARP recruit called Eric. 'He's asked me to go out with him tonight to the cinema,' she whispered, her green eyes glinting and her expression rather bemused as she added, 'I can't imagine what he sees in me 'cos he's ever so posh. He went to university and has a good job in Buchanan's.' She sat back to judge Molly and Anna's reaction, her smile slipping as she said, 'I might not go though. I'm not sure I'm good enough for him.'

'Don't put yourself down, Lily. He must like you if he's asked you out,' Molly said.

'You're as good as anybody, Lily,' Anna assured her. 'Just because he's had a university education doesn't make him better than you. Don't let that put you off, just meet him tonight, and be yourself. He must like what he's seen so far.'

'Yeah, dead right,' Lily agreed, flushed with renewed confidence. 'He's seen me at me worst and that didn't put him off. I'll give him a go 'cos he's ever so good looking and I really fancy him.'

Lily's love life sorted, they chatted about fashion and films, talking like old friends and Anna's liking for the two girls grew by the minute. She really did feel more at home here in Weaver Street than any other place she had ever lived.

She spent the afternoon tidying her bedroom and sponging and pressing her uniform. Jack arrived promptly at five thirty to share the baked fish in a creamy parsley sauce, even though Mavis had grumbled at having to make it with reconstituted dried milk. In the evening they listened to *In Town Tonight* then *Geraldo and his Orchestra* on the wireless, the clicking of Mavis's knitting needles interspersing their conversation. Anna went up to her room to have an early night in a comfortable bed. The mattress in the dormitory at Derby House had been rock hard. She read a chapter of *The Good Earth* then fell into an untroubled sleep.

On Sunday morning when Anna opened her bedroom curtains, she saw that the sky was blue and the sun shining. Only the huge puddles in the lane were evidence of the torrential rain. She heard Mavis moving down below. As she dressed, Anna debated whether or not to accept Mavis's invitation to go to the church at the top of the street with her. Anna had told her she wasn't a Catholic; she wasn't anything. Jane and Norman hadn't been at all religious but Mavis had said it didn't matter. She thought Anna might enjoy the mass. 'It's very soothing,' she'd said. Anna looked at her wristwatch. It showed ten past nine. The mass Mavis attended wasn't until twelve, plenty of time to make up her mind. She went down to the kitchen.

'Well, this is a better day, I must say.' Mavis acknowledged the sun's rays streaming through the window with a flourish of the spoon she'd been using to stir the porridge.

Anna agreed and asked, 'Will I make the toast?'

* * *

In the house next door, Jack pulled on his wellington boots ready to go and see what damage the rain had done to the seedlings he'd planted. He limped across the lane into the allotment to inspect the saturated plots of cabbages, onions, green beans and turnips. The green beans were straggling loose from their canes but the others had survived all right. He walked past the potatoes, no harm done there, and then to check Kitty's plot at the far end near the trees.

Several paces before he reached it, he stopped and stared. His blood ran cold. He knew straight away what it was. He'd seen enough of them in France in the first war. He'd have to do something about it, and quick. Turning back the way he'd come then out into the lane, he headed straight for Kitty's house, his gait awkward at the speed he was travelling.

He knocked on the back door and walked in, calling out, 'Is John about?'

'In the kitchen,' John called back. He was sitting at the table eating a fried egg. Kitty was by the oven stirring a pot. They both gave Jack enquiring looks. He rarely called without Mavis, and then only on special occasions.

Jack jerked his head towards the door impatiently and said, 'Have you a minute, John? There's summat I want to show you.'

'What is it?' Kitty asked, her curiosity aroused. Jack ignored her and limped from the kitchen. John gave Kitty a confused grin, shrugged, then followed him. Kitty rolled her eyes. Jack could be a funny bugger at times.

Outside, John asked, 'What's it about, Jack?'

'A bloody great unexploded bomb in the allotment.'

John's stride faltered. 'Oh my God! Are you sure?'

'Course I'm bloody sure. I saw enough of 'em last time round.'

John's eyes registered panic as he looked into Jack's grim face.

'Whereabouts in the allotment?' He set off at a run.

'Hold on,' Jack shouted. 'Don't go anywhere near it. Vibrations might trigger it.'

John slowed his pace. He and Jack crept into the allotment, walking slowly to what had been Kitty's vegetable plot. There, poking through the mud and slime was the cone-shaped nose of the unexploded bomb. John's breakfast curdled in his stomach.

'Stay well back,' Jack warned, repeating how the least little thing could set it off.

'How long has it been there?'

Jack shrugged. 'No idea, but not long I'd say. Kitty was digging here afore the rain set in. If it had been here then...' Jack silently cursed his lack of tact.

John felt his heart lurch inside his chest. *What if...?*

Slowly, the initial shock wore off.

'Back off carefully, Jack,' muttered John unnecessarily. 'We've got to get help – and quick.' He was trembling, his training with the ARP now seeming totally inadequate. He'd dealt with the aftermath of exploded bombs on many occasions but not one waiting to go off at any given moment. And this one was far too close to home and all those he loved.

Holding their breaths, the two men stepped back steadily then when they were at a safe distance they hurried out into the lane.

'I'll go and ring the report centre and tell them to get the reconnaissance boys out here bloody sharpish.' John was aware that his voice was shaking. 'You go and rouse Lily. Tell her to start clearing the street. She'll know what to do.' By now he was walking rapidly towards his own house, Jack struggling to keep up with him. 'Oh, and get somebody sensible like Stanley to guard the allotment gate and not let anybody in. He'll not panic.'

John dashed off, and Jack limped up number nine's path to

get Lily Stubbs. He hammered on the door, and Stanley answered. Jack wasted no words.

'What's a UXB?' Maggie asked.

'Unexploded bomb,' Stanley barked. 'Get your Lily out of bed.'

Maggie screamed and ran to the stairs.

Jack hobbled to Mavis's door. 'There's an unexploded bomb on the allotment,' he croaked. 'The bomb squad are on their way.'

'Lord o' mercy!' Mavis screeched, and seeing the strain etched into his face and hearing the wobble in his voice, she pulled him close. 'Are you all right, love?'

Anna tossed aside her book and sprang to her feet. 'A UXB? Has somebody reported it?'

'John's doing it right now. You'll need to get clear. It could go off at any minute. Go and take shelter in the church.'

'What can I do, Jack? I'm trained for emergencies,' Anna asked.

'Just keep Mavis safe,' he growled and stomped off.

Anna and Mavis hastily packed a bag with essentials: Mavis's knitting, Anna's book, a flask of tea and packets of biscuits and blankets. Mavis said the crypt would be chilly.

Kitty had put John's half-eaten breakfast in the oven to keep warm and was nibbling toast and pondering on Jack's unexpected visit when John burst into the kitchen. Her jaw dropped and she stared, round-eyed as he told her the reason for Jack's visit.

'Good God in heaven!' Kitty blessed herself then ran to the foot of the stairs and yelled, 'Robert! Get down here. Now!'

John hurried to the telephone. His palm was slick with sweat and his finger fumbled as he dialled the report centre's number. He jigged impatiently from heel to toe as he waited for an answer, fully aware that the bomb could be detonated if it shifted in the oozing mud, or a bird landed on it. His heart thudded in his chest.

Robert jumped out of bed, pulled on his clothes and tumbled downstairs, his eyes bleary with sleep and his hair tousled.

'What's all the shouting for?'

His eyes lit up with fear and excitement when his mother told him. They stood and listened to John's urgent voice as he reported the finding. When he put down the phone he turned to his wife and son. 'You need to get out of the house. Now!' Robert thanked God that he wasn't still wearing his pyjamas. Five minutes earlier and he would have been.

Minutes after Maggie had given her daughter a vigorous shake, Lily was out in the lane dressed in her ARP uniform and carrying her haversack. John ran to meet her with Kitty and Robert at his heels. *A bomb in my veg plot. What can I do to be of use?* Kitty was thinking as she followed her husband. *John will know. He always does.*

'Lily! I've telephoned the report centre, the BRO are on their way,' John panted. The Bomb Reconnaissance Officers were the incredibly brave men who would attempt to make the bomb safe. 'We need to clear the area. Do your job, and try not to let them panic.'

'Aye, aye Captain.' Lily saluted then took the handbell out of her haversack.

'What do we do?' Kitty asked through gritted teeth as she tried to ignore the tight hand of fear that clutched her chest. That bomb was only a few yards from her lovely home.

'Start knocking on doors. Get everybody out and up to the crypt under the church. That should be big enough to hold everybody.' John was referring to the large vaulted space beneath St Joseph's that was regularly used as a shelter.

'Jesus, Mary and Joseph!' Kitty gasped. 'Ten o'clock mass will still be on; the church will be packed. I'll away up there and let Father McLaughlin know. And you, Robert' – she grabbed his arm frantically – 'get our Molly and Ronan out.' Robert didn't drag his feet. This was something important he could do, and tingling with excitement, he dashed to his sister's door.

Hot and bothered, Kitty sped to the church, a lump coming in her throat as she raced past a frail old couple being gently led up the street by a boy: the young and healthy helping the old and infirm. There was still goodness in the world.

At the church door, Kitty paused to catch her breath. The sweet strains of 'Hail, Holy Queen, the Ocean Star' floated through the open doors.

Kitty thrust back her shoulders and marched inside, down the central aisle and up to the altar. The elderly priest gave her a strange glare as she genuflected then stepped up beside him.

'Save us from peril and from woe,' the congregation sang.

'Stop the mass,' Kitty hissed. 'Get everybody into the crypt. There's an unexploded bomb on the allotment in Weaver Street. A big one.'

Father McLaughlin's eyes boggled. He ran distracted fingers through his grey hair.

'Hail Holy Queen, star of the sea, pray for the wanderer, pray for me.'

'Mrs Halloran,' the priest bellowed, 'stop the music.'

The organist almost fell off her seat. The pipes wheezed and fell silent. The choir petered into silence. The congregation, alarmed by the disruption, turned their heads, shuffled to their feet or sat frozen in the pews. *What was Kitty Sykes playing at?*

'Stay seated and listen carefully.' The priest's rumbling voice bounced off the stained-glass windows and walls, his soft West of Ireland accent more pronounced than usual. 'I want ye all to make your way quietly down to the crypt. Don't be pushin' an' shovin' now. Do it in orderly fashion like the dacent souls ye are.'

'What is it, Father?'

'I've a dinner to cook.'

'I don't hear any sirens.'

'Silence!' Father McLaughlin's roar increased the confusion. People began pushing their way out of the pews. Was this a daytime raid or what?

Kitty clambered up the steps into the pulpit and waved her arms. 'Listen, everybody!' she yelled above the hubbub. The congregation, shocked by her audacity, stared open-mouthed. Seeing that she had their attention she continued, her voice clear and confident. 'There's an unexploded bomb in the allotments behind my house in Weaver Street. It could go off at any minute. The bomb squad's on its way. Ye must all take cover, an' the safest place is here in the crypt so do as the good Father has asked ye to do.'

Only when Kitty had finished speaking was she aware that she was trembling like a leaf and that her grip on the pulpit had turned her knuckles white. She let out a deep breath.

By now, Lily's enthusiastic ringing of her handbell had brought people to their doors to see what the commotion was, and she or John or Jack gave them their orders.

'What the hell...?' Bill Walker demanded when he saw Jack. 'I'm in the middle of me breakfast. What's to do?'

Jack told him, and Bill's bluster immediately changed to concern as he warned May to get ready to leave the house. He hurried next door to Rose's. His son Joey would have his guts for garters if he let anything harm his precious grandson and daughter-in-law.

Anna saw Molly emerging from her house with Ronan. She ran to her.

'This is awful,' Molly gasped, hugging Ronan tighter to her chest.

'Give me your bag.' Anna unhooked the bag full of baby

things from Molly's shoulder. 'Go back inside and out through your front door into the street. We'll get to the church quicker that way.' Molly did as Anna suggested and they hurried out into Weaver Street. All along the street, front doors that were rarely used were open wide as their neighbours made a hasty exit.

'Come on, I'll walk with you up to the church.' Anna linked Molly's arm, felt her trembling and realised how hard it was to be a young mother with no man by her side. They hadn't walked far when a woman with dark auburn hair overtook them. Beautifully attired in a smart grey flannel coat and green silk scarf, she walked calmly ahead, looking as though she was on her way to a garden party rather than seeking shelter in the church crypt.

'Is that Rachel Dyson?' Anna asked Molly, recalling how Maggie had likened the colour of her hair to a woman who lived at number seven. She had yet to meet her.

'Yeah, that's her,' Molly panted. 'She's a cold fish, never bothers with anybody.'

'She's very elegant,' Anna said, admiring the back of the slender well-dressed figure.

Molly didn't reply, for just then Mavis and Maggie came alongside, Mavis doing her best to calm Maggie who was cursing the Germans and panicking in case she didn't have enough cigarettes to last the enforced evacuation. Beth and Stuart stepped out of their front door, Stuart with blankets over his arm and Beth carrying baskets filled with emergency supplies that she always had at the ready.

'Look at you, dead organised, aren't you?' Maggie said pettishly as Beth greeted them with a nervous little smile.

'Better safe than sorry. We could be out for ages,' Beth said primly.

'Come on, get a move on!' Lily's raucous shout had them hurrying up to the church. 'A UXB isn't going to wait for you to stand gossiping.' She felt the thrill of being in command as she urged them on. Satisfied that they were all on the move, she ran back to the bottom of the street. 'Weaver Street all clear,' she shouted to John who was standing on the corner by the Weaver's Arms.

'Well done, Lily,' he praised. 'I've got the back lane cordoned off and the BRO will be here any minute. Broad Green should have been cleared by now so you get up to the church and keep yourself safe.'

Lily could see that more ARP wardens had arrived and were shepherding the people who lived above and behind the shops in Broad Green past the end of the lane. Her heart gave a flutter as she remembered that Eric was on duty today. She ran down the lane, keeping her eyes peeled for him. Last night, bolstered by Anna and Molly's advice, she had let him take her to the Astoria to see *Gone with the Wind* and then for a walk in the Botanic Gardens. She had enjoyed every minute, so different from the nights out with other chaps that usually involved too much drink followed by fighting off over-amorous sweaty hands. She had never gone out with anybody like Eric. He was lovely. He'd talked about things she knew very little about, but he did it in a way that didn't make her feel uneducated. Instead, he made her feel precious and respected. Now, her heart flipped when she saw him hurrying towards her.

John, Jack and Stanley stood guard at the end of the back lane awaiting the arrival of the BRO. They looked from one to the other, their faces drawn and fearful and their nerves stretched to the limit. The roar of engines and the screech of brakes drew their gaze down Broad Green where a lorry swung round the corner and hurtled to where they stood. John signalled for them to go up the lane, running alongside the leading lorry until it arrived at the allotments. He waved them to a halt.

Out jumped six men wearing dark blue battledresses and steel helmets stamped with a large 'R' for Rescue; the bomb reconnaissance officers had arrived. Close behind the lorry came three others piled high with sand. This would be used to muffle the explosion.

'Blackstock.' The leader of the BROs stuck out his hand. He was a military type with a clipped moustache and a piercing gaze. Handshakes and names were exchanged then John and Jack cautiously led the way into the allotment while Stanley stayed in the lane. The team followed, each man taking the utmost precaution as they approached their nemesis, its ugly metal nose protruding from the churned mud and debris from the sycamore trees.

'By Jove!' The words whistled out from Blackstock's lips. 'She's a big one all right. SC 1000, or a Hermann as we call them – after Goering you know.'

John and Jack knew fine well who Field Marshall Goering was. The German military leader of Hitler's army, and one of the most powerful members of the Nazi Party was the perpetrator of atrocities like this, and many others.

'Most likely tip-and-run,' another member of the team remarked. 'All that rain and mud probably prevented detonation.' Tip-and-run referred to a German pilot offloading his bombs at random before heading for home.

'We'll dismantle it where it is. It's too risky to move it,' Blackstock said. He turned to address John. 'I presume the area's been cleared and all the necessary agencies notified.'

'I raised the alarm myself,' said John. 'We got everybody to go to the crypt under the church. The report centre will have told the police to divert the traffic, and call out the lads who shut off the gas, water and electric supply. Everything should be in order.'

'Good man. Well done. Off you go then.' Dismissing John and

Jack with a flick of his hand, he gave orders to his men. 'We'll dig trenches and fill them with sand then...'

Two of the team headed back to the lorry and John and Jack followed them. 'Rather them poor buggers than me,' Jack growled.

'Aye, one false move,' John replied morosely. 'I wouldn't fancy digging anywhere near it. If your spade hit a stone the vibrations alone could trigger the bugger.'

By the time John and Jack reached the gate, the two officers were coming back carrying picks and spades. They grinned as they passed by. John and Jack stood outside the allotment looking back at the scene. Jackets off, sleeves rolled up and helmets on the ground, the reconnaissance team were busy digging the trench. John shuddered. He dearly hoped it went well for them. They were somebody's sons, husbands and fathers putting their lives on the line to save others. Would this bloody war never end?

Suddenly he had the urge to be with Kitty. 'I'm going to the church,' he said.

'I'll come with you,' Jack replied.

* * *

The crypt was packed to capacity, bodies huddled together for comfort and to ward off the damp chill of the ancient stonework. At one end a group gathered round Father McLaughlin saying the Rosary. Kitty and Maggie had filled jugs with water in the sacristy and raided the cupboard where the Legion of Mary ladies kept teacups for their weekly meetings. Moving through the crush, they were doling out drinks to whoever needed one.

'Hey, thems our cups,' a stalwart of the Legion bawled as Kitty offered her a drink.

'Aye, an' aren't we blessed that ye have them on the premises for times like this,' Kitty said sweetly. The woman flushed.

'Ungrateful bugger,' Maggie hissed.

The air had grown fetid, people grumbling at those who had lit cigarettes. 'It isn't right in God's House,' moaned a woman piously clutching her string of Rosary beads but not pious enough to give up her seat on one of the few old pews that were stored in the crypt and stand with those who had gathered round the priest.

Hearing this, Maggie deliberately took out her Woodbines and lit up.

Mavis was comforting an elderly couple who had left their dog behind, and Anna went to help a young mother with four crying children find somewhere comfortable to sit. Finding a pile of old curtains, she spread them on the ground then went and sat on the floor on a blanket with Molly and Ronan, who was sleeping. Rose and May sat close by, doing their best to pacify young James. He was tetchy and crying, 'I want to go home.'

'We all do, love, and we will when it's safe,' May cooed.

Robert had found some of his mates and was playing cards under the baleful glare of those who didn't approve. Stuart would have joined them but Beth didn't allow it.

A sweet tenor voice began to sing 'Faith of Our Fathers' and people joined in, the old hymn having a soothing effect on those who were becoming restless. One hymn led to another. Maggie didn't attend the church, and didn't know the hymns but she fancied herself as something of a singer. When the last verse of 'Holy, Holy, Holy' faded, she raised her voice and began singing, 'Keep Right on to the End of the Road'.

'You can't sing that in church,' an irate voice called out, but many of the congregation were familiar with the song from the

Great War and gradually they joined in, their voices swelling and one of the loudest was Father McLaughlin's.

Thrilled with her success, Maggie broke into 'It's a Long Way to Tipperary', Kitty helping her out when she forgot the words. Before long songs old and new were warbled tunefully or otherwise and the long hours of waiting and wondering shortened.

John and Jack hadn't gone straight to the church, although John was anxious to know if Kitty was safe. Even so, common sense had kicked in. The defusing or detonating of the bomb would take hours so instead he suggested that they make sandwiches with anything they could find in the cupboards in Kitty's, Mavis's and Maggie's kitchens. Almost an hour later they walked to the church with bags filled with jam, spam and mashed egg sandwiches. Before they left the lane they had peered into the allotment. Under an innocent blue sky the brave BROs were still toiling in the mud.

Kitty's heart surged when she saw John enter the crypt. She ran and threw her arms round him. 'Thank God ye're safe.' Relief flooded her veins. Her love for him and the pride she felt knew no bounds when he presented her with the bags of sandwiches. 'Ye're a godsend, John Sykes, that's what ye are,' she cried.

Mavis hugged Jack. 'And you made all these yourself,' she said, surprise colouring her words. Jack wasn't known for his culinary arts. 'You're a good man, Jack Naughton.'

The sandwiches were shared out, those who had brought nothing with them grateful for the small offerings, and those like Beth who had come prepared shared out their supplies, the spirit of goodwill infectious. The afternoon dragged its heels into evening and gradually accepting that they had nothing to do but wait the anxious crowd in the crypt found things to occupy them, mums playing I-spy with their young children, while the older boys and girls played cards or made up guessing games about favourite films. The women who had had the foresight to bring their knitting clicked their needles, and the men discussed football. Some of the elderly just dozed.

Anna and Molly had talked of many things in the past hours, and when Molly asked whether Anna had got a boyfriend, Anna casually told her about Simon but she didn't mention the heartbreak she had suffered. Funnily enough, she discovered that the pain she had felt wasn't there any more, that she didn't see Simon's face or hear his voice. There had been a time when there was no other image in mind; when she slept, when she woke, and even at work, and not because she summoned it there. It just wouldn't go away. But tonight, in the gloomy chilly crypt, she didn't see or hear him at all. It was as if she was telling a story about some other poor, unfortunate girl and her cheating lover. Simon Grant no longer mattered.

Fed and watered, the congregation settled down, and those who could slept. Father McLaughlin plodded round the crypt giving each a blessing, and thanking John for the welcome repast. Then he went and sat with a pale young woman whose nerves had got the better of her, soothing her hysterics with soft gentle words.

As the long day drew to a close, Lily and Eric came into the crypt. They were exhausted having patrolled the area making sure nobody was left in danger in case the bomb exploded. After saying a few words to Maggie, they found a corner and sat down, Eric with his arms round Lily and her head resting on his chest.

'He's university trained and has a good job at Buchanan's,' Maggie whispered proudly to Kitty. 'And he seems dead fond of our Lily.'

Kitty smiled and snuggled up to John. 'I hope it lasts,' she whispered back, too tired with the strain of the day to say any more.

In the early hours of Monday morning, word came to say that the bomb had been made safe. A loud communal sigh of relief rushed through the crypt and everyone scrabbled to gather their belongings and go home. Bleary eyed and dishevelled, Father McLaughlin insisted that they gave thanks to God for seeing them safely through the night. They stood, feet shuffling or edging towards the stairs to be first out.

'He might have kept us safe but he didn't work a miracle and give me any cigs. I smoked me last one hours ago,' Maggie grumbled as the priest intoned the prayer.

'I heard that heaven had run out of Woodbines,' Kitty quipped as Father McLaughlin announced, 'The Lord be with you.' Kitty replied, 'And also with you,' then blessed herself.

'I've had enough of this mumbo-jumbo,' Maggie snapped, pushing her way to the front of the crowd.

'Come on, love, let's go home,' said John, easing Ronan onto his shoulder and taking Kitty's arm. Molly and Anna followed with Jack and Mavis.

Lily was on cloud nine as, linking her arm with Eric's, they waited their turn to mount the stairs. He had asked if she would be his regular girlfriend, and told her he had never felt like this about any other girl. He'd said he thought he'd fallen in love. Lily knew she had.

8

Later that morning, Anna arrived at Derby House pale and hollow-eyed.

'My, somebody lived it up last night,' Denise sniped. 'You look as though you're three sheets to the wind.'

'You do look shattered,' Primrose agreed.

'Oh, there's nothing like spending a night in a crypt to make you feel how I look.' Anna told them about the UXB, and how the Bomb Squad had managed to dismantle it safely so that there was only a minor explosion. 'No lives lost, no damage to any houses. The only damage is the bags under my eyes and an inability to stop yawning,' she said, clapping a smothering hand over her mouth.

'Don't let Razor Sharp see you doing that,' Susan said. 'She'll think you had a night out on the town and give you the third degree.' The group captain was suspicious if her WAAFs reported for work looking the worse for wear.

'Yeah. She gave me a lecture on good living the other day when I was late for duty. Two minutes, that's all,' Diane protested.

They left the cloakroom and made their way to the ops room,

Anna feeling like death. After she had left the crypt, she'd managed to snatch a couple of hours' sleep but it wasn't enough. She was also mulling over what she'd told Molly about Simon, surprised to recall that when she'd wakened first thing, she hadn't given him a thought for the first time in ages. It made her feel free. Confession must be good for the soul.

However, feeling good about that couldn't mask how tired she also felt. Twice she miscalculated a vital reference as the team round the table worked frantically to protect one of the Atlantic convoys under threat from German U-boats. Red faced, and angry at her own inefficiency, she brushed away threatening tears with the back of her hand.

'Are you all right, Anna? Do you feel ill?' Ross's concern was so sincere that Anna hadn't the heart or the energy to raise the barriers that she summoned up whenever he approached her. She looked up at him despairingly, her bottom lip trembling pitifully.

'I didn't get much sleep last night,' she said. He raised his eyebrows speculatively, no doubt having the same thoughts as Denise. Anxious to dismiss such a notion, Anna told him about the unexploded bomb and the long night in the crypt.

'You poor thing.' Ross's lips curved in a sympathetic smile. 'Leave it to me.' When he walked away from her, Anna suddenly felt bereft. She shook her head, pushed back her shoulders and tried to concentrate on the incoming information, aware that the Wrens and Primrose were watching her carefully. She risked glancing across the room to where Ross was in conversation with Group Captain Sharp. She quailed inwardly.

A short while later, no more than five or ten minutes, Ross came up to the table and gently gripped her elbow. 'You're to come with me, WAAF Carswell.'

Anna's heart lurched. What had he been saying to Razor

Sharp? Had he complained she wasn't fit to be working? Anger flared. Head held high, she let him steer her out of the ops room. Out in the corridor she turned to him, her eyes blazing.

'I don't need your interference, or your false pity,' she snapped. 'What did you tell Group Captain Sharp?'

Ross raised his hands in surrender, his grey eyes twinkling. 'I told her the truth,' he said. 'And she agreed with me that a strong coffee and a walk in the fresh air was what was needed if you're to stay on your feet for the rest of the shift.' He caught Anna's arm and marched her down the corridor. 'So that is exactly what we're going to do.'

Shrouded in embarrassment, her cheeks red, and feeling decidedly ungrateful, Anna let Ross take her to the canteen.

'Now, WAAF Carswell, I know all about your night in the crypt but I know nothing about the real Anna Carswell, so enlighten me,' Ross said as they sat drinking strong black coffee thick as sludge. He gazed deep into her eyes.

'There's nothing to tell,' she muttered.

'Come off it! You've been antagonistic towards me ever since the dance at the Grafton.' His patience had worn thin. 'I told you your hair was the colour of autumn leaves, which it is, and you bit my head off.' He gave her an imploring smile. 'It wasn't an insult, and I want to know why you felt offended.'

Anna was consumed by ingratitude. He'd been nothing but pleasant to her since they had met, and today he'd been kind enough to wangle a release for her from the pressures of the ops room. She realised how stupid she was being, but being faced with solicitude from a handsome man abraded the sore spot that Simon Grant had inflicted: it was too soon, too raw to ignore.

'Let's say you remind me of someone I'd rather forget, and leave it at that,' she said ungraciously. 'Thanks for putting a kind word in for me with Razor Sharp, I appreciate it. Now, if you don't mind, I'll get back.' She pushed back her chair.

'Not before you've had a breath of fresh air.' Ross stood. 'We'll take a walk round the block, clear your head, and you'll do me the courtesy of being nice to me.' He reached for her hand, and feeling like a recalcitrant child, Anna let her hand rest in his as they left the canteen.

Outside, they walked away from Derby House into Rumford Street, Ross talking easily about his home in a Yorkshire village called Flockton, and about missing his mother's cooking and his collie dog, Shep. 'What about you?'

Somewhat begrudgingly, Anna told him she came from Salisbury, and that her parents were dead.

'Is that what makes you sad and touchy?'

'Not really. We didn't have a great relationship.' Anna spoke flippantly.

'Ah! Then it must be the person I remind you of.' Ross's eyes glinted wickedly.

'Something like that,' Anna said huffily at the same time thinking she was behaving like a proper cow but she couldn't help herself.

Ross changed the subject to films and books, and by the time they had reached the top of the street and turned to make their way back to Derby House, Anna realised that she was enjoying his company. They seemed to have a lot of shared interests and they laughed a lot.

'What do you say to an ice cream?' Ross asked as they came level with a small Italian ice cream parlour.

Before she could prevent herself, Anna replied, 'I didn't know that's what my soul was crying out for, but now that you mention it, I'd love one.' They smiled at one another.

They bought large cornets, and licking and talking, they returned to Derby House.

Before they went back into the ops room, Anna paused and looked into Ross's eyes. 'Thanks,' she said because she really did feel much more alive. 'That was the best medicine I've had in ages.'

Ross smiled. 'Glad to administer it,' he said lightly. 'Now, are we friends?'

'I suppose we are – friends that is.'

* * *

By Monday evening, a day in which all the neighbours in Weaver Street went about their business relieved to be alive but weary from lack of sleep, the remains of the bomb had been shifted. Huge lumps of twisted metal had been dumped behind the sycamore trees whilst other bits of the bomb had been carted away for the BRO to investigate; learning more about how Jerry constructed them and how to safely defuse them was vital.

On Tuesday morning, Kitty stood in the allotment, staring at the crater that had been her vegetable patch. She'd thanked God over and again for saving her house, that it had escaped with no more damage than cracked windows in the parlour. The brave boys in the BRO had managed to dismantle the bomb, and the minor explosion that finished it off had done no more than throw up mountains of churned earth and rip the branches from the sycamore tree. Her thoughts strayed to the German pilot. Didn't he know that the people who lived in the houses where he'd offloaded his evil cargo were just ordinary people like his family back in Germany? That they just wanted to live in peace and get on with their lives?

Jack left off hoeing weeds and hobbled over to Kitty. 'It's a mess, lass, but nowt that a hell of a lot of shifting and shovelling won't put right. It could have been worse. No lives were lost, and that's summat to be thankful for. Tell John I'll give him a hand,' he said gruffly.

'Aye, what's losing a few onions and cabbages when you think of all the lads who've lost their lives in this bloody war,' Kitty said dismally, and thought of Patrick. *God, don't let him be one of them.* 'Will this war never end, Jack? I'm sick of it.'

'Keep your spirits up, lass. We're still all here,' he said, patting her shoulder before she trudged back to her house.

Later that morning, Kitty went over to Molly's. She popped in and out several times a day to see her daughter and grandson, and now she was calling to remind Molly to go over to her house at teatime to turn on the oven and heat the food she'd put in earlier so that John and Robert had a hot dinner to come home to from the factory.

'I'll not be back till near seven,' she said. 'The casserole's half-cooked so if ye go over about five an' set it on low it'll be done for 'em when they come at after six.'

'I'll not forget,' said Molly, handing Ronan over for a cuddle with his granny.

'Ye look down in the dumps,' her mother remarked.

'Is it any wonder? What with the bomb and everything else this rotten war does, and I haven't had a letter from Mickey for nearly three weeks.' Molly's eyes moistened.

'Don't take on, love, ye know what the post's like. Nothing's as it should be any more, an' just because ye haven't heard from him doesn't mean he's not thinking about ye.' Kitty paused, searching for more comforting words. 'An' ye know he's safe an' well otherwise ye would have heard. No news is good news, so they say.'

The suggestion that Molly could have been the recipient of a telegram telling her otherwise made her blanch. 'Oh, Mam, I know you mean well but sometimes you can be awfully tactless,' she cried.

'Aye, me an' me big mouth. But you know what I mean, love. Get ye out into the fresh air, take wee Ronan for a walk. Ye could go by way of the towpath an' keep an eye on my café an' see how Sheila's getting on.'

'I might just do that,' Molly said without enthusiasm. Then, on a brighter note, she added, 'I've asked Anna to come round tonight for a bit of supper. I really enjoy her company.'

'That's grand, an' I'm sure she'll be glad of yours. Everybody needs a friend.' Kitty handed Ronan back to his mother. 'Look, love, I'll have to dash if I'm not to keep Elsie waiting. Ta-ra, I'll see you later.'

Molly slowly waltzed Ronan round the kitchen, humming the tune to 'Red Sails in the Sunset' which had become a favourite of hers, the words summing up how she felt without Mickey. She was looking forward to Anna's visit. She'd be able to talk to her about Mickey, tell her what he was like and why she loved him. It wouldn't be like talking to her mam or Lily – they already knew everything, and although her mam was sympathetic, Lily was too busy trying to find a love of her own to care – but Anna would be hearing it for the first time and Molly had a feeling that she'd understand what it was like to miss somebody so much.

Kitty walked briskly along Edge Lane. Three times a week she worked a split-shift at the munitions factory sharing the twelve-hour stint with Elsie Cooper from Nuttall Street who worked from six in the morning to midday; it suited them both. Elsie needed to be at home for when her six children came out of school, and Kitty needed the time to bake baps and buns for the café.

The sun was shining, a pleasant change after all the rain, but Kitty didn't feel like rejoicing. She was worried about Molly. Mickey's departure seemed to have sapped her spirit. She had always been a confident, lively girl who knew her own mind and had shown great promise at nursing. She'd had to give that up when she got married. The hospitals were taking married women back now there was a war but Molly had Ronan to think of, and although she was using her skills with the ambulance service three nights a week, it wasn't the same.

Kitty heaved a sigh as she reached the factory gates. Her poor Molly's life hadn't turned out quite as expected; neither had married life. Molly and Mickey had married on 2 September 1939; the next day war was declared, and in January 1940 Mickey had been conscripted into the RAF. *Such a pity*, thought Kitty. Mickey was a bricklayer and had been thinking of starting his own business when they whisked him off to a training camp in Lincolnshire. Now he was in darkest Africa, never having seen the son who had been conceived on his embarkation leave, let alone held him. Life wasn't fair. *But at least we're alive*, she told herself, then thought of Patrick. *God spare him*, she prayed as she hurried on.

The sharp stink of TNT bit her nose as she entered the factory, and the buzz of machinery echoed in the corridor as she walked to the changing room. Strict rules forbade the wearing of any metal items in the 'clearways' where shells, bullets, hand grenades and bombs were assembled, and to this end before leaving home Kitty always removed her wedding ring and cross and chain, and left her hair unpinned. Hiding her tawny locks under the hideous mob cap they were obliged to wear then stripping off her blouse and skirt, she put on her biscuit-coloured twill uniform, a stiff and unflattering ankle-length dress with a broad belt and long sleeves. As she buttoned the cuffs, she told herself that in her experience, life surely did have a habit of tossing the unexpected your way and expected you to just get on with it.

In the ops room at Derby House, Anna was perched on the ladder reacting speedily to incoming information then plotting the movement of the Allied convoys on the giant map of the Atlantic Ocean that covered the entire wall. She'd had a much better night's sleep and felt bright and alert. Standing on the ladder was precarious enough but plotting the coordinates was even more so. They had to be precisely exact otherwise it could lead to the sinking of a ship, and the loss of lives. She also felt more at ease whenever she came into contact with Ross. He'd made no mention of their walk the day before, but she could tell that he too appreciated the new footing they had established.

'Eyes to the floor, sailor,' Ross admonished the cheeky young rating who was peering up Anna's skirt as he handed her a list of coordinates. The rating scurried off, his neck red. Ross grinned and winked at Anna. She raised her eyebrows and grinned back. Then pulling the lever that moved the ladder, she glided further along the wall to another area on the huge map, a risky task if distracted. Primrose had fallen off the ladder performing this same manoeuvre the week before. Ross watched Anna go. *She has a lovely pair of pins*, he thought.

Lily kept her eyes on the shuttle on her loom, its repetitive advance and retreat weaving khaki twill but her mind was on what Eric had said in the early hours of Monday morning. Had he really meant it when he'd said he thought he'd fallen in love with her? Or had the excitement caused by the bomb in the allotment and all the rushing around clearing the streets and getting people safely into the shelter made him speak without really thinking? After all, they hardly knew one another and she worried that if and when they did, he might decide she wasn't good enough for him.

The cacophonous roar of the machinery in Holroyd's weaving shed didn't prevent Lily from thinking one awful thought after another. What if he met one of her old friends and they told him about how wild she used to be, drinking and dancing and going with one chap after another? What was it Molly had said? *You change your boyfriends more often than you change your knickers.* And what about her mam? Would he think Maggie was rough because she smoked and cursed too much? She'd bet her last penny that Eric's mother didn't do that. He'd had a proper upbringing with a mum and a dad. He'd been to university, and he lived in a grand house in the nicest part of Wavertree. She couldn't bear to think that the difference in their backgrounds might come between them – not when she knew for certain that she was in love.

She reached out to catch a loose end of thread and automatically fixed it. Weaving was second nature to Lily; she'd worked in the mill since leaving school. Now she wished that she had an office job, one that let people know you were clever and destined for better things, the sort that was more fitting for a girl who was going out with an educated man. She glanced at the huge clock on the wall at the end of the shed. Nearly clocking off time.

The girl working on the loom across the weaver's alley caught Lily's eye. She raised two fingers to her lips, indicating she was about to speak. The constant clacking of the looms made ordinary conversation impossible and the women communicated by mouthing the words. 'Are you coming to the pictures tonight?' she asked.

'No,' Lily mouthed back. 'I'm going out with the most wonderful man in the world.'

Anna left the bunker at the end of her shift and hurried to the tram stop. She was looking forward to her evening with Molly. Through no fault on her part, she had been dropped out of the social loop that the WAAFs had formed. She didn't live in the city, unlike Primrose and Susan, and seeing as they were billeted in houses close to one another they were in the habit of walking to and from work together. This had led to them spending their free time in one another's company. Poppy was billeted with wealthy friends of her family and she socialised with them, and Denise spent her free time chasing soldiers, in the hope of finding one who wanted to marry her. However, Anna didn't feel as though she was missing out on having friends; Mavis was a dear, and although her friendships with Lily and Molly were still in the early stages, the brief time she had spent in their company more than made up for it; an evening with Molly would be a pleasant end to a busy day.

At the tram stop she was surprised to see the auburn-haired woman that Molly had told her was Rachel Dyson, and even more surprised when the woman said, 'Hello, you're the girl who lives with Mavis Robson, aren't you?' Anna said she was and when the tram came, they sat together and fell into easy conversation. They talked about the bomb in the allotment and about the changeable April weather and then about work. Rachel told Anna she was first sales lady in Blacklers fashion department.

'It must be lovely to be surrounded by all those beautiful clothes,' Anna said. They talked for a while about fashion before Rachel commented, 'I presume you're at Derby House.'

Anna smiled and said she was. Her uniform was a dead giveaway.

'Yes, it's non-stop,' Anna replied when Rachel asked whether she'd had a hard day. Then lowering her voice and thinking it was safe, she added, 'Today it was pretty quiet over the Atlantic but hectic in the English Channel.' She paused, hoping she hadn't said too much. 'But then it always is,' she concluded.

'Whenever I hear mention of the English Channel, it sends shivers down my spine.' Rachel's rather theatrical statement seemed at odds with her expression, and Anna was puzzled as to why she didn't look in the least perturbed.

Then, curious to hear more, and thinking that perhaps this was Rachel's way of dealing with what must be a particularly frightening memory she said, 'Sorry if I touched a nerve, but if you don't mind my asking, what is it about the Channel makes you feel like that?'

Rachel curled her lip and Anna thought that she seemed more annoyed than upset. 'Dunkirk. My son was there. He came very close to losing his life.' And although she had claimed to feel unnerved, Rachel spoke so dispassionately that Anna was completely taken aback by her explanation. She made it sound as though it was an affront to her own peace of mind rather than concern for her son's life.

Even so, Anna couldn't prevent herself from gasping, 'Oh my God! I'm so sorry.' Still stunned by Rachel's lack of compassion, she imagined a young man on the beach or wading in water up to his chin as he waited to board one of the many boats that had rushed to rescue Britain's vanquished forces. She had seen photographs and newsreels of the lines of men queueing to board rescue boats as German pilots strafed the beach and British Spitfire pilots did their utmost to protect the troops below. The Germans had decimated the Allied forces in Calais and to prevent the loss or capture of thousands of trained soldiers, rescue was vital. Anna hadn't been closely involved in Operation Dynamo, but her work as a teleprinter operative at Harwell had let her know some of the detail. The rescue operation had been launched by Winston Churchill in late May, and hundreds of small boats had answered the call to sail across the Channel alongside the naval ships and pick the men out of the water.

'Yes, poor Philip.' Rachel's tone verged on sarcasm. 'Some people refer to the rescue operation as "The Miracle of Dunkirk" and I suppose it was nothing short of a miracle because Weaver Street has its own Dunkirk story. Joey Walker, Rose's husband, was in command of the ship that rescued Philip. He saw him struggling in the water and threw him a lifejacket. Philip managed to stay afloat until he could board the ship.'

'What a wonderful coincidence, and how marvellous for you,' Anna gushed, even though Rachel had showed no signs of emotion as she told the story. 'How old is he?'

'He's just celebrated his nineteenth birthday, although celebrated is a silly word to use considering he's back in France, fighting again.'

'Two years younger than me,' Anna said reflectively. 'So young to be putting his life in danger every day.'

'He was very restless after his father died and he joined the army before war was declared. He craved adventure and needed to be with like-minded boys.' Rachel sounded bitter. 'I think he found living with just me rather boring and restrictive.'

Anna didn't quite know what to say to that and lamely said, 'Boys are like that.' By now the tram had rattled its way to their stop and as they alighted in Broad Green she added, 'I'm going to Molly's for supper tonight. I'm looking forward to it.'

'That's nice,' Rachel said as they walked up the back lane. 'Maybe you could spend an evening with me some time. I'd like the company. I'm in danger of becoming a lonely old lady.' She gave a grim chuckle.

'I'd love to,' Anna said, and meant it. She found Rachel rather intriguing.

Rachel smiled. 'Then what about Saturday?'

'It's a date,' Anna said perkily.

* * *

Molly plumped the cushions in the chairs then cast a critical eye over the supper she had set out on the table: tiny fish paste sandwiches and home-baked eggless sponge buns. Ronan was sleeping peacefully in his pram, and Anna was due to arrive soon. Molly had washed her hair and changed her dress, and now she glanced wryly at her reflection in the mirror above the fireplace. *Anybody would think it was a special occasion*, she giggled. But in a way it was. Without Mickey by her side, and having a young child to care for, her social life had drastically reduced and nights spent with Lily, and now Anna, were something to look forward to. The last night out she had had was at the dance in the Grafton, and before that she couldn't say when. Even on the nights she spent with the crew on the ambulance she was too busy tending to the sick or injured to make real friends, and although her mother and Mavis were always on hand, it wasn't the same as having someone her own age to chat with and laugh about things that interested younger women. When she was younger, and before she had married Mickey, she'd had Lily to fill this need; they had been inseparable and had shared hopes and dreams, and there wasn't a thing they didn't know about one another. Then Lily had gone wild, her crazy social life not to Molly's liking. Now, she seemed to have calmed down and these days Lily was either out with the ARP or busy furthering her relationship with Eric. When Molly heard the knock on the door, she almost skipped across the floor to answer it.

'Come in, I'm glad you made it,' she cried, leading Anna into the warm, cosy kitchen.

Anna grinned at the enthusiastic welcome. 'I've been looking forward to it all day.' She looked at Molly for her approval before carefully approaching Ronan's pram to take a peep at him. 'He's gorgeous,' she gushed softly, 'I'd kill for lashes as long and silky as that.'

'He takes after his dad. He's going to look just like him.' Molly was thrilled at the easy opportunity Anna's remark gave her to talk about Mickey. 'Sit down and I'll get the album,' she said, indicating an armchair by the fire.

Anna sat and looked at photographs of a tall, handsome man with black curly hair and laughing eyes. 'You make a lovely couple,' she commented. The wedding photograph showed Molly and Mickey, hands clasped and smiling adoringly at one another. Unbidden, a lump clogged her throat and when she tried to swallow it, it turned into a sob. *That could have been me and Simon.* She squeezed her eyes together and shook her head. She hadn't thought of him for quite some time, and now here she was back at square one.

'Are you all right?'

Molly's anxious cry broke into Anna's thoughts.

'Just a foolish moment of remembering something I hoped I'd forgotten.'

'Is it something to do with that man you went out with at Harwell?' Molly asked gently.

Anna drew a deep breath and this time she told her everything about Simon. When she had finished, she gave a huge sigh of relief.

Molly had listened without interruption. Now she said, 'That's a cruel story.'

Anna grimaced. 'It is, isn't it? And you're the only person I've told it to in all its gory detail. Strangely enough, I feel better for telling it. There was a time when I'd have been blubbing at the very mention of his name and howling about how he'd deceived me, but talking about him like this is helping to get him out of my system.' She gave Molly a perky smile. 'It felt the same when I told you I was adopted. You see, I've hidden things for so long it became a habit. I never told anyone how awful my adopted parents were. I felt ashamed, as though I was to blame for not bringing them the happiness they were looking for. I know now that's not true. I was just one of my mother's whims, nobody could make Jane happy.' She shrugged helplessly. 'I've been guilty of putting too much faith in people who let me down.'

'I know what you mean. I once thought I was in love with a man who used to live in our street.' Now it was Molly's turn to tell Anna about Heinz Muller. 'It was just infatuation on my part, the need to be loved,' she said, getting to her feet and putting on the kettle to make tea as she explained how Heinz had drawn her into the struggle against the government during the Depression. 'We went on hunger marches and rallies. It wasn't until he abandoned me at a rally against that horrible Oswald Mosley and I was being attacked by a policeman that I realised he cared not a jot for me. I could have been killed, you know,' she exclaimed. 'Then I knew he'd just been indoctrinating me and using me as a sounding board to advance his own political ideals.' Her voice had risen, and she rolled her eyes at her own foolishness. 'There was I drooling over a drippy, boring German when the love of my life was right across the street.'

They moved from the chairs by the hearth to the table to eat their supper. Anna asked, 'When did you realise you were in love with Mickey?'

Molly giggled. 'Even after he'd rescued me from the policeman, I still thought of him as the boy I'd grown up with. But then we started to go out together and I realised that I'd always been a bit in love with Mickey O'Malley. Me and Lily used to fight over him when we were young. Falling for him properly was like baking a Christmas cake, you know, let it cook slow and steady then when its baked feed it with brandy every week until it's sweet and rich and just perfect. That's me and Mickey.'

Anna's heart went out to Molly. *She must miss Mickey dreadfully*, she thought, but she refrained from putting her thoughts into words. They were having a good time, sharing confidences and getting to know one another. It made Anna feel warm inside. They chatted until the clock struck eleven.

'I'd best be going, I've work in the morning,' she said and pushed back her chair. 'The supper was lovely, and I really enjoyed tonight. What do you say to making it a regular thing?' She looked hopefully at Molly.

'I'd like nothing better. I can't remember when I last had such a lovely evening.'

They parted with a hug, both girls feeling that they had cemented a true friendship.

* * *

Meanwhile, Lily had left the house next door wearing a smart green costume that showed off her red hair to its best advantage. She had insisted on meeting Eric in the city. He had wanted to collect her from home but she didn't want him there, not just yet. When she stepped off the tram in William Brown Street, a man leaning at the corner gave a piercing wolf whistle. Pleased, Lily tossed her head and sauntered past, swinging her hips jauntily.

Eric was waiting on the steps outside St George's Hall. His handsome face broke into a wide smile as she approached. 'You look lovely,' he said warmly. Lily linked her arm in his, and as they walked down the street, Eric shared his suggestions of how they should spend the evening. 'This lunchtime I met a fellow I went to university with. He's performing in a play tonight and he wondered if I'd go and support it. What do you think?'

Lily had been hoping they would go to a smart hotel like the Adelphi and have a drink before going to the cinema. *Destry Rides Again* was showing at the Scala, and Lily loved Marlene Dietrich. However, when she saw how eager Eric was to go to the theatre she said, 'I'll leave it up to you. I'll like whatever you choose.'

They made their way through the streets to a church hall, outside which a short queue of people awaited admission. This didn't bode well. No Marlene Dietrich fans here. Inside it was rather depressing, the fusty smell and rows of hard wooden chairs facing a small stage with shabby curtains reminded Lily of school. She thought it didn't look very inviting, but if this was the sort of entertainment Eric liked she'd better get used to it. The scattered audience whispered as they waited for the curtain to rise and the play to begin. Lily felt out of place in the sepulchral surroundings, but Eric was perfectly at ease as he acknowledged a greeting from a dowdy girl with glasses, and a peaky-looking chap with a beard.

'Friends from university,' he said, and Lily couldn't help thinking that these were not her sort of people.

'What's the play called?' she whispered.

'*For Services Rendered*. It's about the aftermath of the First World War and the effect it has on a dysfunctional family.'

Aftermath. Dysfunctional. What on earth was she doing sitting here when she didn't even understand a word Eric had said? She knew why. She loved him and dearly wanted to fit into his world. But right now she didn't know how to go about it.

The play was just as dreary as she had imagined it would be. The women characters were simpering and stupid, and the men stuffy. In Lily's opinion, they let silly things happen when all they needed to do to prevent them was to apply a bit of common sense and a lot of backbone. In one of the main character's long dull speeches she nodded off only to be roused by his strident voice declaring, 'This old England of ours isn't done yet, and I for one believe in it and all it stands for.' The curtain fell.

'Brilliant, wasn't it?' Eric gushed and almost lifted Lily out of her seat as the audience got to their feet applauding enthusiastically. The curtain rose and they joined in with the cast and sang 'God Save the King'. Eric turned to Lily, his eyes shining. 'Did you enjoy it?'

'Er, yes... it was very... meaningful.' *Now where did I think that word up from?* she asked herself. Feeling rather pleased she added, 'It showed how awful war really is.'

'Exactly,' Eric crowed. 'I knew you'd get the message. Somerset Maugham's a brilliantly emotive playwright.'

Once again she juggled with unfamiliar words. Emotive. Playwright. Well, whoever Somerset Thingumajig was he couldn't have been more wrong. Ordinary people weren't at all like that in Lily's book.

'Come on,' he said, taking her elbow. 'We'll go backstage and congratulate Henry.'

'So, you made it then,' Henry cried, sticking out his hand and pumping Eric's vigorously.

'Wouldn't have missed it for the world, old chap. It was a triumph.' Eric pulled Lily closer. 'Let me introduce you to Lily Stubbs, my partner in crime,' he chortled.

Lily blushed. He'd called her his partner. She dismissed the crime bit. He couldn't possibly know she used to shoplift in Woolies when she was a kid. Suddenly she felt happy again.

They went with Henry and the rest of the cast to a nearby pub; this was more to Lily's liking although the talk centred on the play. Eric repeated Lily's summation of it and added, 'Lily's no stranger to war. She's a warden in the ARP. That's how we met.'

Full of admiration and curiosity, the actors bombarded her with questions, Lily acquitting herself admirably by telling a few amusing anecdotes and making them laugh.

Eric glowed with pride and gave Lily an encouraging smile. She smiled back. *I'm learning*, she told herself. *I am right for Eric even if I do come from the wrong side of the tracks.* And she was even more convinced when in a dark corner at the end of lane behind Weaver Street he took her in his arms and kissed her, a long meaningful kiss or so Lily thought. Until now the kisses they had shared had been tender and respectful, lacking in passion. Yes, Eric loved her and she loved him.

9

Anna found it hard to believe that two months had gone by since she had come to Liverpool. The time had flown, and she felt more at home in the city than she had in any other place. Her friendship with Molly was progressing nicely – what was it about these people on Weaver Street that had her opening her heart and feeling she had found true friends? – and although she had yet to have supper with Rachel, she had a feeling that it would be a pleasant evening even though there was an age gap of some twenty years.

'Are you off then?' Mavis asked as Anna put on her coat ready to walk down the lane.

'If that's all right with you,' Anna said tentatively. Had she heard a hint of disappointment in Mavis's tone or had she imagined it?

''Course it's all right, I'm pleased you're making friends. There's nothing more valuable than friendship. I don't know where I'd be if I didn't have Jack and Kitty and the others to keep me going.' Mavis spoke sincerely. 'Jack'll be in any minute for the *Saturday Variety Show*.' The programme on the wireless was a favourite of Mavis and Jack's and Anna had listened to it with them on two previous Saturdays. Pleased that her fears at abandoning Mavis for Rachel were groundless, Anna said she hoped Mavis would enjoy the show and slipped out of the house. Jack was halfway up the path.

'Going out, Anna?'

'Just down to Rachel's.'

'Well, have nice evening.' Jack gave a satisfied smile.

'You too,' Anna said, stepping aside to let him pass, and getting the distinct feeling that Jack welcomed her absence, not in any nasty way; he just preferred to have Mavis all to himself. As she walked down the lane, she mused yet again about the full extent of their friendship. They were lovely people, and she found herself hoping that theirs was a romantic relationship in every sense of the word. It made her giggle. Whatever would Mavis think if she knew her lodger was speculating about her love life?

Rachel had hurried out in her lunchtime and queued to buy two mock cream pastries, and now as she awaited Anna's arrival, she wondered if she should have bought twice as many. No, of course she shouldn't, she told herself sharply. There's a war on, and she'd been lucky to get these two. Flour was in short supply so most bakers stuck to making only the staples: loaves, baps and plain rolls. And unlike Kitty, Mavis and Molly, she never baked. Cooking was low on Rachel's agenda.

In answer to Anna's knock on the back door, Rachel welcomed her inside. 'Come on through,' she said, leading Anna out of the neat and tidy kitchen into the parlour that overlooked the street. This took Anna by surprise. Mavis rarely used her parlour, and Maggie's was a workroom dominated by a large mending frame. Even more surprising was the artful decoration and furnishings: walls a deep shade of plum red made a backdrop for a large cream rug, two elegant wing chairs and a small octagonal table. Against one wall was a finely crafted bureau, and under the window a small escritoire, every piece elegant and gleaming with a rich patina. Intricately embroidered throws draped the arms of the chairs. The entire room glowed with a warm ambience.

'My gosh!' Anna gasped. 'It's magnificent. I wasn't expecting anything like this.'

'I'm glad you like it. I'm afraid it's a passion of mine.' Rachel gave an apologetic little smile and carefully adjusted the folds of a scarlet throw. 'I grew up in a house furnished with beautiful things, and when I married George and moved to Carlisle I began collecting things. I hunted the antique shops and junk shops for pieces other people had thrown out then George and I cleaned them up or refurbished them.' She moved a porcelain figurine an inch to the left. 'He was very good with his hands, and I learned a lot from him, or taught myself. Those chairs were covered in horrible brown velvet, worn and torn, so I borrowed an upholstery book from the library and gave them a new lease of life. All they needed was love.'

Anna's gaze roamed the room as Rachel talked and fiddled lovingly with her collection, describing each piece in detail and how she had come by it; some she had bought and some were pieces she had inherited from her parents. With genuine admiration for Rachel's skills, Anna said, 'It's so creative, a work of art like something you'd see in a magazine.'

'That's praise indeed.' Rachel beamed at the compliment. 'Now, sit down and I'll bring in the supper.' She went into the kitchen while Anna perched on the edge of the seat of one of the wing chairs, almost afraid to wrinkle the velvet or dislodge the embroidered silk cushion. Rachel returned carrying a silver tray laden with delicate china. 'It's not much,' she apologised, pointing to the two pastries in a filigree dish. 'George and Philip used to laugh at my baking; I'm a poor housewife in that respect.'

'Maybe so, but you're great at making wonderful rooms like this,' Anna said.

Over supper they chatted convivially about furnishings, fashion and rationing, laughing at the struggle to save enough coupons to buy anything decent, whenever there was even a choice. Things got scarcer by the month.

'Will you go back to Wiltshire?' Rachel asked after she had enquired where Anna had lived before coming to Liverpool.

Anna paused thoughtfully. 'I don't really know. I don't think I will. I feel much more at home here, but then...' She gave a little lopsided smile. 'I suppose it's only natural. I was born in Liverpool.'

'Oh... where? What part?' Rachel seemed eager to know.

Anna gave a pathetic shrug. 'I can't claim to have lived for very long in any particular part of the city,' she said, and taking a deep breath and lowering the barriers yet again to divulge the nature of her birth she said, 'You see, I was adopted.'

Rachel gave what Anna took to be a sympathetic smile, the sort that she had encountered before when people learned that she hadn't been reared in what they considered to be 'a normal family'. But deep inside, Rachel was struggling to hide a gamut of emotions.

'I only found out that I'd been born here when I needed to produce my birth certificate to join the WAAFs,' Anna continued. 'I've always known I was adopted but I don't know how my parents came by me and took me to live in Salisbury.' She said it lightly with a bemused grin. 'We never talked about such things.'

'Did you have a happy childhood?' Rachel didn't quite manage to hide the urgency in her voice.

Again, Anna hesitated then made a decision to be honest. 'Not really,' she began, then in a casual manner, she went on to tell Rachel about the dysfunctional Jane and Norman. 'It wasn't that they were deliberately cruel or anything like that. They just didn't know any better,' she said, excusing them and feeling sad at having had to paint such a woeful picture; but it was the truth. Not wanting Rachel's pity, she hastened to say, 'But please don't feel sorry for me. It taught me to be independent and make the best of things. I'm doing that now.'

Rachel didn't speak for some time. She sat with her eyes half closed and the strange expression on her face was unfathomable. Anna began to feel uneasy, and wishing she could retract her story, she was relieved when Rachel eventually said, 'You've come out of it well, Anna. You're a lovely girl, one any mother would be proud of.' Anna flushed at the heartfelt compliment. She admired this creative, elegant woman and thought that Philip was a lucky lad to have a mother like Rachel even though, to Anna's surprise, she hadn't mentioned him all evening. Mothers usually liked to talk about their children, especially when they were away fighting in a war. She was just about to enquire after him when Rachel intervened.

'What did you think to the pastry? Mock cream's not a patch on the real thing, is it?' Rachel blurted this out in a desperate bid to change the conversation and quell the disturbing thoughts that Anna's information had aroused.

* * *

On Monday morning, Anna arrived at Derby House ready for another week, the last in April. As she entered the cloakroom she was met with a flurry of questions from Poppy and the other WAAFs. Ross was returning to his squadron on Wednesday. They couldn't let him go without giving him a send-off so what should they do?

'I think we should go to the Grafton,' Denise suggested.

'Perhaps a meal at the Adelphi, just the six of us,' Poppy volunteered. 'We could all chip in and treat him.'

'We'll miss him, won't we, Susan?' Primrose said, looking for Susan's agreement. The two of them had grown very close. They were both rather old-fashioned, their shared interest in knitting – they were members of a knitting and sewing circle at the church near their billets – evoking sarcastic comments from Denise.

'I think he'd like to go dancing,' Anna said, recalling the night they had first met.

'We can ask some of the other chaps if they'd like to join us, make it more of a party.' She also thought that Ross would prefer that rather than sitting in all-female company at the Adelphi. It would be an easier way of spending the evening.

'Good for you, Anna.' Denise was pleased that she supported her idea. 'Let's vote on it.' Susan and Primrose looked at one another. They didn't mind where they went, and a disgruntled Poppy reluctantly said, 'Okay.'

When they put it to Ross he accepted, and thanked them for their thoughtfulness.

'Will you promise not to storm off and leave me floundering in the middle of the floor if I ask you to dance?' he said as they made their way to their workstations, Ross to Air Control and Anna up the ladder.

Anna giggled. 'I'll try not to,' she said.

* * *

Kitty was baking baps for the café when she heard the knock on her front door. It wouldn't be a neighbour. They always used the back door. Thinking it might be a travelling salesman, she wiped her hands and went to answer it.

The elderly man on the doorstep looked vaguely familiar, but she couldn't immediately place him. Only when she heard the thick Birmingham accent did she realise who he was. Startled, she felt a cold shiver run down her spine. Why was he calling on her after all these years? It must have been twenty since she last saw him.

'Your daughter told me I'd find you here,' he said. 'She also told me you're no longer Mrs Conlon, so are you going to invite us in, Mrs Sykes?' He emphasised Kitty's title.

Flustered, Kitty gestured for Detective Inspector Horace Baxter to step inside. He turned round and beckoned for the man sitting in the car at the gate to join him. A young man jumped out and walked up the path. Both policemen wore fawn belted raincoats and brown trilby hats. Kitty thought they looked like characters in a gangster film. She led them into the parlour, and remembering that Horace Baxter had a voracious appetite for tea and buns, she left them there and hurried to the kitchen to put on the kettle. Her nerves jangled as she waited for it to boil. Their visit must surely be something to do with Tom's murder but she couldn't imagine what. The last time the detective had called round was about seven years after Tom's death, and then only to report they still had no leads as to who had killed Tom. It was what he called 'a cold case'. Her hands trembled as she carried the tray into the parlour.

'Thank you, Kitty.' Horace reverted to using her Christian name as he had done in the past. 'Now I'll not beat about the bush.' He attacked the plate of ginger snaps and slurped a mouthful of tea before continuing. 'It's a bad old business to rake up after all this time, but new evidence has come to light and I thought you should be made aware of it.' He took another biscuit and nodded at the young detective. 'This is Detective Vincent Scott. If you're willing, he'll give you the detail.' He sat back, chomping and awaiting Kitty's reply.

Her heart missed a beat, and her breathing came quick and shallow. Did she want to resurrect the awful memory of Tom's murder? Did she need to know the detail? It wouldn't make a difference. Tom would still be dead. She had long since stopped asking herself why someone had killed him, although she was sure it was something to do with his shady dealings at the race-tracks. She twisted her hands in her lap and bit down on her bottom lip. There would always be a corner of her heart that belonged to Tom Conlon, and perhaps she owed it to him to finally lay him to rest.

'Go on,' she said flatly, 'tell me what you know.'

'Right, Vinny, get on with it.' Horace nodded again at the young detective. 'You'll be surprised when you hear what he has to say.'

Surprised! I'm being torn apart, Kitty thought as she steeled herself to listen.

The young detective coughed then loosened his shirt collar. Then, in a very formal manner, he read from his notebook. 'On 20 March 1941, I arrested Clarence Bennett on a drunk and disorderly charge. He was in a very consumptive state and later when questioned, he told me he was dying and wanted to confess to a crime he regretted.' Vinny glanced at Kitty, and receiving a desperate frown in return, he glanced at his superior officer. When Baxter smiled and nodded, Vinny closed his notebook. 'It's like this, Mrs Sykes,' he continued in a rather relieved tone. 'Your brother, Shaun...'

Kitty gasped. 'Shaun? What has this to do with him?' She clasped her hands to her face, the blood leaching from her cheeks.

'Stay calm, Kitty,' Horace urged. 'Shaun is safe on his farm in Ireland. We spoke with him the day before yesterday to further our investigation. He'll no doubt write and tell you about our visit. Roscommon's a pretty place, isn't it?'

Her mind reeling, Kitty didn't reply. It was like being in the middle of a nightmare.

'Go on, Vinny, get it over with,' Baxter growled.

'Your brother and Bennett served time together in HMP Birmingham after the Easter Rising in Ireland. Your brother was a political prisoner, a member of the Free State Irish Republican Army. Bennett was a common criminal but he was also a member of Ulster Volunteer Force.' Vinny looked at Kitty to check that she understood. She nodded.

'Well, I'm sure you were aware that there was no love lost between the men who fought for Ireland's freedom and those who were loyal to the crown.'

'I was,' Kitty said, having gathered her wits. 'Shaun told me about the appalling treatment he suffered at the hands of those black-hearted Protestants from the North, and how the prison warders stood by and did nothing to prevent it,' she said bitterly.

'Well, it would appear that after your brother was released, Bennett and an accomplice, Samuel Sneddon, tracked him down to Liverpool to carry out a vendetta against him.' Vinny paused, then, the words rushing out of him, he concluded, 'They killed your husband by mistake. Bennett told me that the man they had killed was very similar in appearance to your husband, and on the night of the murder in the dark alley they didn't realise they had got the wrong man until his hat fell off. He said that the man they had battered to death had black hair and that your brother had red hair.'

Kitty closed her eyes. 'As red as a fox's pelt,' she murmured. 'The Fox, that's what his IRA compatriots called Shaun. An' didn't meself see the likeness in my Tom an' Shaun? Tall, lean, hard men. Fine men, handsome men,' she intoned as her mind registered all that Vinny had told her.

She opened her eyes. 'I lost me husband but kept me brother? Long runs the fox.'

Disturbed by Kitty's ramblings, Baxter and the young detective exchanged anxious glances. Baxter cleared his throat. 'Yes, Kitty. It was a case of mistaken identity. A terrible waste that should never have happened, but believe me when I say Bennett and Sneddon will pay for their crimes, and I didn't want you to find out about them by reading it in the newspapers. I thought it only right to warn you.' Poor Baxter looked distraught. 'I'm beginning to think it was a bad idea telling you all this. It won't bring your husband back.'

'Don't upset yourself, Horace,' Kitty said calmly as she reflected on the fact that Tom would have left her anyway in pursuit of his grand life. 'Tom wasn't mine to keep.'

'Er, no,' Baxter muttered, recalling what she had told him at the time of the murder. He cheered up. 'But you're happy now, Kitty, with your new husband and your new home.' He looked admiringly around the parlour.

'Oh, very happy,' she replied. 'An' as for letting me know, ye were only doin' your duty.'

She saw them out, standing on the step until the car drove out of sight then she went back into the parlour where she huddled on the couch and cried until she was empty.

When John came home, he found her red-eyed and in a very strange mood. He comforted her the best he could, inwardly cursing Horace Baxter for stirring up such distressing memories. And what good did it do Kitty? Baxter's revelations didn't change a thing. 'It's all in the past, Kitty. You've put it all behind you,' John soothed. 'Let it stay there, and look to the future.' She gave a wan smile and told him he was right, as usual.

Tuesday night at the Grafton was a roaring success. Anna and Ross and the girls were joined by three naval officers working in Derby House, and they danced and laughed, and drank in moderation – they all had to work the following day – and Ross had to make the journey back to his squadron in Lincolnshire. Denise left the party early with a soldier, and when it was time for the others to leave, they hugged Ross and wished him well. Poppy left in a car driven by a friend of the family she was staying with, Primrose and Susan walked arm in arm back to their billets, and Ross offered to walk Anna to the tram stop. She accepted willingly.

The night was warm and stars studded a deep purple sky. A 'bomber's moon' cast its light over the streets but thankfully the heavens were not disturbed by the drone of black-winged German Heinkels, and Anna and Ross strolled through the city for most of the time in companionable silence, Anna feeling safe and content.

'I'm going to miss you, Carswell,' said Ross as they waited for the tram.

'I'll miss you, Wing Commander Penhaligon.' Anna really meant it. She had tried to steel her heart against feeling anything for a member of the opposite sex – they couldn't be trusted – but Ross was different and she couldn't help but value his friendship.

'If I write to you, will you promise to write back?' Ross was serious now.

'I promise,' she said.

'And if I should find myself in Liverpool again, will you keep a lonely airman company and make his leave something to look forward to?'

'I'd like to do that very much. I can't have you wandering round the city all alone.' Anna's voice was light, but her heart was heavy. She suddenly realised she didn't want Ross to go. She turned to look directly into his face and he returned her gaze, his silvery grey eyes filled with longing and regret.

Anna slipped her arms round his neck and brushed his lips with hers. Ross responded so passionately that he took her breath away, his kiss lasting until the tram rattled to a halt. Reluctantly, they broke apart.

'Goodbye, sweet Anna. I'll be seeing you.'

Anna climbed aboard. Ross saluted. Anna waved back and called out, 'Goodbye, Ross. Don't forget to write.' Her lips tingled with the feel of his kiss.

* * *

'I near cried my eyeballs out after he'd gone,' Kitty told Maggie as they walked to the shops on Wednesday morning.

'I should think you did. It was dead rotten of Baxter to come back after all this time and tell you all that bloody awful stuff.'

'He wanted me to hear it from him first. He didn't want me to read it in the papers. He was only doing his duty.'

'Yeah, I suppose so. Bloody coppers, eh?'

They walked into Broad Green and joined the queue at the butchers. Kitty hated queueing and then finding there was nothing much left when it came to her turn. She bought eight ounces of scrag end to make a stew and Maggie bought a quarter pound of mince. In the chemist's, Norman Hopkinson told them there was no soap.

'How are we supposed to keep clean if we can't get soap?' Kitty moaned as they left the shop. She was feeling more depressed by the minute. Earlier, she'd gone to the cemetery and put flowers on Tom's grave, then it being the first day of May, she had gone into the church and placed a posy on the Virgin Mary's altar. She didn't usually attend mass during the week but May was the month to celebrate Our Lady and Kitty had asked her for a special intention: please keep my family free from harm. But rather than finding the solemn sanctity of the mass and a few prayers uplifting, she had come away downhearted.

'I feel as though I'm in a deep, black pit an' I can't climb out of it,' she told Maggie as they queued in the grocers. 'Like all the misery is swallowing me up an' eatin' away at me.'

'Bloody hell, Kitty!' Maggie's eyes widened. 'It's not like you to let things get you down.' She thought of the times she'd been at her lowest ebb, when Kitty had been the one with the strength to raise her up.

'I know, but I just can't shake off this awful feeling that things are only going to get worse.'

Anna buttoned her jacket then looped the strap of her bag over her shoulder. She smiled as the weight of a jar of Mavis's precious bottled pears bumped against her hip, her landlady's contribution to the meal Anna was going to share with Susan and Primrose in Susan's billets. They had finished their shift at six and she was looking forward to the evening ahead.

The girls had persuaded her to go to a sale of work in the church hall where the sewing circle they attended each week held their meetings. 'It's all for a good cause,' Primrose had told her. 'When people buy the stuff we've knitted, we put the money in the wounded soldiers' fund at the hospital, and maybe a pair of my socks will warm the feet of some poor lad in a trench in France.' How could Anna refuse?

'Are we ready for the off?' Susan asked as she adjusted her cap.

'Ready and able,' Primrose replied.

They left Derby House and walked through the city towards Bold Street and Susan's billet. Her landlady was also a member of the sewing circle and had no objection to Susan inviting her friends for a meal. She had agreed to provide the tea, and Susan and Primrose the bread and margarine and a tin of spam. Anna's pears would be a tasty treat to finish off.

Maggie and Stanley were sitting on the couch, his arm round her shoulders and Maggie nestled into his side like they were a pair of young lovers. The wireless played softly in the background and they were half listening to it but not talking; theirs was a comfortable silence. Stanley was a man of few words, and Maggie had grown used to these quiet moments in the three years they had been married. She blessed the day she had accepted his proposal. He wasn't at all like the men she'd had relationships with in the past. There was nothing flashy or exciting about Stanley with his balding head and paunchy stomach, but Maggie loved the bones of him. He was kind and dependable, slow to act, not like her first husband, Fred, who had beaten her senseless on more than one occasion, the last on the night he'd learned that Lily wasn't his daughter. She was the result of one of Maggie's many flings during the last war when Fred was serving in the army. Lily had inherited her flaming red hair from that casual lover.

'Do you have to go out tonight, love?' Maggie asked as noises up above broke the silence. Lily was getting ready to go on duty and Stanley was going with her.

'Aye, I do, lass, if I'm going to keep you and our Lily and them two mares in Toxteth safe,' Stanley replied firmly. Maggie loved the way he said 'our Lily' as though she was his. The two mares he referred to were his daughters from his first marriage. They hadn't been best pleased when he'd married Maggie but neither Maggie nor Stanley let it bother them.

'Are you ready, Stanley? Let's go and spend another night mooching the streets and banging on windows shouting keep your blackouts drawn.' Lily sounded positively cheery. She would have Eric to keep her company. What more could she ask for?

Stanley pecked Maggie's cheek then got to his feet. 'It'll most likely be a quiet night,' he said to allay her fears. He didn't know how wrong he was.

'Ta-ra, Mam,' Lily said and marched to the door.

'Take care now,' Maggie called after them. It was just before eight o'clock.

The church hall was busy with women and children gathered round stalls displaying a wide variety of handmade goods. Anna bought a pretty embroidered tray cloth for Mavis, and then lingered at the stall where a wizened old man was selling beautifully crafted leather wallets. Should she buy one for Ross? she wondered. The thought surprised her. He had yet to write to her, and she dismissed the notion. *It's just that I noticed his wallet was frayed at the edges*, she told herself irritably. The old man looked at her, his eyes bright with hope of making a sale and wanting to please him she bought a black one with a finely tooled pattern on it.

'It'll never be empty, even when it has only a photograph of you in it,' he said, presuming that she was buying it for a special man in her life. 'My wallets bring good luck.'

'We could all do with some of that,' Anna said as she paid him.

'It's true. A woman was telling me only the other day that the wallet she bought for her husband saved his life. He had it in his breast pocket packed full of her letters and it stopped the bullet that would have gone to his heart. There now, what do you think of that?'

'I think it's a beautiful story,' she said, gesturing to the wallet. 'I'll treasure it.'

The sewing circle celebrated the success of the sale with a cup of tea, and Anna let Susan cajole her into staying for one. She left the hall much later than she had intended and there were no streetlamps so the waxing crescent moon gave only a little light as she hurried through the streets back to the city centre to catch her tram.

She was in Cook Street when the siren blared and panic shot through her. Why had she left it so late? She slowed her pace, dithering, unfamiliar with this part of town. Should she run back to the church hall, or should she go on, find a shelter and wait for the all-clear? She just didn't know. She decided to press on.

As she raced forward, she heard the bombers roaring overhead. Seconds later the world seemed to turn upside down as massive explosions assaulted her ears. She stopped. Cringing against the gable end of a house, she looked back. A conflagration of flames and smoke was rising from the docks. Above her head, German planes swooped and turned then swooped again like huge black gulls as they dropped their deadly cargo.

She suddenly became aware of shouts and the thud of feet, and peering round the gable end, she saw people rushing to the far end of the narrow street. There must be a shelter nearby, she thought, deciding to follow them. She had taken no more than a few stumbling steps when she heard a hissing followed by an almighty crash. The ground shook beneath her feet. The end house on the opposite side of the street had taken a direct hit from an incendiary bomb.

Anna cowered in a doorway as she watched the house disintegrate in a mass of flames and rubble, the fire so intense she could feel its heat on her face. She staggered out of the doorway and started to run. A young boy of about six came haring towards her shouting and crying. 'They can't get out. They're stuck inside.' He flung himself at Anna and she caught him and held him steady.

'Who? Where?' she asked urgently. 'Tell me so I can help you.'

'Me mam an' the little 'uns,' he sobbed, 'over there in that house.' He pointed to a house partway up the terrace. Only then did Anna notice that the incendiary explosion had caused the other houses in the row to lean into one another, the force of the blast pushing their window and door frames at a crooked angle. 'I climbed out of the window,' the lad cried, 'but me mam's too fat.' Anna looked at the small hole edged with jagged glass that the boy pointed to.

'Did you cut yourself?' She stooped to check. His shirt was ripped and underneath it was a long scratch above his hip, but no blood. 'Good boy. You're okay. Now let's get your mam and the youngsters out,' she said, her fear forgotten, and sounding far braver than she felt.

Crunching over smashed bricks and broken glass, she inspected the window the boy had climbed through. Bits of glass dangled on the broad tapes that had been stuck over the pane to prevent it from shattering. The frame was twisted. Then she looked at the door. That too was twisted but the blast had caused the panels to crack.

'Right,' she said. 'We're going to break in.' She stepped back a few paces then took a running kick at the door but although it shuddered it stayed jammed. She kicked and kicked again, terrified that she might bring the entire row of houses down. To cries from the excited boy of, 'You're doin it, missis, you're doin' it,' she kicked with all her might, her legs and feet throbbing and sweat blinding her. The door panels caved in and she shoved against them till they broke free from the frame. Splinters flying, Anna pushed her way inside.

'Oh, thank God! Thank God!' A panic-stricken young woman clutching a baby in one arm and hugging a toddler to her side with the other tottered towards her. Anna lifted the toddler and led the way outside. The boy was jumping up and down yelling with relief.

'She did it, Mam. The airman woman kicked the door in.'

At his amusing description of her, Anna looked at her uniform. Bits of splintered wood clung to the dark blue serge and there was a ragged tear in her right sleeve. She then realised she'd lost her cap. She glanced round for it. 'Here you are, missis airman.' The boy handed over her cap. 'It fell off when you were kicking,' he said.

'I can't thank you enough for saving us,' the woman said, 'but we should make a run for the shelter. I think I smelled gas.' As she spoke there was a creaking, groaning noise from the houses. The bombed house had collapsed into its neighbour and slowly its roof fell in and its front wall burst open. Bricks spewed on the pavement. Too late, a team of firefighters roared up, and leaving them dowsing the flames, Anna and the little family hurried to the shelter. In the distance beyond the rooftops the sky burned and the city shuddered with the sound of one explosion after another as the relentless bombardment did its worst.

In the shelter, the young woman wasted no time in telling

those inside how Anna had rescued her. Someone gave her a seat on a bunk and with their praises ringing in her ears she closed her eyes and settled down for the night.

'Robert, come inside and close that damned door,' Kitty barked, her cry almost lost in the roar of enemy planes passing overhead on their way to the docks. The sirens had blared their sharp intermittent warning some twenty minutes before and now she was in the shelter at the bottom of her garden trying to calm a very anxious Mavis.

'She went to a sale of work down by the docks,' Mavis was telling the neighbours. They all knew that she now looked on Anna as the daughter she'd never had, just as she had Rose when she'd taken her in after a disastrous love affair had gone terribly wrong.

'Robert! I won't tell ye again,' his mother said threateningly.

'There's dozens of 'em,' he called back excitedly as high in the sky, German planes circled the docks and thuds and thunderous eruptions echoed across the distance. 'The docks are on fire, Mam, and there's loads of smoke and flames nearer the city centre.' Robert would have loved to be in the thick of it doing his bit like his dad, out on patrol with the ARP, and he railed at being left to mind a shelter full of women and little children.

'Get inside, now,' Kitty roared. 'It's not a bloody game. Ye never know where the next bomb'll land.' She shuddered, recalling the unexploded bomb that had landed on the allotment. They'd been lucky then, but the awful feeling of impending doom and gloom that plagued her had her fearing the worst.

Reluctantly, Robert stepped inside and slammed the door,

preparing himself for another night listening to the mindless chatter of the women and the snuffling and crying of babies.

'That's better,' May Walker said. 'At least the bombing's not near enough to harm us.'

'Not yet, it isn't,' Maggie groused, 'but them bloody Germans don't care where they drop 'em as long as they think they're killing somebody.'

'And poor Anna's in danger in the city,' Mavis cried.

'Nay, don't take on. She most likely went back to Derby House when it started,' said Jack. 'She'll be safe enough there.'

Mavis wasn't to be comforted. Rose sat with James on her lap, remembering how kind Mavis had been to her after she had made the foolish mistake of running away from home with a man that she thought had loved her. Home had been a mansion in Buckinghamshire, her father a wealthy horse breeder and her mother a cruel, heartless woman with no love for her daughter. Rose had led a sheltered life of luxury and had a scant knowledge of the wider world. She had been easy prey for the charming confidence trickster Lewis Aston. He had taken her to Liverpool, and after two horrendous nights in the Adelphi Hotel he had robbed and abandoned her, leaving her penniless and pregnant. It was there that Mavis had come to her rescue. Luckily for Rose, Mavis had been at work that day and when she learned of Rose's predicament she had brought her to live with her in Weaver Street and given her a whole new meaning to life. When Rose had learned she was pregnant she'd almost lost her mind, and one evening in blind panic she had wandered into the path of an oncoming lorry. She had miscarried the baby, but with Mavis's help she had found the strength and courage to overcome her loss, earn her own living and make something of herself. For the first time in her life, Rose had felt loved. Marrying Joey Walker had been the icing on the cake, and her happiness was due to

Mavis. Anna was a lucky girl to have Mavis worrying about her. She wondered if Anna felt that she had found a second family in Weaver Street just as she, Rose, had. She hoped that Anna was safe.

Mavis and Rose weren't the only ones anxious for Anna's safety. Molly looked on her as a special friend, and Rachel Dyson also had her own interest in the girl. Sitting apart from the others, she was now mulling over a part of her life that she thought she could never recapture. She rarely thought of those terrible days, but now when her life felt threatened and the arrival of Anna had stirred unpleasant memories, she found herself dwelling on them.

Ronan started to wail and tug at the neck of his siren suit. He found the one-piece garment intended to keep a baby warm and well-padded against flying debris restrictive. Molly undid the fastenings and jiggled him up and down. She looked close to tears.

'Give him here,' said Kitty, lifting the little boy into her own lap. She cuddled him to her breast. *Dear Lord, let no harm befall this child an' him not yet baptised*, she prayed. Another massive fulmination sounded close by and her premonition that things could only get worse now seemed a reality and the thought of what the future might yet hold made her feel nauseous. She pressed her mouth to Ronan's cheek, and ruffling her lips, she fluttered them against his tender skin. His crying ceased, and he chuckled. Evenings spent in the shelter were now a part of everyday life and they just had to make the best of it.

'Let's play a hand of cards,' Maggie said, unnerved by the cacophony, and worrying if Stanley and Lily were safe.

* * *

Anna arrived at Derby House early the next morning looking somewhat dishevelled and decidedly lacking sleep. The first person she met was Group Captain Sharp.

'My, my, Carswell,' she said, her eyes raking Anna from head to toe. 'We're not looking our best this morning, are we?' Anna's heart sank at the thought of a dressing-down.

'I got caught up in the raid last night and had to spend the night in a shelter near Cook Street,' she explained timorously.

'Cook Street? What were you doing there, Carswell? And how did your uniform come to look like something one might see on a rag tatters stall?'

Anna hadn't intended telling anyone about rescuing the little family, but Razor Sharp's glowering face made her change her mind. Modestly, she explained the best she could.

'Well done, Carswell. You're a credit to the WAAF,' the group captain praised, her expression softening. 'I like to think my girls will do their duty no matter the circumstances.' She smiled warmly. 'Come with me. Get yourself cleaned up. We'll find you another jacket.' She took Anna by the arm and marched her down the corridor. 'We should find one to fit,' she said as she unlocked a storeroom. The jacket was on the small side, and when Anna left the top buttons undone Elsie Sharp frowned but let it go. In the ops room, she beckoned Corporal Somerville. 'Light duties for Carswell on this shift, Somerville,' Elsie ordered. 'She had a rather traumatic night.' Anna breathed a sigh of relief. Razor Sharp had a heart after all.

The blitz on Liverpool that had begun on that first day in May 1941 continued for seven long nights. Thousands of civilians had been killed or injured, their homes flattened or burnt out. Each time Anna left Derby House to return to Weaver Street she stared in horror at the devastation the Germans had wreaked on the city. Piles of rubble and blackened holes were all that remained of some of the city's finest buildings, and the docks were almost in ruins.

The tram service was disrupted, the driver on more than one occasion shouting, 'That's it, folks, I can't go no further,' leaving Anna and the other passengers to travel home on foot. Everywhere she looked gangs of men were searching through mountains of debris or dousing fires, and distraught families were wandering the streets clutching the few possessions they had managed to save as they hunted for new accommodation.

The words on every tongue told of the destruction and carnage that was taking place.

'Huskisson Number Two dock's totally destroyed,' John reported as Anna sat with Mavis in Kitty's kitchen. 'The SS *Malakand* was docked there, loaded with tonnes of ammunition. When it caught fire the bombs on board exploded. They're saying bits of the *Malakand* have been found more than a mile away.' He shook his head in disbelief.

'There'll be nothing left at this rate,' Mavis moaned. 'The Corn Exchange has gone...'

'Aye, and Custom House, and St Nicholas's Church,' Kitty intervened.

'And there's not much left of John Lewis's,' Anna added.

In the weeks following the blitz, they learned that almost two thousand people had been killed, and nearly fifteen hundred seriously injured. Rumour had it that seventy thousand people had been made homeless, and when Mavis repeated this to Anna, Anna said she could believe it, for every day on her journey to work she saw families taking shelter in the wreckage of what had once been their home or someone else's as they struggled to carry on.

'The rotten bastards even bombed Liverpool Cathedral,'

Maggie expostulated at one of the tea drinking sessions. 'All that lovely stained glass smashed to smithereens.'

Kitty giggled darkly when she repeated this to John. 'Maggie never darkens the door of any church, but to hear her ye'd think she was in line to be the next pope,' she told him.

'Aye, the next thing she'll be complaining about is not being able to buy her summer frocks in Blacklers.'

Kitty laughed out loud. Maggie didn't have a good word to say about Blacklers. It was one of the most expensive stores in Liverpool and she regularly denigrated the people who could afford to shop there. It had been extensively damaged two nights before.

'She'll be all right as long as they don't bomb Woolworths,' Kitty quipped, thinking that you had to have a laugh sometimes because if you didn't, you'd end up crying.

John joined in the laughter, relieved to see Kitty smiling. Just lately her downcast attitude had worried him. He blamed much of it on Baxter's visit, and that she lived in fear for Patrick and Mickey's safety. Twice she had turned her back on him in bed and told him she didn't need his affection, something she had never done before. Now, he pulled her into his arms and looked deep into her hazel eyes. The golden flecks that spoke of laughter and her zest for life were no longer there and he felt his heart lurch.

'Tell me this, Kitty, are *we* all right?'

She saw the love and hurt in his deep brown eyes, and felt the strength in his arms and knew exactly what he meant. She leaned her head against his broad chest and heard the thud of his heart. What would she do without the love of this good man?

'I know I've not been meself lately, John,' she said against his shirt, 'but there's times when I'm so sick of everything that's going on that I can't be bothered to be cheerful and strong. Baxter an' all that bother over Tom set me back.' She pulled away from John, her voice rising with anxiety as she looked imploringly up into his face. 'Then there's our Patrick risking his life in the sky an' our Molly left like a widow, an' that child not yet baptised. It worries me something shockin' to think he might be taken from us an' him left in purgatory. There just seems no end to it,' she cried, 'and what's it all for, John? What's it all for?'

John's arms tightened round her and he rocked her like a child as his lips brushed against her hair. Darling Kitty, everybody expected her to be there for them, but had there been anybody there for her? In the last few weeks, she had been so miserable and detached that now he felt shrouded in guilt. He had dismissed Baxter's revelations with a few words, and he'd given more thought to his factory and his ARP duties than he had to the love of his life. It was time to make amends.

'I'm sorry, Kitty. Sorry for neglecting you. It was thoughtless of me not to realise how upsetting painful memories can be, and that no matter how old your children are you still share their unhappiness or fear the danger they are in. I feel it too, even if I don't show it.' He tucked his finger under her chin and raised her face, his own so full of love and remorse that Kitty thought her heart might break. 'You're not alone, Kitty. You have me to lean on. We have each other and our sons and daughter, and our friends and neighbours, and although none of us are as happy as we have a right to be, we are still here. All we have to do is keep looking to the future.' He covered her lips with his own and kissed her tenderly.

Kitty felt a loosening in her chest as though John had gently reached into her heart and set it beating to a different rhythm. She had been foolish to dwell on the unthinkable. She had a wonderful man to lean on, a man she loved with every bone in her body, and children who were in good health and making the best of this terrible war. Then there were her friends. How could she have thought she was alone in these dark times?

'You're a very wise man, John Sykes,' she said and returned his kiss fulsomely.

Later that evening, John went across to Molly's. He couldn't make the war come to a sudden end but he could do something to ease his darling Kitty's worries. Gently and thoughtfully, he told Molly that the next time her mother raised the subject of Ronan's christening she must agree to it. *Give her a day to be joyful*, he said.

The next day, Kitty, having aired her fears to John and feeling better for it, also paid Molly a visit. The recent bombings had made her all the more aware that *ye never know the minute God will call ye* as her own mother had been fond of quoting and Kitty was determined to rid herself of one problem.

'Tomorrow we'll go see Father McLaughlin and make arrangements to have Ronan christened,' she announced as soon as she entered the kitchen.

'But Mam,' Molly protested, 'I want to do it when Mickey's here. You know—'

Kitty silenced her with a glare. 'Ye don't know when that'll be, if ever,' she growled, 'so no more prevaricating. May is the month for The Blessed Virgin, she'll watch over him.'

Molly thought about what her stepfather had asked her to do the night before, and how much her mother had always done for her. Did she have the right to deny her happiness? No, she didn't, she decided, and anyway, there was little point in arguing with her mother when her mind was made up.

'All right,' she said brightly. 'We'll go and ask him to do it next Sunday.'

Kitty's eyes widened and her lips parted in a huge smile. She had expected an argument. 'Thanks, love,' she gushed. 'Ye've made me a happy woman.'

Molly nodded and smiled. *Oh, where are you now, Mickey, when I need you?*

* * *

Anna was thrilled when Molly told her about the christening. 'I'd have liked you to be one of his godmothers,' Molly said once the arrangements had been made, 'but seeing as how you're not RC, Father McLaughlin says you can be a Christian witness, and that's just as good in my eyes.'

During the week that followed, Anna had little time to think about anything but work. For one horrible week, the last in May, Germany's flagship, *Bismarck*, dominated the seas and on the night of the twenty-fourth it sank HMS *Hood*, the pride of the British navy. The loss of almost fifteen hundred men plunged the ops room into a desperate bid to seek revenge, and two nights later in the Denmark Straits victory was theirs when the HMS *Dorsetshire* sent the *Bismarck* to the bottom of the ocean.

Anna had rejoiced with the rest of the team in Derby House, and the next Sunday as she stood in St Joseph's Church with Molly and her family, she gave a special thanks to God. Her eyes moistened and she swallowed a lump in her throat as Lily placed Ronan in her arms. He gave her a gummy smile before she handed him to Mavis who then passed him to Robert. He stepped forward, smart in his best grey flannel suit, and taking his role as godfather very seriously, he placed his nephew in the priest's large hands. Father McLaughlin sonorously intoned the time-honoured words and tenderly applied the oil and water. Ronan let out a roar that made everyone laugh.

'There now,' said his grandmother as the priest gave Molly her howling son, 'he's one of us in the family of our Good Lord.' Relief shone in Kitty's eyes and her beaming smile, and as the sunlight streaming through the stained-glass windows behind the altar bathed the party of worshippers in its golden glow, Anna felt that she also was now a member of the most loving, wonderful family on earth. Choking back tears, she joined her friends and neighbours in congratulating Molly and Ronan. Despite the terror of war and the sadness all around them, life had never felt so good.

10

Maggie walked across the lane, down the side of the house to the back garden. Kitty looked up from the flowerbed she was weeding and smiled a welcome. It was a balmy evening in early June and she was taking the opportunity to enjoy the fresh air after her shift in the munitions factory. Sitting back on her heels, she waited for Maggie to speak first, the look on her friend's face letting her know that whatever she was about to say wouldn't be anything to lighten the mood.

'I don't know what's eating our Lily these days but she's dead miserable,' Maggie said. 'She's as prickly as a bloody hedgehog. She near bit me face off when I asked her what was wrong, then just now she stamped out of the house with a face like thunder. She can be a right mardy cow when she wants to be.'

'Aye, John mentioned that she'd been a bit short with him the last couple of times they've been on duty together. He wondered if working all day in the mill and doing ARP four nights a week was getting too much for her.'

'It never bothered her before,' Maggie said, sitting down on the grass and lighting a cigarette. 'She loves the ARP, and since she started going out with Eric she's been as happy as a sandboy, but now...' She blew out a cloud of smoke and watched it spiral into the air, the frown lines above the bridge of her nose deepening. 'We've yet to meet him, but she says he's lovely, a proper gentleman, so it can't be owt to do with him that's making her crabby.'

'She's more than likely just overtired, an' ye know how it is when we feel like that. We always take it out on them closest to us,' said Kitty, pulling out a clump of chickweed as she attempted to raise Maggie's spirits. 'I take me temper out on John an' our Robert when they've done nothin' to deserve it, an' you do the same on Stanley so don't be getting all het up 'cos your Lily's had a go at you.'

'Yeah, I suppose you're right.' Maggie heaved a sigh. 'It's just that she's been so much nicer since she met Eric. She's stopped all that gadding about and picking up one chap after another, and she doesn't drink like she used to. She'd turned into a proper little lady and...' Maggie choked back what sounded like a sob then added, 'I liked that about her, Kitty. I was happy for her.'

Kitty saw the disappointment in Maggie's eyes. She knew of old that her friend had always craved for something better than life had dealt her, and that Maggie was investing those hopes and dreams in Lily. Her kind heart ached for her friend.

'She's a lovely girl, Maggie, no matter that she can be a bit moody at times. She'll not let ye down. Just wait an' see.'

* * *

Lily walked to where she was meeting Eric, her heart as heavy as her tread. Each step she took caused a pain in her chest and the cruel words she was repeating inside her head made her brain feel as though it was about to burst. Why did there always have to be something in her life that got in the way of happiness? A cold sweat turned her skin clammy, and she was tempted to turn back, leave Eric waiting and wondering why she was putting an end to their romance. The thought brought tears to her eyes. She plodded on, practising her lines.

Her mother might not know what was troubling Lily, but Lily did and it made her feel dirty and nauseous. She had done just what she had always promised herself she would never do. She'd followed in her mother's footsteps and got pregnant without first getting a husband.

Eric's face cracked into a smile so wide as she approached him that she felt the urge to run back the way she had come, but before she could do so he hurried towards her, clasping her hands with his and pecking her cheek. 'I was beginning to think you'd let me down,' he said.

Oh, I've let you down all right, and I've let meself down, Lily thought bitterly.

'What will it be then? The cinema or the new play at the little theatre? The choice is yours,' he said gallantly.

She couldn't possibly say what she must in either of these venues so she mumbled, 'It's a lovely evening. Let's go for a walk round the Botanic.'

'What a splendid idea.' Eric linked her arm through his and as they strolled towards the Botanic Gardens, he told her how the city corporation had created the garden as a place where people who toiled in the city could come at their leisure to enjoy the fresh air and admire the many different plants that had been brought from different parts of the world. 'It's even been visited by Queen Victoria. She opened an exhibition here.' He sounded impressed.

Lily was only half listening. 'Fancy that,' she said. 'I've been here loads of times and I never knew that.'

They walked along the neat pathways bordered with box hedging, and paused to gaze at the ruins of the conservatory that had been destroyed by a German bomb the year before. As they walked, Eric bemoaned the loss of the conservatory, and Lily's thoughts were in turmoil. *Is this what a condemned woman feels like before they hang her for murder?* She wished that Eric would shut up. When they came to a bench in a sheltered corner and he suggested they sit down, Lily slumped onto the seat, dreading having to say the words that were jangling in her head and burning on her tongue. Eric draped his arm over her shoulders. It felt good and she allowed herself to relish the moment.

'I've been thinking,' he said enigmatically, 'that if you and I are going to make a go of it then it's about time I took you home and introduced you to my mother.'

Lily's insides churned. She took a deep breath. 'I don't want to meet your mother, Eric. In fact...' She shrugged his arm away and got to her feet. 'I don't want to see you ever again.'

He looked as though she had slapped him. 'But... but I thought...'

'I don't know what you thought, but I know I can't keep on pretending to like you. You and your boring plays and your hoity-toity friends, I can't stick any more of it. You're just a namby-pamby posh boy.' The lies spewed out, but she knew this was the best way to end it. Let him think she hated the sight of him so that he wouldn't come looking for her and try to change her mind.

Eric jumped up. 'You don't mean that, Lily. I told you I loved you and you said you loved me. We've been happy together.' He looked as though he might cry.

Lily steeled herself and warmed to her theme. 'You might have been happy. Personally, I've been bored to death,' she scorned. 'I'm not your sort, Eric, and you certainly aren't mine.'

She spun on her heel and hared down the pathway, tears streaming and her broken heart crumbling in her chest.

Eric stood, mesmerised. Lily had spoken the truth when she'd said she wasn't his sort, but he'd fallen in love with her, rough edges and all. From the moment he'd worked alongside her as they carried out their ARP duties, he'd admired her fiery spirit and her wicked sense of humour. He was rather namby-pamby, he knew that, but he found it hard to believe that was the reason for her to so cruelly end their romance. Torn between chasing after her or owning up to the fact that much of what she had said was true, he stayed where he was nursing his broken heart.

Lily cried all the way home. She barged into the house and in answer to Maggie's anxious cry of, 'What's matter, Lily?' she yelled, 'Nowt to do with you. Keep your nose out.'

'Bloody hell,' said Stanley. 'She gets worse.'

'Yeah, she does. I was saying to Kitty that she was proper narky but it couldn't be owt to do with Eric, but she's just been with him and look at the state of her.'

'They'll sort themselves, love. She's a big girl. Stop worrying.'

* * *

The following evening in the ARP headquarters Lily said to John, 'Don't double me up with that chap called Eric tonight or any other night.'

'I couldn't even if I wanted to. He called in and said he wasn't free for any more duties.' He gave Lily a quizzical stare. 'I thought you and him were getting along just fine.'

'Well, you thought wrong. He bored me to death,' she snapped, slamming on her helmet and marching into the little kitchen where the other wardens were gathered. She felt like death, and the job that had given her so much pleasure and made her feel important and worthy now seemed like an unwelcome chore. She'd have to give it up anyway when the baby started to show. It felt like swallowing stones as she acknowledged the truth of what she had yet to contend with in the months ahead.

* * *

'Letter for you, Carswell,' the Wren on the reception desk called out as Anna entered the foyer in Derby House. She waved a blue envelope beckoningly.

Anna felt a little thrill of anticipation. It must be from Ross. He was the only person who would write to her at Derby House. She tucked the letter into her bag then hurried down to the cloakroom to read it before she went on duty.

Dear Anna,

I said I would write, so here goes. I hope you and the rest of the girls are in good spirits and that Razor Sharp is not working you too hard. I'm back with my squadron, putting all I learned in Derby House into practice and making preparations to travel to far-flung places. I fondly remember the farewell party at the Grafton, it was great fun. We have a dance hall near our base but it's poor stuff compared to the big bands at the Grafton, and the girls are not as pretty. I'm careful not to remark on the colour of their hair when I'm dancing with them just in case… But believe me, your hair is the colour of glorious autumn leaves.

I'd appreciate a reply, if you can find the time to write to a lonely wing commander.

All the very best to you and the girls. Give them my regards.

Yours sincerely, Ross

The brief one-page letter was no more or less than she had expected. It was friendly and impersonal, but he had mentioned the colour of hair, and his clear intentions for her to pass on his felicitations to the other girls meant he had chosen to write to her alone. Or had he? You couldn't trust men. Perhaps Primrose, Susan and Denise had all received similar letters. She was fairly sure he wouldn't have written to Poppy. She'd made it very plain that her flight lieutenant was the only man for her. Still, Anna thought, he had written to her and she would write back in the same light-hearted manner. She tucked the letter into her breast pocket to show the other girls at breaktime.

'I knew he was keen on you,' Primrose said after reading the letter.

'It's really for all of us,' Anna replied, her cheeks pinking.

'He hasn't mentioned the colour of my hair,' said Denise, patting her bleached blonde chignon and grinning wickedly at Anna.

'Will you write back?' Poppy asked briskly.

'I will; it would be impolite not to.'

Anna's diffident response made Primrose giggle. 'Do I smell the beginning of a long-distance romance?' she asked.

'He's going abroad,' Anna replied. 'I'll probably never see or hear from him again.'

Lily could neither eat nor sleep. She had to let Barry know. He'd want to know, wouldn't he? She couldn't write to him. She didn't know where he was stationed. But it was his baby as much as hers, and he'd have to do something about it. Would he offer to marry her? Did she want to be married to him? No, she did not. She wanted to marry Eric. She had set so much store by that becoming a reality that it made her insides ache to think that now it would never happen. Slowly, her heart heavy and her head throbbing, she climbed out of bed. Today she'd hunt Barry down; she couldn't leave it any longer.

Washed and dressed, she went over to the dressing table to put on her make-up. At one end was the large encyclopaedia she'd borrowed from the library before she was certain she was pregnant. She glanced at it malevolently then shoved it to the floor where it landed with a thud. So much for hopes and dreams. She had intended to borrow a book each week in order to be able to talk to Eric about the things she'd learned. Now there was no point in trying to better herself. She'd take back the encyclopaedia and borrow a book on how to rear a baby, she thought bitterly.

Downstairs, she popped her head round the front room door. Maggie was bent over her mending frame. 'I'm off out,' Lily said.

'Where are you off to?' Maggie raised her head and looked into her daughter's dismal face. Her loss of appetite, red-rimmed eyes and violent mood swings had Maggie worried.

'Never you mind,' Lily growled.

Outside the shabby house in Hood Street where she had spent the night with Barry, she paused. Would his mate, Davy, even remember her? They had only met fleetingly before she and Barry had fallen into the bed in his spare room. She knocked on the door.

Davy did remember her; who could forget that head of flaming red hair? He looked rather taken aback. 'Lily, what are—'

'Have you heard from Barry lately?' she asked urgently.

Davy's jaw dropped and his face paled. He wiped his hand over his eyes. 'You mean to say you don't know?' His voice shook.

'Know what?' A cold hand clutched Lily's heart.

'Bas went an' got himself killed in Italy... about a month ago. His wife came round to tell me.'

Now it was Lily's jaw that dropped. She felt dizzy, and grabbed for the doorpost.

'His wife?' She spoke barely above a whisper.

'Yeah,' said Davy, his cheeks reddening. 'Didn't he tell you he was married? They've got a kid. He's nearly two and...'

Davy's last words were spoken to thin air. Lily was running down Hood Street as though the hounds of hell were after her.

* * *

The summer dragged on, sunny days and balmy nights doing little to cheer the friends in Weaver Street. The war in Europe and Russia still raged with no signs of it ending, and rationing was increased by the week. The 'Spitfire Summer' of the year before when the British had been sure that The Battle of Britain would put to an end to the slaughter, was a distant memory.

'I couldn't get any margarine this week in any of the shops,' Kitty complained to the friends assembled in her kitchen one Saturday afternoon in August.

'The same with condensed milk,' Mavis moaned.

'And dried peas,' Beth added.

'Rose managed to get two tins of corned beef didn't you, love?' May Walker beamed at her daughter-in-law.

Rose grinned back. 'I got them from a chap who came into the shop,' she said referring to Betty's Bijou Bazaar. 'He had a box full. No doubt he'd pinched them off the docks, but I didn't care where they came from if it meant we could make a few tasty meals.'

'You should have sent him up to us, given us a chance,'

Maggie grumbled. She had been tetchy for the past few days and now she looked as though she wanted a fight.

Rose's cheeks reddened. 'Sorry, Maggie. I wasn't thinking. I'll send you up a few slices.'

'Oh, don't bother your arse on my account,' Maggie snapped.

'Now, now, Maggie, don't ye be takin' out whatever's eatin' away at ye on Rose,' Kitty admonished. 'Ye've been like a bear all week, so ye have.'

Maggie screwed her face then snorted. 'You might as well know before you see it for yourselves... our Lily's gone and got herself pregnant.' She puffed furiously on her cigarette and blinked rapidly to ward off threatening tears. 'She's nearly five months gone.'

The silence that followed was so deep that Maggie felt as though she was drowning in it. Then they all started talking at once.

'Well, she's not the first, and she certainly won't be that last,' said May, alluding to girls who got pregnant outside marriage.

'It'll be a Christmas baby, how lovely,' Mavis twittered.

Rose silently recalled the unwanted baby she had miscarried and how Mavis had wanted it more than she herself. Then, thanking God for giving her a second chance, she leaned forward and ruffled James's hair. He smiled up at her as he played with a toy car at her feet. 'I wish Lily all the best,' she said softly.

Beth sniffed. 'It's not ideal, but then... Is her young man going to marry her?'

'Aye, is Eric standing by her?' Kitty gave Maggie an anxious look.

Maggie swallowed noisily. 'It's not his! It's that bugger Barry's, him she used to go out with,' Maggie snarled as she fought back tears.

There followed another lengthy silence before Kitty broke it.

'I thought she gave him up a long time ago,' she said, her heart aching for Maggie.

'She did,' Maggie muttered. 'But then she met him one night at the Grafton.'

'An' will he marry her?' Kitty was desperate for a happy solution to Lily's predicament.

Maggie finally let her tears flow. 'He can't,' she wailed, 'he's dead. Killed in Italy.' A chorus of gasps and Maggie's hysterical sobbing filled the kitchen and Kitty pulled Maggie into her arms.

'There, there,' she soothed, 'it's not the end of the world. We'll manage, darlin'. We've been through worse, an' we've always come out smiling.'

Maggie hiccupped and clung to Kitty as she gave a wan smile. 'Yeah... we have... haven't we?' She forced a proper smile as she looked from one to another of the women. 'This baby's gonna have more aunties than spots on a leopard,' she croaked.

* * *

Across the lane, Lily had just finished telling the same story to Molly and Anna.

'Don't cry, Lily. It's not as though you've committed a crime,' Molly pleaded.

'Lots of women bring children up on their own.' Anna didn't add that the war would leave thousands of children without fathers.

'I know that,' Lily grunted. 'It's just that having this baby means I can't have Eric.' She choked back a sob. 'I really did love him, you know.'

'Did you tell him about it, let him choose what he wanted to do? He might have forgiven you if he really loved you.' Molly was clutching at straws, desperate to help her friend.

Lily shook her head. 'I was too ashamed. Eric's not the sort to...' She began to cry again.

'You don't know that for certain,' Anna pressed.

Lily shrugged. 'When I told him I'd finished with him he didn't come looking for me, did he? If he really wanted me, he'd have come by now.' Lily's green eyes flashed and she tossed her mane of red hair angrily. Anna and Molly didn't know what to say to that.

* * *

In a rather grand house in Wavertree, Eric Kitson paced his bedroom floor. Several times in the past few weeks he had been tempted to seek Lily out, beg her to come back to him. Then he thought of all the cruel names she had called him, and told himself he would be wasting his time. And, of course, there was the matter of pride. He wouldn't let her hurt him again.

But he missed her dreadfully.

11

The sycamores in the allotment had lost their leaves and stood stark against the autumnal sky. Banks of grey clouds scudded overhead as Anna walked up the lane. She waved to Molly standing at the window with Ronan in her arms. 'See you later,' she mouthed, flicking her hand to her chest then at Molly. Molly nodded and grinned.

'Your tea's ready, love,' Mavis said as Anna entered the kitchen. The fire was blazing and a delicious smell of stew pervaded the air. Anna smiled gratefully. It was lovely to return after a hard day's work to such a warm welcome. She couldn't have wished for a better billet.

After she had eaten and washed up, she sat down at the table with her writing pad and pen, and Ross's third letter. Tapping her pen against her teeth, she gazed thoughtfully into space, deliberating on how she should word her reply.

'Writing to Ross, are you?' Mavis asked from her chair by the fire as she clicked her needles in and out of the cardigan she was knitting for Anna. His last two letters had been addressed to

Weaver Street so she knew that Anna was corresponding with him.

Anna frowned. 'I'm trying to, but I don't know quite what to say. He's coming to Liverpool the weekend after next and he's asked me to meet up with him.'

'And is that a problem?' Mavis put her head to one side, looking for all the world like an inquisitive little sparrow.

'In a way, yes. I don't want to start something that might get complicated.'

'What's complicated about spending time with an old friend?'

'He might read more into it if I agree, and I'm not sure I'm ready to get involved with anyone again,' Anna said gloomily. She had told Mavis something about her broken romance with Simon Grant without divulging how heartbroken she had been.

'You mustn't let one bad experience colour the rest of your life,' Mavis advised. 'If you enjoy Ross's company then tell him you'll meet him. That way you'll find out how you feel about him, and no doubt he'll do the same about you. You don't have to commit yourself to anything that doesn't sit well.'

Mavis's homespun wisdom struck a chord. *It's me who's reading too much into his invitation to meet up. He's most likely just looking for company in between whatever business he has at Derby House,* Anna thought and started to write. She told him she'd be delighted, and asked where she should meet him.

'Did you say yes then?' Mavis's beady eyes twinkled. When Anna affirmed that she had, her landlady gave a satisfied sigh. It was only natural for a lovely young thing like Anna to have a young man in her life.

* * *

Now that her mother and her friends and neighbours knew about her pregnancy, Lily resigned herself to the fact that there was no turning back. She had lost her slender figure, and soon she would have to give up working in the mill until arrangements could be made for somebody to care for the baby, but not once had she considered any other options. She knew girls who'd had back-street abortions, and others who had given up their babies for adoption. Lily wasn't prepared to do that. This baby was hers, nobody else's and when it was born, she'd love and care for it with every breath in her body, and maybe with luck on her side she'd be able to give it some of the advantages that she had never had. She wouldn't be like Maggie, always looking to replace one man for another in the hope that one might turn out to be a decent husband and a dad for her child.

'I'll be all right, you know,' she told Molly and Anna. 'I've always been able to look out for meself. With a mam like mine I had to.' Lily grimaced then gave a little chuckle.

'Your mam always loved you, Lily, even if she spent most of her time looking for somebody to love her,' Molly said affectionately.

'Yeah, you're dead right there. She did love me in her own way but I'd have liked a dad as well. I'd like this baby to have one.' Lily's voice was thick with emotion. 'Do you remember the time you told me I could share John with you 'cos I didn't have a dad?'

'The love of one parent is better than no love at all,' said Anna, reflecting on her own childhood. 'I had two who barely knew I existed half the time. If you give your baby all the love in the world it won't need a dad. You didn't have one and you've turned out all right.'

'Yeah, except for being an unmarried mother having a baby with a dead man who was already married to somebody else, and losing the man I'd have loved to marry, I've done bloody brilliantly,' Lily crowed and burst out laughing. Molly and Anna joined in.

'You'll be fine. You've your mam and Stanley and all of us looking out for you, and if I know you, Lily Stubbs, you'll not let this spoil your life.' Molly got to her feet and put the kettle on. 'Now, enough baby talk. I'm going to make another pot of tea and Anna's going to tell us all about the chap she's meeting this weekend.'

* * *

Anna looked at the clothes scattered on the bed. Should she wear the bottle green soft wool dress under Mavis's camel coat or the grey tweed skirt and cardigan with her service issue greatcoat? Then again, Ross might expect to see her in full uniform. She knew which she looked most attractive in and before she could change her mind, she pulled on the green dress, smiling wryly as she looked at her reflection in the mirror. Mavis had said the dark green dress brought out the colour of her hair. Would Ross think so too?

When she went downstairs, Mavis clapped her hands and told her she looked beautiful. 'I know you have to keep your hair up for work, love, but it's a proper picture when you leave it loose. You look like Rita Hayworth in *Only Angels Have Wings*. That was a lovely film,' she enthused, 'but then anything with Cary Grant in makes my heart beat a bit faster.'

Anna laughed at the idea of her landlady swooning over the handsome film star. 'I'm borrowing your camel coat again if you don't mind,' she said. 'It's so much nicer than my greatcoat.' Mavis had bought the well-tailored three-quarter-length swing coat in the twenties. It had a velvet shawl collar, and made Anna feel rather glamorous.

'Wear it all you like, love. I'll not be wearing it again. My flapper days are over.'

'I can't imagine you as a flapper, Mavis.' Anna was laughing again.

'I never was. I just bought it in a moment of madness in Cripp's sale. I've always been a bit of a Plain Jane when it comes to fashion,' Mavis said wistfully.

'There's nothing plain about you, Mavis. You're lovely inside and out. I wish I'd had a mother like you.'

Anna couldn't have said anything more pleasing and Mavis's eyes moistened and her lips quivered into a wide smile. 'Go on, you get off and enjoy your day out.'

Anna was meeting Ross at eleven outside Lime Street Station. She still didn't know why he was coming to Liverpool. Maybe he had business at Derby House. Perhaps he'd just take her to lunch and nothing more. *You're not looking for anything more*, she told herself crossly as she was sitting on the tram. *Once bitten, twice shy. Or had you forgotten that, Anna Carswell?* She tried to remember the last time she had felt the pain of losing Simon. It seemed ages ago.

Ross was waiting outside the station. It was the first time Anna had seen him in civvies and she thought he looked devastatingly handsome and carefree in his seaman's jersey and navy pea coat. She also reckoned that if he wasn't in uniform then he mustn't have any business at Derby House. His face broke into a wide grin when he saw her and he hurried forward to meet her.

'It's good to see you, Anna, and might I say you look delightful.' His eyes admired her from top to toe.

She blushed and said, 'It's good to see you. What brings you to Liverpool?'

Ross's eyes widened in surprise. 'You,' he said. 'I came to see you.'

Anna's heart fluttered. He sounded and looked so sincere that she felt guilty at having thought he was just killing time with her in between whatever else had brought him to the city. 'Well, here I am,' she said, feeling rather flustered. Ross seemed not to notice.

'What would you like to do first?' he asked. 'How will we spend the day?'

Anna was still feeling rather discombobulated by the fact that he had made the journey specially to see her, and that they were to have the entire day at their disposal. They hadn't yet moved from the station entrance, and as everyday commuters and servicemen coming and going swirled past them, she quickly gathered her wits and thought about what she would like to do.

'Let's not go into the city centre. The damage is so depressing, and I see it every day. We could take the ferry to New Brighton and walk on the sands. I'd like that.'

'Then New Brighton it is,' Ross said, tucking her arm into his, 'and as we go you can tell me all about that awful week in May, the one I missed. Seven nights of bombing. Your nerves must have been wrecked.'

Anna liked the feel of her arm in his; it didn't stir any unwanted memories. And as they walked, she told him about kicking in the door to rescue the woman and her children. She made it sound ridiculous rather than heroic and Ross laughed. 'You amaze me, Carswell. You really are something else.' Anna took it as a compliment and felt pleased.

Ross then told her about the time he was inspecting a Wellington bomber when he slipped and his foot went through the skin of the plane. 'I felt an absolute fool,' he said, 'and the rest of my crew are still ribbing me about it. Luckily, we were on the ground when it happened.'

Laughing and chattering all the way, they soon reached the

ferry station and boarded the *John Farley* within minutes of their arrival.

They stood at the ferry's rail, a crisp breeze blowing tendrils of Anna's hair across her cheeks. Ross thought she had never looked lovelier. He'd thought about her often after leaving Liverpool, but he had deliberately kept his letters light-hearted; he had sensed at their first meeting on the dance floor at the Grafton that she was sensitive to a chap coming on to her too strongly. He had an idea that she'd been badly hurt in the past.

Anna watched the white wake of the ferry as it streamed across the Mersey and thought how easy she felt in Ross's company. Not once had they run out of conversation. With Simon she had sometimes felt as though he was doing her a favour by taking her out for a ride in the countryside or a meal before rushing her back to his quarters, and into bed. But then she had been so in love with him, she had buried the feeling.

When the ferry docked, they walked hand in hand along the pier then along the promenade and down onto the strip of sand that wasn't cordoned off by barbed wire and other sea defences. They ran like children as far as they could go, and as they retraced their steps, strolling this time, Anna picked up shells and pebbles that caught her eye. The sun, the sea and the sand made it feel like she was on holiday – Jane and Norman had never taken her to the seaside; they didn't do holidays – and now Anna felt as though she was having the best time of her life. She tucked the shells and pebbles in her coat pocket then set off at a run, skipping over the sand and hallooing, her hair flaring rebelliously. Ross kicked up his heels and ran after her, laughing.

When he caught up with her, he threw his arms round her, pulling her to his chest. Then he kissed her. The kiss tasted of salty air and a sweetness that made her head spin and her heart beat all the faster. She felt the thud of his heart against her own.

He withdrew his lips and she gazed up at him. He saw her expression flit through surprise, then wariness before her face broke into a rapturous smile. Ross's breath whooshed out with relief.

'I've waited a long time to do that,' he said.

'I'm glad,' she whispered into his shirt. 'I wasn't ready before, but I am now.' They kissed again then strolled up to the promenade, both of them feeling that they had surmounted a barrier and cleared the way to the future.

They ate fish and chips, walked round the shops and visited the New Brighton Tower then caught the ferry back across the Mersey. Daylight was fading, the sky streaked with pink and purple and the last of the sun's rays glinting on the water. 'It's magical,' Anna breathed.

Ross was unsure whether she meant the scenery or their newfound relationship but he hoped it was the latter. 'Which bit in particular?' he asked, his pure grey eyes almost silver and filled with hope.

'All of it,' Anna said. 'Every single little bit of it.'

'We'll make it even better tomorrow,' he said, and Anna thrilled at the prospect of sharing another day with him.

'Where are you staying tonight?' she asked.

'Derby House. I begged a bunk from Razor Sharp. She has a soft spot for me.'

She's not the only one, Anna thought, and said, 'I suppose she can't help herself.'

They had tea in a café then caught the last performance at the Odeon. By some strange coincidence, the film was *Only Angels Have Wings*. Anna giggled and told Ross what Mavis had said about Rita Hayworth. 'You knock her into a cocked hat,' he said gallantly.

Cocooned in the warmth of the cinema with Ross's arm round her shoulders, Anna drew comparisons with what was happening in her own life as the images rolled across the silver screen. The male characters flew aeroplanes like Ross, and Rita fell for one of them only for him to leave her in the end. Would that be the story of her love life? Anna wondered, but when they left the cinema and walked to her tram stop, such thoughts were dispelled as Ross kissed her goodnight. 'See you tomorrow for more of the same,' he whispered against her hair as the tram rolled up and he handed her aboard.

Mavis was waiting up, her beady eyes bright with curiosity as Anna entered the kitchen.

'Well, was it the right thing to do? Did you have a good day?'

'It was wonderful,' Anna said, pulling off the camel coat and draping it over the back of the chair before sitting by the fire, and aware that Mavis expected a blow-by-blow account, she told her all about it. 'And you'll never guess what the film was,' she giggled, her eyes shining as she relived the day.

'I'd say it was meant to be,' Mavis said sagely.

But later, in bed, Anna was filled with doubt. Was she too eager to feel loved? Was she trying to fill the emptiness and loneliness she had always felt when living with Jane and Norman that made her susceptible to the charms of men like Simon and Ross? *Ross is nothing like Simon*, she told herself irritably as she tossed and turned. *He's interested in you as a person not just somebody to warm his bed.* With that, she fell into a restful sleep.

Rain had fallen during the night, and although it had ceased by the time Anna was ready to go and meet Ross, the heavy sky threatened more. Anna put on her greatcoat; she wouldn't risk spoiling Mavis's camel coat. Mavis was busy at the sink preparing vegetables to go with the rabbit Jack had caught in the allotment the day before, the delicious smell of slowly braised meat scenting the air.

'This'll be a proper treat,' she crowed, smacking her lips in expectation of the tasty meal. 'Jack and me will have ours about one, and you can have yours when you get back.'

'I don't know what we'll do today; there's not much to do in the city on Sunday and if it rains, I don't know where we'll go,' Anna said dismally, going to the door as a splatter of raindrops wet the window. 'Ross's train doesn't leave until six.'

Mavis dropped chopped carrots into a pan then spun round to face Anna, her beady eyes alight as she said, 'Train journeys can take forever these days, bring him back here before he goes halfway across the country. Let the lad have a tasty dinner and a seat by the fire.'

Anna paused, her hand on the doorknob. 'Could I?' she asked, sounding amazed, and very tempted by the offer. It would be far more preferable to traipsing the bombed-out streets in the rain.

''Course you can, love. There's plenty for four of us, and Jack'll enjoy having another man about the place.' Mavis's delight at having made the suggestion was palpable.

'It's a brilliant idea, and thanks, Mavis. I'll ask him, but I don't know if he'll agree.'

'He'd be daft to turn down my braised rabbit,' Mavis said perkily.

Ross didn't refuse Mavis's invitation. He was interested to see where Anna lived. It would bring them closer, he thought, as they caught the tram back to Weaver Street in the pouring rain. The dinner was a royal treat and the conversation lively. Jack reminisced about his experiences in the first war and, fascinated, Ross told him what being a wing commander involved. Anna and Mavis exchanged satisfied smiles as they washed the dishes, Mavis proud at the way in which Jack was acquitting himself, and Anna delighted by Ross's easy manner with the older couple. She had done the right thing in bringing him to Weaver Street. By doing so it had confirmed what a decent man he was and she found him all the more endearing.

But all too soon it was time for Ross to leave.

The rain had stopped, and as Anna walked Ross down the lane to the tram stop on Broad Green, she pointed out the houses of the friends she had made in Weaver Street.

'You seem very much at home,' said Ross. 'I won't have to worry about you when I'm in Africa.' Anna recalled that his first letter had mentioned going abroad, but in her excitement at meeting him again it had slipped her mind. Her spirits sank. He would be very far away.

'When do you go?' she asked plaintively, wondering if she would ever see him again.

'December fifteenth. My squadron's joining the West Africa Campaign in Takoradi. That's on the Gold Coast. We'll be supporting the chaps in the north where the real fighting is, taking in supplies and maintaining aircraft.' He had no qualms at giving Anna such detailed information; she dealt with far more sensitive stuff every day, but his heart lurched as he divulged it. They would be separated by thousands of miles just when he thought that he was in love with her. The thought stopped him in his tracks. Puzzled, Anna stopped too.

'Give us a moment,' he said, gently pulling her into the shadows of the grocer's shop doorway. He cupped her face in his hands and looked deeply into her eyes. 'I'm going to miss you, sweet Anna. Will you miss me?' Anna was about to say yes but his kiss smothered the word, a kiss so deep and passionate that she felt as though her insides were melting. The kiss was different from the playful kisses they had shared yesterday, and as she returned it, it felt just right and she never wanted it to end. Breathless, they broke apart and gazed at one another, their dazed expressions turning into joyful smiles that said a thousand words.

Ross broke the magical silence. 'I'll get embarkation leave before I go. Can I come and see you again? And will you promise to write and not forget about me?'

'I couldn't forget you if I tried,' Anna said, her voice shaking with emotion. They kissed again then as they walked to the tram stop, she said, 'I wasn't in a good place when we first met. It's a long story and one day I might tell you about it. Getting to know you has changed all that and there's nothing I'd like more than to see you again and write to you. I have a feeling I'm going to miss you dreadfully the minute you get on the tram.'

They heard it in the distance rattling towards them and he hurriedly made arrangements to write and let her know the dates of his embarkation leave. 'Try to get a few days off. Tell Razor Sharp you're meeting me,' he urged.

'Won't she be jealous?' Anna giggled, but her heart was aching at the thought of letting him go. The tram rumbled to a halt.

'See you in December, sweetheart,' Ross said and brushed his lips against hers.

Anna waved until he was out of sight then walked back up the lane on feet that felt as though they didn't belong to her. Already she was missing him. He had restored her faith in love and for that she was glad, and although this rotten war would keep them apart, she felt that even if in the fullness of time their brief romance failed to bloom into a full-blown love affair, she had found a wonderful friend in Ross Penhaligon.

12

November was cold and foggy, and daylight hours so short that Anna got used to going to and coming home from Derby House in the dark. On the bright side, Jerry seemed to have lost interest in Liverpool and there had been no further catastrophic raids since the May Blitz.

As she neared the end of the lane, she caught sight of Rachel Dyson and quickened her pace to catch up with her.

'Hello, Rachel. How are you?' Anna felt a spike of guilt at not having visited the widow again. Many of her free evenings on these dark November nights were spent in the comfort of Mavis's kitchen, sometimes chatting with Kitty and Maggie, but mostly she went and sat with Molly. They shared so many interests and were happy to talk about Mickey and Ross, like two teenage girls rhapsodising about their first romances.

'Oh, hello, Anna.' Rachel gave her a distracted smile. 'I haven't seen you for some time.'

Your fault as much as mine, Anna thought, sweeping aside her feelings of neglect. Rachel rarely chose to be neighbourly. She didn't pop in and out of the houses like the other women in the street, and they in turn respected her privacy.

'Foul weather, isn't it?' Anna said. 'Going to work this morning I could barely see my hand in front of my face the fog was so thick.'

Rachel appeared not to have heard her. Making no mention of the weather, she blurted, 'Will you call round this evening if you have time?' By now they were level with her gate.

Anna hesitated. She had been going to spend it with Molly, but hearing the anxiety in the older woman's voice she said she would call after she had had her tea.

'Thank you,' Rachel said, sounding grateful. Somewhat bemused, Anna hurried to Mavis's door.

'You've a letter from Ross,' Mavis chirped as soon as Anna entered the warm kitchen. Anna smiled. Her landlady was taking almost as much interest in Ross as Anna was.

'You are a true romantic, Mavis Robson,' Anna laughed, taking the letter from Mavis's outstretched hand.

'Love makes the world go round, or so they say,' Mavis quipped as she poured Anna a cup of tea and set it next to the plate of corned beef hash on the table. Anna took off her coat and sat down, Mavis hovering and waiting for her to open the letter. To please her, Anna did so and skimmed the single page.

'He's got leave the first week in December,' she said, her eyes sparkling.

'Well, isn't that just lovely,' Mavis said, her curiosity satisfied. She had formed a great opinion of Ross and was keen for the friendship to develop. Anna deserved happiness.

After she had eaten and changed out of her uniform, Anna told Mavis that Rachel had asked her to call. 'I'll get straight off, that way I'll still have time to go into Molly's before bedtime. We're making a Christmas tree out of cardboard for Ronan.'

'That's nice. It's a shame you can't get the real thing these days. Jack says the War Ministry's taken over all the forests for timber for the war effort. They'll be taking control of how many times we use the lavatory before they're done,' Mavis groused. 'And what with wool being on coupons, I'll not be able to knit half the things I usually do for presents.'

'You can have my old blue cardigan to pull back now that you've knitted me that lovely cream one,' Anna offered.

Mavis visibly cheered. 'Thanks, love. It'll be grand for gloves and scarves.'

Pleased to have made Mavis happy, Anna went off to Rachel's house. Rachel welcomed her warmly, and after some inconsequential chatter, she said, 'Yesterday I had a letter from Philip,' her tone suggesting that her son didn't write very often. 'He's coming home next week. He has seven days' leave.' Anna was surprised by Rachel's lack of enthusiasm. She almost sounded as though she was dreading it.

'Oh, that's lovely. I'm sure he's looking forward to it,' Anna replied brightly. 'Where is it he's coming from?'

'He's in Aldershot for some reason. He was in France.' Rachel sounded deliberately vague. She gave Anna a wan but hopeful smile. 'He finds my company rather boring. I was wondering if you might spend some time with him, maybe take him to the Grafton or the cinema. I think he'd enjoy his leave in the company of someone young like yourself.'

Startled, Anna didn't know what to say. Was this the reason Rachel had invited her?

'I... I've never met him,' she said. 'He might not want to...' Realising how ungracious she sounded, she meekly added, 'Well, if you think he'd like that you could introduce us...'

'What a good idea,' Rachel agreed as she got to her feet, her manner indicating that the visit was over. Then, in a faraway voice, she said, 'You remind me of me when I was young, Anna.' She walked over to the outer door and opened it.

Anna stood, feeling thoroughly confused. As she walked to Molly's, she tried to make sense of what had taken place. She felt concerned that Rachel was using her, and it diminished the respect she had for her.

Anna told Molly, but Molly didn't know Philip either so she couldn't enlighten her as to what he was like. 'I know he's paid her a flying visit once or twice but none of us have met him.'

'I'd have thought Rachel would be thrilled to have him home, but if she is she certainly didn't show it,' Anna said.

'I think it 'ud take lot to please her. She's that full of her own importance she has no time for anybody else. Mam tried to make a friend of her like we always do in Weaver Street, but Rachel has always been stuck-up and stand-offish, if you know what I mean. It's like she had something to hide.' Molly chuckled. 'And if my mam and Maggie can't get her to open up then nobody can. They've noses on them longer than Pinocchio.'

Anna laughed. 'Have you seen that front room of hers?'

Molly looked puzzled. 'No. I don't think anybody has. What about it?'

Anna went on to describe the splendour of Rachel's front room, Molly's eyes widening in surprise. 'She's a dark horse if ever there was one.'

'And she's a cold fish into the bargain.'

* * *

After Anna had gone, Rachel went into her front room. Sitting in a wing chair in the dark, she mulled over what she had asked Anna to do. She wondered if she had been entirely fair. Anna was a lovely girl even if she hadn't had the best start in life, she thought, playing with the notion that she might have contributed to Anna's unhappy childhood. It did seem rather far-fetched but it wasn't impossible. The girl had been born in Liverpool; she was about the right age. Rachel closed her eyes, picturing yet again the evening Anna had spent in this very room. As she had watched her it had been like looking into a mirror from the past. The slender figure, the auburn hair and the way she moved. It could have been herself twenty or so years ago.

But I must take my time, Rachel told herself as she opened her eyes then stood gazing around the room. *I could be wrong, and open a can of worms that crawl out, bringing with them things that neither she nor I can deal with. I must go slowly if I am to uncover the truth without damage to my reputation and her peace of mind. She's blossomed into a beautiful, independent young woman with a worthwhile career. I wouldn't wish to do her harm. Maybe with Philip's intervention I can get closer to the girl and...*

Irritated by the troublesome notions, Rachel went into the kitchen and made a cup of tea. As she sipped, her thoughts dwelt on Philip. She had seen very little of him since he had joined the army. He had come to Weaver Street on only three occasions, each one a flying visit. Would this one be the same? And when she insisted that he abided by her rules in her beautiful house would he show his dissatisfaction by being sarcastic and deliberately untidy as he had done before? He was such a difficult boy. Yet, if Rachel believed what she thought might possibly be true he could prove useful on this occasion. There were still a lot of questions to be answered and she'd ask them all in good time. Hopefully Anna would provide the answers.

* * *

November was drawing to a close, and on a Friday morning in the same week that Anna had agreed to Rachel's strange request, Kitty was hurrying along the towpath to deliver the baps she had baked earlier that morning. The café did very little trade at this time of year but she was feeling grateful for the mild weather and the bags of flour she had managed to get the day before. The mill workers preferred her home-made baps and Kitty didn't blame them because she suspected that the local bakery padded out the flour with sago and the bread was stodgy. Seeing as how the lasses and lads from the mill were her main source of income, it paid to please them.

She smiled as her café came into view, its bold blue and white paintwork lending a touch of the seaside and jollity to the towpath. It always had that effect on her, even if there were no customers sitting out on the veranda built to extend the seating area for what had been a busy weekend trade in the spring and summer months before the war. She had fought hard to make her café a success but in the past two years what with food shortages and people more concerned with just getting by and staying alive, trade was poor. Taking leisurely walks on the riverbank and dropping in for tea was a luxury now, and for Kitty, keeping the café open was a matter of personal pride and not a money-making venture.

'Fresh baked baps,' she announced as she walked inside and past the empty tables to the counter. 'Ye can use the last of the fish paste for some, an' fill the others with spam or corned beef.' She put the bags on the counter.

'You got the flour then?' Kitty's assistant, Sheila, began emptying the bags as she grinned at her employer, one brown eye meeting Kitty's, the other wandering off to the right. Mrs Sykes was a living wonder in her opinion. Sheila had been born with a hump on her left shoulder and a dreadful squint that denied her a job in the mill, or anywhere else for that matter. But when she'd applied for the job in the café, lovely Mrs Sykes seemed not to notice these impediments. Sheila was truly grateful of her position and did her utmost to please.

Kitty took off her coat and began slicing the baps in half. 'How's your mam?' she asked. Sheila's mam was a widow who had never recovered from losing most of her hair and part of her scalp in one of Holroyd's weaving looms. Sheila was her only means of support, yet another reason to be grateful for her job.

'As well as can be expected, Mrs Sykes.' Sheila opened the tub of margarine and began smearing each cut bap sparingly. Kitty mashed the corned beef with brown sauce to make it go further. 'Tell her I asked after her,' Kitty responded.

Sheila nodded then said, 'Has Lily Stubbs had her baby yet?'

'Not yet, she's a week or so to go,' said Kitty, twisting the lids off jars of fish paste.

'There's three new babies been born on our estate,' said Sheila, referring to the council maisonettes that had been built in the Depression to give employment to some of the thousands of men out of work at the time. 'The girl who lives next door to us had hers yesterday. It's black. Her mam says nobody has to see it, but she let me in.'

'Jesus, Mary an' Joseph, they can't keep the poor mite hidden forever,' Kitty exclaimed, dolloping an overly generous amount of the mushed corned beef onto one half of a bap.

'That's what I said,' Sheila replied, 'and it's not as if it's the only black baby on our estate, there's two others. Their dads are foreign fellas off the boats. When they're in port they get daft lasses pregnant and then just beggar off. They never see 'em again.'

'Did ye ever hear the likes of it? It's not right the poor wee souls grow up without fathers all because their mothers don't have a bit of common sense.'

'Lily Stubbs doesn't have a dad for hers, does she?' Sheila asked slyly, her wandering eye disappearing into the corner and her good eye glinting wickedly.

'Every child has a father, Sheila, sure an' ye know that,' Kitty said tersely. 'It just happens that Lily's man was killed before he could marry her.' Inwardly blessing herself for telling the lie, she hastily washed her hands and put on her coat. 'Now, I have to dash. I've less than fifteen minutes to get to the factory.'

Kitty ran down the steps onto the towpath, still stinging from Sheila's cutting remark. She felt protective of Lily and didn't want Sheila to denigrate her.

Kitty arrived at the factory to be met by Elsie. 'You're late by nearly ten minutes.'

Making her apologies, Kitty began patrolling the rows of long tables where girls making bullets sat, heads bent and fingers nimble. She was glad that this time round in munitions she was supervising rather than tamping shells as she had done in the last war. As her eyes roved the benches on the lookout for shoddy work, she wondered if any of these young women would fall for the charms of a foreign sailor, only to be left high and dry if they became pregnant. The war was making all sorts of changes in society, and not for the better. She couldn't wait for it to be over.

At the end of her shift, she hurried home through the dark streets, the chill late afternoon air lending impetus to her steps. As she entered the lane, she saw a young man a few paces in front of her dressed in RAF blues and carrying a kitbag. Her heart leapt. Was it Patrick? A closer look told her the lad wasn't tall enough and her fleeting euphoria evaporated. The man turned in at Rachel Dyson's gate. *It must be Philip. Lucky woman to have her son home for a while*, Kitty thought.

Anna had told Molly of Rachel's request, and Molly had told Kitty. 'I think she has a nerve asking Anna to go out with him. Anna's Ross's girl,' Molly had said hotly. 'She doesn't need to give up her time entertaining a lad she's never met.'

'Can ye just see your brother's face if I made arrangements for some young lass to keep him company when he comes on leave,' Kitty had scorned.

Molly had replied, 'Our Patrick 'ud tell you to mind your own business.'

Kitty thought about popping in to let Anna know that Philip had arrived then she changed her mind. John and Robert were expecting her, and Anna would find out soon enough.

Rachel had left work early pleading a headache and now she was sitting in her neat and tidy kitchen reading when the back door was pushed open. She sprang to her feet as Philip entered. 'Philip! I wasn't expecting you until tomorrow.' It sounded like an accusation. She stood by her chair, frowning and wringing her hands. Her mouth had gone dry and a knot of annoyance formed in her chest.

'And lovely to see you too, Mother,' Philip sneered. He dumped his kitbag on the floor and unbuttoned his greatcoat. 'Am I to apologise for disturbing your sanctity, or will I go away and come back some other time?'

'No, no, you've just taken me by surprise, that's all,' Rachel stammered, eager to redress the situation. 'Please, sit down, make yourself at home. What can I get you?'

Philip tossed his greatcoat over the nearest chair. Instinctively, Rachel snatched it up and hurried into the hallway to hang it up. Her son watched her.

'Make myself at home, you say, but don't ruffle the cushions or drop any crumbs, and above all don't leave your clothes lying about,' he scoffed as he sprawled into a chair by the fire. 'Oh, Mother, you certainly make a chap feel welcome.'

Rachel made a pot of tea, and they exchanged a few desultory comments, Rachel asking why he had come, and Philip replying that it was a duty visit, after which they ignored each other. Philip leafed through the pages of a newspaper he had brought with him and Rachel prepared a plate of spam, tomatoes and buttered bread. Philip gave a wry smile at the sparse offering then sat at the table to eat it, and she lingered by the kitchen window watching for Anna to return from work. As soon as she spied her, she rushed to the door and called out, 'Anna, do you have a moment? Philip's arrived. I'd like you to come in and meet him.'

Anna's heart sank but she could hardly refuse. *Best get it over with*, she thought, and reluctantly followed Rachel. Philip was sitting at the table, the remnants of a meal in front of him. He glanced round, curious, as his mother ushered Anna into the kitchen.

'Philip, this is Anna.'

'Ah! One of the girls in blue,' he said affably, and pushing back his chair he stood and stuck out his hand. Anna shook it, feeling uncomfortable and foolish.

'Pleased to meet you, Philip.' She was going to add that his mother had told her about him but she swallowed the words. Rachel had told her nothing other than he was coming on leave, and that he found her company boring.

'Anna's billeted with one of my neighbours and is working at Derby House,' said Rachel enthusiastically, breaking the silence that had followed. 'She's going to show you where you can find some entertainment whilst you're in Liverpool.'

Oh, am I. How nice of me. Anna's discomfort was making her feel hot and irritable.

'That's very kind of you.' Philip didn't sound overly interested but Anna thought she saw Rachel sag with relief before she beamed at her son and then at Anna.

'Are you free this evening, Anna?' Rachel's desire to make arrangements was palpable.

Anna unscrambled her thoughts. 'Er... no... but... what about tomorrow night.' *Get it over and done with, satisfy the silly woman.*

'That's splendid, isn't it, Philip?'

'If you say so, Mother, and Anna is willing.' He didn't bother to conceal his sarcasm.

'See you tomorrow about eight then,' Anna mumbled, eager to escape.

She ran up the lane and burst into Molly's in a flurry of bad temper. 'She was watching out for me, waiting to drag me in, then bulldozing me into saying I'd take him somewhere tomorrow night,' she gabbled, her cheeks red with aggravation. 'I felt a proper fool.'

'Was he all for it?' Molly put Ronan in his pram and gave her attention to her irate friend. 'What's he like?'

'Hard to say, in answer to both your questions.' Anna gave a gusty sigh, relieved that she had Molly to confide in. 'He seemed pleasant enough, but the air between him and Rachel positively crackles. She was gushing like a waterspout and he was bristling with sarcasm.' She burst out laughing. 'Oh, what am I like, Molly? I'm getting all hot and bothered, and I've only myself to blame. I should have said no at the start.'

'But you didn't because you admire Rachel, and you don't want to let her down.'

Anna screwed her face. 'I did admire her. She's so elegant and in control of herself. Look at the way she dresses, all smooth and sleek and never a hair out of place. Not like the rest of us who only do that on special occasions, and don't care if people see us out of sorts. I rather fancied myself being like that one day, but now I'm not sure.' Anna's green eyes flashed with annoyance. 'I think she's a scheming, selfish woman who's using me for her own ends.'

'I told you she was a dark horse,' said Molly.

* * *

'I've agreed to go out on the town with Philip Dyson,' Anna told Mavis as she ate her dinner.

Mavis looked surprised. 'Whatever for?' Her face crumpled. 'What about Ross?'

Anna groaned. 'It isn't like that, Mavis. I couldn't care less about Philip Dyson, or he me if I judged him right. It's all his mother's doing. She bamboozled me into it.'

'Well, if you're sure you know what you're doing,' Mavis murmured anxiously.

'Oh, I know what I'm doing about Philip,' Anna replied firmly, 'but I'm at a complete loss to understand why Rachel Dyson thinks she can organise my life.'

Anna didn't dress up for her night out with Philip. She had no intentions of going to the Grafton. She'd suggest they went to the cinema. They had a choice: *Billy the Kid* or *How Green Was My Valley*. She'd let Philip choose.

He was ready and waiting when she knocked on the door. Rachel hovered at his shoulder, smiling and telling them to have a lovely evening. 'We will, Mother, if only to please you,' he said as he walked down the steps. He was wearing civvies, a dark blue shirt under a tweed jacket, and with his stocky frame and mousy brown hair, in no way did he resemble his mother. *He must take after his father*, Anna thought as they walked down the lane and out into Broad Green in silence.

'The tram stops over there,' Anna said, and before she could suggest that they go to the cinema, Philip stopped walking and said, 'You don't have to do this if you don't want.'

Caught off guard, and resigned to spending the evening with him, Anna was at a loss. He grinned. 'Look, I know you're only taking me on to please my mother, and I agreed because I'm doing exactly the same. I need to keep in her good books, but if there's somewhere else you'd rather be I'll take myself off to the pub for a couple of hours and when I go home I'll tell her what a wonderful evening we had.' He put his head to one side and gazed quizzically at Anna as he waited for her response.

Anna burst out laughing and Philip joined in. 'Are you telling me to get lost?' she said.

'No, I'm simply saying you don't have to kow-tow to Mother's wishes.'

'Why do you think she's so keen for us to get to know one another?' Anna bristled with curiosity.

'I haven't the foggiest.' Philip held his hands palms upward in bewilderment. The night air had turned even chillier and Anna shivered. 'Look, we can't stand here all night trying to understand the elusive Rachel Dyson's machinations; let's go to that pub on the corner.'

'Yes, let's,' said Anna. Her opinion of Philip was changing by the minute and she found herself liking his irreverent attitude. And she was intrigued. Why was Rachel dragging her into the prickly relationship she had with her son? What did she hope to gain?

The Weaver's Arms was warm and welcoming after the bitter coldness of Broad Green. They found seats by the roaring fire, and Philip went to the bar and ordered a pint of beer for himself and a port and lemon for Anna. Whilst he waited to be served, Anna mulled over the questions she wanted to ask. She had an idea that Philip would answer them honestly.

'Cheers,' he said, handing over the port and lemon and taking a swig of his pint before sitting facing her across the small table. 'This is more like it. It's far better to get acquainted in convivial surroundings.' Anna agreed and sipped her drink.

'Tell me about yourself,' she said.

'Not much to tell, really,' Philip replied easily, not at all fazed by her request. 'I suppose you already know we used to live in Carlisle.' Anna nodded. 'Well, after Dad died Rachel decided to come back to Liverpool and I joined the army. Cadet training, then when war broke out, I was singled out by Wosbees as officer material. I'll get made up soon,' he said proudly then softened his pride with a silly lopsided grin.

'What's Wosbees?' Anna asked, her brow furrowed.

'War Office Selection Board. They pick out the chaps who will lead their troops bravely and wisely into battle so that Jerry can finish them off with a sniper's bullet or a well-aimed hand grenade, or blow them to kingdom come with an MG42,' Philip told her dryly. When Anna frowned again, he explained, 'MG42, a massive shell capable of a lot of damage.' He gave a bitter snort and drank deeply from his pint glass. 'Another drink?' he asked, standing ready to go to the bar.

Anna mused on what he'd told her of his present life, but she wanted to know about his past... and Rachel's. That woman had really got to her.

When Philip sat down again with the refilled glasses she said, 'So after you lost your dad you left home?' She gave him a sympathetic smile in an attempt to draw him out.

'It was the best option,' he replied flatly. 'You see, Dad was a wonderful man.' Philip's brown eyes misted and he shrugged as he added, 'When I had him on my side, I managed to tolerate Mother's pernickety ways, her fussiness about doing everything exactly as she wanted, but once he'd gone...' Philip raised his eyes and shook his head.

Anna felt for him. 'Yes, I had noticed her liking for perfection,' she said, thinking of the way Rachel dressed, and the beautiful front room with all its splendid furnishings.

'Perfection's the word. Let's make everything perfect.' He shrugged again. 'You know the sort of things I mean. Don't do this, do that. Sit up straight, don't slouch. Wear this not that.' He began to laugh as he warmed to his theme. 'Get top marks in school, don't play with the rough boys, and don't get dirty and trail mud indoors.' He guffawed loudly. 'I was dizzy with rules, Anna.'

'That must have been hard for you. Growing up knowing that you didn't please her.'

Philip smiled wryly. 'Don't get me wrong. In her own way she loves me, but she's always tried to mould me into something I'm not. Dad saw it, and he understood when I deliberately misbehaved – that it was my way of fighting back, trying to be my own person. That didn't stop him siding with Rachel though. Dad worshipped her, put her on a pedestal. He worked himself to death trying to meet her demands. I, on the other hand, never matched up to them.'

'I know what you mean,' Anna said wholeheartedly. She went on to tell him about her adoptive parents. 'I always felt that I disappointed them, that I didn't give them the happiness that I should have, no matter how much I did for them.'

'God! We have more in common than I would ever have imagined,' Philip chortled. 'And to think I was prepared to dislike you.'

'That makes two of us,' Anna giggled. 'I was going to be coolly polite and ditch you at the first opportunity.' This set them off laughing again.

* * *

To Rachel's delight, Philip and Anna went out on two more occasions before he returned to Aldershot. Anna told him about Ross, and he told her about Sally, an ATS girl he was madly in love with. Neither Anna nor Philip was any the wiser as to why Rachel had wanted them to meet, or why their continued friendship seemed to make her so happy.

'Ross will be here this weekend. I can't wait to see him again,' Anna said to Philip on the last night of his leave as they arrived back in Weaver Street after a trip to the cinema. Outside Rachel's house she asked, 'When do you think you'll be back?'

'I can't say. We never know these days, do we? But...' Philip's eyes twinkled wickedly. 'I'll allow enough time for Rachel to erase my presence from her house so that she can smooth the rumples out of the cushions and sanitise the room I slept in.' They both laughed at this, and wishing one another all the best and saying they looked forward to their next meeting whenever that might be, they said goodnight.

As she walked up the lane, Anna noted not for the first time that he never referred to the house in Weaver Street as 'home' and that he often called his mother by her Christian name and never 'Mam'. She felt saddened by this; he was a lot like she *had* once been, a lost soul desperately wanting to be loved by the person they *thought* should love them.

But I don't feel like that any more, Anna thought as she mounted the steps to Mavis's door and 'home'. Coming to live here had changed all that. *Now I have my friends and allies, offering wise advice and warming me with genuine affection, and what's more I have Ross.* A thrill of excitement made her heart flutter; three more days and she'd be back in his arms where she belonged. He had ten days' embarkation leave, and she had managed to wangle five of those days to spend with him. Razor Sharp had been quite sympathetic.

'Well, how did it go tonight, love?' Mavis dropped her knitting and stood. 'I'll put the kettle on. You warm yourself at the fire then you can tell me all about it.'

Awareness of how much she had grown to love her kind landlady and living in Weaver Street wrapped round Anna like a blanket.

13

'How do I look?' Anna asked, giving a twirl for Molly and Lily to offer their opinion. She smoothed the skirt of the new green dress bought with the coupons she had saved specially for such an occasion. 'Do you think he'll still fancy me?'

'If he's coming all this way, he must,' said Lily, easing her swollen body into a chair at Molly's kitchen table.

'You look beautiful,' Molly said, admiring Anna's slender figure and her glossy auburn hair that hung in waves to her shoulders. 'That tailored dress suits you. Those little shoulder pads and that white V-neck collar are very smart.'

'I've forgotten what it's like to dress up and look glamorous,' Lily groused. 'I look like a barrel of lard in whatever I put on.' She was finding the last weeks of her pregnancy hard going, and wished that she could get it all over and done with.

'It won't be long now,' Molly said sympathetically. 'Come Christmas you'll be back to how you used to be, the gorgeous, glamorous Lily Stubbs that has all the fellas chasing after her.'

'You must be joking.' Lily wasn't appeased. 'Fellas don't want a woman with a kid, unless it's theirs,' she grumped.

'But you want it, Lily, and that's all that matters.' Anna didn't like to see Lily down in the dumps when she herself was floating on cloud nine.

'I know, I know,' Lily snapped irritably, 'it's just that I feel like I've been blown up and stuffed, and I'm crippled with wind. I could fart for Britain. The War Office could use me as a weapon against Jerry.' She laughed at her own discomfort and Anna and Molly joined in.

'What time are you going into the city to meet Ross?' Molly lifted Ronan from his pram then sitting him on her knee she began spooning a mush of bread soaked in warm milk and sprinkled with sugar into his greedy mouth.

'I'm not, he's coming here.' Her voice was high with surprise. 'I got a note yesterday telling me to sit tight, he'd pick me up at Mavis's.' Anna looked rather bemused.

'You've got a right gentleman there, Anna,' Lily said, her thoughts straying as they so often did to Eric. Although she dearly wanted her baby, there were nights when she cursed her missed opportunities.

'He is, and I'm lucky to have found him,' Anna agreed.

Lily raised her backside off the chair and let out a ripping fart. 'Sorry about that.' She didn't sound in the least penitent.

Amid gales of laughter, Anna said, 'On that sweet note, I'm off to keep an eye out for Ross.' Still laughing, she ran back to Mavis's, her fluttering stomach feeling as though it had been invaded by a swarm of butterflies.

In the early afternoon, Anna stood at the kitchen window watching and waiting for Ross to arrive. Her eyes widened in amazement when a rather shabby Austin 7 came to a halt outside the house, and Ross stepped out. She had been expecting him to arrive on foot. She flew to the door and opened it, bounding down the steps into his open arms.

'Surprised to see me travelling in such style?' he laughed as Anna's eyes strayed to the car. In answer to her 'Whose is it?' he told her he'd borrowed it from a friend of his father's, a retired miner who never used his petrol coupons. 'I did a deal with him, gave his daughter a parachute to make her wedding dress.' As he told her this, Anna was filled with an immense tenderness. She led him indoors, curious as to why he was in full uniform when he was on leave. 'It makes it much easier getting through army checkpoints,' he explained. 'I suggest you wear yours when we set off tomorrow.'

'Why? Where are we going?' Her excited cry made Ross laugh again.

'I'm taking you to meet my parents.'

'What!' Anna was startled to the roots of her hair. She had thought they would spend the four days together in Liverpool.

'They need to give their approval,' he said, his eyes twinkling mischievously. 'We'll stay here tonight then drive to Flockton tomorrow morning and spend a couple of days there. I want to show you Yorkshire in all its splendour. That's if you're up for it.'

'I wasn't expecting that,' she gasped. Ross's face fell. Seeing his disappointment, she quickly added, 'Not that I don't want to go. I'd love to meet your parents and see where you live.'

After a cup of tea and a sandwich, they walked up to the top of Weaver Street and down to the towpath. The air was crisp, and a brittle sun glimmered on the river's dark surface. The willows, stripped of their leaves, dangled black fronds in the water and moorhens careened gracefully. Hand in hand, Anna and Ross strolled along the riverbank talking easily. He was here, he was real, and he wanted her to meet his parents.

When they passed by the blue and white café, Anna told Ross about Kitty. 'She's a lovely brave woman who goes out of her way to be a friend to everyone,' she said, and went on to tell him about her friendship with Kitty's daughter, Molly.

Ross's heart warmed as he listened to Anna's tales about the people in Weaver Street. It gave him immense pleasure to know that she was happy living there, and it lessened the pain of having to be parted from her when he left for West Africa. He tried not to think about it. Pulling her into the shadow of an overhanging willow, he kissed her, his lips warm and tender. Then he rested his forehead against hers and gave a deep sigh of happiness. 'When I'm with you everything feels right and I don't want to be or go anywhere else,' he said.

Anna read his mind for in the back of hers she had been thinking of his imminent departure. Refusing to let it mar their happiness, she said, 'We have four whole days and nights ahead of us. Let's make the very best of them.'

'Oh, believe me we will,' Ross said, kissing her again.

When they retraced their steps, Anna suggested they go into the café for a cup of hot cocoa. The sun had gone down and she was feeling chilled, not only by the nippy wind but by the knowledge that time was flying, each moment precious.

Kitty greeted them. She had given Sheila the day off to tend to her sick mother. 'Anna darlin', good to see ye.' She came from behind the counter, her smile warm and welcoming. 'And this must be Ross.' She stuck out her hand. 'We've heard all about ye,' she said roguishly as he grasped her hand in his.

'Nothing bad, I hope,' he chuckled, his steely grey eyes crinkling at the corners in obvious amusement.

Kitty winked mischievously. 'That 'ud be tellin'. Now, what can I get ye?'

She brought three steaming mugs of cocoa to the table by the window and sat down with them. Ross liked her immediately. She asked him whereabouts in England he came from, and he asked her about Ireland and the café. As they chatted, Ross's dispiriting thoughts of leaving Anna in the city that wasn't hers, and with no real place to call home, were lightened. Mavis was an absolute dear, and if this woman, Kitty, was anything to go by, it was no wonder Anna felt at home amongst her friends and neighbours in Weaver Street.

When they arrived back at the house, Mavis had returned from the Adelphi where she had been making pastries, and Jack came to join them. After tea they played cards, Jack and Ross challenging the women to a game of rummy, and Mavis and Anna laughingly protesting when they thought the men were cheating. Anna felt utterly content. The game over, Mavis disappeared into the front room. On her return she whispered to Anna, 'I've lit the fire,' and in a louder voice she said, 'Now off you two go into the front room and leave me and Jack to listen to *ITMA*. We never miss Tommy Hanley. He makes us laugh,' she added for Ross's benefit as she gently shoved him towards the hall door, her beady eyes bright with thoughts of romance.

Cuddled in Ross's arms, Anna made a mental note to give Mavis extra money for the blazing coals in the grate – coal was an expensive and scarce commodity – and in between kisses she asked him about his parents and told him something about hers, the exchange bringing them closer as they explored each other's past.

Eventually, it was time for Ross to go with Jack to his house for the night. Up in her bedroom Anna lay with her eyes wide open contemplating the days ahead.

* * *

They left Weaver Street early the next morning, a watery sunshine and high white clouds with no threat of rain making driving conditions pleasurable. Anna's heart stepped up its pace as they left the bombed-out city streets behind and bowled along the road to Warrington then past the urban sprawl of Manchester, driving through soot-blackened towns with towering mills dominating the skyline until they reached Saddleworth Moor. Vast expanses of bracken and heather lined either side of the winding road, and Ross pulled into a lay-by so that Anna could admire the view. He plucked a sprig of purple heather and threaded it into the buttonhole of her blue greatcoat and kissed her.

'Something to remember me by,' he said, his grey eyes speaking a thousand words.

'As if I would forget,' Anna replied, her voice choked with emotion.

The sun was high in the sky as they drove over the Pennines and into Yorkshire, passing through sleepy little towns that on the surface appeared to be untouched by war, the rows of little stone houses and cottages and farms dotting the hillsides, basking peacefully in the wintry sunshine. 'Jerry mustn't know these places exist,' Anna said, her tone a mixture of bitterness and wonder.

'Too rural, nothing worth bombing,' Ross replied as the car topped a rise in the road. Again, miles and miles of moorland stretched out on either side of the road. In amongst the heather and bracken and the rocky escarpments, ragged sheep grazed the rough grass or wandered aimlessly along the verges. Ross slowed to let two elderly ewes on Anna's side of the car meander across the tarmac then slammed on his brakes when they changed their minds halfway and darted back on to the moor.

'Jeepers!' Anna jolted forward. 'That was close,' she gasped, her hands flying to her cheeks as she slid back into her seat.

'Are you all right?' Ross asked, concerned. When Anna said

she was, he laughed. 'Typical of the female sex,' he joked, nudging her with his elbow.

Laughing, she nudged him back. 'Hey, be careful what you say. I'll have you know I rarely change my mind when it's made up.'

'And have you made up your mind about me?' Ross asked as he slowed the car to a snail's pace behind a tractor and trailer loaded with silage.

Anna risked distracting him by leaning over and pecking his cheek. 'Definitely,' she said.

Ross smiled and picked up speed as the tractor rumbled into a muddy lane, leaving the long winding road clear.

'Almost there,' Ross said as he manoeuvred the Austin through the busy traffic in Huddersfield and then out again into rolling countryside and pretty little villages until finally, they arrived in Flockton. 'That's where my dad works.' He pointed to the blackened structure of the pithead winding gear in the distance. 'And this is my local, the George and Dragon,' he said as they drove past a public house, its Tudor frontage painted white and black.

'That's rather impressive,' said Anna, picturing him standing at the bar with his family and friends. She'd ask him to take her there.

'And here we are,' Ross said as he swung round a corner into a narrow side road. 'This is home.' He brought the car to a halt in front of a house in the middle of a short row of dwellings built from mellow York stone, each one sporting quaint porches and well-tended gardens. *This is where Ross grew into the wonderful man he is today*, she thought, gazing at the bright red door and the tangle of clematis creeping over the porch roof. Her heart softened as she imagined the young boy with tow-coloured hair and silvery grey eyes running in and out; it seemed such an ordinary setting for the man who was now a wing commander in His Majesty's forces. She had an idea that his parents must be awfully proud of him.

'Come on, let's see what they make of you.' Ross gave her his hand. Anna prayed that they would find her more than suitable. He pushed open the red door and shouted, 'I'm back, and see who I've brought with me.' Anna's worries immediately faded as Esme Penhaligon came, arms outstretched, ready to embrace her.

'Hello, Anna. We've heard so much about you I feel as though I know you already,' she said, hugging Anna to her ample bosom. Letting go, she stepped back and smiled appraisingly. 'And you're just as lovely as he said, isn't that right, Tam?'

Ross's father stepped forward and shook Anna's hand. 'That be so, Esme,' he said, his thick Devonian accent making Anna smile all the more.

'I only told you what was true,' said Ross, laughing.

Ross went to bring in their bags, and Anna was ushered to a chair by the roaring fire – no shortage of coal here in a mining village, she thought, as she sat down and held her hands to the blaze. As Esme and Tam asked about the journey from Liverpool, Anna took in the cosy living room-cum-kitchen with pine dressers, chintz armchairs and raftered ceiling and at the same time she assessed Ross's parents. Esme was plump and motherly but her heart-shaped face still held the beauty of her youth, and her bright blue eyes shone with a zest for living. Tam was lean and craggy, his knotty muscles and sinews letting Anna know that here was a man who toiled deep underground digging for coal that, like now, was warming her bones. The faint blueish scar on his right cheekbone where coal dust had penetrated some minor injury lent his handsome face a rakish image, and his steely grey eyes, tow-coloured hair and rangy physique were those that Ross had inherited.

During the next few days Anna was to discover that whilst Tam and Esme Penhaligon were so unalike in appearance they were as well-matched as the pair of pot Staffordshire dogs that sat either end of their mantelpiece. Their love and respect for one another and their mutual love for their son had made Ross the kind, uncomplicated loving man that he now was. More than once in her stay she found herself comparing Esme and Tam with Jane and Norman, and she envied Ross.

In her conversations with Esme, she learned more about his older brother, Jack, now living in Canada and married with two children, and his sister, Mary, now in the ATS and stationed down south whilst her husband was serving in the army in France. Esme's blue eyes had filled with tears as she spoke of the grandchildren she had never seen, and the daughter who was so far away. And now Ross was bound for far distant places as well. Anna's heart went out to her. She had created such a happy family and for one reason or another – wanderlust in Jack's case, and the rotten war in the other – she was being deprived of the children she so obviously loved. Anna did her best to offer what comfort she could, her heart aching, for all too soon she also would be bereft.

The three days passed by in an almost dreamlike state, and elated at simply being together, they went for long walks in the countryside well wrapped up against the frosty December weather or spent the evening in the George and Dragon, laughing and chatting with Ross's friends. They were lads he had gone to school with, most of them now coal miners – a reserved occupation that fuelled the war effort. They found it highly amusing that he was now a wing commander in the RAF.

'Ah, here comes Bomber Blue Boy,' a voice shouted on their first visit to the pub. A big, burly fellow making a loud droning noise hurtled towards them, arms outstretched. His broad hands, fingernails blackened with coal dust, clapped Ross's back. Laughing, Ross threw a friendly punch at the bearded jaw.

'Get back below ground, Ernie, you big hairy mole. Keep digging,' he retaliated, his grin wide as he fielded mock salutes and ribald comments about flying aeroplanes from his friends at the bar. Anna was introduced and she joined in the laughter at the risqué remarks asking how Ross had managed to attract such a beautiful girl.

'Why Bomber Blue Boy?' she asked when she got the chance. She wondered if it was a snide nickname because Ernie and his mates thought of Ross as Esme and Tam's blue-eyed boy.

She was glad when Ross said, 'The colour of my uniform. They howled the first time they saw me wearing it. I've been trying to live it down ever since.'

A few more hours in the company of Ross's friends let her know that they genuinely admired him, and that the camaraderie he shared with them was yet just another facet of his life that had shaped him into the lovely man he was.

The days and nights went by with terrible speed. As Anna lay in bed in the pretty little bedroom under the eaves and separated from Ross by only the thickness of a wall, she wanted time to stand still. And waking each morning to the sound of his voice, and Esme's motherly warmth made each day the most perfect she had ever known.

On the last afternoon, Ross asked his mother for the keys to Mary's cottage at the other end of the village. 'I'll go down and light a fire, keep the place aired,' he said, his neck reddening slightly as he gave his reason.

His mother's eyes twinkled wickedly. 'Aye, off you go and warm the place up,' she said, giving Anna an eye-rolling smile.

Mary's cottage was very much like her mother's, although the furnishings were more modern. Ross lit a fire in the grate and then joined Anna on the comfortable couch in front of it. The shadows lengthened as they kissed and cuddled, and Ross stood to light the lamps and draw the curtains. Anna wished that it was their home and that he wasn't going to West Africa. Cocooned behind drawn curtains that shut out the leaden sky and warmed by the rosy glow of the flickering fire and the softly gleaming lamplight, Anna felt safe and utterly content.

Ross didn't sit back down beside her, instead he clasped both her hands in his and gently raised her. Then folding her in his arms he lowered her until they were both lying on the thick soft hearthrug in front of the fire. She felt the length of his long, hard body pressed against hers and her blood tingled. For a while he kissed and caressed her, Anna revelling in his touch and the taste of his lips as he stroked her face and arms, bare below the sleeves of her blouse. Then he propped himself up on his elbow and gave a warm, half-sleepy smile that immediately made her aware of her skin under the layer of clothes.

'Can we?' he asked softly, his eyes meeting hers in a gaze so deep that she felt as though she was drowning. She nodded, her throat too constricted to even say 'yes'.

He knelt over her and slowly removed her blouse then her skirt and her underwear. She let him do it, taking pleasure in his admiration. When he stripped off his shirt and trousers, she admired his broad chest and taut abdomen, and when he covered her body with his own, she felt the rippling muscles in his back under her fingertips as their naked bodies conjoined.

She could tell that it wasn't the first time he had made love but she didn't care, and Ross's lovemaking was so different to Simon's that it unlocked delicious feelings that she had never before experienced. In fact, she mused afterwards, had she refused she might easily never have learnt the language of such pure and joyous love that in the end came so naturally.

They drifted into a light sleep wrapped in each other's arms, and when they wakened Ross gave her a slow sweet smile. 'No regrets?' he asked.

'None whatsoever,' she said dreamily.

* * *

The journey back to Liverpool the following day was miserable. Anna's tearful farewell to Esme's eager 'You will come again,' and Tam's 'Make sure you don't forget about my boy,' had left an ache in her heart that would not go away. Ross was silent for much of the time, and when he spoke it was with forced jocularity.

'I'm going to miss your snippy little moods,' he said, harking back to the night she had left him stranded on the Grafton's dance floor, and other occasions when she had disagreed with him.

'And I'll miss you, Wing Commander,' she said flippantly. 'I'll have no one to bully me into being sensible.' She was referring to the day he had taken her for a walk through the streets near Derby House and made her realise that it was wrong to take her disappointment with life out on other people. They both knew exactly what the other meant, and whilst they tried to laugh about it their hearts weren't in it, and they lapsed once again into silence.

After tea with Mavis and Jack, the older couple deliberately left them alone to make their final farewells. Standing in a close embrace in Mavis's hallway they spilled the thoughts uppermost in their hearts and minds.

'I love you, Anna Carswell. Promise you'll wait for me and marry me when I come back.'

'I'll wait forever if I have to, and I'd marry you tomorrow if I could.'

As they broke apart their brave smiles creased their woebegone faces. 'I love you. I love you,' they cried simultaneously as Ross plunged down the steps and into the car. Anna stood in the street waving until the car drove out of sight. He was gone, and all that she had left was to keep their love alive with letters and hopes and dreams.

14

'She's beautiful, Lily,' said Molly as she lifted the day-old baby from her crib and handed her to her mother.

'Yeah, she's dead gorgeous, isn't she? She looks like me, but there's a bit of Barry in her as well,' Lily replied and silently wished that she could have said that her daughter looked like Eric. She didn't have one regret about becoming a mother but she still yearned for her lost opportunity of spending her life with the only man she had ever truly loved. Cradling her daughter and dropping a kiss on her downy head, she wondered where Eric was now.

'Her hair's not as red as mine, thank God,' Lily continued, fondling the pale red-gold wisps on her daughter's scalp. 'It must be Barry's fair hair that's cooled it down, and she's got his nose an' all.' Her eyes filled with tears as she thought of poor, dead Barry. He'd never know he had a daughter. And his wife would never know, and neither would his son. Tangled thoughts played in Lily's head as she unbuttoned her nightdress and latched the baby onto her nipple. *I've made a right mullock of my own life*, she mused, *but I'll make sure that hers is as good as it can be.* The baby sucked ravenously.

Molly took a nappy from the pile on the dressing table. Like everything else Lily had bought for the baby, it was brand new and good quality. She had spared no expense where her baby was concerned. Molly laid the nappy on the bed then placed one of the soft cotton lawn nightdresses beside it. She was pleased to demonstrate the techniques she had learned from Kitty after her own baby was born and was keen to pass them on to Lily. To her mind, Maggie wasn't much use when it came to caring for babies. Kitty had told her the stories about how she had practically had to rear Lily when Maggie failed to cope.

Ronan was crawling at her feet and she lifted him to her knee as she sat down on a chair by the bed. 'What are you going to call her?' she asked.

'Catherine Erica,' Lily said, easing her daughter on to her other breast.

'Erica?' Molly couldn't hide her surprise.

'Yeah. I can't have him but I can give her a bit of him even if he's not her dad.'

'Catherine Erica Stubbs. It has a nice ring to it,' said Molly.

'It'd be nicer if it was Catherine Erica Kitson,' Lily said plaintively. 'I'd be over the moon if she was Eric's. As it is she'll have to make do with Stubbs, like it or lump it.'

'Don't dwell on what can't be, Lily. Just love her to the moon and back.'

* * *

Anna was missing Ross more than she had thought possible. Although their work had kept them apart for weeks on end they had, at least, been separated by miles in the same country not the

Atlantic Ocean that washed the shores of a different continent. The sight of his sloping handwriting on his first letter had reduced her to tears, and she kept the letter in the breast pocket of her tunic, next to her heart and near to the sprig of heather pinned on the underside of the lapel on her uniform jacket.

'Here, let me hold her while you get washed.' Anna held out her arms for Lily to put the wailing Cathy in. In her free time, to stop herself from moping, she had taken to dropping in on Lily, glad of the distraction and pleased to help out her friend.

'Any more word from Ross?' Lily asked as she climbed out of bed to go to the bathroom.

'Not yet. It's only been two weeks since he went and he must have written his first letter whilst he was still in England. I suppose by now he's in West Africa, and letters from there will probably take ages to get here.' Anna nuzzled the soft folds of Cathy's sweet-smelling neck to hide her misery.

'I won't be a tick,' said Lily, hurrying to the bathroom. Stripped of her nightie she sponged her tender, engorged breasts and the rest of her body. She dreaded the idea of germs. *But I survived, and there were plenty of them*, she thought, reflecting on Maggie's dirty kitchen and her grandmother Vi's fug of filthy cigarette smoke and clutter of messy make-up. She towelled her body roughly. But that was all in the past. Maggie's marriage to Stanley and her own maturity meant that the house was cleaner than it had ever been. Nothing but the best for Cathy.

Back in the bedroom she smiled fondly at her sleeping daughter and then at her new friend. She knew that Anna missed Ross dreadfully, but with luck on her side she'd get him back once the war was over. She had no hope of being reunited with Eric. Pigs would fly over Edge Hill before that happened.

'Thanks ever so,' she said, relieving Anna of the baby and putting her in her crib. 'It's grand having friends like you and

Molly to give me a hand. Me mam's no use, but then I never expected anything else. I just hope she turns out to be a better granny than she was a mother.' She climbed back into bed feeling fresh in her clean nightdress and comforted by having a friend to chat with.

'Your mam might not have been perfect,' Anna said, her thoughts straying to Esme who was the complete antitheses to Maggie, 'but she loves you, and that's what matters. Mine didn't even do that. Neither did Jane.'

Molly had told Lily all about Anna's adoptive parents and now Lily asked, 'Did you ever think about finding your real mam?'

Anna fastened her lower lip between her teeth and screwed up her eyes. 'Molly asked me that, and to be honest I didn't use to think about. But then I met Ross's lovely mum and it got me thinking about mine – not Jane – I mean my real mum.'

'If you know which bit of Liverpool you were born in, you could ask around there. Somebody might remember and be able to put you in touch with her.' Lily's green eyes gleamed at the notion of finding Anna's real mother.

'I have a birth certificate and an adoption one that might help,' said Anna, caught up in Lily's enthusiasm. 'I put them all in a big envelope when I packed up the house, but I've never had the heart to go through them.' Her own eyes were twinkling now at the thought of uncovering her roots.

'Where's the envelope?' Lily was all set to begin the search.

'With my things at Mavis's. There's not much else in it, just documents about the house and insurance stuff, I think.' Anna's shoulders slumped, her excitement fading.

'You should go through them tonight,' Lily urged, 'then we'll scour the Pool and find her.' She gave Anna a confident grin and clapped her hands as though the problem was already solved.

'It's only a week to Christmas. You might get a mam as a present.'

* * *

Less than a week later, on Anna's day off, she and Lily were glumly walking away from St Monica's Home, 30 Grove Street. Anna had done what Lily suggested and together they had carefully perused her birth certificate that gave them her mother's name and the address they had just visited, but Anna's request for information about Florence Rigby and the daughter she had given birth to on 3 February 1920 had been curtly refused. 'The child was adopted and our policy does not allow us to reveal information about the birth mother or the identity of the adoptive parents without their permission,' the ancient, sour-faced nun informed them.

'I don't need to know who the adoptive parents were,' Anna protested, 'I'm the child they adopted. I'm the child on this birth certificate and it's Florence Rigby I want to trace.'

'Then I can be of no further use to you.' The nun smiled benignly, and opening the door that led out to the pavement, she indicated that the interview was over. Anna and Lily looked at one another, defeated. They had both been expecting to be invited into an office and a search for documents to take place in answer to their enquiry. Instead, they had got no further than the lobby and were none the wiser. They began walking back the way they had come.

'Well, that was a complete bloody waste of time,' Lily grumbled. 'The snotty-nosed cow should be ashamed of herself. She hardly looked at your birth certificate.'

'I shouldn't have expected anything else,' Anna replied dismally. 'Hundreds of unmarried mothers must have given birth there and then just carried on with their lives after their babies were adopted. There's no reason why they should know my mother's whereabouts after all this time. I just hoped the nuns might have had an address for where she lived before ending up with them. That would have given us something to go on but...' She shrugged. 'It doesn't really matter. I've lived without her for twenty-one years, and it's not as if I need her. And she certainly mustn't have needed me. She didn't even bother to give me a name.'

Anna stopped walking and fished the birth certificate from her bag. 'Look!' She pointed to where the word 'girl Rigby' was written under the heading 'name of child' then at the insertion 'father unknown'. 'Not much to go on, is it?'

'No, but you know her name,' said Lily, unwilling to give up the search too easily. 'We could ask round to see if anybody knows any families called Rigby and if they ever had a daughter called Florence.'

'Don't bother your backside,' Anna scoffed. 'I'm not that interested.'

On Sunday afternoon Anna went for a walk on the towpath, consoled by memories of the walk she and Ross had taken only a few weeks before. She had still to receive a second letter from him although she had written three and addressed them to the RE (PS), the Royal Engineers Postal Section. The saying 'no news is good news' was no comfort today and she mooched along trying to take pleasure from cracking the ice that filmed the puddles, and making a mental note of where the holly berries were thickest so that she could come back nearer Christmas Day with a pair of snippers and gather sprigs to decorate the house.

She was walking back down Weaver Street when she met Rachel coming in the opposite direction. Rachel greeted her cheerily. 'I haven't seen you in an age,' she said. 'What have you been doing with yourself?'

'I had a few days' leave. I spent them in Yorkshire with Ross.' Anna hadn't spoken with Rachel since Philip's visit and was surprised when Rachel, chattering profusely about the chilly weather, linked her arm through hers and began walking back with her down Weaver Street and then up the back lane. Confused, Anna accompanied her to her gate wondering why Rachel had abandoned wherever it was she had been going.

'Do come in if you have a moment to spare.' Rachel tugged Anna's arm, urging her up the path to the house door. Anna wanted to refuse, but curious as to Rachel's intent she went in.

Rachel busily began making tea and asking about Anna's trip to Yorkshire. Anna told her that she had met Ross's parents and Rachel raised her eyebrows. 'As serious as that, is it?' she remarked then enquired if Anna had had any word from Philip and Anna said she hadn't. 'Neither have I,' Rachel replied tartly.

They sat by the fire with their tea, neither of them seeming to find anything to say until Rachel broke the uncomfortable silence. 'I've been writing my Christmas cards.' She gestured to a pile of cards and envelopes on the table. 'I'd send one to Philip if I knew where he was,' she said, giving Anna a quizzical look as though she suspected her of being dishonest when she had told her she hadn't received a letter from him telling her of his whereabouts.

Anna's patience was wearing thin. She was annoyed at having let Rachel chivvy her into the house when all she had wanted to do was spend the rest of her day off with Molly and Ronan, and maybe Lily and Cathy. The girls were often in one another's houses, and here she was listening to what, in her opinion was a decidedly odd woman prattling on about greetings cards.

'I like sending cards, particularly birthday cards,' Rachel continued. 'I choose them very carefully so they reflect what I want to say to the recipient.' She gave a strange little smile.

I'll bet you do, thought Anna irritably, reminded of Rachel's pernickety ways.

'When is *your* birthday, Anna?' Rachel's voice was high with curiosity and Anna was mystified as to why her reply should have such importance.

When she said, 'The third of February,' she was puzzled even more by Rachel's reaction.

A sharp intake of breath was followed by an enigmatic smile and half-whispered, 'Of course it is.' Rachel fluttered her eyes and shook her head.

'And yours?' Anna asked although she didn't really care to know.

'Oh, I don't do birthdays any more, dear. One doesn't like to think about growing old,' Rachel simpered then added, 'It's in July.'

This woman is as odd as ninepence, Anna thought and asked herself why she had once been so impressed by her. She supposed it was her elegant dress sense and self-assured manner that had initially claimed her admiration, but since then each meeting had only confirmed that she didn't particularly like or understand Rachel Dyson.

Anna drained her cup and got to her feet. 'Thanks for the tea, Rachel. I must be getting off. I've lots to do,' she said, feeling rather guilty at wanting to escape. Maybe the woman was simply lonely and clutched at any opportunity for company.

Rachel made no attempt to detain her and as Anna walked up to Molly's she mulled over what had just taken place. She couldn't make up her mind whether Rachel was indeed lonely – or completely stark raving bonkers. And the more she thought about it the more she was convinced that Rachel's odd behaviour was driven by ulterior motives. But she couldn't for the life of her think what the hell they were and why they should involve her.

15

Three days before Christmas Eve, Anna arrived home from Derby House to find she had received two pieces of mail. Her heart leapt as she recognised Ross's sloping handwriting and she brushed the flimsy blue envelope with her lips.

Mavis watched out of the corner of her eye as she dusted the mince pies that she had baked earlier with the precious icing sugar she had sneaked out of the Adelphi kitchen. *They'll never miss it, and I've earned it with all my years of service*, she consoled herself, feeling slightly disturbed by the petty theft. But it wouldn't be Christmas without mince pies.

'They look and smell delicious,' Anna said as she slipped off her overcoat and scarf. 'Where did you get the mince?'

'I concocted it out of Jack's apples, some old currants and plenty of cinnamon all mixed up with a drop of brandy that Jack found in his medicine cabinet,' Mavis said proudly. Then, nodding at the letters in Anna's hand, she added, 'They've put a smile on your face.'

'They have indeed,' said Anna, and curious to know what was in the stiff white envelope she opened it first.

The Christmas card from Esme and Tam had a picture of a pretty cottage on it, not unlike their own. The bright red door sported a holly wreath and the snow was thick on the porch roof and the garden path. A cheeky robin redbreast perched on the windowsill, and Anna wished with all her heart that she was back in Flockton with Ross by her side. Inside the card Esme had written how much they had enjoyed her visit, that they looked forward to the next, and were happy that Ross had found such a lovely girl. Tears sprang to Anna's eyes. She held out the card for Mavis to look at.

'Ooh, that's ever so nice,' she said, handing it back. 'Now look, love. You get upstairs and read your letter in private 'cos if you start crying it'll set me off and I'm all behind as it is. I haven't even christened what we're having for tea.'

Anna climbed the stairs thinking how kind and thoughtful Mavis was. She did want to read Ross's letter alone.

My Dearest Anna,

Oh, how I miss you. You'll never know how much. I'm so grateful for those last few days we spent together in Flockton. Lots of beautiful memories to look back on now we are so far apart. I've never been in love before but now I know what the poets that I always thought of as maudlin meant when they wrote about love. You make it all make sense although it doesn't stop me aching with longing to hear your voice and hold you in my arms. I love you, Anna Carswell.

Thank you, my darling, for your letters, and the beautiful wallet. How did you know I needed one? Better still is the gorgeous photograph of you. Was it taken when you were at Harwell? You were lovely then and you are even lovelier now. I posted your Christmas present separately so I hope you receive it before the day. In some ways it's not dissimilar to your gift for me. Great minds think alike, eh? They don't do Christmas here in Takoradi but the NAAFI will be putting on a dinner and entertainment. It's as hot as hell and sand gets into everything. I'm plodding about in baggy khaki shorts and a sweat-soaked vest for much of the time when I'm not flying. I'm not a pretty sight, I assure you. The sun's turning my skin brown and bleaching my hair. I'll be as blonde as Jean Harlow by the time I come home to you – and that can't come soon enough. At night we have to sleep under mosquito nets because the blighters are everywhere and their buzzing lulls me to sleep and then I dream of you.

I wish with all my heart that we could spend our first Christmas together but sadly that is not to be. However, don't let it prevent you from having a jolly good time. Do keep in touch with Mam and Dad now and then, and please, please, please keep writing to me and carry me in your heart as I carry you in mine.

Your ever loving, Ross.

He had filled the rest of the second page with clever little sketches of things they had done in New Brighton and Flockton: little figures running hand in hand on the beach or walking a country lane past a church, and sitting in the pub surrounded by friends. Each one was enclosed in a heart and they were so evocative that Anna's tears streamed down her cheeks. It was the most beautiful letter she had ever received and she knew she would treasure it all her life, come what may.

Anna was glad she had posted her last letter and the wallet she had bought at the sale of work in time for Ross to have already received it. She wondered what his gift for her would be. It seemed an age since she had bought the wallet and rescued the woman and children on that dreadful night of the bombing. Both had been impulsive actions. She had put the wallet in a drawer, too embarrassed to give it to Ross in case he thought she was reading too much into their relationship, that they were simply friends and nothing more. Now she knew different and the wallet had served its purpose.

* * *

'Jim Dobbs from across the road's home for Christmas,' Lily announced as she walked into Molly's kitchen with Cathy in her arms. 'Lucy's over the moon. She didn't know he was coming.'

'Lucky her,' Molly groused, clattering crockery into the sink. 'My poor husband's sweating it out in a desert millions of miles away and I'm freezing me socks off here afraid to light the fire in case I run out of coal before the next delivery.' She plunged a pan into the sink. Water slopped over the edges onto her apron, and Molly groaned. 'Christmas isn't the same without Mickey. In fact, nothing's the blooming same. Mr Stinking Hitler has a lot to answer for, and I hope his Christmas will be as miserable as mine – or his last.'

'Yeah, you're dead right, the rotten bugger,' Lily agreed and fished her cigarettes out of her smock pocket. 'Poor us, eh? I'm not expecting mine to be up to much either.' She settled Cathy in the corner of the armchair and put the cushions round her. 'Get the kettle on, kid,' she said to Molly, 'I'm dying for a cuppa and a fag.'

Molly couldn't help smiling. She lit the gas under the kettle. Lily's request took her back to the time when Maggie used to shuffle into what was then Kitty's kitchen and say the same thing. 'Hey, do you remember when your mam used to bring you round here on Christmas Day and we'd look at one another's presents and sometimes swap 'em?'

'Yeah, I swapped my girl's annual for your cut-out paper dolls and your mam went crackers 'cos she'd gone to a lot of bother getting 'em.'

'I always liked books best,' Molly said, feeling in a lighter mood. 'Here, hang on and I'll show you what I got from Mickey.' Molly darted out of the kitchen into the front room and returned with a beautifully crafted small brass leaf-shaped dish and a hand-painted headscarf patterned in red, green and gold. 'Aren't they lovely? He says he got them at a market in a place called Monrovia. He's dead sorry he won't be home for the Boxing Day party.'

Lily grinned. 'Yeah, come hell or high water, your mam'll have her Boxing Day party and sod Mr Hitler. She'll not let him spoil Christmas.'

Molly laughed. 'You've got to give her that. She never gives in. She's managed to get some dried fruit and she's baked two lovely cakes, but the tarts she made out of caramelised carrots are proper sickly.' Molly pulled a face. 'I'll be giving them a miss.' Ronan toddled on shaky legs over to the little cardboard tree she and Anna had decorated with cut-out white paper snowflakes and red and gold tinsel. 'Don't touch, darling, just look,' she warned as he plopped down in front of it. 'Now he's walking he's into everything but that'll keep him quiet while we have a cuppa.' She poured the boiling water on the leaves in the pot.

'Stanley got a rabbit for our Christmas dinner,' Lily said, 'and if me mam doesn't burn it to a cinder it'll make a nice change from spam.'

'Mavis and Jack are having rabbit, and me mam got two ox hearts,' said Molly, handing Lily her cup of tea. 'Anna's having hers at Derby House. Seeing as Ross's not here she's volunteered to do double shifts on Christmas Eve and Christmas Day to let the women with kiddies be at home. She's off on Boxing Day though, so she'll be at the party.'

Lily took a slug of her tea. 'God, I needed that!' She lit another cigarette and puffed contentedly. 'I love being a mam but it's harder bloody work than weaving khaki for Holroyd's.'

'You're making a smashing job of it, Lily. Your Cathy's a lucky girl. She's the best Christmas present you could ever ask for, and we'll make this one extra happy,' said Molly, lifting the baby and cuddling her.

Ronan looked away from the tree then toddled over to his mother, his bottom lip jutting. He raised his arm. 'My mammy,' he wailed. Molly and Lily burst out laughing.

* * *

Anna worked her double shifts on Christmas Eve and Christmas Day, pleased that she was letting other workers in Derby House enjoy the comforts of their own firesides. The canteen staff had done their best to bring some festive cheer into the long, bare room with a few streamers and sprigs of holly pinned around the serving hatch, and a bunch of mistletoe above the doorway into the canteen.

'Give us a kiss for Christmas,' said a young naval rating as he and Anna entered side by side. He puckered his lips and Anna obliged with a peck on his cheek. 'You missed the mark, Carswell,' he protested.

'I'm saving my kisses for someone special,' she said, laughing at his disappointment.

'And we all know who that is,' the rating said. 'How is Wing Commander Penhaligon?'

'Basking in the sunshine and eating sand in his dinner. Apparently, it gets everywhere,' Anna quipped. 'Other than that, he's fine.' She might have sounded cheerful but her heart ached for Ross.

When the postman had delivered Ross's gift to her the day before, she had clutched it to her lips, breathing in its exotic scent and imagining Ross handling it; it brought him closer. A note inside told her that he had watched the local women in a Takoradi market weaving the small folding writing case, beautifully woven in red, gold and green stripes. *Keep my letters in it along with the piece of my heart that I have placed there*, he had written. Anna's tears had smudged the ink.

At the end of her double shift, Anna hurried out of Derby House into the dark, empty Christmas Day streets. The night air was crisp, and a handful of stars twinkled in a purple sky. Anna made a wish on the brightest one as she walked briskly to the tram stop: *Please God keep Ross safe and send him back to me as soon as you can.* She didn't know how much danger there was in West Africa, and of course Ross had never mentioned it. She knew from what she had read in the newspapers that most of the fighting in Africa was in the north and she hoped that Ross's job didn't take him there, but she had no idea whether or not it did because everything had to be kept secret from the enemy. Thankfully, the Germans had lost interest in Liverpool and there had been no serious bombings for months. Now she hoped that Jerry was too busy celebrating what they called '*weihnachten*', or so she'd been told. She was looking forward to sleeping in her own bed rather than the bunk in the dormitory, and hearing how Mavis and Jack had spent the two days she had been away. She realised that she'd missed them and the company of her friends almost, but not quite, as much as she was missing Ross.

As the tram trundled along Edge Hill Lane, she recalled what Molly had said on the night they had been at the Grafton then travelled home together. *You'll find a family of sorts now you're living in Weaver Street.* Anna smiled fondly at the memory then settled more comfortably in her seat and closed her eyes. Molly's prediction had come true.

* * *

'There, that's me done for the night,' Kitty said as she hung the dishtowel over the oven door. Molly was putting the last of the plates they had used for dinner and tea into the cupboards. Molly and Ronan had spent Christmas Day with Kitty, John and Robert, and now father, son and grandson were ensconced in the parlour whilst mother and daughter cleared the kitchen. The outside door opened, and Lily sauntered in.

'I thought I'd pop over for a bit of a jangle. I've put Cathy down for the night, me mam's snoring her head off and Stanley's listening to some bloody awful music on the wireless.' She sat down at the table and took out her cigarettes. 'It was bad enough having to listen to the King's speech, him rambling on about the war and humming and hawing, and Stanley standing to attention and saluting like a regimental sergeant major,' she groused.

'Ah, now the King can't help his stammer, an' ye shouldn't make fun of Stanley. He's just bein' patriotic,' Kitty chided. 'Did ye get your dinner over rightly?'

'Me mam put too much salt in the rabbit, and me mouth's been as dry as a bone ever since. Apart from that it was all right.' Lily lit a cigarette then asked, 'Any chance of a cuppa?'

'Ours was just grand, wasn't it, Mam?' Molly said as she put the kettle on. 'I didn't think I'd like ox hearts but they were ever so tender.'

'That's 'cos I soused them all last night in a drop of stock an' let 'em sit while we were at midnight mass, talking of which, Father McLaughlin's holding special prayers all week for them that's lost loved ones to this damned war. Thank God we're not among 'em.' Kitty heaved a huge sigh and blessed herself.

'You can say that again,' Molly replied in a shaky voice.

'Yeah, dead right there,' Lily agreed and fleetingly thought of poor dead Barry's wife and their son.

'I'll leave you two to it,' Kitty said and went into the parlour where John and Robert were putting together a model toy car kit. At the sight of the two brown heads bent over the table, their faces creased in concentration as they glued and screwed the parts together, Kitty was suffused in a sudden rush of tenderness and going over to the table, she lightly dropped kisses on her husband and son's heads. 'Enjoying yourselves?' she asked.

'It's been a lovely day,' John replied, gazing up into her eyes, his own filled with love.

'Aye, it's been as good as it gets,' Kitty replied with a fond smile. And hopeful that tomorrow's party would be just as successful, she went over to where Ronan was sleeping on the settee, his long dark lashes feathering his rosy cheeks. As she watched her grandson's small chest rising and falling, she prayed that soon the war would be over and that her Patrick would come home safe and sound and that Mickey would come back to be with his wife and the son he had yet to hold.

* * *

In sheer defiance of Hitler and all the misery that war had brought, Kitty's Boxing Day party went with a swing. Everyone contributed something to eat, games were played and carols sung, but the absence of their loved ones put a damper on the celebrations for Anna, Molly and Rose.

'Just look at them two lovebirds,' Molly said as Kitty and John waltzed to the tune of 'White Christmas'.

'I never thought I'd hear myself say I was jealous of May, but she's got Bill, and while my Joey's at sea I envy her,' said Rose as her in-laws shuffled to the music.

'Even Mavis and Jack have got one another.' Molly nodded over to where the couple stood swaying dreamily. 'It's times like this that I miss Mickey most.'

'I agree,' said Anna. 'This should have been mine and Ross's first Christmas together and now we're thousands of miles apart.'

'Think yourself lucky you've got chaps even if they're not here,' Lily moaned. 'Me, I've got nobody.' She looked so woebegone the others couldn't help laughing.

'You'll get somebody someday,' Anna reassured her friend as the music ended and Maggie jigged into the middle of the floor, dragging Stanley with her and shouting, 'Robert, put Glenn Miller on. Me an' Stan are in the mood.' Robert changed the record on the gramophone and the four lonely young women got to their feet and danced with each other.

16

Nineteen forty-two dragged itself in on its heels and the winds of war were still blowing. Anna went back and forth to Derby House, her love for Ross and his for her kept alive by letters of endearment and news of Weaver Street on her part and West Africa on his bringing them closer together with each delivery. *I dream of holding you in my arms and feeling your lips on mine*, he wrote, and she answered, *With every passing day I pray that we will soon be together again so that I might show you how much I love you.*

For her birthday in February, he sent her an intricate little statue of an African man standing with a spear in his hand. *The spear is a symbol of the one that penetrated my heart the first time I set eyes on you, my darling Anna*, Ross had written in the card that came with it. She also received a card from Rachel. Of late, she had seen little of her and the hand-painted card of a baby in a cradle nestled in a bower of delicate flowers – most likely Rachel's own work – left her feeling rather bemused. Even more confusing was the odd little verse inside.

On a birthday cold and grey

My little seed was blown away
Oh, joy of joys in shining hour
A light has come into my bower
And on this happy, happy day
Bright is my beautiful, glowing flower

Absolute gobbledegook, thought Anna, as she'd read the verse and Rachel's florid signature. It left her feeling disturbed and embarrassed, and without showing the card to anyone she'd stuffed it in a drawer in her dressing table. What on earth did it mean? She'd made a point of thanking Rachel when she next saw her and came away feeling even more bewildered when Rachel had given her a searching look and said, 'You did understand the sentiments, didn't you, Anna?' Anna hadn't, but she had nodded before hurrying away. The less she had to do with Rachel Dyson, the better.

On the home front, the friends in Weaver Street pulled together to make life easier, but they still couldn't help moaning and grumbling about the impingements on their daily lives. 'Did you ever hear the likes of it?' Maggie groused when the 'Plimsoll line' on bath water was introduced. 'No more than two bloody inches deep in the tub. It barely covers my arse.'

'It'd take Lake Victoria to cover your arse you've put that much weight on,' Lily retorted as the women sat drinking tea in Kitty's kitchen.

Maggie reared up. 'It's not my fault. It's middle-aged spread,' she roared, 'and I can't do owt about that.'

'I never thought I'd live to hear the day ye thought of yourself as middle-aged, Maggie.' Kitty chuckled at her old friend's chagrin for she was well aware that Maggie was terrified of growing old.

'You're not really fat, Maggie, you're just pleasingly plump,' Anna volunteered, 'and I'm sure Stanley loves every inch of you.'

Appeased, Maggie gave her an agreeable smile.

Mavis, eager to follow Anna's example and pour oil on troubled waters asked, 'Is that a new lipstick, Lily? It's a striking colour.'

'Is it bloody hell. It's beetroot juice. You can't buy a cheap lipstick for love nor money.'

'Along with a lot of other things,' Beth concurred, pursing her lips in disapproval before adding, 'And have you seen how short skirts are now we have to conserve material? I'll stick to my old ones. I don't fancy showing so much leg.'

Molly, Anna and Lily giggled at the thought of prim and proper Beth flaunting her legs, and Kitty said, 'Aye. John was telling me that when a young chap who works for him at the factory went to get measured for his wedding suit, the tailor told him he'd been advised to make trousers without turn-ups.'

'That's nowt compared to being told you can only have a cardboard wedding cake,' Lily said, then went on to tell them that a girl from the mill had received this news from the baker.

And so, the weeks and months ran their course, the friends in Weaver Street accepting that this was what they had to contend with for the foreseeable future.

But it wasn't all doom and gloom.

'We're really showing Jerry what we're made of,' Robert crowed one evening in May as he sat at Kitty's kitchen table with the newspaper. 'Bomber Harris and his lot have blanket bombed Cologne and Dusseldorf. They've wiped out loads of factories making arms and bombs.' He pushed the newspaper over to John. 'Just read that, Dad.'

John, not long back from his own factory, scanned the front page and smiled. 'Where would we be without the RAF, eh?'

'We'd have our Patrick at home where he should be,' Kitty said stonily as she loaded three plates with shepherd's pie, 'and just ye wait. Jerry'll get his own back. This damned war is all tit-for-tat. There's nothing to be glad about.'

Sadly, Kitty was proved right. The Germans retaliated by bombing Exeter, Bath and York along with other cities and towns in an attempt to stamp out the best of British history and culture. There seemed to be no end to the events that were changing the face of the British people's beloved country, and when those changes occurred closer to home they caused quite a stir.

In the summer of 1941 Britain had signed an alliance with Russia and following on from that President Roosevelt had promised a stronger commitment to the allied forces. Now, under General Eisenhower's command of US forces in Europe, the military camp at Burtonwood on the outskirts of the city was overflowing with American soldiers.

'You can't walk down a street in Liverpool without bumping into gangs of the arrogant buggers in their posh uniforms chasing our lasses,' Stanley grumbled, his primary objection being that 'the Yanks' held the opinion that they were a superior force and that the British couldn't manage without them. And he wasn't the only one to voice his complaints about the way the war was turning out.

'I thought that when the Russians pushed the Germans back and beat them at every turn it'd put an end to all this killing,' Mavis moaned as she sat drinking tea with Kitty and Maggie, 'but now we know what they're doing to the Jews in Poland and Russia, and even in their own country, it's like the world is coming to an end.' She sniffed into her hanky then wiped her eyes, her face a mask of disbelief. Her eyes filled with tears and she shook her head, frustrated. 'I can't believe what's happening to the human race. Man's inhumanity to man 'as never been so evil.'

But it wasn't all doom and gloom. As Mavis lamented the situation in Europe, Leading Aircraftsman Mickey O'Malley, thousands of miles away on an airstrip in Monrovia, was waiting to board the Wellington that would fly him home to Molly. He grinned widely when he heard the shout, 'Ready for off,' and nicking his cigarette then putting the butt in his pocket he took the steps into the plane two at a time, barely able to believe his luck: three or four days and he'd be back where he belonged.

* * *

While Mickey was winging his way back to Molly, Anna and Lily were shopping in the city so that Lily could spend her wages from the mill on buying clothes for Cathy.

'She'll be the best dressed baby in Liverpool,' Anna commented as they took a short cut back to the tram stop in William Brown Street.

'You're dead right, kiddo. She might not have a dad but she'll have a wardrobe to die for,' Lily boasted as they made their way between the empty warehouses on either side of the narrow alley. They'd almost reached the end when three smartly uniformed American GIs rounded the corner. Their arms swinging and their voices loud, they broke step when they saw Anna and Lily.

'Hey, guys, look what we got here. Two pretty dames. Waddye say we have some fun.' One big and beefy, one short and ugly and the other tall and skinny, they crowded in on Anna and Lily, blocking their way, leering and whooping and breathing beery fumes into their faces. Anna glanced back down the alley. It was empty.

'Get out of our way and let us pass,' she snapped, pushing away a groping hand.

'Yeah, bugger off! We don't bother with drunks,' Lily snarled.

'Gee, we got two gutsy dames to play with,' said the short one, making a grab for Anna who pushed him off roughly. 'Aw, come on now, play nice. We got nylons and cigarettes for pretty girls who play ball.'

'Hey, Ginger, I bet you give a great blowjob.' Beefy pushed his face into Lily's, making slurping noises with his lips, and grabbed a handful of her long red hair. If there was one thing that made Lily mad it was being called ginger. She landed a hefty swipe across his leering face. Taken completely by surprise, the soldier reeled back. His expression turned ugly. 'So, you wanna play nasty, do you?' He bunched his fists.

'Hey, guys…' The skinny GI with a bad case of acne hung back.

Anna and Lily exchanged urgent glances. Anna's green eyes glinted like emeralds as she hissed, 'Combat training,' and yelling like a banshee and using the tactics she'd learned in self-defence at the training camp, she grabbed the raised arm of the GI who was threatening Lily and twisted it behind his back, at the same time delivering a few sharp kicks to his shins.

'Yaaay!' Lily screeched, and following Anna's example, she delivered a mighty clout that sent his short mate reeling. Skinny pleaded with them to stop but his brawnier mates sneered and bunching their fists, they moved in for the kill.

Anna's spirits sank only to be raised by the roar of a military police jeep screeching to a halt alongside. She hadn't heard it coming. An MP leapt from the jeep, wielding his baton and laughing. 'I'd say you guys picked on the wrong dames,' he chortled. Then, dropping the smile, he barked, 'You men, back to camp. Now!'

Like chastened schoolboys the soldiers boarded the jeep.

'Ma'am, are you okay?' the MP asked, giving Lily an admiring look as she combed her fingers through her tangled locks.

'Never better, thanks to her,' Lily crowed, her cheeks red as she nodded at Anna who was tucking her blouse back into her skirt and straightening her jacket. 'Somebody should have warned your boys you don't mess with a British WAAF.'

The MP turned his attention to Anna. 'Are you a member of the armed forces, ma'am?'

'AC2 WAAF Carswell serving with Western Approaches at Derby House,' she retorted.

A deep frown creased the MP's face. He stood to attention. 'Ma'am, on behalf of the United States Army, I offer you our sincere apologies.' Looking decidedly embarrassed he added, 'And perhaps you could be so kind as to not report the incident. They won't inconvenience you again, ladies.' Saluting smartly, he jumped back into his vehicle and it stormed off down the street.

'Oh my God!' Lily doubled up with laughter until Anna joined in.

'Aw, Anna, you should have seen that brute's face when you tackled him. I thought he was going to shit himself.'

'Proud to be of service, ma'am,' Anna mocked in an American accent and brushed the palms of her hands together. 'I'll admit I was a bit scared, but I think we showed them what for.'

'I nearly pissed myself.' Lily flapped her hands against her chest. 'We must be mad!' They looked one another up and down and Anna burst out laughing again.

'You can say that again. I'm not sure what would have happened though if the MP hadn't arrived when they did.'

'You'd most likely have killed him, kiddo,' chortled Lily, her voice thick with admiration. She pulled a face. 'Bloody Yanks. I'll steer clear of 'em from now on.'

'They can't all be bad,' Anna said as they set off walking.

'Yeah, you could be right. I suppose not all fellas are bad. There are some decent ones out there,' Lily said sagely, her thoughts dwelling on Eric. 'It's pigs like them Yanks and Simon bloody Whatshisname that'd put you off men for life.'

'I once thought that,' said Anna. 'Then I met Ross and you...' She paused and gave Lily a tender smile. 'And you met Eric. I'm sorry things didn't work out with him, Lily.'

'Yeah, so am I.' Lily's face crumpled. 'He was the one chap who loved me the way I want to be loved,' she said dreamily. Then reasserting her hard shell, she tucked her arm in Anna's and cheerily added, 'We make a good team, don't we, me and you?'

'You'd better believe it,' Anna said, wishing with all her heart that Lily had never met Barry at the Grafton, and that Cathy was Eric's baby.

* * *

In the garden at number eleven, Weaver Street, Molly was taking washing from the line. It had been a glorious late summer's day, not a cloud in the clear blue sky. Breathing in the fresh smell of the crisply dried sheets and pillowcases, she piled them into the clothes basket and skipped back indoors. She'd fold them and put them straight into the airing cupboard before Kitty brought Ronan back from his walk on the towpath. Her mother would be horrified; she insisted that everything should be ironed.

Molly glanced into the pram where Cathy was sleeping before she hurried upstairs. Lily was working part-time in the mill and Molly minded the little girl three days a week. At eight months old she was no bother, and Lily needed the money.

Mickey O'Malley leapt from the tram as soon as it slowed on Broad Green then ran full pelt up the lane, his heart almost bursting with love. Any minute now he would hold his son in his arms and be with his darling Molly again. The back door was open and he darted into the kitchen, hoping to find her there, but the kitchen was empty save for a rosy-cheeked baby with red hair asleep in a pram.

His heart plummeted. *God, no!* It couldn't be.

What had Molly been up to whilst he was away? He stared at Cathy, his heart pounding and he thought he might be sick. He'd heard tales about other chaps whose wives had strayed in the long years apart. Why, only last week a chap in his unit had received a letter from his wife telling him she'd got fed up of waiting for him and was moving in with the insurance man. Had his Molly found somebody else to fill the long lonely years? He felt his blood turn to ice as the sound of footsteps on the stairs mingled with his tortured thoughts.

'Mickey! Oh Mickey!' Molly's euphoric cries could have wakened the dead. She flung herself against his chest and twined her arms round his neck smothering his face with kisses. Mickey stood rigid, sneering bitterly. Then he gave the pram a hefty shove. It banged against the wall. Startled out of sleep, Cathy began to wail. Aghast, Molly let go of him, her tears of joy turning to sorrow as she cried, 'Mickey, what's the matter?'

His eyes black with anger, he turned them on the pram. Cathy was roaring by now. 'When did this happen, and who's the filthy bastard that fathered her?' Mickey shouted above the racket.

Molly felt faint. She stared at him, her expression a mixture of confusion and utter misery. Then, as she desperately gathered her wits she began to laugh hysterically, and hiccupping with relief she gasped, 'Oh, Mickey! She's not mine! She's Lily's.'

Mickey sagged visibly, and a dull redness suffused his cheeks. He hung his head, too ashamed to meet Molly's flashing blue eyes. How could he have thought...

Molly voiced his thoughts for him. 'Mickey O'Malley, how could you ever think I'd do something like that?' she raged.

Mickey pulled her into his arms and buried his face in her hair and she didn't resist. His tears dampened her ear and neck, and she felt his grief.

'God, Molly. I've been too long in the desert. It's driven me mad. I'm sorry, sweetheart, so sorry,' he sobbed. 'Forgive me, please. Let me go out and come in again.' Turning quickly from her, he dashed out of the door. Standing on the step, he berated himself for the fool he was. Wiping his face with his hands then tugging at his RAF tunic, he prepared to go in again.

In the kitchen, Molly wasted no time in cooling her anger. It had been a silly mistake, one which hurt but not one that couldn't be put right, and her Mickey was here for her to love and cherish, and she'd do just that. She brushed the tears from her eyes and smoothed her tangle of thick black curls ready to welcome him home.

When Kitty arrived back with Ronan, she found Molly and Mickey snuggled up on the couch, blissful smiles on their faces. Mickey leapt to his feet, his long dark lashes moistening as he looked at the little boy with black, curly hair and blue eyes so like his own. A choking sound escaped his throat. Ronan, still holding his grandmother's hand, gazed up at the tall, sunburned man in the blue uniform and Mickey fell to his knees and opened his arms. Solemnly, his son looked from his mother to his grandmother. 'He doesn't know who I am,' his father said brokenly. Molly's heart twisted in her chest. 'This is your daddy, Ronan. Say hello and give him a big kiss.'

'Dadda? My dadda?' Ronan stared at the wedding photograph on the mantelpiece. Was this man kneeling in front of him the same man his mammy was always telling him about? He turned his gaze on Mickey and his lips curved into a smile. 'My dadda come home,' he marvelled as Mickey caught him in a huge hug. 'Yes, son, your dadda's come home,' Mickey whooped, swinging

Ronan high in the air then clutching him to his chest again. Ronan giggled and said, 'Again.' His father obliged, and Kitty and Molly blew their noses and dried their tears.

'Did ye know he was coming?' Kitty asked as Molly made a pot of tea.

'I only knew meself three days ago,' Mickey answered for his wife. 'Our squadron leader has a bad bout of malaria and they picked me to accompany him back to Blighty. I left him in hospital in London and came straight up here.'

'Malaria?' Kitty shuddered and glanced at Ronan. 'It's not catching, is it?' Mickey's assurance that his squadron leader was no longer infectious but just very weak settled her mind and she sat down to drink her tea and ask a hundred questions about Africa.

Molly made no mention about Mickey's misunderstanding to Kitty but she did tell Lily and Anna. They thought it was hilarious, and Anna wondered if Ross would be having strange notions about her fidelity. Maybe, as Mickey had told Molly, the sand and the heat and the flies really did drive men crazy.

Molly and Mickey's idyllic reunion came to an end when the squadron leader was declared fit for duty and he and Mickey returned to the Gold Coast in the last week of October. 'My bed's half empty again,' Molly moaned to Lily and Anna.

'Mine's permanently empty and I've no hope of filling it,' Lily groused.

'So is mine,' Anna said, 'and until Ross comes back it'll stay that way.'

Just lately she had paid particular attention to the news about the North Africa campaign. Although Ross was stationed in the west, she knew that he made regular flights north. When Rommel's advance in the north was stopped at El Alamein and

General Montgomery's Eighth army overpowered the Axis Forces she felt sure it couldn't be long before Ross came home.

An entire year had gone by since she had waved goodbye to him, a year of keeping love alive with letters and hopes and dreams that one day soon this rotten war would be over.

She wasn't entirely unhappy. She had Mavis's motherly comforts and Molly and Lily's sincere friendship, and she was now an established member of the team in the ops room at Derby House, no longer afraid of not pulling her weight and honouring the good name of the RAF. She'd had no contact with Rachel during the past year other than to wish her the time of day whenever their paths crossed. There had been no further invitations to spend the evening together and for that Anna was glad. She couldn't say exactly why but she just didn't trust her.

17

'I need a night out. I haven't had one in ages,' Lily said to Anna and Molly one evening in as they huddled at Molly's fireside. 'Will you come to the Grafton with me? I want to let me hair down.'

'Look what happened to you the last time you went there. You let more than your hair down,' Molly replied tartly.

'I know but...' Lily's pleading softened Molly and Anna's hearts and they agreed to go at the weekend. When the time came, Molly dithered but persuaded by Kitty and Anna, she got ready. 'Mickey won't mind ye having a night out,' her mother told her, and Anna said she'd partner Molly if she felt uncomfortable dancing with a man.

The ornate ballroom was just as Anna remembered it, the music blaring and the dance floor crowded with whirling bodies. 'Table over there,' Lily yelled and scooted round the edge of the floor to an empty table. Anna and Molly followed and sat down. Only then did Anna realise that the empty table was at the side of the dance floor where the American troops had congregated and that the British servicemen were over at the other side. Anna wondered if she should point this out. Gossip in Derby House had it that there was no love lost between the British troops and the Americans, and Anna felt it would be tantamount to letting down their own men if they were to stay sitting there.

'Let's find somewhere else,' she said, pointing to the other side of the ballroom, but before Molly or Lily responded, Lily accepted a big, beefy GI's offer to dance and skipped away. 'We should be sitting with our lads, not the Yanks,' Anna said to Molly.

'Let's wait till Lily comes back then we'll move,' said Molly.

'May we join you, ladies?' A swarthy, pleasant-looking GI who looked about thirty and a blond, skinny much younger soldier hovered at the table, and hearing no refusal they sat down. Anna looked at Molly and raised her eyebrows as Lily came back on the arm of her sweaty red-faced partner and flopped down in a chair grinning happily.

'Hi there, Rod, you gonna join us?' The older GI indicated an empty chair.

'Don't mind if I do, Sarge,' Lily's partner drawled like a rough, tough cowboy in a film.

'Ladies, allow me to make the introductions. I'm Staff Sergeant Tony Morelli,' the dark-haired, older GI said, tapping his chest, 'and these guys are Corporals Buddy Haynes and Rod Garner.' Flaxen-haired Buddy blushed, and Rod thumped his barrel chest.

Anna and Molly sat like rabbits caught in the headlights of a fast-moving vehicle as they muttered their names but Lily took it all in her stride. When Tony asked, 'What are you pretty ladies drinking?' she replied, 'G and T for me.' Molly and Anna ordered lemonade. It seemed rude to refuse and Buddy went to the bar.

Over drinks they established that the GIs had been based in Burtonwood for almost two months, and Anna and Molly feeling slightly less uncomfortable – the older GI was affable and extremely polite – they took to the floor, dancing in turn with Tony, Buddy and Rod, each of them declaring in hushed tones that Rod's style of dancing was like tackling a wild bear.

'Tony's a terrific dancer, but Rod seems to think it's a wrestling match,' Anna panted as she came back to her seat. When Buddy asked her to dance again, she readily agreed, leaving Lily to dance with Rod and Molly with Tony.

Molly hesitated. 'I don't know how to do this one,' she said, her eyes on the dancers' energetic footwork as they rotated and swung out to the music.

'It's the Lindy Hop,' Tony said. 'Let me show you.' Despite feeling guilty about dancing with a man other than Mickey, Molly didn't refuse. They took to the floor, and with Tony's expert guidance, Molly found she was at last enjoying the evening. Breathless and invigorated, she was ready for more, but then the band changed the tempo and a slow, sinuous melody oozed into the ballroom. Tony pulled her closer as they danced to 'I'm in the Mood for Love'. Molly stiffened. She felt as though she was betraying Mickey. When Tony's lips brushed against her ear she leapt away as though she'd been stung.

'I shouldn't be here,' she cried, forcing her way through the dancers and rushing back to the table to collect her handbag.

Tony ran after her and caught her by the arm. 'Gee, Molly, I'm sorry.' His dark eyes begged her to listen to him.

'So am I,' she said brokenly. 'It's not right. I'm a married woman. It was just...'

'And I'm a married man,' Tony interjected. Gently, he persuaded her to sit down.

'Look, I've said I'm sorry. I guess I just got carried away. For one stupid minute I thought I was dancing with Della.' His face crumpled. 'That's my wife and the mother of my two kids. Gee, do

I miss them.' He looked so genuinely contrite and miserable that Molly forgave him.

'I know how you feel,' she said. 'I was remembering what my husband's arms felt like.'

They looked at one another and smiled sadly.

'Gee, we're a couple of lost souls so we are, Molly, but it doesn't mean we can't be friends.' He didn't wait for her response. 'Tell me, where is your husband and what do you call him?' His tone was warm with sincerity.

They sat the rest of the evening out, Tony showing her photographs of Della and two small boys, and Molly telling him about Mickey and their son, Ronan.

'This is one of Ronan at a week old,' she said, handing him a snap, 'and this is him now. Mickey went to Africa before he was born, and he's had just one leave since so he's only spent a few days of his life with him.' She sounded tearful.

'Oh, honey, that must be hard on the poor guy. I miss my boys, and I hate to think of them growing up without me. Giuseppe – we call him Gyp – starts school after the summer and I won't be there to take him, and Carmelo's just two. He'll have forgotten me when I get back.'

'This rotten war has a lot to answer for,' Molly said heatedly, her heart aching for Tony as much as for herself, Mickey and Ronan, and Della and the little boys. Then not wanting to dwell on it she asked, 'They're Italian names, aren't they?'

'Sure. I'm second-generation Italian.' Tony told her about his extended Italian family living in Fairfield, New Jersey and Molly responded by telling him about Kitty and John and Robert, and that Patrick was a Spitfire pilot. Tony was impressed. 'Those guys surely earn our respect. Me, I'm just bomber crew. I don't fly the plane.'

'You're still in danger though,' Molly said, reluctant to let him make little of himself. She'd warmed to him and thought he sounded like a real decent family man, not one of the men the girls joked about wanting to get into your knickers.

All the time they had been talking, the others had made several trips back to the table for refreshment. Anna felt safe dancing with Buddy. He was just a boy making the best of being away from his family and his college friends. Even so, she still felt like a traitor entertaining the Yanks. After Anna and Lily danced the last waltz all the girls went to the cloakroom to collect their coats and as they headed towards the exit door, Molly saw Tony pushing his way through the crowd towards her.

'I really appreciated your company tonight, Molly,' he said when he reached her side. 'I hope we meet again someday.'

'I enjoyed it as well. Best of luck, Tony, to you and Della and the boys.'

'Thanks, Molly. And the same to you and Mickey and Ronan.' They exchanged warm smiles and farewells.

'You two certainly found something to talk about,' Lily remarked as they made their way to the tram stop. Molly smiled. 'He's in the same boat as me and Anna, poor chap, only he's missing his wife and kids like we're missing Mickey and Ross.'

* * *

A few days later, Anna found herself in the same queue as Rachel at the tram stop. Anna boarded the tram first and was surprised but rather relieved when Rachel chose not to sit next her. When the tram arrived in Broad Green, Rachel scurried into the hardware store and Anna walked up the lane alone, blissfully ignorant of the fact that Rachel was, and had been for many months, deliberately avoiding her.

Rachel lingered in the hardware shop until she was sure the

path was clear then hurried home to her empty house. Leaving the lamps unlit, she sat down in the dark room. Seeing Anna always caused her to feel distressed, and Rachel detested not being in complete control of her emotions. She had been plagued by indecision ever since that fateful evening she had entertained Anna in her front room and it did not sit well with her.

Although Rachel was convinced the child she had given birth to in St Monica's House was Anna, she was still unsure that she wanted to reclaim her. Month upon month, her thoughts in turmoil, she had fluctuated between telling Anna what she believed to be true and letting the matter rest. Initially, she had hoped to forge a relationship whereby Anna would open up sufficiently for her to ask the questions that had since kept her awake on many nights, but the girl had been unforthcoming. Forcing her into a friendship with Philip had come to nothing, and sending the birthday card had been an error of judgement. She had laboured long and hard over the illustrations and the poetic message but clearly it had triggered nothing in Anna's mind. And now, on reflection, it was perhaps just as well.

In the immediate aftermath of giving birth to her daughter she had been relieved to learn of her adoption, but over the years, in her darkest moments, she had been tortured by misgivings. In a perfect world a mother cared for her child but she had all too readily abandoned hers. It had left her feeling flawed when all she had ever strived for was to be seen as faultless. George had understood and rescued her, and he had believed that when Philip was born her torment would be alleviated. But he could not see into her soul and the guilt that she carried. Suppressing her culpability had led to bouts of depression and a constant striving for perfection. It had driven George to despair and alienated Philip.

Now, faced with with accepting or disowning Anna, she

weighed up the pros and cons. The girl was pleasant, attractive and successful. *She might be thankful to find her birth mother. I would no longer be plagued with guilt. But what of my reputation? There would be gossip once the truth was out; those garrulous women who meet up in one another's houses would have a field day. Philip would have to be told. What would he make of my youthful indiscretion?* Rachel's head was beginning to ache and she stormed from the room and up to her bedroom, no nearer to reaching a solution to her problem.

I could be putting myself through all this for nothing, she thought, stripping off her clothes and crawling into bed. *She might not be my daughter at all. Short of demanding to see her birth certificate I have no proof.* On that unhappy note, she fell into a troubled sleep.

18

A hard frost had iced the puddles and a chill wind blew into Anna's face as she trudged down the lane to catch the tram that would take her to Derby House. Yesterday, the loss of several ships and men in a convoy on its way to Archangel had upset them all and as she mused on yet another Christmas without Ross, she was reminded of all the families that might never see their loved ones again. At least Ross was alive and reasonably safe in West Africa according to his last letter.

Kitty was standing at the sink behind her kitchen window, and Anna waved to her as she passed by. Kitty waved back. What a lovely girl Anna was, and how well she fitted into Weaver Street, Kitty thought, hurriedly drying her hands when she heard the telephone ring. Who could it be calling so early in the morning? John and Robert had just left for the factory so it couldn't be either of them. A sense of foreboding clutched at her heart.

'Hello, who's speaking?' Kitty heard the wobble in her voice.

'Mam, it's me.'

Kitty's knees buckled and she plopped into the chair by the telephone table.

'Patrick, oh, Patrick! Are ye back?' she cried. She'd lived for his phone calls when he was based in England but since he had been transferred to Malta there had been none, just a few postcards and a letter now and then.

'Yes, I'm back in Duxford. Is everything all right? You sound a bit strange.'

'Oh, never mind me, son. It being so early I didn't know what to expect,' she said, her heart rate slowing then overflowing with love for her firstborn. 'Are ye well?'

'Fine and dandy. What about everybody? Are they okay?'

After hearing the latest news from Weaver Street, Patrick said, 'Listen, Mam. I've got ten days' leave over Christmas. I'll be home on Christmas Eve. Is it all right if I bring a friend to stay?'

Kitty's heart thrilled. He was coming home. ''Course it is, love. I can't wait to see ye.'

'Me too. I just thought I'd let you know. Got to dash now, I'm on call. Hops on a wimpy and all that,' he jested. 'Give my love to everybody and most of all to you.' The line crackled and just before it went dead Kitty blurted, 'I love you, son.'

She sat still, clutching the telephone and tears streaming down her cheeks. Her beloved son was coming home. She couldn't wait to tell John.

The news that Patrick Conlon was coming on leave spread like wildfire and all the neighbours were delighted for Kitty. They all knew how much she missed him and worried about his safety; Spitfire pilots were in constant danger. His imminent return seemed to have knocked ten years off his mother, and her friends listened and watched with amusement as Kitty made preparations for his homecoming.

* * *

Mavis trotted up the lane, her lips pursed and her brow furrowed. She had been to one of her WVS meetings and had come away feeling thoroughly discombobulated. She'd joined the Women's Volunteer Service shortly after war broke out, but she hadn't attended meetings regularly. Now, she was wishing that she hadn't attended this one. At Kitty's gate she slowed her pace. She'd pop in and ask Kitty's opinion.

'Hello, Mavis. You're just in time for a cuppa.' Kitty gestured with the teapot she'd been about to set on the table.

'Hiya, Mavis.' Maggie flourished her cigarette.

When Mavis was settled with a cup of tea and a ginger biscuit in front of her, she offloaded her problem. 'You know Hetty Vickerman, her what's president of our WVS?' She looked from Kitty to Maggie and they nodded. 'Well, she's having two American soldiers for Christmas and she thinks we all should do the same.' Two pink spots flared on her cheeks, and her beady eyes anxiously sought her friends' opinions.

'Bloody hell! I hope they're tender. I don't think I could eat two Yanks,' Maggie hooted.

Mavis giggled. 'You daft ha'p'orth. I mean she's invited them for tea on Boxing Day, and she thinks we should all do the same. She says it'd be a nice way of thanking 'em for helping us out with the war.'

'I suppose it is a nice idea; after all, they are far from home an' it's times like Christmas when ye miss your family the most,' Kitty said.

'If I didn't have Stanley, I wouldn't mind entertaining a couple of Yanks, if you know what I mean,' Maggie said lewdly. 'I'd get me Christmas stockings filled in more ways than one. Just think, nylons, chocolates and them long American cigs.' She rolled her eyes.

'Maggie Pickersgill, will ye ever grow up?' Kitty expostulated.

'Ye'd think ye were a seventeen-year-old floozy instead of a respectable married woman in her forties.'

'Cheeky sod,' Maggie scoffed.

Mavis was well used to Kitty and Maggie's friendly and often crude banter, but it didn't help to solve her problem.

'Let's put Maggie's respectability aside for a moment and concentrate on what I should do. I let Hetty bully me into agreeing to have two of them on Boxing Day but what Jack'll say, I don't know.' Mavis looked quite flustered.

'He'll say over-sexed, over-paid and over here,' Maggie quipped. 'That's what Stanley says whenever they're mentioned.'

'I can understand people being narked by some of 'em 'cos they do have a bad reputation,' Kitty said thoughtfully, 'but it is the season of good will to all men an' I'd like to think that somebody would invite my Patrick to celebrate with them if he couldn't come home.' Her eyes misted at the thought of his imminent return. 'An' seeing how I always have a bit of a do on Boxing Day, an' my house is bigger than yours, Mavis, I'd say you should go along with Hetty's idea. Let 'em come here and celebrate with the rest of us.'

Relief shone from Mavis's face. 'Ta, Kitty. I knew you'd have an answer. You see, when I agreed I thought of Anna. She has no home to go to but here, and I'd hate to think that the only celebrating she would do was in Derby House. It's not the same as being with family.'

Kitty and Maggie agreed and over the next few days the three of them set about planning the Boxing Day party.

In between making the necessary preparations befitting the season the friends also celebrated Cathy's birthday with a tea party in Lily's house. It was a merry affair with buns and jelly and custard for the children and tea and sardine sandwiches for the grown-ups. 'Never let it be said that the folks in Weaver Street can't manage to put on a spread,' Kitty said, waving a magnanimous hand over the table to acknowledge that everyone had made a contribution then turning in her chair to smile fondly at Lily who, proud as punch, was watching her bonny little daughter play with Ronan and James on the rug in front of the fire, and thinking that her neighbours always managed to make things turn out right even if they'd got off to a bad start. Cathy might not have a dad, but she had a wealth of people who loved her.

During the days prior to Christmas Eve everyone in Weaver Street was gearing up for the festivities, but none more eagerly than Kitty and her family as they waited for Patrick to arrive from the airbase in Cambridgeshire. He was bringing a friend with him.

'His friend can have what used to be your room,' Kitty had told her daughter early in the week as she was helping her clean the house from top to bottom. 'No doubt it's just some lonely wee lad with nowhere else to spend Christmas,' Kitty had continued. 'Ye know how thoughtful our Patrick is when it comes to his mates.' Molly did. Her brother had inherited his mother's kind nature.

'The return of the number one illustrious son,' Molly had joked to Anna and Lily later that same night as they sat wrapping presents in Molly's house. But she was just as excited as her mother. Molly loved Patrick.

By late afternoon on Christmas Eve, Kitty was fidgeting in her neat and tidy kitchen unable to settle to anything. 'I can't believe a year and more has gone by since I last saw him,' she said to John as she polished the sink for the umpteenth time. It warmed John's heart to see Kitty so happy and he took her in his arms and waltzed her round the kitchen. Robert laughed out loud at the pair of them, but he too was just as excited. His half-brother Patrick was his hero.

Even Anna, in the kitchen at number fifteen was beginning to anticipate Patrick Conlon's homecoming because for all she had never met him, Mavis talked of little else. Anna knew every detail about the time Molly had succumbed to scarlet fever and she and Kitty had been quarantined for weeks in their house leaving Mavis to care for four-year-old Patrick in her own home. As Anna had listened she had, not for the first time, thought what a wonderful mother Mavis would have been if she had ever married. Now, as for the umpteenth time Mavis wondered out loud if Patrick had arrived, she voiced her curiosity.

'Why did you never marry Jack?' she asked as she put on her coat ready to go round to Molly's to spend Christmas Eve with her, Lily and their children.

Mavis's smile was poignant. 'He never asked me,' she said. 'We both have our own ways of going and we have a beautiful friendship. If something's not broke don't try to fix it. Now, you get off 'cos Jack'll be in any minute for the carol service on the BBC.'

Anna loved her all the more because it was Mavis's uncomplicated way of looking at things that were helping Anna to deal with the complications in her own life. After giving Mavis a peck on the cheek then slipping out of the back door, she ran the short distance to number eleven, the chill night air exhilarating.

'Has Patrick arrived?' she asked Molly as soon as she entered her kitchen.

'Oh, he's arrived all right, and you should have seen my mam's face when she saw his friend,' Molly chortled as she buttoned Ronan into his pyjamas. Lily joined in the laughter.

Anna looked bemused.

'There was my mam all ready to make some wee lonely lad

welcome,' Molly continued, 'and her eyes went out on stalks when she saw the friend was a cute, little blonde with an hourglass figure called Fionnuala.'

'A girl!' Anna gasped. 'Has Patrick never mentioned her in his letters?'

'His letters are just scribbled notes, and Paddy boy likes to keep things close to his chest,' his sister mocked.

'It's all right though,' said Lily, deliberately rolling her tongue as she added, 'Fi... onn... uala... scores nine out of ten in Kitty's book just for being from an Irish family – and she's a WAAF like you.'

'I'm looking forward to meeting her,' said Anna.

'An' I'm looking forward to meeting the Yanks,' Lily drawled, a speculative gleam in her eyes. 'Do you think they'll bring fags and chocolate, and maybe some nylons?'

'Aye, and when one of 'em instantly falls for you then whisks you off to America when the war's over don't come crying back to me,' Molly said, her sarcasm making them both burst out laughing.

'Poor Mavis is a bag of nerves as to what to do with them when they come for the party,' said Anna. 'She's as flustered as if it was Adolf himself.'

'Leave 'em to me,' said Lily. 'If they bring nylons and them long American ciggies, I'll make sure they have a good time, but staying sober doesn't half take the fun out of it.' She sipped her tea then puffed on her cigarette reflectively. 'Do you know, before I had Cathy I was always as sozzled as a fart on Christmas Eve, singing an' dancing an' behaving badly. Last Christmas I didn't touch a drop 'cos I didn't want to spoil me milk.'

'Aye well, don't be getting carried away with them Yanks or you might end up spoiling more than your milk,' Molly warned.

* * *

Late in the afternoon on Boxing Day, a military jeep came to a halt outside Mavis's front door and two American soldiers dressed smartly in full uniform climbed out. They each carried a brown cardboard box. 'You guys are to be collected at ten tonight,' the driver of the jeep called out. The older and shorter of the two GIs gave him the thumbs-up. 'Okay,' he called back.

Mavis was busily putting mince pies and small iced buns into tins to ferry them over to Kitty's for the party when she heard the knock. Ruffled, she glanced at Anna.

'I'll go,' Anna said, leaving aside the knife she had been using to spread potted meat on sandwiches. 'Will I put them in the parlour or bring them in here?'

'The parlour,' Mavis squeaked, rattling the tins one on top of the other.

Anna opened the front door, her eyes widening in amazement when she saw who was standing on the step. 'My goodness,' she exclaimed. 'I never imagined it would be you two.' Tony Morelli and Buddy Haynes grinned back at her. 'Come in, come in,' she said, still barely able to believe that the two Americans they had met at the Grafton were to be Mavis's guests at the Boxing Day party.

'Gee, is this a coincidence or what?' Tony's surprise equalled Anna's.

'Good to see you again, ma'am.' Buddy gave her a shy smile.

Forgetting all about Mavis's instruction to put them in the parlour, Anna led them through into the kitchen. 'Mavis, meet Tony and Buddy. Boys, this is Miss Mavis Robson, the lady who kindly invited you to celebrate with us.'

Mavis flushed to the roots of her hair. She wiped her hands on her apron ready to shake hands but Tony and Buddy were still holding the boxes so she let her hands fall to her side. 'Pleased to meet you, I'm sure,' she said, looking like a startled rabbit as her eyes silently asked why Anna hadn't shown them into the parlour.

'We can't thank you enough, ma'am, for letting us share your Christmas,' Tony said. 'Now where would you like us to put these?' He proffered his box.

'Put them on the table. What's in them? What have you brought us?' Anna excitedly eyed the boxes as the soldiers set them down.

'Just a few things we know you folks have been going short of this while back,' Tony said. 'We did a favour for a guy in the stores and in return he gave us the run of the place.'

Anna peeled back the tape securing one of the boxes and opened the lid. A large, juicy pink ham was nestled in a bed of paper napkins. 'Oh, Mavis! Look! Look what we've got.'

Anna's squeals made Tony and Buddy laugh.

Mavis peered into the box. 'Oh, in heaven's name, I haven't seen one of those outside a butcher's shop since before the war,' she declared, sniffing appreciatively. 'Wait till Jack sees this.' The second box contained everything that Lily had said she hoped they'd bring and Anna imagined her delight when she got her share of it; she knew that Mavis would spread the happiness.

Now the ice had been broken, Tony and Buddy sat down to cups of tea and Mavis's famous ginger biscuits. 'Did you smell the teapot?' she enquired tartly as Jack walked in. Introductions were made and after Anna had explained how she had met Tony and Buddy at the Grafton they sat swapping stories about their homes and families, and how they had celebrated Christmases before the war. Tony and Buddy were rather in awe of the veteran of the Great War, and they quizzed Jack about his experiences. As Jack regaled them with stories, Mavis fluttered round the GIs like a mother hen. Anna felt relieved for Mavis's sake that everything was going splendidly. She imagined Molly and Lily's surprise when they discovered who the American guests were, and she was pleased to think that just like it had for her, Weaver Street was working its magic on two soldiers who were far away from their loved ones at this special time of year.

After the tea and chatter, Mavis and Anna crossed the lane with Tony and Buddy at their heels, toting the ham and the goodies to Kitty's house. 'This is where we're holding the party,' Mavis informed them. 'Kitty and John Sykes are our very good friends, and their house is bigger than mine.'

John and Kitty gave the Americans a hearty welcome, and the boxes were handed over.

'Oh, sweet mother of Jesus,' Kitty exclaimed when she saw the contents. 'Look, John,' she urged, lifting the glistening ham from its wrappings and placing it on a large platter. 'Did ye ever see the likes of it?'

'Not since before the war,' John agreed. 'Thanks, lads. We really appreciate it.'

'Compliments of the US Army, sir,' Tony told him with a naughty wink and John grinned. He knew that the soldiers at Burtonwood were well catered for, and that neither the ham nor the chocolates, cigarettes and stockings would be missed. John led the soldiers into the parlour leaving Kitty, Mavis and Anna to put the finishing touches to the food on the long dining room table.

The large ham, now partially sliced, was at one end of the table and plates of sandwiches, mince pies, Christmas cake, carrot tarts and dishes of jelly and custard covered the rest. Kitty clapped her hands. 'Aw, isn't that just grand? A proper coming together with the best we can manage,' for Rose and May had made the jellies and some of the sandwiches, Mavis the mince pies, and Kitty and Beth the cakes and tarts.

* * *

Further down Weaver Street at number three, Rose Walker gave a final glance in the mirror and liked what she saw. She didn't get much opportunity these days to dress up, and wanting to look her best for the party she had put on a soft blue wool dress that showed off her slender figure and complemented her blue-grey eyes and long, blonde hair. The dress wasn't new, she'd bought it before the war and it was Joey's favourite. *You look like a princess but you're the queen of my heart*, he'd said the first time she'd worn it. Her eyes misted as she thought of her husband somewhere out at sea instead of being with her and their son James.

Brushing her hand over her eyes, she put on a brave smile and lifted James off the bed. 'Come on, darling. Let's go and collect Granny May and Grandpa Bill and go to Auntie Kitty's party.' James tucked his toy truck under one arm and toddled out of the bedroom. They were halfway down the stairs when they heard the back door open and footsteps in the kitchen. 'Oh, they must have beaten us to it,' said Rose, thinking it must be her in-laws. Holding James's free hand, she quickened her pace and hurried into the kitchen. She stopped dead in her tracks, her breath caught in her throat and James's squeals ringing in her ears.

Joey Walker embraced his wife with one arm and with the other he hoisted his little son to his shoulder. Rose felt the delightful tickle of his beard as he kissed her and she flung her arms about his neck and kissed him back. James clung to the lapel of his father's navy greatcoat and breathed in the smell of tobacco and the sea.

'Where did...? What...?' Rose's euphoria was such that she couldn't find the words.

Joey released his hold on her but kept James at his shoulder, his son fiddling with the gold strap on his dad's peaked cap then putting the cap on his own head.

Joey set his son down and James marched proudly round the room wearing the cap.

'She took a bit of a bashing and we had to come in for repairs,' Joey said casually, referring to the ship he commanded.

Rose blanched. 'You're not hurt, are you?' she gasped although it was quite obvious that the broad-chested, tall handsome man was perfectly hale and hearty.

'Five minor casualties that's all, and a bloody great hole to starboard,' he assured her with a grin. 'Couldn't have happened at a better time.' Rose breathed a sigh of relief.

Joey ran his eyes over her lovingly then enquired, 'And where are you off to, dressed to kill and looking gorgeous?'

Rose blushed prettily. 'Kitty's party. Mavis let the WVS chivvy her into entertaining two Americans so we're going over there for the evening.'

Joey raised his eyebrows. 'It seems I arrived just in time. I can't have damned Yankees sniffing round my beautiful wife.'

Rose knew he spoke in jest and casting her eyes to the ceiling she whispered, 'I know what I'd rather do than go to a party.'

Joey laughed. 'My thoughts exactly. We'll save it for later.'

* * *

The party was in full swing, everyone eating, laughing, singing and dancing like old times. Robert had wondered if boys of sixteen were destined to feel lonely and left out at Christmas. He was too old for Santa Claus and too young for drinking and dancing, and he'd been prepared to be bored to death. However, he found himself enjoying it immensely once he fell into conversation with Buddy who was only two years older. Tony had found a ready listener in May and was showing her photographs of his family. Bill had left earlier to babysit James.

'I'm glad I invited them. They're lovely young men,' Mavis declared rather proudly, gesturing at what she now thought of as 'her Yanks'.

'You're glad? We all are.' Lily patted her handbag stuffed with nylons and cigarettes.

After they had all partaken of the food, John put one record after another on the gramophone and Anna, Lily and Molly took turns to dance with Tony to 'I'll Be Seeing You', 'White Christmas' and 'Somewhere Over the Rainbow', Anna thinking of Ross, Molly of Mickey and Lily's mind on Eric.

Rose and Joey had eyes only for each other, as did Patrick and Fionnuala. However, Patrick did give his mother a whirl round the room much to her delight. Stuart, like the biddable son he was, danced with his mother, Beth, much to Robert's amusement. He couldn't help smirking, glad that his own mother had his dad for a partner. Even Mavis and Jack and Maggie and Stanley took to the floor. Kitty's heart swelled. It was grand to see everyone having a good time after so much hardship and suffering.

'I did invite Rachel, but she must have thought better of it,' Kitty told Anna as she helped her replenish the drinks.

'I don't think anybody missed her. She's as odd as ninepence.'

'Ye can say that again, but when everybody else's here ye'd think she'd want to join in.' She patted Anna's arm consolingly before saying, 'It's sad that Mickey and Ross aren't here, but maybe this time next year, eh?'

'Oh, yes please, let's hope they come back long before next Christmas.'

As the party drew to a close, they all lustily joined in with 'We're Going to Hang Out the Washing on the Siegfried Line' before finishing off with a round of carols. As everyone was preparing to leave there were plenty of hugs and thanks, and cries of 'Merry Christmas' rang in the crisp night air when Tony and Buddy went to await their jeep back to Burtonwood. In indecent haste, Rose and Joey scampered across the lane to their own house and up to their bedroom, and the others wended homewards all declaring that the party had been as merry as they could have wished for, that Americans weren't all obnoxious, and that for a few short hours they had laughed, sang and danced and forgot that the country was still at war.

* * *

Over the rest of the festive season the fun was high. Kitty floated on a cloud of pure happiness now that she had her eldest son back where he belonged, and Anna did her shifts in Derby House then came home each night ready for another enjoyable evening. She got on with Fionnuala like a house on fire, swapping tit-bits about their jobs and commiserating over having to keep their love affairs alive through letters.

'My heart was in my mouth every day that Patrick was in Malta,' Fionnuala confided, and whilst Anna said she couldn't claim that Ross's job was as dangerous as Patrick's – reassembling aircraft in Takoradi where there was no fighting sounded much safer than flying a Spitfire – she said she felt the same because he was so far away and she didn't really know how good or bad things were on the Gold Coast. 'I just hope they send him back next year, safe and sound,' she said, showing Fionnuala the pretty shell bracelet that was Ross's Christmas gift to her.

She also got on well with Patrick, a lovely uncomplicated man at ease in his own skin. He reminded her of Ross and there were moments when her heart ached with loneliness and more than a touch of envy whenever she was in Patrick and Fionnuala's company. As the church bells rang out the old year and welcomed in 1943, all the friends and neighbours shared their hopes that the war would soon be over.

There were tears on New Year's Day as Kitty and John and Molly and Robert said goodbye to Patrick and Fionnuala. 'Thanks for making her so welcome, Mam. I'm glad you like her 'cos if nothing goes wrong, she's going to be your daughter-in-law.'

If nothing goes wrong. Kitty's heart missed a beat. Then smiling bravely and hugging Patrick in a fierce embrace, she said, 'I'm pleased for ye son. She's a lovely girl an' I wish ye both all the happiness in the world.'

* * *

Winter days were dark and gloomy, snow fell then turned to slush, making the pavements treacherous and journeys to work or to the shops to stand in long queues all the more unpleasant. There had been no further air raids on the city for almost a year but this did little to lighten people's hearts.

'Ne'er mind, if winter's here spring can't be far behind,' Mavis chirped as she and the friends spent a Sunday afternoon doing yet another session of mend and make do in Kitty's dining room. By now they were all inured to the shortages of food and new clothes and the fear of the air raids starting up again, but somehow life went on and people did their best to keep their spirits up.

Molly waited impatiently each week for Mickey's letters, and every time they played 'We'll Meet Again' on the wireless she prayed that it would be true. In the meantime, she took great delight in seeing Ronan grow into a sturdy little boy who learned something new every day. She reported all this in her letters to Mickey along with the photographs she sent so that they might lessen the disappointment he felt at missing seeing Ronan's progress at first hand. General Montgomery's successes in North Africa against the Germans had her living in hope that her husband would soon be sent back to England.

Lily also took great pride in rearing her daughter. Now a delightful toddler Cathy was the darling of the house and Maggie and Stan doted on her. Lily still often thought of Eric and what might have been, so much so that she had no interest in finding anybody to take his place. She was quite content to spend her nights out with Molly and Anna at the pictures laughing at films like *Yankee Doodle Dandy* and *Road to Morocco* or crying over Rick's lost love in *Casablanca*.

Anna and Ross kept their romance alive with loving, newsy letters. However, Ross made no mention of the rumour that was flying round the camp on the Gold Coast; his squadron was to be transferred back to Britain in the spring of 1944. Had Anna known this she would have been over the moon and wishing for the months to pass like greased lightning. Instead, she concentrated on her job in Derby House, grieving for the loss of British ships and aircraft and cheering grimly in May when Barnes Wallis's bouncing bombs destroyed the Möhne and Eder dams, wreaking havoc and destruction to the German factories making weapons of war.

The Dambusters, as the brave pilots who flew in what was called Operation Chastise, became the focus of Robert's imagination and he reported daily to Kitty the successes the RAF and the Allied Forces were having. It gave them both hope.

Along with growing vegetables and keeping chickens, going

out to their various places of work, and running their homes, Kitty and her friends found that the time passed quickly enough. They took advantage of a few days in summer to make day trips to New Brighton and before they knew it another Christmas was on the doorstep begging to be celebrated: 1943 had run its course.

19

SPRING 1944

Anna alighted from the tram on Broad Green and pulling up the collar of her greatcoat against the driving rain, she walked briskly towards home. March was proving to be both wet and windy. At the end of the back lane, she saw Rachel hurrying ahead of her trying to avoid the puddles on heels too high to cope with the muddy ground. She was almost at her gate when she misjudged her stride and fell. Anna gasped and quickened her pace.

'Oh, Rachel! Let me help you,' she cried. Standing astride the unfortunate woman sprawled face down in the mud, and putting her hands under Rachel's armpits, Anna hauled her upright. Rachel's fine woollen coat was covered with slime, and her face was puce with annoyance and embarrassment as Anna helped her into the house.

Mortified at being seen in such a mess, Rachel blurted, 'I'd better go and clean myself up.' She darted from the kitchen up to the bathroom. Anna didn't know whether she should go or stay, and decided on the latter to ensure that Rachel wasn't hurt. She perched on the edge of a chair by the hearth. On a small table next to it was a pile of books and as Anna waited for Rachel to return, she picked up the topmost book.

Its embossed cover stated that it was a collection of poetry and idly, Anna flipped it open. There was an inscription on the flyleaf:

> *To my dear daughter Florence Rigby on her seventeenth birthday, 9 July 1919 from her loving father Isaac Rigby.*

Anna began to tremble as she read the fine italic script again, and again. Then she stared at the bold black words, juggling the names and the date in her fevered brain. This was her mother's name. And the date seemed about right. Her birth mother could have been that age in 1919. But why did Rachel Dyson have the book? Feeling decidedly hot and bothered, Anna fumbled for an answer. Maybe Rachel had picked it up in a second-hand bookshop, or perhaps she had known Florence Rigby. Her thoughts swirling, Anna was still clutching the book when Rachel entered the kitchen. Spying the book in Anna's hand, she trilled, 'Ah, I see you're a poetry lover like me.'

Lost for words, and feeling as though she was holding a red-hot cinder, Anna placed the book back on the table and gaped at Rachel. Then, gathering her wits, she mumbled, 'Who's Florence Rigby?' The floor seemed to shift under her feet as she waited for an answer.

'That's me – or was,' Rachel said softly, her calculating stare judging Anna's reaction. Did she know the name of her birth mother? Anna stared back but her face gave nothing away. Rachel's emotions seesawed between disappointment and relief but she maintained her cool calm demeanour and instantly made a decision.

She forced a little chuckle then said, 'My parents named me

Florence but my late husband always called me Rachel because we met at a place called The Wishing Well. It was George's little joke, you know, Rachel at the well in the Bible story.'

Anna didn't want to hear any more. Curtly refusing Rachel's offer of tea, she hurried from the house and hared up the lane, thoughts bouncing inside her head. *Is that woman my mother? No! There's bound to be more than one Florence Rigby. But I look like her, and she said I reminded her of when she was young.* By the time she entered Mavis's kitchen, Anna's head was spinning. Making a hasty excuse that she needed the lavatory, she rushed upstairs to her room and flopped on the bed, clutching her head in her hands. She didn't particularly like Rachel, and she wasn't sure she wanted this strange woman to be her mother.

Minutes ticked by as, trawling her mind, she tried to make sense of the implications: the peculiar interest Rachel had initially shown in Anna's past, her insistence that Anna should meet Philip, and the way she had ferreted for other details such as Anna's birth date. Anna got to her feet and scrabbled in the dressing table drawer for the birthday card Rachel had sent. She found it underneath her scarves and handkerchiefs. This time she carefully perused the card. Rachel had asked her had she understood the meaning of the illustration and verse, and Anna had lied and said yes though she'd dismissed it with barely a glance. Was the illustration of the baby and the poetic mush about the lost seed meant to be her, Anna, and was the bit about the bower referring to the time Rachel had invited her into the lavish front room? She groaned out loud.

'Your tea's ready,' Mavis called from the foot of the stairs.

'Coming,' Anna called back, and taking off her greatcoat that she was still wearing then brushing her hair, she thought of the way Rachel had almost ignored her for the past year. And why hadn't she told Anna that she thought she might be her mother?

Surely that meant that Anna was letting her imagination run riot. Whatever, she certainly wasn't going to mention what she had discovered on the flyleaf in the book or the suspicions it had aroused to anyone. She'd let sleeping dogs lie.

Although uncomfortable thoughts plagued her waking hours, they completely escaped Anna's mind when a few days later she received a letter from Ross. His squadron was being transferred from the Gold Coast back to England.

Her screams of delight resounded in Mavis's kitchen followed by tears of joy as she read that he would be returning before the end of the month. Mavis too was delighted and took Anna's hands in both her own and jigged her round the kitchen.

Molly was pleased for Anna, if not a little envious. Why couldn't it be Mickey coming home? It took only a matter of days for her jealousy to turn to rejoicing when she learned that Mickey's squadron was also returning to Britain. After that, Molly and Anna talked of little else and made endless preparations for when they would be united with the men they loved.

Ross arrived first to a rapturous welcome from Anna. Tanned by an African sun, he looked twice as handsome, and Anna fell in love with him all over again. Mickey came two days later and for one glorious week the two young couples made the most of their time together. They picnicked in the Botanic Gardens, took the ferry to New Brighton and played on the sands then came home to sit long into the evenings catching up with news of how they spent their time apart.

Mickey was thrilled that this time his son remembered him, and Molly was made up as she watched them play together. Ronan, no longer confused by a strange man in their house, enjoyed having his daddy back where he belonged.

Anna and Ross spent several undisturbed and magical evenings sealing their love in Mavis's front room, each one just as wonderful as the one before and afterwards as they talked Anna deliberated over the wisdom of telling Ross about Rachel; she desperately needed to confide her suspicions in somebody she could trust, and he was that person. When she told him what she had discovered, Ross was concerned by her obvious distress. Wanting to alleviate it, he said that there could be several women called Florence Rigby, and that Anna was perhaps making too much of her likeness to Rachel; it could simply be a coincidence. He advised her to wait and let Rachel make the first move. Once again, Anna tried to dispel the worrisome thoughts so as not to spoil being with Ross.

'Something big's coming up,' said Ross on the last night of his leave as they sat in Molly's house drinking beer and playing cards. 'We haven't been told what, but we've been warned it will be all hands to the pump when we return to base.'

Mickey had heard the same story. 'We're back here to support whatever it is and though it's all hush-hush, the rumour is it could put an end to the war.'

Anna and Molly both chorused that they hoped that was true.

The next day, having to say goodbye again to their men was heart-breaking and the worry of what 'something big' might mean for Ross and Mickey left them grateful for the time they had shared but anxious about what the future might bring.

* * *

In Derby House, Anna kept a close ear and eye on the activities that suggested something important was about to happen. Of late, the threat of German U-boats to the convoys in the North Atlantic had diminished, much to the ops team's relief, and whenever Anna was deployed to work on the Aircraft State Board that showed the present situation of all RAF stations and the ongoing operations it made her feel closer to Ross, him being a flyer.

Top brass from the Royal Navy, the Allied Forces and the RAF came and went and by the end of May, Anna knew what Ross's mention of 'something big' was all about.

Of course, she couldn't tell anyone, not even Molly, but her fears for Ross, and Mickey, and Joey Walker's safety mounted by the day. Although she didn't yet know the exact detail of the operation in progress, she understood that it was of the utmost importance. Getting to grips with the manning of the complexities of the Aircraft State Board took all Anna's time and attention and that, along with the tense situation in the ops room, made her worries about Rachel fade into insignificance.

Come the first week in June, all personnel in Derby House had been ordered to stay on duty day and night and Anna was missing her comfortable bed in Mavis's back room. Her bunk was hard, her sleep restless, and her hours on duty fraught with nerves.

The 'something big' had begun.

For the past few weeks RAF Bomber Command had been attacking road and rail links to the battle areas, and Anna now knew for certain that Ross's squadron was involved in the operation. As she monitored the Aircraft State Board she prayed, then sagged with relief when at the end of each sortie his squadron reported that all their aircraft had returned safely to base.

On 5 June 1944, Anna climbed out of her bunk in Derby House feeling like a tightly strung violin. Today was the launch of Operation Overlord, or D-Day as they were calling it. When she entered the ops room shortly after dawn, she was immediately aware of the tense situation. The air was thick with cigarette smoke and human sweat, the cloying stink exacerbating the tension as she relieved her co-worker on the Aircraft State Board.

'It's been one hell of a night, and it's gonna be one hell of a day,' the WAAF muttered as she staggered off to get some sleep.

During the previous evening the weather had worsened. The Met Office had reported dense cloud cover over Northern France and rising winds which would seriously hamper the operation. The Air Operation required clear skies and a full moon for good visibility, and the Navy needed low winds and calm seas to safely transport the troops ashore. With the forecast being what it was, things were hanging in the balance.

Anna took up her position on the board and along with the senior officers, Wrens and WAAFs, she waited for orders from High Command. Teleprinters rattled in the room next door and in the ops room the atmosphere was electric. Anna could feel the hairs on the back of her neck standing to attention as she monitored the activity of RAF stations throughout the country.

Eventually word came that High Command had made the decision to delay D-Day until the weather improved. The sudden anticlimax left many in the ops room feeling cheated, and Anna couldn't decide whether she felt relieved or disappointed. She wondered if Ross and his crew now at RAF Bisterne were feeling the same. Along with the rest of the team she resumed her normal duties for the rest of the day, all waiting with bated breath for orders of how they should proceed, and at the end of her shift she crawled into her bunk, exhausted.

Shortly after dawn the next day, 6 June, the ops room tingled with excitement. The cloud cover of the previous day had lifted. It was all systems go!

At six thirty that morning, the RAF raided Normandy and Northern France and Belgium, paralysing the German war machine and giving no clue about what was to come. Feeling exhilarated and fearful at one and the same time, Anna kept a vigilant watch on the Aircraft State Board, her nerves jangling as one squadron after another took flight. Operation Overlord was underway and the Normandy Landings were going ahead. Naval officers and Wrens converged around the large table in the ops room, monitoring the movement of ships in the English Channel that were carrying thousands of infantrymen to Utah and Omaha beaches.

On board LCI *Glenvale*, a landing craft for infantrymen, Joey Walker stood on a deck awash with vomit. The crossing was rough and men from every regiment had been seasick as huge waves tossed them and the landing craft to their destination. They had Joey's sympathy; years of service in the navy made him immune to such discomfort. Utah Beach was in sight and high overhead allied airmen were bombing German gun emplacements along the shoreline. When the LCI lowered its ramps, the soldiers on board swarmed ashore, racing for the shelter of the low cliffs as the Germans retaliated with shot and shell.

Up above the sun-split clouds Patrick Conlon's Spitfire whirled and soared as he guarded the activity below against enemy Heinkels or any of the Luftwaffe that had been alerted to the scene. Adrenaline rushed through Patrick's veins as, grinning widely, he topped a windswept forest with easy grace, on the lookout for Jerry.

Suddenly, the grin slipped into an anxious grimace as a sickening thud on the Spitfire's tail sent the plane spinning down, down, down.

* * *

The combined forces of land, sea and air made this the largest invasion in history and for twelve savage weeks the Allied Forces battled against the might of the German army.

Of the 12,000 aircraft that supported the Normandy Landings

and the 14,000 sorties that took place on D-Day, only 127 planes were lost. One of them was Patrick Conlon's Spitfire.

Kitty was standing at the sink when through the kitchen window she saw the military vehicle come to halt at her gate. Two uniformed officers stepped out. Her blood ran cold.

20

Everything had stopped. The ticking of the clock, the gushing of water in the pipes, the voices of those comforting her, and the beating of her heart. Kitty sat as if turned to stone. She couldn't weep, yet inside she felt all her hopes and dreams disintegrating into ashes.

The neighbours came and went, but none of it made sense to Kitty, no matter what they told her. Patrick was dead. Dead. No matter how many times she said it, it wouldn't sink in.

Today she sat by the window in the parlour, gazing out across the garden to the sycamore trees beyond and struggling to come to terms with life without Patrick. Her unwashed hair clung to her scalp in greasy strands and her crumpled, stained dress was the same one she had been wearing for the past week. There had been days and nights when she'd thought she would never sit down again as she wandered aimlessly from room to room, always ending up in Patrick's, lying on his bed and breathing in what she imagined was the faint sweet smell of him. Then there were other days when inertia claimed her and she could neither move nor speak as she tried to forgive God for His terrible blunder. He had let her precious son die.

'He's reported missing, Kitty, not dead,' John pleaded for the umpteenth time.

'If our Patrick was dead, I'd feel it in here,' Molly stoutly declared, thumping her fist over her heart and begging her mother to live in hope.

'He could be a prisoner of war,' Maggie suggested.

'Until you know for certain you shouldn't grieve unnecessarily,' Mavis advised.

Whilst Kitty mourned the loss of her son, the battle for supremacy in Europe raged on. Less than two months later, Paris was liberated, and German resistance weakened as the Allies pushed steadily eastwards in a hard-fought campaign that enabled the American forces to stage a breakthrough in the west. Thanks to the influx of troops and equipment, D-Day marked a massive turning point in the war but all this meant nothing to Kitty and her family and friends. Patrick was still missing, presumed dead.

Gradually, Kitty was learning to live without him. She washed and dressed each day and went about her chores but she was now a pale shadow of herself, no longer the life and soul of the company she kept.

John felt as though he had not just lost his beloved stepson, he had almost lost his wife. Patiently, and lovingly, he tried to comfort Kitty through that awful summer.

* * *

The leaves on the trees on the towpath were turning golden and russet and that distinct damp, earthy smell that Kitty always associated with autumn reached her nose as she walked to the café on a morning in mid-September. This had always been her favourite time of year; now that Patrick was gone, she didn't think she had one. As she served her customers, the talk was all about the latest successes in Europe and predictions that the end of the war was in sight, but Kitty shut her ears to the chatter. For her the war would never be over.

As Kitty went about her business, an amazing coincidence was taking place at Liverpool Lime Street railway station. Hissing and clanking, the overcrowded train from London ground to a halt and the doors flew open, disgorging its passengers, many of them in uniform. Ross Penhaligon leapt to the platform and was pushing his way through the throng when he heard someone shout, 'Hey, Ross, wait up, mate.'

Glancing over his shoulder Ross saw Mickey O'Malley shouldering his way towards him, a big grin stretching his lips. 'I guess we're heading in the same direction,' Mickey said as they clapped each other's backs silently acknowledging that they'd made it home safe after D-Day. They stopped at the WVS stall where a motherly woman handed them cups of weak tea, and as they quenched their parched throats, Mickey saw a tall lad with tawny hair sticking out from under his cap limping towards them.

'Holy Mother of Christ!' he spluttered. 'As I live and breathe, it's Patrick Conlon.'

* * *

Less than an hour later, Weaver Street echoed with joyful cries as Kitty, Molly and Anna welcomed home their loved ones. Rose Walker, saddened that it wasn't her Joey, had volunteered to run to the café and get Kitty, who had almost fainted with shock and relief as Rose imparted the wonderful news. On legs feeling as though they belonged to someone else, Kitty had rushed back home alongside Rose, laughing and crying and thanking God.

When she arrived at Molly's house, Maggie, Mavis, Jack, Rose and May were all there to share her joy. After the noisy, tearful reunion in Molly's house, they each went to their own homes, Kitty clinging to Patrick as though she'd never let go again. An almost hysterical telephone call to the factory brought John and Robert home with tears in their eyes while Anna and Ross took sanctuary in Mavis's front room where they kissed and cuddled and talked about the future to their hearts' content.

Later that evening, they all gathered in Kitty's house to hear Patrick's story, and for the second time that day for the benefit of the neighbours – he'd already told his mother and stepfather and his brother and sister – he repeated what had happened.

He began by describing how his Spitfire had been pranged as he was flying west of Utah Beach and he explained how he'd bailed out – 'took to the silk' as he put it – and then lost consciousness as he plummeted earthwards. 'The next thing I know I'm dangling upside down from my parachute that had got caught up in a tree and my right leg wedged between two branches,' he continued, his lopsided grin letting them know that he'd felt rather foolish, 'and a little voice is telling me' – here Patrick adopted a squeaky French accent – '"Stay! I get help."' His audience chuckled.

'I was about to say I didn't have much option. I was stuck fast, but the girl, who was about twelve, ran off. Then I was shit scared. I was afraid she'd come back with Jerry – they occupied a lot of the farms round there. Anyway, an old boy and a younger one appeared with a ladder and got me down. The pain in my leg was excruciating and I blacked out,' he said, grimacing at the memory.

Patrick gave his captivated audience a wistful smile then told them how the French family hid him in a barn and the old man had put his broken leg in splints. 'He do it wiz zee cow and zee horse,' he said, mimicking the girl who had translated her grandfather's words, 'so if I suddenly break into a gallop you'll know why,' he joked, his grin slipping as he added, 'They were risking their lives for me. The girl brought me food each day, and when I could walk with a stick the young man and his mates – all members of the Resistance – helped me escape.' He took a deep breath. 'That bit was hairy I can tell you. We tramped night after night in the pitch black through dense forests, me limping along with my stick, scared to death we'd run into the Germans, but those Resistance chaps were marvellous and when we got to Cherbourg I teamed up with the British and' – he punched the air – 'here I am safe and sound back in Blighty.'

Kitty squeezed his hand and blinked her tears away as the others cheered loudly.

* * *

It felt like no time until Ross and Mickey had to return to their units, and once again Anna and Molly comforted one another while Kitty was in her element nursing her son. Her joy knew no bounds when Patrick was still at home for Christmas, deemed unfit for duty.

Whether it was the spirit of the season that made Anna heed Ross's advice she would never be sure but on New Year's Day she came to a decision. Ross had told her it was foolish to torture herself with uncertainty about her possible relationship to Rachel and the sooner she resolved the issue, the better.

Rachel greeted her with a disinterested smile and reluctantly invited her in. The welcome being what it was, Anna saw no reason to prevaricate.

'Rachel, my birth mother was called Florence Rigby,' she said firmly, her cheeks hot and her breathing shallow. 'The name on the flyleaf in your poetry book is the same. Is it just a coincidence? Or are *you* my mother?'

Rachel gasped, the colour leaching from her face, and her eyes widening with shock. Her hand clawed at her throat then her lips. 'You'd better sit down, Anna,' she croaked as she herself flopped into the nearest chair.

But Anna remained standing and in the tense silence that followed she could feel her heart thudding against her ribs. Forcing herself to maintain eye contact with Rachel, she waited for an answer. None forthcoming, she persisted, 'Is that why you took an interest in me when we first met, and was the birthday card your way of trying to tell me that you are my mother?'

Rachel sat upright, her composure regained, the skin around her mouth taut and her eyes cold. She looked Anna up and down then shrugged carelessly and gave a simpering smile. 'I have to admit that when we first met I was curious about you, and after we got to know one another I did toy with the notion that you might be my daughter. You see...' she floundered. 'I did... give birth to... er... a child I... gave up... for adoption.' Her eyes searched Anna's face, waiting for her reaction.

Anna stood, her arms folded across her chest and her expression blank.

Rachel gave a brittle laugh then carried on talking as though it was some sort of game she was playing and that Anna was rather stupid. 'It's because you so closely resemble me when I was young,' she said coyly, 'and then when you told me your birth date I allowed myself to get carried away with the idea. Foolish of me, I know, and once common sense prevailed, I realised that it was purely coincidence.' She looked directly into Anna's face, her eyes glinting and the playful attitude she'd adopted suddenly vanishing as she said, 'I'm not your mother, Anna.'

Was that a satisfied smirk on Rachel's face?

Anna's mind curdled with contempt as the cold, hard words registered. 'But what about your name?' she cried. 'You were Florence Rigby before you married. That's my birth mother's name. You did live in Liverpool, and we do look alike.'

'There could be dozens of girls in Liverpool with that name.' Rachel's expression verged on a sneer and her voice was harsh as she added, 'And furthermore, Anna, I don't need a daughter. I didn't want one then and I certainly don't need one now.'

The words were like a slap in the face. Anna gasped at the blatant cruelty.

'As I said, it was all a silly mistake.' Rachel stood, her arrogance restored and her expression one of dismissal. 'Now if you don't mind, Anna, I'd like you to forget all about this nonsense, and I'd appreciate your silence on this matter. I'd prefer to keep it from the gossips in this street. It would damage my reputation. Let's keep it just between us.' She gave a conspiratorial smile. 'We both made mistakes thinking we'd found something we thought we wanted, but we were wrong.'

Rachel strutted past Anna and held open the door. For a moment, Anna stayed rooted to the spot as she struggled to understand what had just taken place. Mixed emotions surged through her and she didn't know what to make of them. Anger struggled with an unexpected feeling of disappointment; she still hadn't found her birth mother. Then, turning slowly she fixed her eyes on Rachel and her confusion was dispelled by an overwhelming sense of relief. Thanking her for her time, Anna marched out of the house. She didn't look back. She didn't want Rachel to be her mother.

21

Lily was window shopping outside Blacklers department store in Great Charlotte Street, gazing enviously at beautiful dresses and shoes that she couldn't afford. Cathy tugged at her hand, impatient to be on the move; the lively three-year-old wanted to get to the pick-and-mix stall in Woolworths.

'All right, you bossy little mare,' her mother rebuked more in jest than anger. Lily adored her daughter and was proud of her confident manner. Cathy had a mind of her own, and Lily liked that. She knew from experience that it would stand her in good stead when others pointed the finger at her precious little girl, born out of wedlock. Molly had told her that it would go unnoticed. *Hundreds of kids will be without fathers after this war*, she'd said. But it still bothered Lily. Taking hold of Cathy's hand, they set off to Woolworths.

They had just rounded the corner into Church Street when Lily saw a familiar figure walking towards them. Her heart lurched painfully.

Eric Kitson stopped in his tracks. Lily pulled Cathy to a sudden halt.

'Hello, Lily,' Eric said softly, a slow smile curving his lips.

'Long time no see,' Lily mumbled, her heart thudding. He was just as she remembered him and she wanted to throw herself against his chest and cry.

Cathy looked from Eric to Lily and lisped, 'Mammy, pick-and-mix.' She had no time for gossiping.

'Who's this then?' Eric sounded forcibly cheerful as he squatted down to Cathy's height. 'What do they call you?'

'Caffren Erica,' she lisped, and pleased to be the centre of his attention she gave him a bright smile. He patted her golden curls then came upright his legs unsteady.

'Catherine... Erica?' He looked at Lily, his face masked in confusion.

'She's my little girl.' Lily wanted the ground to open and swallow her.

'So, you're married... and a mother,' Eric said hollowly.

Lily shook her head then blurted, 'I'm still single.'

Eric drank in her words then stammered, 'Did... did you... name her... after me?' His incredulous tone was a mixture of delight and disbelief.

Lily nodded. Her cheeks had pinked and she shuffled her feet uncomfortably.

'Oh, Lily, you'll never know how much I've missed you.' He spoke so sincerely that Lily had trouble holding back her tears.

'I've missed you too,' she said, her voice barely above a whisper. 'An' I'm sorry I said all them rotten things to you. I didn't mean any of 'em.'

'Didn't you?' Eric's eyes moistened and he blinked then gave her a wobbly smile. 'Look, I think we need to talk,' he said urgently. 'Do you have time?'

They went to Woolworth's and bought dolly mixtures, jelly babies and fruit gums. Then to a teashop where Eric bought

Cathy an ice cream sundae large enough to keep her occupied whilst he spilled out his heart. Lily did likewise, weeping openly and not giving a jot that people were staring. Eric still loved and wanted her.

'You've made my mammy cry,' Cathy piped through lips smothered in cream.

'I'm crying 'cos I'm happy,' Lily sobbed.

* * *

'I can't believe it,' Lily crowed as later that evening in Molly's house she told Anna and Molly about her meeting with Eric. 'He said he understood! That me getting pregnant before I met him didn't matter one bit. He said he still loves me and that he'll love Cathy as though she was his own.' Her eyes wide with the wonder of it all, she looked like a child whose Christmases had come all at once.

'He bought me ice cream but he made my mammy cry,' Cathy informed them.

'They were tears of joy, Cathy,' said Anna. 'Sometimes we cry when we're happy.'

'I don't,' Cathy retorted, 'but he was a nice a man.' Lily jumped up and hugged her.

'Looks like she'll soon have the daddy you always wanted for her,' said Molly.

'I bloody hope so,' Lily cried as she danced her daughter round the room.

* * *

'Rachel Dyson's up and gone,' Mavis told Anna when she entered the kitchen a week after Anna had asked Rachel if she was her mother.

Anna gasped. She had made no mention of her visit, but she had written all about it in a letter to Ross. 'Gone! You mean left Weaver Street?'

'Aye, May Walker said a van came late last night and shifted all Rachel's stuff. The curtains are down so I noticed when I went up to the church this morning. She always was a strange one, was Rachel. You'd think she might have come to say goodbye.' Mavis poured boiling water over the leaves in the teapot. She'd no sooner done that than Kitty, Molly, Lily and Maggie trooped in with Ronan and Cathy.

'You must have smelled the tea brewing.' Mavis pretended to look put out.

Kitty chuckled at the riposte then asked, 'Have you heard the news? Rachel packed up and left last night.'

'I was just telling Anna,' Mavis said, filling cups on the worktop.

'That means number seven's empty,' Lily chirped. 'I wonder if I can persuade Eric to rent it for us, for when we get wed. I'd like to stay in Weaver Street.'

'Ooh, go on. Ask him.' Maggie was all for keeping Lily and Cathy close by.

'I don't suppose we'll ever see Rachel again,' Anna said, her eyes taking on a faraway look as she juggled with her emotions.

'She'll not be missed,' said Maggie scornfully.

'Yeah, she was a right stuck-up cow,' Lily agreed.

The others clamoured to voice their opinions, but Anna sat deliberating on whether or not to tell them about her last meeting with Rachel.

'Weaver Street 'ull not be any the worse without royal, regal Rachel,' May commented dryly and deliberately rolling her 'r's'.

'She's not called Rachel. Her name's Florence – Florence Rigby.'

'But... but that's the name on your birth certificate, Anna,' Lily cried.

'Yes, it is, Lily. I'm pretty sure she's my mother,' Anna said softly.

The others gasped, staring at her wide eyed. Then they all began to gabble at once, eager to know all the ins and outs, and disgusted when Anna told them about the cruel way Rachel had denied being her mother.

'The heartless mare,' Maggie growled.

'I could be wrong about her, but I don't think so,' said Anna, and after she had told them more of what had taken place between her and Rachel then shown them the birthday card, they all nodded their heads and agreed she might be right.

'I aways said there was a distinct similarity between ye,' Kitty remarked.

'And you were the only one she ever showed an interest in,' Mavis added.

'But the evil sod denied it even though her name fits the bill,' Lily blustered.

'It doesn't matter, Lily.' Anna smiled, grateful for her friend's support but not wanting any pity. 'I think she changed her mind. In the end she was more bothered about saving her reputation than finding a daughter, and do you know what, I don't care. What you never had you never miss, and in a way, I've found a mother right here.' Anna reached out and squeezed Mavis's hand. 'That's if she'll have me.'

'Oh, Anna!' Mavis burst into tears, and flinging her arms round Anna, she sobbed, 'I'd be proud to call you mine.'

* * *

The following evening, when Anna was sitting with Molly and Lily in Molly's cosy kitchen, Lily, never one to let things drop, lit a cigarette then asked, 'Do you honest and truly think Rachel's your mother, Anna?' She jabbed with her cigarette towards Anna like a barrister might jab his pen at a witness in a court of law.

Anna, caught off guard, didn't answer immediately. With her brow puckered and her bottom lip jutted she gave the question some thought before saying, 'Yes, I really do think she is but...' She gave a careless shrug. 'I've reached the conclusion that it makes no difference to me. She made it quite plain that she didn't want me in her life, and I certainly don't need her in mine. And don't go thinking I'm being bitter,' she hastened to add, 'because I've got everything I want right here.' A smile twitched the corners of her lips. 'I can't say I've lost her now she's gone 'cos I never really found her so I'm neither better nor worse off than I was before.' Her smile broadened as she gave one friend then the other a smile of utter contentment. Molly and Lily acknowledged it with smiles of their own.

'Do you think she'll bother to let Philip know she's moved? You did say they didn't have a loving relationship,' said Molly, her tone suggesting that she thought Rachel was selfish enough to leave her son in the dark as to her whereabouts.

'I've no idea what she'll do,' Anna replied. 'She's a law unto herself, but I know what I'm going to do.' Her eyes lit up and she spoke firmly. 'I've no idea where Philip is but it won't be hard to trace him. I can do that through the RAF postings. After all, if I'm right in believing Rachel's my mother then Philip's my half-brother – and even if he's not – I'd like to meet him again. We got on really well that time he was here.'

'Maybe that's because blood's thicker than water,' said Lily with a gleam in her eye.

* * *

After that, whenever Anna looked back on the events of the past twelve months, she was amazed by what had happened. Ross had returned from Africa safe and sound and for a few precious days they'd gloried in being together again, as had Molly and Mickey. Patrick Conlon had returned from the dead, his mother beside herself with joy, and Lily was now on her way to becoming Mrs Eric Kitson and giving Cathy the father she so craved. Wonders never ceased.

Sadly, for Kitty, her joy had been all too short-lived when Patrick was declared fit for duty and went back to flying his Spitfire. And as for her own strange and unsettling dealings with Rachel Dyson, Anna had put all that behind her, with no regrets. She had Mavis for her 'mother' and her friends as her family, and although she missed Ross dreadfully and often found her work with Western Approaches saddening whenever they lost a ship or an aircraft, there was always something happening in Weaver Street to raise her own and everyone else's spirits.

'I'm thrilled for Lily and Eric, but I can't help feeling envious,' Anna said as she adjusted her cap in Molly's bedroom mirror. At Lily's request she was wearing her uniform and would be glad of her greatcoat because it was a bright but chilly day in February.

'Your day will come, Anna. If Ross was here, he'd marry you tomorrow,' Molly told her comfortingly as she wrapped a warm woolly scarf round Ronan's neck then pulled on her gloves. 'Now, we'd best get a move on. We don't want to be late at the church.'

* * *

Lily's wedding was a beautiful, simple service in St Peter's Church of England. Eric looked smart in his dark grey suit and Lily looked a picture in Molly's dress, her flaming red hair a mass of luxurious waves caressing her shoulders as she walked down the aisle on Stanley's arm. Behind them came Cathy, everyone declaring she was the prettiest bridesmaid they'd ever seen, and Cathy reminding anyone who would listen that Eric was now her daddy.

Eric's mother laid on a splendid reception at her sister's house in Wavertree, Molly and Anna glad that Mrs Kitson had readily accepted her son's choice of wife. 'He's been pining for her ever since they split up,' she'd confided, 'but he's happy now.'

'It's not everybody who'd welcome a girl with another man's kiddy for a daughter-in-law,' Maggie whispered as they tucked into egg and cress sandwiches.

'She's obviously sensible enough to realise that if Lily's the girl Eric loves then it would be foolish to object,' said Anna, recalling the warm welcome Ross's parents had given her. She was looking forward to seeing Esme and Tam again when Ross came home. Keeping in touch by letter was all right but it wasn't the same as being in their home in Flockton.

'A good mother-in-law's worth her weight in gold. I couldn't ask for better,' Rose commented, giving May's arm a playful nudge. May flushed with pride.

Lily paraded the room with her arm linked into Eric's and his free hand clasping Cathy's. 'They're a proper little family already,' Kitty observed.

* * *

Winter days lingered with frost, snow and freezing fog, and preparing to face another year without their loved ones was almost more than Anna, Molly, Kitty and Rose could bear. Shortages of food became more acute, but as usual they all pulled together to make the best of it. Letters from Ross, Mickey, Patrick and Joey told of the hazards they faced daily in drifting snowstorms, biting wind and intense cold. The letters couldn't say much more, but the recipients knew from listening to news bulletins that the Allies were fighting for their lives, and winning.

'Things are really looking up, Mam,' Robert told Kitty one afternoon in March 1945. 'We won the Battle of the Bulge when Hitler tried to split our troops up, but us and the Americans were more than a match for 'em, an' now that they're running out of men and weapons we're giving 'em a right pasting.'

'I'm pleased to hear it, son, but I won't be happy until it's all over. This war's hanging on like grim death even though they've lifted some of the restrictions. I'm glad we've got rid of the blackout and the street lights are on again.' Kitty gave Robert a big smile. 'Still, the man on the wireless said our lads are winning in Ardennes.'

And they were. The boldest and the bravest of the allied infantry forces made beach landings, and up to their armpits in swirling water, they raced over the rippled sand, seeking cover while all hell broke loose around them. Orders that had been crystal clear now seemed utter nonsense in the chaos of German machine gun fire and explosions ripping up the beach. Each man was now intent on self-preservation as they watched their comrades blown to bits but they remained undeterred. If they were to survive and win the war, they had to fight on.

Meanwhile, Patrick Conlon continued to storm the skies in his Spitfire, his job to protect those below as he swooped and dived then blasted Heinkels and Messerschmitts to kingdom come. In Bomber Command, Ross Penhaligon and Mickey O'Malley patrolled the heavens, keeping the enemy at bay and frustrating their advance as they bombed rail and road networks to halt the German advance. And out at sea, Joey Walker scoured the ocean on the lookout for U-boats to torpedo as he escorted the convoys bringing vital food supplies to English shores. All this done out of love for their families and friends at home, all praying for their safe return.

* * *

Good news travels fast, and by the end of April, reports that the Allies had taken Berlin and achieved great success in Germany lifted everybody's spirits. Listening to the news now became something of a pleasure as one victory followed another. When it was announced that Hitler had committed suicide Lily was so ecstatic that one might have believed that she'd had a hand in his demise.

'Bloody good riddance to the hateful bugger,' she'd crowed, dancing round the front room at number seven, waving a cleaning rag victoriously. Eric flinched at her choice of words, then dropping his paintbrush, he jumped up and danced with her.

The friends in Weaver Street and people in every town and city held bated breaths, the tension almost unbearable as they waited for the official declaration of peace. Only Maggie still found something to moan about.

'They're saying everybody has to buy red, white and blue bunting without coupons,' she carped to her neighbours in Kitty's kitchen.

'I'd willingly spend money on a million flags if it means the war's over,' Anna retorted.

A few days later, in the first week in May, she was out on the street waving just one flag and rejoicing along with everyone else in Weaver Street. Hitler was dead, the Germans had surrendered and a new world for every British man, woman and child was beginning to take shape. After years of danger and doing without, the joy was indescribable. Liverpool throbbed with patriotism and emotion. In every street people were singing and dancing. On her way home from Derby House, Anna was hugged and kissed by strangers as she made her way to the tram stop.

'I'm going to miss driving this tram,' the woman at the wheel shouted to the passengers as they rattled along, for like many of the women who had taken the place of men, they now knew they would be redundant.

'I'll miss the lasses in munitions,' another woman called back before adding, 'but at least I'll not get blown up when I'm back in me own kitchen.'

'You will if you leave the gas on without lighting it, Nellie. You've done that before.'

This was met with a gale of laughter.

'It's been the most exciting time of my life.' The young girl in an ARP uniform caught the passengers' attention.

'Aye, it hasn't all been about making jam an' knitting socks,' an elderly woman wearing her grey suit and bright red WVS jumper proudly agreed. 'We've done our bit an' done it well, an' when our brave lads are all home safe, we can celebrate an' let the world know that we Liverpudlians'll never be beaten.'

A huge cheer went up, and although Anna cheered as loudly as any of them, she couldn't help but wonder if she would ever hear from Ross again. She hadn't had a letter for ages.

* * *

'This is dead bloody marvellous,' Lily cried to Anna and Molly as they put plates of meat paste sandwiches on the tables set out in

Weaver Street. Front doors were open wide, a huge banner declared 'VICTORY IN EUROPE' and garlands of red, white and blue bunting were draped from one side of the street to the other. The landlord of the Weaver's Arms had organised for the older members of the local brass band to provide the music, and young and old merrily danced the hokey-cokey up and down the pavement. It seemed amazing that after six terrible years of seeing their city bombed and burned the horrors were finally over.

The celebrations roared on, the sun fading as dusk fell, but it didn't dim the light in the hearts of John and Kitty, Maggie and Stan, Lily and Eric, Mavis and Jack, and May and Bill as they danced to the oom-pah-pa beat of 'We're Going to Hang Out the Washing on the Siegfried Line.'

Anna and Molly and Rose watched on. Their men had yet to come home.

22

After all the excitement of the VE celebrations the days and weeks that followed were something of an anticlimax. There were still shortages and shabbiness wherever they looked without any immediate signs of things improving, but the war had ended and the wonderful sense of freedom the friends in Weaver Street felt was not diminished. However, waiting for the return of their loved ones was almost beyond bearing.

Anna's impatience mounted by the day. In Derby House she assisted in winding down Western Approaches operations in the Atlantic, but the war still raged in the Pacific and now the focus was on achieving victory over Japan. It seemed as if for her the war would never end. Ross had written to say he would possibly be demobbed by the end of August and had advised her to prepare for an autumn wedding.

'I want nothing more than to marry Ross,' she said to Mavis one evening, 'but I can't help worrying that we don't really know one another. You can't say that a few days on leave is the same as living together full-time. Suppose I annoy the hell out of him by wanting to read in bed, or that he hates my cooking and I don't like his snoring?'

'Then you'll be no worse off than lots of other couples. Nobody knows what it's like to live with somebody until they do,' Mavis said sagely. 'And if you love one another then those things don't matter. You work them out as you go.'

Anna yet again accepted and appreciated her landlady's wisdom. She did love Ross and she was sure he loved her, but she had been let down so many times before by people that she had thought loved her that she still had her doubts.

The word 'demobbed' seemed to be on everyone lips as the demobilisation of troops got underway. The government was issuing all serving men with a suit, two shirts, a raincoat and felt hat, shoes and underwear. When Anna and Lily dropped into Molly's one evening in July, she waved the letter that she'd received that morning at them.

'Mickey says he's got his demob suit so they should be letting him come home any day now,' she said, her eyes shining with excitement.

'That's wonderful,' Anna said, smiling fondly at her friend but wishing that she was the one imparting such good news. Ross was still based somewhere down south.

'Woo-hoo!' Lily threw her arms up in the air. 'It's been one hell of a war but you'll soon have your men back, and I've got mine so we're on the up-and-up, girls,' she yelled, and as Molly made a cup of tea Lily sang Eric's praises and the wonders of married life.

Over in Kitty's house she and John were celebrating her last day at the munitions factory.

'I can't say I'm sorry to see you out of that place,' John said heartily. 'I dreaded every day in case you were caught up in an explosion.'

'An' ye not there to rescue me,' Kitty joked, referring to the time in the last war when she had run back into a blazing shed to rescue her workmates and John had saved her from being killed just in the nick of time as another explosion had roared through the building.

'You were an impulsive young thing – and you still are,' he teased, slapping her playfully on her backside. 'I don't think I'll ever tame you, but now you'll just have to be content with minding your café.'

'Aye, business can only get better.'

'If there's one good thing this war's done for us it's keeping my factory in business. Those government contracts have set us up for life. We'll have no more money worries, Kitty, and the kids won't want for anything.'

'Aye, that's true, but at what cost? I'd as soon be a pauper than think of all them young lads who'll never come home again. We nearly lost our Patrick, an' no amount of money brings ye happiness if you lose the ones you love.'

'You're right, Kitty. We can't buy happiness. We have to make our own, and we will.'

The VE Day bunting came down and the 'Welcome Home' banners went up.

Anna and Molly had painted a gaily coloured banner on strips of old sheet and suspended it from Molly's upstairs window to a tree near the allotment gate so that it could be seen the minute anyone entered the back lane. They'd also made four smaller banners to attach to it. Mickey's name was the first to go up in readiness for his homecoming and sure enough he arrived two days later.

His rapturous reception from Molly and Ronan was somewhat spoiled when, letting him go, Molly had a fit of giggles. 'You look like a spiv,' she chortled, eyeing the three-piece grey worsted pinstriped suit that was too tight across Mickey's broad shoulders and the trousers too short in the leg.

'You should have seen some of the other blokes,' said Mickey, 'theirs only fitted where they touched. The raincoat's all right though, and the suede shoes are smart.'

'I'll get me mam to let the turn-ups down and you can wear it for Anna and Ross's wedding. She's already booked the register office for when Ross gets back. I'm sure he'll not be far behind you. He wants them to get married straight away.'

'I don't blame him,' said Mickey, grabbing Molly round her waist and pressing himself against her. 'He doesn't know what he's missing.'

'Ooh, but I do,' Molly giggled, wriggling in Mickey's arms as the back door opened and Kitty and John came in. 'Just be patient. It'll be worth it,' she whispered in Mickey's ear. He groaned as he let her go and turned to greet his in-laws.

The rest of the evening was spent entertaining the family and friends who called to welcome Mickey back. At close to midnight, Kitty went home with Mickey's trousers under her arm, and Molly and Mickey climbed the stairs to bed.

'I've waited a long time for this,' said Mickey as they hurriedly undressed. 'When I was in the desert, I used to dream about it.'

'Well, you're not dreaming now,' Molly said as she lost herself in his embrace.

* * *

Three days later, Mickey's banner was replaced by Joey Walker's. Rose had rushed up the lane the night before to let them know that Joey was arriving the next day. One celebration seemed to roll into another, but Anna and Kitty were still waiting even when victory over Japan was announced and they all celebrated VJ Day.

'My mam can't wait to kill the fatted calf but there's still no word about Patrick coming home,' said Molly one evening as she and Anna sat in the garden enjoying the dying rays of a sunny August day. The weather had been as changeable as Anna's moods, one day gloriously warm then the next thunderstorms and cold snaps.

'I can't imagine what's keeping Ross,' she said. 'His letters keep on saying any day now, but that day never seems to arrive. I was worried that his squadron might be deployed to the Pacific, but now that America's dropped those awful atom bombs on Hiroshima and Nagasaki, that's not likely to happen.' She heaved a deep sigh. 'I know being a wing commander means he has a lot more responsibility than some of the other men but they'll have to demob him sometime, and I can't help thinking perhaps he's got cold feet, that he's just delaying letting me know he's not coming back for me.'

'Don't be daft. He's head over heels in love with you, anybody can see that,' Molly protested, saddened to see her friend so downhearted.

'But we've been apart for so long, and fighting a war does funny things to some men's minds. Why, only the other day one of the cleaners in Derby House told me that her husband had barely spoken a word since he came home and that he hated her going out to work even though they need the money.'

'Yeah, I know what you mean. Nellie across the road's husband accused her of being too independent. He said her place was at home minding the kids not driving a tram.'

'She'll have to give that up soon enough once things get back to normal 'cos the men will want their jobs back. Personally, I can't make up my mind whether to leave the WAAFs or stay on, but I'm not sure what else I can do, I've only ever worked in an office.'

'You won't have to work once you're married to Ross.'

'If he ever marries me.' Anna looked woebegone. 'And I don't know what sort of a job he'll get. I suppose Mickey will go back to bricklaying.'

'He starts next Monday with his old boss. There's lots of building going on what with all the damage the bombs did.' Molly sounded pleased.

When Anna stepped outside much later to go home, she felt the darkness thicken and gather round her. It seemed to be pushing its way into her very soul and all her fears that she might never see Ross again clamoured inside her head and heart.

* * *

Anna couldn't shake off the feeling that she had lost Ross, that it had just been another wartime romance and now the fighting was over he was planning a future without her. She hadn't had a letter from him in over two weeks, and now as summer days waned and the leaves on the trees began to shrivel, so did her heart.

He'd told her to plan for an autumn wedding and she had made a few tentative arrangements. She was going to borrow Molly's dress – Lily commenting, 'It's getting some bloody hammer.' Mavis had offered to make the cake and Kitty to hold the reception, and Jack to accommodate Tam and Esme Penhaligon when they came to the wedding from Flockton. She even had a list of vacant slots at the registry office for the months of September and October, but as the days went by, she couldn't help thinking that her preparations were surplus to requirement.

Mavis's kind heart ached for Anna. As she put two eggs into the pan for their breakfast, she mulled over what she had learned about her lovely WAAF lodger during the years Anna had lived with her: a baby of an unmarried woman, given up for adoption at birth and into the hands of two feckless people who didn't deserve to look after a dog let alone a child. Then a broken romance with a heartless cad that had left her devastated, and to cap it all, that carry-on with Rachel Dyson who was more than likely her real mother but didn't want to tarnish her reputation by admitting it. Now there was this to-do with Ross.

The water in the pan bubbled and as the eggs boiled so did Mavis's blood. Life wasn't fair. Anna had had too much bad luck. *If I ever come across that Ross fella again, I'll wring his bloody neck.* Shaking her head in despair she went to the foot of the stairs and called out, 'Anna, your breakfast's nearly ready.' Would Anna stay with her if Ross broke off the romance? she wondered, putting two slices of bread into the toaster. Yesterday had been Anna's last day in Derby House as Western Approaches no longer needed her services, and now that it was beginning to look as if Ross was about to let her down, she still hadn't decided whether or not to continue being a WAAF. And if she did decide to stay in the services they'd transfer her somewhere else, Mavis thought disconsolately as she brewed a pot of tea. And, looking on the bright side, if Ross married her he'd take her to live with him. Whatever happened, Mavis knew she would miss her.

Upstairs, Anna heard the sound. It broke through a tangle of dreams. She had been in a desert looking for Ross, but every time she caught sight of him the sand had whirled up and blown in her eyes and when her vision cleared, he was nowhere to be seen. Surfacing slowly, she looked blearily round the familiar room and as she got dressed, she gloomily dwelt on her own past. Her birth mother had given her away, and Jane and Norman Carswell had barely known she existed. Then Suzy, a girl she'd thought was a true friend had betrayed her with that arrogant prat, Simon Grant who had carelessly tossed her aside, and Rachel had disappeared leaving her still wondering if she really was her mother. And now Ross...

Did nobody want her for keeps?

'Your toast's going cold.'

Anna gave a wan smile. Dear Mavis. She was here, and so were Molly and Lily and all her friends in Weaver Street. Her spirits lifted and she tripped downstairs to find a boiled egg, toast and tea waiting for her along with Mavis's warm smile. She'd get by.

Later that morning, Kitty called to say Patrick was expected that day. Yet again the banner was changed but Ross's banner lay where Anna had placed it weeks ago. Would it ever be used, or would she eventually put it in the bin along with all her hopes and dreams?

* * *

'Letters get lost,' Lily told Anna as she sat with her and Eric in their new home. It looked very different from when Rachel had lived there, and Anna couldn't help but recall the opulent front room and their last strange meeting. She wondered where Rachel was now and thought of Philip.

'Philip's didn't,' Anna said irritably. She'd managed to trace him and in reply to her letter he'd told her he hadn't heard from his mother in ages, but that he was thrilled to hear from Anna and would be delighted to accept the invitation to her wedding. She'd made no mention of her suspected relationship to Rachel; she preferred to do that face to face when the time was right. 'He says he's going to do his best to make it to Liverpool in time for my wedding,' she continued before sourly adding, 'That's if it ever comes off.'

'Oh, Anna, don't be like that. Ross's crazy about you,' Lily exclaimed. 'Of course he'll come back and marry you.'

'Then why doesn't he write and tell me so?'

'He's most likely too busy. The most senior officers have more to do when they're winding down operations. Ross is a wing commander so he'll be one of the last to be demobbed.' Eric's rational response gave her no comfort but pretending that it had she forced a smile and began complimenting them on changes they had made to the house.

Anna had also written to Esme Penhaligon to ask if Ross had returned home and Esme had replied saying they hoped to see him any day now and were looking forward to Anna's next visit. But were they telling the truth or just being kind and letting her down gently? Now, as she accepted a cup of tea, she felt envious of Lily and Eric's happiness. Lily was positively blooming in her role as his wife, and Eric was clearly a devoted husband and father to Cathy. Things had come right for Lily, and as she sipped and chatted, Anna wondered if they would come right for her.

'You've a face like a slapped arse,' Lily admonished, glancing in Eric's direction and reddening. She was trying to be more refined now she was married to a university man. 'It's Patrick's welcome home party tonight so put a smile on it.'

* * *

Kitty hadn't quite killed the fatted calf but she had trawled the butchers and the grocers for the best they had to offer. Her delight was poignant as she watched her beloved son mingle with her neighbours. When Anna got the opportunity to welcome Patrick, she couldn't help but voice her fears about Ross.

'He'll see all his squadron off first, and if he's thinking of staying on in the Air Force like I am there'll be other things to arrange. He's most likely chasing his tail at the moment so writing letters won't be a priority until he knows for certain where he stands,' Patrick told her. He sounded so knowledgeable that it went some way to settling Anna's nerves.

The days dragged by, and Anna felt at a loss as to what to do. She was no longer a WAAF with an important role in the war effort – that war was over – but the one that kept her awake at night still raged on. If Ross had given up on her, should she stay with Mavis and look for work in Liverpool, or seek pastures new, become a regular in the WAAF and go wherever they sent her? It would be a wrench to leave all she had in Weaver Street behind but perhaps it would make it easier to make a fresh start and forget all about Ross Penhaligon.

To cheer herself up, she went into the city to spend her clothing allowance. Whereas the government had provided every serving man with a ready-made suit and other items of clothing when he was demobbed, women were given money to spend as they chose. It was a dry sunny day, the last in September, and although many of the streets still bore the scars inflicted by German bombs, the city thronged with people. Feeling quite uplifted by the prospect of buying a new set of clothes that she wasn't paying for, Anna's first port of call was Marks & Spencer in Church Street. The store at Compton House had an impressive facade built with reddish stone and rows of arched windows lined the upper floor that were topped with two tall towers. At ground level, canvas awnings jutted over plate-glass windows displaying a wide variety of goods. Anna window-shopped before entering the store and making for the women's fashion department, her excitement mounting.

Taking her time, she lingered at the counters and perused the racks. Oh, what a joy it was to purchase a satin brassiere and two pairs of silky camiknickers, a change from the heavy-duty cotton drawers the WAAF had issued. Next, she bought a cream silk blouse and a gorgeous two piece in dark green, its neatly tailored jacket and pencil skirt in the new shorter length showing off her shapely calves. She still had enough money and coupons left over for a pair of shoes.

'I'll wear the blouse and suit now,' she told the assistant.

'I don't blame you. It suits you to perfection,' the assistant gushed.

Feeling rather glamorous, Anna set out for Lord Nelson Street and the shoe shop Mavis had recommended. To get there she had to pass Lime Street Station.

Ross Penhaligon strode across the station platform to the exit, looking awfully smart in his new group captain's blue uniform. Passers-by, still grateful for the supreme efforts of all serving men for saving them from being ruled by the Germans, smiled at the tall handsome man to say thank you. Ross acknowledged them with a nod and a cheery grin. He was feeling particularly buoyant. After all, he was on his way to claim the girl he loved.

Outside the station, he paused to get his bearings. That was when he saw her: a tall girl wearing a dark green suit that showed off her curves. His breath caught in his throat. He knew the sway of those shapely hips and that glorious mane of auburn hair. They had filled his dreams on many a night in the past four years.

'Anna! Anna!' His cry lost in the hum of the traffic he broke into a run.

'Anna! Anna Carswell,' he roared.

Anna's step faltered. Had she heard someone calling her name?

She glanced behind her then came to a sudden halt.

Her heart leapt into her throat, and tears misted her eyes.

'Ross! Oh Ross!'

She longed to run and throw herself into his arms but instead she stood rooted to the spot, incapable of doing anything other than stare at the man running towards her. Her heart raced, and all the fears that had tormented her days and nights flew away like birds suddenly startled into flight, and as they soared they left behind them the most wonderful luxurious feeling of warmth, happiness and love.

Ross skidded to a stop panting for breath and gazing into Anna's face, drinking in her beauty and wondering how he'd managed to live so long without her by his side.

She gazed into his silvery-grey eyes, alight with love.

Then, the spell broke as he swept her up into his embrace, and regardless of the amused, sympathetic glances from passers-by, they kissed and laughed and cried for pure joy.

'I thought I'd lost you,' Anna said as they walked to the tram stop. 'You didn't write and I had the idea that you'd changed your mind about us.'

Ross's expression was incredulous. 'I did write,' he protested, 'and as for changing my mind, I could never do that. I love you, Anna Carswell, and I always will.'

'And I'll love you forever,' Anna replied, feeling as though her world was just perfect for quite suddenly the drab grey streets of Liverpool had taken on a rosy glow and she almost felt faint with happiness.

* * *

On the day Anna was to marry Ross, her friends and neighbours in Weaver Street were preparing to make it a day to remember for this lovely girl they had taken into their hearts and their homes. She was now one of them.

Outside number five, Bill Walker stood with his car doors open ready to take May, Rose and Joey, and Stanley and Maggie to the registry office. May came out looking resplendent in the blue suit that Kitty had made her for Rose and Joey's wedding. They followed on, Rose's yellow dress bright against her husband's smart naval uniform.

On the steps at number seven, Eric stood awaiting his lift with the Sykes family. His wife and daughter were key players in today's celebrations and he felt immensely proud. Like Anna, he too had been made to feel at home in Weaver Street.

In number nine, Stanley carefully combed his sparse hair over his bald patch and glued it in place with Brylcreem, at the same time as holding his belly in to prevent the buttons on his waistcoat from popping. Maggie, trying not to wrinkle the skirt of her gaudy flowered two-piece outfit, was squeezing her feet into a pair of high-heeled shoes she hadn't worn in ages. 'I'll be crippled before the day's done,' she moaned, tottering over to the mirror to put on her hat which was bright yellow with a cartwheel brim. She'd worn it for Beth's wedding almost twenty years before, and Kitty had said it looked like a dustbin lid, but Maggie didn't care.

In number thirteen, Beth adjusted Stuart's tie then flicked his hair back from his forehead with her fingers. Blair polished his spectacles then buttoned the jacket of his brown pinstriped demob suit. Beth gave her husband and son the once-over and smiled. 'You both look as handsome as the day is long,' she said, ignoring Blair's drawn, pallid cheeks and scrawny frame, evidence of the long years spent fighting on the Western Front. She'd soon fatten him up, she told herself, as she put on her neat navy-blue coat with the velvet collar.

Two doors up in Jack's house, Ross nervously paced the floor.

'Calm down, lad. You'll wear t'floorboards out,' Jack ordered the tall handsome man, splendid in his group captain's dress uniform. Anna had calmly accepted his decision to stay on in the RAF, and after the wedding they would go to live in married quarters in Lincolnshire. Esme and Tam Penhaligon had arrived the night before and now they gazed proudly at their son.

'Aye, don't wear yourself out. You've a long night ahead of you,' said Mickey with a naughty wink. He wriggled his shoulders in his too-tight demob suit jacket thinking that as Ross's best man he could have looked smarter if he had still been in uniform.

Ross responded to Mickey's wink with a wicked grin then said, 'Do you remember how we felt just before take-off when we were going on a bombing raid? Well, that's how I feel.'

'Ah, but think what's waiting for you when you land.' Mickey's dirty laugh put wry smiles on the faces of the men. Esme's cheeks pinked and she gave a discreet cough.

Across the lane, Kitty and John were also admiring their sons: Robert looking very grown-up in his best grey suit and Patrick wearing his flight lieutenant's uniform. He too had signed on to stay in the RAF. Next spring, he was marrying Fionnuala and they'd all go to the wedding in the west of Ireland. Kitty was looking forward to that and visiting her brother Shaun again. 'You look as pretty as a picture,' John told Kitty, admiring her dark green suit that complemented her tawny hair. 'I could marry you all over again.'

Meanwhile, in the hallway at number fifteen, Mavis peered into the mirror and tilted her fussy little pink hat over one eye. Then, deciding it looked rather risqué she pushed it back firmly until it sat square on top of her mousy brown curls. A thrill of excitement mingled with anxiety as she checked the overall appearance of her best grey box-pleated skirt and matching jacket, and the satin blouse the same colour as her hat. Today was important and she wanted to look just right. At eleven o'clock she would walk into the registry office with Anna on her arm and give her to Ross to love and cherish.

In the kitchen, Cathy, looking adorable in pink taffeta, stood prim and proper ready to play her role as flower girl, and Ronan and James fidgeted in their crisp blue shirts and navy trousers. 'Don't get all crumpled before the wedding, boys,' Mavis gently reprimanded as she came in from the hallway.

Upstairs, Molly and Lily put the finishing touches to Anna's dress. Anna felt bathed in love as she stood between her two bridesmaids, gazing at their reflections in the long mirror. Then, as her bridesmaids crossed to the window to check on proceedings, she stood lost in her own thoughts. The war had changed her life and the lives of thousands of women. They had shared their anxieties as war had threatened, and when it became a reality and their husbands, sons, brothers and boyfriends had answered the call of duty they had watched them go with heavy hearts. They had struggled with shortages of food, the blackout, and the fear of being blown to kingdom come in the bombing raids, and taken on new roles as they went to work in munitions factories, joined the services or became ARP wardens and ambulance crew, anything to help the war effort and defeat Adolf Hitler. Through the long years they had borne whatever the Germans threw at them, all the while living in fear for their own safety and that of the men they loved. A generation of young men had given their lives so that they might have freedom and Anna felt truly blessed that their menfolk had returned safely home. She glanced over at Molly and Lily who were chattering excitedly as they peered through the window, and her heart swelled with love and pride for the two brave girls who had given her their unstinting friendship.

They had seen their city decimated by German bombs, and had seen buildings they had loved lying in heaps of rubble, but gradually their city was being restored and life was returning to normal; nothing could vanquish the spirit of these Liverpudlians who supported one another throughout the darkest days. The war had touched all their lives, but now they had so many wonderful things to live for: marriages, the births of children and grandchildren and bright, new hopes for a future filled with happiness and love.

'Ross's just getting into the car and he looks absolutely gorgeous,' Lily announced as the groom, his parents and Jack and Mickey exited number seventeen. She craned her neck a bit further to get a better view of the cars that lined the lane. 'Oh, me mam's having trouble getting her hat into Bill's car. It's as big as a bloody cartwheel.'

'Doesn't our Patrick look handsome in his uniform?' Molly gushed, leaning over Lily's shoulder. 'And your Eric looks smart,' she added so as not to leave him out.

'He always does,' said Lily, about to pass a cutting comment about Blair Forsythe's awful brown suit as he and Beth and Stuart climbed into a taxi. Then she changed her mind. Today wasn't a day for being unkind.

The cavalcade moved slowly out of sight and Molly and Lily stepped back from the window and looked expectantly at Anna.

'Right, that's it then. They're all away,' said Molly. 'Are you ready to become Mrs Penhaligon, Anna?'

'More than ready.'

Anna and her bridesmaids descended the stairs.

Mavis and the children gasped with delight when Anna walked into the kitchen.

'You look beautiful,' Mavis said, her voice wobbling as she blinked back tears.

'I feel it,' said Anna. 'When the WAAF transferred me to Liverpool I never imagined that they were sending me to the place where I'd find out just how beautiful life can be. It's here that I found Ross and all of you.' She opened her arms wide to embrace them.

They hugged her in turn then Molly and Lily shepherded the excited children out to the waiting cars.

Anna's eyes were bright with unshed tears as she slipped her arm through Mavis's and stepped outside. On the pavement she let her gaze drift from one end of the street to the other. 'No matter where Ross takes me, I'll always look on Weaver Street and you as home,' she said, then dropped a kiss on Mavis's cheek.

Mavis flushed with pleasure. 'Home is where the heart is and there'll always be a place in mine for you, Anna.'

'And in mine for you, Mavis. Thank you for giving me a family.'

And so the jubilant bride and groom and their family and friends made their way to the registry office. They had survived a war and now they were going to celebrate in the best way they knew how.

ACKNOWLEDGEMENTS

Many grateful thanks to my magnificent agent Judith Murdoch and the wonderful team at Boldwood for all their support in bringing the stories of the folks in Weaver Street to my faithful readers. Particular thanks to Sarah Ritherdon, Candida Bradford and Sandra Ferguson for their expert editing and advice that always makes a better story. Thanks also to Clare Fenby, Nia Benyon, Isabelle Flynn, Marcela Torres and the marketing team for getting it out there. Where would we be without them?

Thanks also to the Veterans' Association for their photographs and useful information that enhances any World War 1 or 2 story, and the numerous Liverpool archives that help to set time and place.

Special thanks to my family who support me in all I try to do. I love all of you.

ABOUT THE AUTHOR

Chrissie Walsh was born and raised in West Yorkshire and is a retired schoolteacher with a passion for history. She has written several successful sagas documenting feisty women in challenging times.

Sign up to Chrissie Walsh's mailing list here for news, competitions and updates on future books.

Follow Chrissie on social media:

ALSO BY CHRISSIE WALSH

The Weaver Street Series

Welcome to Weaver Street

Hard Times on Weaver Street

Weaver Street at War

Standalones

The Midwives' War

Printed in Great Britain
by Amazon